Annie lay in the darkness, listening for any sound at all from Pete Taylor.

"Taylor—you awake?" she whispered.

"Yeah."

"This is weird," Annie said. "Kind of like the first night of college with a new roommate."

From where Pete lay on his bedroll, he could hear the rustling of her sheets as she sat up in bed.

"When's your birthday?" she asked.

"February 6," he said.

"What's your favorite color?"

Pete had to think about it. "Blue," he said finally. The color of the sky. The color of Annie's eyes…

"When you were a kid, what did you want to be when you grew up?"

"Honestly? I wanted to be president. How about you? Did you always want to be an archaeologist?"

Annie stared at the ceiling. "When I was eight, I realized that most kids didn't live out of suitcases. I developed a longing for 'TV normal.' Suburbia, lots of kids. I love what I do. But I can't help wondering what it would be like to do something different."

She was silent for a moment. "Do you like your job, Taylor?"

Pete didn't answer. Yeah, Pete loved his job, since it meant lying there in the dark with Annie…

ASSIGNED TO PROTECT

NEW YORK TIMES BESTSELLING AUTHORS

Suzanne Brockmann

AND

Elle James

Previously published as *Hero Under Cover*
and *Hot Combat*

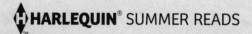

HARLEQUIN® SUMMER READS

Recycling programs for this product may not exist in your area.

ISBN-13: 978-1-335-00826-8

Assigned to Protect
Copyright © 2019 by Harlequin Books S.A.

First published as Hero Under Cover by
Harlequin Books in 1994 and Hot Combat by Harlequin Books in 2017

The publisher acknowledges the copyright holders of the individual works as follows:

Hero Under Cover
Copyright © 1994 by Suzanne Brockmann

Hot Combat
Copyright © 2017 by Mary Jernigan

This edition published by arrangement with Harlequin Books S.A.

For questions and comments about the quality of this book, please contact us at CustomerService@Harlequin.com.

® and TM are trademarks of Harlequin Enterprises Limited or its corporate affiliates. Trademarks indicated with ® are registered in the United States Patent and Trademark Office, the Canadian Intellectual Property Office and in other countries.

Printed in U.S.A.

HARLEQUIN®
www.Harlequin.com

CONTENTS

Suzanne Brockmann is an award-winning author of more than fifty books and is widely recognized as one of the leading voices in romantic suspense. Her work has earned her repeated appearances on the *New York Times* bestseller list, as well as numerous awards, including Romance Writers of America's #1 Favorite Book of the Year and two RITA® Awards. Suzanne divides her time between Siesta Key and Boston. Visit her at suzannebrockmann.com.

Books by Suzanne Brockmann

Not Without Risk
Night Watch
Taylor's Temptation
Get Lucky
Identity: Unknown
The Admiral's Bride
Hawken's Heart
Harvard's Education

Visit the Author Profile page at Harlequin.com for more titles.

HERO UNDER COVER

Suzanne Brockmann

For those fabulous Kuhlmans—Bill, who's been trying to teach me simply to be happy, and Jodie, who's been showing us all how to be happy for years.

Chapter 1

"You're going to do *what!*"

"A strip search," the FBI agent said, heading for the door. "Please follow me."

Dr. Annie Morrow crossed her arms and planted herself firmly. She wasn't going anywhere, that was for damn sure. "You've gone through my luggage with a fine-tooth comb, you've X-rayed the hell out of my purse, and now you want to do a *strip* search? This is harassment, plain and simple. You've held me here for nearly five hours without letting me contact an attorney. My civil rights are being violated, pal, and I've had damn near enough."

On the other side of the one-way mirror, CIA operative Kendall "Pete" Peterson stood silently, watching Dr. Anne—nickname Annie—Morrow, renowned archaeologist and art historian, professional artifact authenticator. According to her file, she was thirty-two years old, and one of the world's foremost experts on ancient metalworkings—coins, statues, works of art, jewelry. The daughter of two archaeologists, she'd been born on a dig in Egypt. She'd lived in thirteen different countries and participated in nineteen different excavations, and that was *before* she'd even attended college.

What the file *didn't* tell him was that she was filled with a seemingly limitless supply of energy. During the course of the five hours he'd been watching her, she had sat still for only a very short time. Mostly she paced; sometimes she stood, she leaned, she tapped her foot, but generally she moved around the small interrogation room like a caged animal.

The file also didn't describe the stubborn tilt to her chin, or the way her blue eyes blazed when she was angry. In fact, the photo included hadn't managed to capture much of anything out of the ordinary, except maybe her long, shining brown hair, and her almost too-sensuous lips.

But in person, in motion, she was beautiful....

"So that's our little Dr. Morrow," came a voice at his shoulder.

Peterson turned to look at Whitley Scott, the man in charge of the FBI side of the investigation. Scott smiled at him, his eyes crinkling behind his thick glasses. "Sorry I'm late, Captain," he said. "My flight was delayed."

Peterson didn't smile back. "We've been holding her for hours," he said. "She's pretty steamed."

Through the speaker system, he could hear Dr. Morrow still arguing with FBI agent Richard Collins.

"I've told you nine million times, or is it ten million now? I was in England to pick up an artifact—a gold-cast death mask from the nineteenth century—for a client. I wasn't out of the U.S. long enough to do whatever illicit crimes you're trying to accuse me of. The shipping papers for the death mask are all in order—you've admitted that much," she said. "What *I'd* like to know is when you intend to let me leave."

"After the strip search," Collins said. He was a good man for this job, Peterson thought. Collins could out-argue anyone. He was solid, steady and extremely patient. And he was absolutely never fazed.

"She's just your type, Pete," Whitley said, with a sideways glance at the taller man. "Something tells me you're going to enjoy this job."

Peterson didn't smile, but his dark brown eyes flashed in Scott's direction for a microsecond. "She's too skinny," he said.

In the interrogation room, Annie Morrow had had enough. She slammed her hand down on the table, pulling herself up and out of the chair she'd recently thrown herself into. "You want to strip-search me?" she said. "Fine. Strip-search me and let me get the hell out of here."

She shrugged out of her baggy linen jacket, tossing it onto a chair as she kicked her sneakers off. A quick yank pulled her loose red shirt over her head, and she quickly unbuttoned her pants.

"Umm…" Collins said, rattled. "Not *here*…."

"Why not?" Annie asked much too sweetly, her eyes bright with anger as she stood in the middle of the room in her underwear. "Oh, relax. I have bathing suits that are more revealing than this."

A slow grin spread across Peterson's face. Man, she'd managed to faze Collins. She knew darn well he had wanted her to follow him to a private room where she'd be searched by a female agent. Yet she'd undressed in front of him, simply to upset him. He felt a flash of something, and realized that he liked her—he liked her spirit, her energy, her nerve. He frowned. She was a suspect, under investigation. He wasn't supposed to like her. Respect, admire even, but not like. But, man, standing there, looking at her, he found an awful lot to like.

Annie turned and gestured toward the mirror, hands on her hips. "Don't you think the rest of the boys want to get in on the fun?"

She knew they were watching her. She was really something, really sharp. Her file said she'd had a 4.0 average throughout college, graduating with a Ph.D. in half the time it normally took. He liked smart women, particularly when they came wrapped in a package like this one.

Her bra and panties were both black and lacy, contrasting the smooth paleness of her fair skin. Her breasts were full, her waist narrow, flaring out to slender hips and long, beautiful legs. "I take it back," Pete said to Whitley Scott. "She's *not* too skinny."

She seemed to be looking directly at him. He could see the pulse beating in her neck. Each ragged, angry breath she took made her breasts rise and fall.

"Do you intend to harass me every time I leave and re-enter the country?" she said.

Pete glanced at Whitley. The older man shrugged. "She's looking right at you," Whitley said.

"You know she can't see me," Pete said, but he motioned for the mike to be turned on. "The Athens investigation," he said, raising his voice so the mike would pick him up, "hasn't been closed."

Annie threw up her hands and began to pace. "Well, there we go," she said. "We're finally getting somewhere. You *are* trying to harass me. You don't give a damn about this death mask. You still think I have something to do with the jerks that bombed and robbed that museum."

Pete tried to keep his attention on her words instead of her body. But it wasn't easy. She moved like a cat, the muscles in her legs rippling....

"How many times do I have to tell you that I am *not* a thief?" she continued. "Shoot, I wish I were. It would make this a whole hell of a lot easier. But I'm not about to confess to crimes I didn't commit."

She stopped pacing, coming back to stare directly up at him again. It was eerie, as if she really could see him through the glass.

"There was an explosion and a robbery at the gallery in England two hours after you left it," Peterson said, his voice distorted over the cheap speakers. "This time, people died."

Peterson watched Annie's face carefully as a range of emotions battled through her. Anger finally won.

"So, naturally, you believe *I* was involved. That's great, that's really great. Innocent people die, and the best you guys can do is to give me a hard time as I get on and off planes. You should be over there chasing the creeps that did the bombing, not playing peekaboo with somebody who gets queasy when she cuts her finger, pal."

"Doesn't it seem a little strange that you should go to European art galleries twice in five months, and within hours after you leave, each of them is hit by a bomb and a robbery?" Peterson had been in this business long enough to know that when there was smoke, somebody was trying to hide a fire. He wasn't buying the indignant act. "How do you explain the fact that you left the Athens convention hours before any-one else?"

"I don't!" Annie countered, eyes aflame. "I've al-ready told the FBI, *and* the CIA, and everyone else who's asked, that I left because I'd seen everything at the exhibit and I wanted to catch an early flight home." She was pacing the floor now, clearly upset. "What ever happened to innocent until proven guilty? Huh? Just what the hell is going on here?" she shouted, right through the glass at Peterson.

There was silence. Big fat silence. It disarmed her as Pete knew it would. Dr. Anne Morrow was low on patience, and impatient people didn't like being made to wait. She turned, gathering her clothes. "If we're through…" she said pointedly.

"But we're not," Pete said. "It's called a strip search for a reason."

What little remained of her patience snapped. "Oh, give me a break," she said, throwing down her clothes and striding over to the mirror. She came up really close—close enough for Pete to see the details of her thick, dark lashes and the streaks of lighter color in the deep blue of her eyes. Close enough for him to see that her skin was as smooth and soft as it looked. If the glass of the window hadn't been between them, he could have lifted his hand and touched her.

Peterson felt Whitley watching him, and somehow he managed to remain expressionless. But, man, it had been a long time since he'd looked at a woman and wanted her this badly. It had been a real long time.

"I assure you that everything I'm hiding in my un-derwear is attached, pal," she said. "No removable parts."

"Sorry," he said. "I'm being paid a lot of money not to trust you."

"What exactly are you looking for?" she asked. "Maybe if you tell me, I can check and see if I've got it on me somewhere."

"You ever hear of mules?" Pete asked.

She froze.

He'd managed to shock her, but somehow he didn't feel triumphant about it. "Mules are people who smuggle illegal substances into the country inside their bodies," he said.

"I *know* what a mule is," she said. "Tell me honestly, do you really think I've swallowed the crown jewels? Whole?"

"Not swallowed," he said, and then was silent, letting her figure it out for herself.

"Oh, Christmas," she said. Her face paled slightly beneath her tan, and her freckles stood out. "We're really trying to go for total humiliation here, aren't we?"

"Just going by the book," Pete said. "And the book says that you'll be searched—completely. We have a physician waiting in another room."

"Oh, you mean you don't want to do it right here?" Annie said. She was furious. He could almost see her pulse accelerating as he watched the vein in her neck. "You sure you trust this doctor to do it right, pal? I would've thought you'd want to watch."

"I'd love to watch," he said, his voice coming out low and intimate, even through the tinny speakers. "And by the way, the name's not *pal*."

"I prefer to personalize the disembodied voices that talk to me," she said. "It helps me feel more human. But you wouldn't know about that, would you?"

She turned away from the window suddenly, but not before he saw the glint of tears in her eyes.

Pete felt ashamed of himself. What was wrong with him? Why did he have to be so rough on her?

He was rough on her because he felt for her, because he found himself believing her. And he had absolutely no facts to back him up, just gut instinct. *Gut,* thought Pete, *yeah, right. Aim a little lower....* He couldn't let himself forget that Dr. Anne Morrow was a suspect, quite possibly a thief, connected to people who wouldn't think twice about killing to satisfy their greed.

He watched her pull on her pants and then her shirt as the female agent led her from the room. With a nod, he ordered the microphone connection cut.

Whitley Scott was watching him.

"She's gutsy," Pete said to him. "You've got to give her that much."

"I think she's hiding something," Scott said. "We've got to find a way to get closer to her. But how?"

"Good question." Pete leaned against the back wall of the room, crossing his arms in front of him. "I'm not exactly qualified to work in her laboratory. Or even on one of her digs."

"Client?" Whitley asked. "You could bring her some rare artifact to authenticate. One thing leads to another—a little dinner, a little who knows what, and she's telling you her deepest, darkest secrets."

"Perfect," Pete said expressionlessly. "Except she never dates her clients as a rule. No exception."

"Next-door neighbor?"

"She lives over her lab in a restored Victorian house up in Westchester County," Pete said. "Expensive neighborhood. Way out of our budget. It would cost us close to half a million to buy one of the houses next door—provided someone was even willing to sell. And I've already checked—no one wants to rent."

Whitley nodded, turning toward the door. "Well, keep thinking," he said. "We'll come up with something sooner or later."

Chapter 2

Annie pulled her little Honda into the driveway and turned the engine off. Damn, she was tired. Damn the CIA and damn the FBI and damn everyone who was working so hard to make her life so miserable.

Five months. The harassment had been going on almost nonstop for five months. And now, after the bombing in England, it was only going to get worse. Already everyone in town knew that she was the subject of an FBI investigation. The agents had talked with everyone she knew, and probably a lot of people she didn't know. Her college roommate had called last month to say that even she'd been questioned about Annie. And it had been five years since they'd last gotten together....

Damn, damn, damn, she thought. And particularly damn that horrible man who'd spoken to her from behind the one-way window. Somebody had referred to him as Captain Peterson. If she ever ran into him, she'd let him have a good swift kick where it counted. Except she didn't have a clue what he looked like. She wouldn't even be able to recognize him from his voice, not from hearing it over those awful interrogation room speakers.

She stepped out of the car and went around to the other side to pull the package from England from the passenger seat. *Damn these gold artifacts, too,* she thought, as she barely lifted the crate. *They always weigh a ton.*

Her assistant's car was still in the driveway, so instead of going up to her apartment on the top floors of the house, Annie went into the lab. She could hear the sound of the computer keyboard clacking and followed it to the back room, where the office was set up.

Cara MacLeish was inputting data at her usual breakneck speed. She didn't even stop as she looked up and grinned.

"Welcome back," she said. Her short brown curls stood straight up in their usual tangle, and her eyes were warm behind her horn-rimmed glasses. "I thought you'd be here sooner. Like six hours ago."

Annie lowered the crate holding the gold death mask onto her desk top, then brushed some strands of hair back from her face. "I was detained," she said simply.

Cara stopped typing, giving her boss her full, sympathetic attention, swearing imaginatively.

"Took the words right out of my mouth," Annie said, smiling ruefully.

"FBI again?" Cara asked.

"FBI, CIA." Annie shrugged. "They all want a piece of me."

"Well, look on the bright side," Cara suggested.

They both fell silent, trying to find one.

"They haven't been able to make any charges stick," Cara finally said.

Annie pulled a rocking chair closer to the computer console and sat down.

"And you haven't lost any business because of this," Cara said, warming up to it now. She stretched her thin arms over her head, then yawned, standing up to get the kinks out of her long legs. "In fact, I think business has picked up. We had a ton of calls while you were away."

Annie watched her assistant cross to the telephone answering machine. Next to it, a stack of little pink message slips were held by a bright red wooden duck with a clothespin for a mouth.

"Jerry Tillit called," Cara said. "He's back from South America, and he's got some Mayan stuff for you to look at."

"Did you talk to him, or get the message off the machine?" Annie asked.

Cara blushed. "I spoke to him."

"Did he ask you out again?" Annie grinned.

"Yes."

"And...?"

"We don't date clients, remember?" Cara said.

Annie corrected her. "Jerry's not a client, he's a *friend.*"

"He's also a client."

"So he's also a client," Annie admitted. "But just because *I* don't want to date clients doesn't mean *you* can't, MacLeish. Will you please give the man a break?"

"I did."

"You... What?"

The taller woman grinned, pushing her hair back from her face and sitting down on top of the desk. "I told him I'd go out with him. He's coming up to drop his finds off this Saturday. We're going out after that."

Annie glanced around the cozy office. The room was really quite large, but with two desks, two computers, a fax machine, a copier and all sorts of chairs and bookshelves, there wasn't much room even to walk. But Cara MacLeish was an essential fixture here. "Don't you be going and getting married, MacLeish," she said sternly. "No running off to South America with Jerry Tillit."

Cara grinned. "I'm only going to the movies with him," she said. "The next logical step might be a dinner date. Not marriage."

"You don't know Tillet as well as I do," Annie muttered. "And that man has a definite thing for you...."

"Speaking of marriage," Cara said, flipping through the phone message slips. "Nick York called—five different times. Something about a party down at the Museum of Modern Art sometime this month."

Annie released her hair from its ponytail, letting it swing free in a gleaming brown sheet. She leaned back in the rocking chair, resting her feet on top of the computer desk. "Shame on you, MacLeish. You know the words *marriage* and *York* cannot be uttered in the same sentence," she said. "York wants only two things from me. One of them is free lab work. And the other has nothing to do with marriage. Who else called?"

"The freight guy at Westchester Airport said a package from France will be in Saturday."

"Great." Annie sighed. "Like I've got any chance of getting to work on it in the next decade." She closed her eyes. "Okay, so I pick it up on Saturday. What else?"

"A guy named Benjamin Sullivan called," Cara said. "Ring any bells?"

Annie's eyes popped open. "Yeah, of course. He's the owner of the piece I just picked up. What did he want?"

"He left a message on the machine, saying that we should ignore Alistair Golden if he calls," Cara said. She laughed. "I didn't recognize Sullivan's name, but it seemed kind of mystically, cosmically correct to get a message from a stranger telling us to ignore Golden. I always ignore Alistair Golden. Ignoring Golden is one of the things I do best."

Golden was Annie's chief competitor, and he usually handled all the U.S.-bound artworks and artifacts from the English Gallery.

"And sure enough," Cara said, snickering, "the little weasel called. He was in a real snit, whining about something—I'm not sure exactly what, because I was working very hard to ignore him."

Annie laughed. "I think I know what the bug up his pants was," she said. "When I got to the gallery, Sullivan's package was already crated and sealed. Golden had assumed he'd be doing the authentication job, so he'd already done the packing work."

"Golden packed the crate for you?" Cara said with great pleasure. "No wondering his whine was set on stun. He wanted you to call him back, but unless you want to subject yourself to a solid forty-five minutes of complaining, I wouldn't. I give you my permission to use the 'scatterbrained employee didn't give me the message' excuse for the next time he catches up with you."

Annie smiled. "Thanks. Did Ben Sullivan want me to call him back?"

"He said something about going out of town," Cara said, glancing back at the phone message slip. "Who is he? How do you know him? Come on, fill me in. Height, weight, marital status?"

"As far as I know, he's single," Annie said, then smiled. "But he's also seventy-five years old, so get that matchmaking gleam out of your eyes."

Cara made a face in disappointment.

"Ben's an old friend of my parents." Annie leaned back in her chair, breathing deeply. "I don't think I've seen him since, wow, since I was about fifteen. Apparently, he was talking to Mom and Dad recently, and they told him about me—you know, that I opened this lab a few years ago. When the offer to buy came in on this death mask, he requested that I do the necessary authentication."

"Instead of Golden," Cara said.

Annie grinned. "Instead of Golden." She sat forward, stretching her arms over her head. "Anyone else call?"

Cara nodded. "Yeah. I saved the best message for last. It came in on the answering machine. Let me play it for you."

Cara slid off the table, handing Annie the message slips, then pushed the message button on the machine. The tape rewound quickly, then a voice spoke.

It was odd, all whispery and strange, as if the caller had deliberately tried to disguise his voice. "The mask you have gained possession of does not belong to the world of the living. It is the property of Stands Against the Storm. Deliver it at once to his people, or be prepared to face his evil spirit's rage. The doors to the twilight world are opened wide, and Stands Against the Storm will take you back with him."

There was a click as the line was disconnected. Cara punched one of the buttons on the machine and the tape stopped running. "So, okay." She grinned. "Which one of your weirdo friends left *that* message? And who the heck is Stands Against the Storm?"

But Annie wasn't laughing. Swearing softly under her breath, she stood up, hoisted the crate containing the death mask off her desk and went down the hall toward the lab. Cara followed, her grin fading.

"What?" Cara asked, watching as Annie locked the front door. "What's the matter?"

"We've got to put this in the safe," Annie said, gesturing to the package in her arms.

"Annie, who *was* that on the tape?" Cara asked, eyes narrowing.

"Some crackpot," Annie said, heading back to the sturdy vault that sat directly in the middle of the house, surrounded by the lab in the front and the office in the rear. It was secure, impenetrable. She would feel a lot better after she locked the gold death mask inside.

"If it was just some crackpot," Cara demanded, "why did you rush across the room and lock the door?"

Annie opened the innocuous-looking closet door to reveal the combination lock of the big safe. She spun the red dial several times before entering the numbers. "Because it would be foolish not to take precautions, crackpot or not." She looked up at her assistant. "You must not have had a chance to read the background info I left you on this project."

Cara shrugged expansively. "I cannot tell a lie. I had about an hour of free time last night, and I spent it watching 'Quantum Leap' instead of reading about nineteenth-century Indian chiefs."

Setting the package on the top shelf of the vault, Annie swung the door shut, locking it securely. "Native Americans, not Indians," she corrected Cara. "In a nutshell, the artifact we're testing for authenticity is supposedly a gold casting of a death mask of a Navaho named Stands Against the Storm. He was one of the greatest Native American leaders. He was a brilliant man who truly understood Western culture. He tried to help the white leaders understand his own people as thoroughly."

Cara followed her back into the office. "How come I've never heard of him?" she asked. "I mean, everyone knows Sitting Bull and Geronimo. Why not this guy?"

Annie sat down behind her desk, frowning at the chaos on its surface. Why was it that paperwork seemed to multiply whenever she went away for a few days? "Sitting Bull and Geronimo were warriors," she said. "Stands Against the Storm was a man of peace. He didn't get as much press as the war party leaders, but not from lack of trying. In fact, he was in England, trying to drum up support for his people among the British, when he died." She shook her head. "His death was a major blow to the Navaho cause."

"If Stands Against the Storm was such a peaceful guy," Cara said, "then why would he have an evil spirit?"

"The Navaho believe that when people die, they become ghosts or spirits," Annie said. "It doesn't matter how nice or kind a person was during his life. When he dies, he becomes malevolent and he gets back at all the people who did him wrong during his lifetime. Chances are, the nicer the guy was, the more evil his spirit would be—the more he'd have to avenge. You know, nice guys finish last and all that."

"But if Stands Against the Storm died in England," Cara said, "then how could his spirit come after you?

Assuming for the sake of this discussion that the Navaho are right about this spirit stuff," she added.

"Death is a major problem for the Navaho," Annie said. She smiled. "Actually, I can't think of too many cultures that look forward to death, but the Navaho *really* don't like it. In fact, if someone dies inside a house, even today, that house will sometimes be abandoned. See, the Navaho believe that the place a person dies in, and the things he touches before dying or even after he's dead, can contain his bad spirit. Making a death mask would be a real invitation to disaster. The Navaho would *never* make something like a death mask. But it was the custom at the time in England, you know, to make a mold of the dead person's face and then cast a mask from it to get a likeness. I guess Stands Against the Storm was something of a celebrity—and certainly a curiosity, a Red Indian from the Wild West—so when he died, they made a death mask."

Annie looked over at the answering machine. What she couldn't figure out was how it had become public knowledge that she was working on authenticating Stands Against the Storm's death mask. Unless Ben Sullivan, or Steven Marshall, the purchaser, had leaked something....

"Hey, Annie?"

She met Cara's worried brown eyes. "It just occurred to me," the taller woman said. "That message on the answering machine is basically a… Well, it's a death threat."

"It was just some nut." Annie shrugged it off. "Besides, I don't believe in ghosts."

"You gotta admit, it's creepy," Cara said. "Maybe we should, I don't know… Call the police?"

Annie groaned, dropping her head onto her arms

on the desk top. "No more police, no more FBI, no way. I'd much rather be haunted by the spirit of Stands Against the Storm."

Annie sat up in bed, wide-eyed in the darkness as the burglar alarm shrieked.

Her heart pounded from being awakened so suddenly. She clicked on the light and grabbed her robe. Oh, Christmas! This damned alarm was going to raise the entire neighborhood.

She ran down the stairs two at a time and turned on the lights in the foyer as she crossed toward the alarm-system control panel.

Oh my God, thought Annie. It wasn't a malfunction! The alarm schematic showed a breach in the system on the first floor. A window in the lab was marked as the intruder's point of entry.

Suddenly she was very glad for the shrieking alarm. Across the street, she could see the neighbors' lights go on, and she knew they'd call the police—they always did. She ran back up to her room and opened the drawer on her bedside table. Oh, damn, damn, damn, where *was* it?

She pulled the drawer out of the table and emptied it onto her bed. *There* it was.

She grabbed the toy gun, unwinding a stray piece of string from the barrel, and headed toward the stairs. She ran down and kicked open the door to the lab. She flicked on the light switch with her elbow and the bright fluorescent bulbs illuminated the room.

No one was there—either human or inhuman.

But the window had been broken.

Feeling just a little silly, she put the plastic gun down on the lab counter and stepped carefully toward the large rock that had been thrown through the window. There was a piece of paper attached to it with a rubber band.

Spinning lights from two police cars caught her eye as they pulled into her driveway. She went to the front door and keyed into the control panel the code to cancel the alarm. The shrill noise stopped instantly. Taking a deep breath, she opened the door to the town police officers.

They came inside and looked at the broken window. One of them made a quick survey of the house, checking to make sure all the windows and doors were still locked, while the other radioed in to the station.

Big doings in a small town. Annie sighed. She went into the kitchen and put on a pot of coffee. Something told her this was going to be a long night.

Peterson woke up instantly and answered the phone after only one ring.

"Yeah," he said, looking at the glowing numbers of his clock: 3:47. He ran one hand across his face. "This better be good."

"It's Scott. Can you talk?" Whitley Scott said in his flat New Jersey accent.

"Yeah, I'm awake," Pete said, sitting up and turning on his light.

"No, I mean…are you alone?"

"Yeah, I'm alone." Pete rubbed his eyes. "If you check my file, you'll see that I haven't been involved with anyone since last March."

"I've already checked your file," the FBI agent said easily. "And *it* says you've got something of a reputation as a tomcat."

Pete was silent, thinking about that new administrative assistant in the New York City office. Carolyn something. She had curly brown hair and legs a mile long. And eyes that made it more than clear that she was interested in him, no-strings-attached. She'd invited him out for a drink last night. If he had gone with her, she'd probably be lying here right now, next to him.

But he'd turned her down.

Why? Maybe because, regardless of the fact that he'd be using her the exact same way, he was tired of being the flavor of the month for ambitious, upwardly mobile women.

Even though he wasn't overly tall, he knew that with his black hair and his dark brown eyes, he had the dark and handsome part down cold.

For years, he'd used his good looks to his advantage, but recently it had been rubbing him the wrong way. His relationships, which usually lasted a month or two, were getting shorter and shorter. And when he'd looked at that administrative assistant last night, he hadn't felt the usual heat from knowing that she wanted him. If he'd felt anything at all, it had been disdain.

More than once over the past few months, the thought of retiring from the agency had crossed his mind. The closer he got to his fortieth birthday, the more aware he seemed to become of an emptiness in his life.

He couldn't figure out what he was looking for. He was far too jaded to believe in true love—hell, he was too jaded to believe in any kind of love. And if he stopped having relationships based on animal attraction, on sex, he was in for a whole lot of cold, lonely nights....

"You still there?" Whitley Scott asked.

"Yeah."

"We've found a way for you to get close to Anne

Morrow," Scott said. "She practically handed it to us on a platter."

Pete listened intently as Scott explained. It would work. It would definitely work.

After he hung up the phone and turned the light off, Pete stared up at the dark ceiling, feeling a wave of anticipation so charged that it was almost sexual. In a sudden flash of memory, he saw black lace against pale skin, and a pair of wide, blue eyes....

"The note said what?" Cara's voice rose sharply.

"It was stupid," Annie said, clearing some of the clutter off her desk. "I can't believe the police took it seriously."

"When someone bothers to send a message via a rock through a window," Cara said tartly, "it should probably be taken seriously."

"But, God, did they *have* to notify the FBI?" Annie said. "You know, the Federal agents got over here really quickly. I'm wondering if they weren't somehow responsible. I mean, they've been hassling me every other way imaginable. Why not a rock through a window?"

"With a note saying 'Prepare to die'?" Cara asked. "I doubt it, Annie."

"And *I* seriously doubt that a Native American group, no matter *how* radical or fringe, would resort to this kind of petty threat," Annie said. "The FBI can go ahead and investigate, but they're just wasting their time." She sat back in her chair, her normally clear blue eyes shadowed with fatigue. "I just don't need the FBI's garbage on top of everything else. You know, they wanted to provide me with round-the-clock protection. Surveillance is more like it. I told them I could protect myself perfectly well, thank you very much."

"I don't suppose you told them that the likeliest suspect is a ghost called Stands Against the Storm," Cara said. "Maybe we should've called Ghostbusters instead of the police." She sang the familiar horn riff to the original movie theme.

Annie laughed, searching for something on her desk to throw at her friend. She settled for an unsharpened pencil.

Cara dodged the pencil and grinned. "Of course, if a ghost isn't a freaky enough suspect, there are always Navaho witches."

Annie tiredly closed her eyes. "I see you finally read the background information I gave you."

"'Quantum Leap' reruns weren't on last night," Cara said. "So I had some free time. Fascinating stuff. I particularly liked the part that said the Navaho believe some people—who appear to be normal during the day—are really witches. And if plain old witches who can cast spells and wreak havoc aren't bad enough, these witches can transform themselves into giant wolves at night and roam the countryside. Very pleasant."

"Most cultures have some version of bogeymen that stalk the night," Annie said. "Werewolves are nothing new."

"Yeah, but *these* werewolves are neighbors, relatives even," Cara said. "And they start doing their witchy business when they get jealous of another person's wealth or good luck or— Hey, that's it." Cara grinned. "Call the FBI off. I've figured it out. Alistair Golden is really one of these witches, and he's cast horrible bad-luck spells on you because you're starting to steal away some of his business. Although, actually he'd make a better weasel man than a wolf man."

"There's a big hole in your theory," Annie said. "Golden's not Navaho."

"Good point." Cara's eyes narrowed, taking in the pale, almost grayish cast to her friend's face. "The guy fixing the window won't be done for another hour or so," she said. "Why don't you go upstairs and take a nap? I can hold down the fort."

The phone rang.

"That's got to be my call from Dallas," Annie said. "I called Ben Sullivan but he's out of touch for a while. He's on a dig in Turkey, so my contact for the death mask is the buyer, Steve Marshall."

Cara picked up the phone. "Dr. Morrow's office. MacLeish speaking." She listened for a moment, her eyebrows disappearing under her bangs. "One moment, please," she said. She covered the speaker with her hand as she gave the handset to Annie. "What, are you clairvoyant, now, too? It's Steven Marshall. Calling from Dallas."

Annie smiled wanly as she took the phone. "Hello?"

"Dr. Morrow," came the thick Texas drawl. "My secretary tells me you've been trying to reach me?"

"Yes, Mr. Marshall," Annie said. "Thanks for getting back to me so quickly. We're having a little problem."

Briefly she described both the threatening phone call and the follow-up note that had come through her window.

"I don't think there's any real danger," Annie said. "But I felt I had to notify you and give you the opportunity to have the artifact authenticated by an establishment with higher security."

There was a moment of silence. Then Marshall said, "But…you're the best, aren't you, darlin'?"

"Well, yes, I like to think so," Annie said.

"I'm more concerned with your personal safety," he said. "Are you frightened? Do you want to get out of this contract?"

"Not at all. It's just that I may not be set up to provide security at the level necessary to protect the piece," she explained.

"Oh, that's just a little bitty problem," Marshall said with the easy nonchalance of the very wealthy. "We can solve that, no sweat. *I'll* provide the security, darlin'. I'll send a man over later this afternoon. He'll be responsible for the safety of the death mask. He'll also act as your bodyguard."

Oh, great, just what she needed. A pair of biceps following her around. She took a deep, calming breath. "Mr. Marshall, that's not necessary—"

"No, no, darlin', I insist."

"But I'm backlogged," Annie protested. "It's going to be weeks before I even get a chance to *look* at the artifact. And the tests I need to perform will take that much time again. My contract states an estimated completion date of mid-December. That's over *two months*—"

"I'll tell the guy to be prepared to stay for a while."

"But—"

"I gotta get back to work now," Marshall said. "Nice talking to you, darlin'. I'll be in touch."

"But—"

He hung up.

"But I don't *want* a bodyguard!" Annie wailed to the buzz of the disconnected line.

"A what?" Cara asked.

Annie hung up the phone with a muttered curse. "I'm going to take a nap," she said, stalking toward the door. "Maybe when I wake up, this nightmare will be over."

"Did you say *bodyguard?*" Cara's voice trailed after her.

Annie didn't answer.

Cara's face broke into a wide grin. A bodyguard. For Annie. This was going to be an awful lot of fun to watch.

Chapter 3

Annie stretched, luxuriating, enjoying having spent the day in bed. It was a real self-indulgence, particularly since she had so much to do in the lab.

But she wouldn't have gotten a whole heck of a lot done if she'd tried to work. Her concentration would've been way off because of her fatigue, and she would have ended up having to do everything over again. So instead she'd slept hard, and now felt much better. And hungry. Boy, was she hungry.

She pushed back the covers and went into her bathroom to wash her face, deciding against a shower. Why bother? Cara would be leaving for home in an hour or so. And the artifacts Annie had to run tests on didn't care if she worked in her pajamas. She brushed the tangles out of her hair and put some moisturizer on her face.

The sky outside the window was dark, she realized suddenly. It must be later than she thought.

She went down the stairs barefoot, calling, "Mac-Leish! Are you still here?"

"No, she went home."

Annie stopped short at the sight of the stranger standing in the shadows of the foyer. How did he get in? What was he doing here? Fear released adrenaline into her system and, heart pounding, she stood on the stairs, poised to turn and run back up and slam the door behind her.

He must have realized that he had frightened her, because he spoke quickly and stepped into the light. "Steven Marshall sent me," he said, his voice a rich baritone with a slight west-of-the-Mississippi cowboy drawl. "My name's Pete Taylor. I'm a security specialist. Your assistant let me in. She didn't want to wake you...."

He was not quite six feet tall, with the tough, wiry build of a long-distance runner. His hair was black, and cut almost military short. His face was exotically handsome, with wide, angular cheekbones that seemed to accentuate his dark eyes—eyes of such deep brown, it was impossible to tell where the iris ended and the pupil began. His lips were exquisitely shaped, despite the fact that he wasn't smiling. Somehow Annie knew that this was not a man who smiled often.

He held out his wallet to her, opened to reveal an ID card encased in plastic.

Annie couldn't keep her hand from shaking as she took the smooth leather folder from him, and she saw a flash of amusement in his dark eyes. He thought it was funny that he scared her. What a jerk.

She sat down on the steps as she looked at the ID. Peter Taylor. Age 38. Licensed private investigator and security specialist. The card gave him a New York City address, in a rather pricey section of Greenwich Village. Across from the ID card was a New York State driver's license. She lifted the plastic flaps and found an American Express Gold Card for Peter Taylor, member since 1980, a MasterCard, a Visa and a Sears credit card. He was carrying over five hundred dollars cash in the main compartment, along with several of his own business cards.

She tossed the wallet back to him and, as their eyes met, she saw another glint of humor on his otherwise stern face.

"Do I pass?" he said. As he tucked the wallet into the inside left pocket of his tweed jacket, she caught a glimpse of a handgun in a shoulder holster.

Annie nodded. "For now," she said, working hard to keep her tone formal, polite. "But just so that it's out in the open, I think you should know that I don't want you here. I consider your presence an imposition, and I intend to speak to Marshall about it tomorrow. So don't bother unpacking—you'll be leaving in the morning."

"When I spoke to Mr. Marshall this afternoon, he was adamant that I remain," he said. "Apparently he's concerned for your safety. Somehow I don't see him changing his mind so quickly."

Annie stared at him. His feet were planted on the tile floor, legs slightly spread, arms crossed in front of his chest. His jeans were tight across the big muscles in his thighs. His belt buckle was large and silver and obviously Navaho in origin. Annie couldn't see it clearly, but there was a silver ring on his right hand that also looked Navaho. He wore a necklace, but it was tucked into his shirt. She would bet big money that he was at least half Native American, and probably Navaho.

"Where did you grow up?" she asked.

He blinked at the sudden change in subject. "Colorado," he said. "Mostly."

His shoulders stiffened slightly. So very slightly, he probably didn't even realize it. But Annie noticed. Something about the question had made him feel defensive, wary. Was it that she'd asked a personal question, or did his wariness have something to do specifically with Colorado, or the "mostly" that followed it?

She was instantly fascinated. It wasn't because he was outrageously handsome, she tried to convince herself. Her attraction toward him—and she *was* attracted, she couldn't deny that—was more a result of his quiet watchfulness, spiced with a little mystery. He had something to be defensive or at least wary about. What was it?

"You ride horses, don't you, Taylor?" she asked, head tilted slightly to one side as she looked at him, hooked into trying to solve the puzzle, hoping for another clue from his reaction.

She was watching him, Pete realized, studying him as if he were an artifact, memorizing every little detail, searching for his flaws and weaknesses.

Her hair was down around her shoulders, parted on the side and swept back off her face. It gleamed in the light. She wore a too-large pair of men's pajamas, with the legs cuffed and the sleeves rolled up. There was no makeup on her face, and instead of giving her that naked, vulnerable look most women have without cosmetics, she looked clean, scrubbed and fresh.

Her eyes were a brilliant blue, and she met his gaze steadily, as if she were trying to get inside his head.

"Yeah," he finally said.

"I figured it was either horses or a bike," she said. "Don't you feel odd, carrying around a gun?"

"No."

"What do you know about death masks?" she asked.

"Not much." She was firing off questions as if this were some kind of interview. He decided to play it her way. It might make her start to trust him. It certainly couldn't hurt—he wasn't going to tell her anything he didn't want her to know.

"How about art authentication?"

"Ditto."

"A Navaho leader from the nineteenth century named Stands Against the Storm?"

"Only the information that Marshall faxed me this morning," he said.

"Have you read it?"

"Of course."

She watched him thoughtfully. "Where did you go to school?"

He shifted his weight. While most people would have been loath to admit their ignorance, it hadn't bothered him one little bit to tell her he knew next to nothing about death masks and art authentication. But *this* question about himself, about his background, made him uncomfortable, Annie thought. Now, why was that?

"NYU," he said. The bio the agency had created for Peter Taylor had him attending New York University from 1973 to 1977. Truth was, he hadn't even set foot in New York until 1980. But he'd been Pete Taylor so many times, on so many different assignments, he almost had memories of the imaginary classes....

"Are you aware that I'm currently under investigation by the FBI and the CIA?" she asked, her blue eyes still watching him.

He was caught off guard by the directness of her question and had to look away, momentarily thrown.

"They think I'm involved in some kind of international art-theft conspiracy," she said.

He glanced up at her and saw that her lips were curved in a small smile. "Are you?" he asked.

He made a good recovery, Annie thought. He *had* known about the investigation. She was willing to bet he had done a full background sweep on her before coming up from New York City. It didn't surprise her one bit. Marshall wouldn't have hired anyone who was less than outstanding.

"Are you hungry?" she said, standing and stretching, arms pulled up over her head, ignoring his question. "I haven't eaten all day, and if I don't have something soon, I'm gonna die."

Pete found his eyes drawn to the gap that appeared between her pajama top and the loose bottoms that rode low on her slender hips. "I ate already, thanks," he said. "Besides, I have an expense account that Mr. Marshall is covering. It's not fair that I should cost you money. After all, you don't even want me here."

"It's nothing personal," Annie said, climbing up the stairs, heading for the kitchen.

"I know," he said, following her.

She turned on the light in the kitchen and opened the refrigerator. She pulled an apple from the crisper drawer and took it to the sink, where she washed it quickly, then dried it with a towel.

The kitchen was a small room, just barely large enough to hold a table in one corner and a counter with a sink, stove, refrigerator and dishwasher in the other. It was decorated in black and white, with a tile floor that reminded Pete of a chessboard.

"I'd like to do a complete walk-through of the building," Pete said, watching her take a healthy bite of the apple. "I checked out the first floor and the basement while you were asleep. Your safe location is good. It would take a significant explosive charge to blow it open. But your general security is—" He broke off, shaking his head.

"Bush-league?" Annie supplied, leaning back against the counter, ankles and arms crossed, watching him as she ate her apple.

It didn't rate a smile, but there was a flicker of amusement in his dark eyes. "Definitely. A professional could get into this house without triggering the alarm system—no problem. Don't you read *Consumer Reports?* The system you have is known for malfunctions. It's unreliable. It's easily bypassed, and it goes off spontaneously."

Annie shaved the last bit of fruit from the core of the apple with her teeth, licking her lips as she looked up at him. "I've noticed." She opened the cabinet door beneath the sink and tossed the apple core into a compost container, then rinsed her hands.

His expression changed slightly. Most people might not have picked it up—it was just a very small contraction of his dark eyebrows. But Annie was trained to pay attention to details, and on a face as expressionless as he kept his, the movement stood out. "What?" she asked.

He blinked. "Excuse me?"

"Something's bugging you. What is it?"

She was standing only a few feet away from him, and he breathed in her natural fragrance. She smelled sweet and warm, with a little bit of baby shampoo, some rich-smelling skin lotion and tart apple thrown in for good measure. Although her pajamas were boxy and made of thick flannel, he was well aware of the soft, feminine body underneath. He felt his desire for her sparking, and he tightened his stomach muscles. Man, his entire office believed that she was a thief....

"I was wondering if that's all you're going to eat," he said levelly. Through sheer force of will he stopped his desire for her from growing. He forced it back, down, deep inside of him, willing it to stay hidden. For now, anyway. "It doesn't seem like very much, considering that you were so hungry. You should eat something more filling."

Annie laughed, her white teeth flashing. "This is great," she said. "A bodyguard who gives nutritional advice. How appropriate."

He smiled. It was actually little more than the sides of his mouth twitching upward, but Annie decided it counted as a smile. Shoot, with a full grin, he'd be as handsome as the devil. *More* handsome...

"Sorry," he said. "But you asked."

"You're right," she said, leading the way onto the landing, "I did. Look, I've got to get some work done."

She flipped her long hair back out of her face in a well-practiced motion, and hiked up her pajama bottoms. Pete wished almost desperately that she would put on some other clothes. It wasn't like him to be so easily distracted, but every time she moved, he had to work hard to keep from wanting her.

For a long time now, he'd gone without sex. Not because it wasn't available, but because he simply hadn't wanted it. Didn't it figure that his libido should suddenly come to life again out here, in the middle of nowhere, while he was alone in this big house with this beautiful woman? Man, as soon as he got back to the New York office, he'd have to look up Carolyn what's-her-name, the administrative assistant with the long legs....

"It *would* help if I could take a look at the top floors of the house," Pete said.

Annie shook her head. "Taylor, I don't mean to be rude," she said, "but I'm already two days behind in my work schedule. Frankly, there's no point in my showing you around, because after I talk to Marshall tomorrow, you're going to be catching the next train back into the city."

"I drove up," he said expressionlessly.

"I was speaking figuratively," she said.

"It's going to be hard for me to do my job without your cooperation," Pete pointed out.

She started down the stairs to the lab. "Why don't you use my phone to call your answering machine," she said, not unsympathetically. "Maybe someone called with a different job for you. You can work for them and get all the cooperation you could possibly want."

Annie stayed in the lab until shortly after two-thirty in the morning. She finished all but the last set of purity tests on a copper bowl that had been found at a southwestern archaeological dig site, believed to have been left by early Spanish conquistadors. That last test would take another two hours, and the thought of spending that much more time under Peter Taylor's unwavering gaze was far too exhausting. Besides, even if she finished the testing, she wouldn't have any conclusive evidence until the sample results came back from the carbon-dating lab.

She switched off the equipment and put the bowl back in the safe, turning to find Taylor still watching her.

He was sitting in a chair by the door. He didn't look tired despite the late hour. He didn't look uncomfortable or put upon or…*any*thing.

Christmas, he was making her nervous.

She thought about just breezing past him, out the door and up the stairs, but her conscience made her stop.

"There's a spare bedroom upstairs," she said. "You can sleep—"

But he was shaking his head. "No."

"Oh," she said. "I suppose you want to stay down here, to be near the safe—"

"The safe's secure," he said, pulling himself out of the chair in one graceful, fluid motion. "You'd need a crane to move it, and a ton of dynamite to get into it. If I sleep at all, it's going to be in your bedroom."

Annie stared at him, shocked. In her bedroom… But his words had been said matter of factly, expressionlessly, without any hint of sexual overtones. Either he had no idea of his physical appeal, or he was so confident, he didn't doubt that any woman would be grateful to share her bed with him. "I don't think so," she said.

He raised one eyebrow, as if he knew exactly what she'd been thinking. "I meant, on the floor."

Annie willed herself not to blush. "You'd be much more comfortable in the guest room," she said.

"But you would be much less safe," he countered. "Your alarm system is nearly worthless—"

"I'll be fine," Annie protested. This was starting to get tiring. Why wouldn't he just accept his defeat and sleep in the guest room?

He was blocking her way up the stairs, his arms crossed stubbornly in front of his chest. "Will you please let me do my job?"

"By all means," she said. "Do your job. Just do it in the guest room tonight."

He wasn't going to move, so Annie pushed past him, starting toward the stairs.

But he caught her arm, stopping her. His fingers were long and strong, easily encircling her wrist. The heat from his hand penetrated the flannel of her pajamas.

Her heart was pounding from annoyance, Annie tried to convince herself, not from his touch. She tried to pull away, but his grip tightened.

"I *am* going to protect you," he said. His face remained expressionless, but his eyes were like twin chips of volcanic glass.

He had pulled her in so close that she had to crane her neck to look up at him. "Maybe so," she said, and to her chagrin, her voice shook very slightly. "But who's going to protect me from you?"

Pete dropped her arm immediately.

"I don't know you from Adam," Annie said, stepping back, away from him, rubbing her arm. "For all *I* know, you're really the guy who's been making the death threats. For all *I* know, you've done in the real Peter Taylor."

"My picture's on my ID, *and* my driver's license."

"Everyone knows picture IDs are easy to fake—" She broke off, staring in fascination at his necklace. She'd noticed earlier that he wore silver beads around his neck, but until now she hadn't caught a glimpse of the necklace. It was clearly Navaho, with small coin-silver hollow beads, and five squash blossoms decorating the bottom half, along with a three-quarter circle design pendant, known as a *naja*.

Ignoring her trepidation, she took a step toward

him, lifting the *naja* in her hand. "This is beautiful," she said, glancing up at him before studying it more closely. Two tiny hands decorated the ends of the *naja*. "Navaho. It's quite old, too, isn't it?"

All of her anger, all of her uneasiness was instantly forgotten as she was caught up, examining the carefully worked silver. She looked at the necklace with real interest, real excitement sparking in her eyes.

Pete laughed, and Annie looked up at him in surprise. It was a rich, deep laugh complete with a grin that transformed his face. She had been right—with his face unfrozen, he *was* exceptionally handsome.

"Yeah," he said. "It's Navaho."

She was standing so close to him, mere inches away, holding the *naja,* but looking up at him. As he gazed into her wide blue eyes, he could feel the heat rising in him. What was it about her that made his body react so powerfully? He wanted to pull her into his arms, feel her body against his. He could imagine the way her lips would taste. Warm and sweet. Man, it would take so little effort....

Pete shoved his hands deep into the pockets of his jeans to keep from touching her.

"Your belt buckle is Navaho, too," she said. "And the ring on your hand, I think... I didn't really get a good look at it."

He pulled his right hand free from his pocket, glancing down at the thick silver-and-turquoise ring he wore on his third finger.

"Do you mind?" Annie asked, letting go of the pendant and taking his hand. She looked closely at the worn silver of the ring, at the delicate ornamentation. "This isn't quite as old as the necklace," she said. "But it's beautiful."

Her slender fingers were cool against the heat of his. She kept her nails cut short but well-groomed, and wore no jewelry on her hands.

"I thought you were a specialist in European metal-works," he said. "How come you know so much about Native American jewelry?"

She turned his hand over, looking at the other side of the ring. "When I was a kid, I spent about six years at sites in Utah and Arizona, one year in Colorado. Out of all the places we ever lived, my favorite was the American Southwest. When I went to college, I even considered specializing in Native American archaeology."

"Why didn't you?"

"I don't know," she said. "I mean, there were a lot of different reasons." She looked down at his ring again. His hand was so big, it seemed to engulf both of hers. He had calluses on his palm, and two of his fingers had healing abrasions on the knuckles—as if he'd slammed his fist into a wall. Or a person, she realized. In his line of work, it could very well have been a person.

He was looking down at her, making no attempt to take his hand away. Their eyes met, and for the briefest of instants, Annie saw the deep heat of desire in his eyes. Fire seemed to slice through her as her body responded, and she dropped his hand, noticing with rather horrified amusement that he had let go of her with as much haste. What had he seen in her eyes, she wondered. Was her own attraction for him as apparent?

She looked away, taking a step back from him, once again heading for the stairs. "Good night," she said, her voice sounding strange and breathless.

But he was in front of her, leading the way up to the second floor. "At the very least, I want to check out your room," he said. "Make sure all the windows are locked—"

"I can do that," Annie protested.

"Yeah, I know," he said as he went into her bedroom. "But I have to see it for myself."

The bed was still unmade from Annie's afternoon nap, and she saw him glance at her bright blue and green patterned sheets before crossing to the bay windows on the other side of the big room.

He pulled back the curtains and looked at each window carefully, checking to see that the locks were secure and the alarm system was working.

Annie stood in the middle of the room, arms crossed in front of her as she watched his broad, strong back. With his conservatively short black hair, she wouldn't have expected him to be wearing jeans with his tweed jacket, but somehow it didn't look out of place. The jacket was well tailored, fitting his broad shoulders like a glove. His jeans were loose enough to be comfortable, yet managed to show off the long, muscular lengths of his legs. Legs that went all the way up to—

She pulled her eyes away, not wanting to be caught staring at Taylor's butt. It *was* exceptional though, she thought, grinning, glancing back at him. Even with his hair cut so short, Taylor would have no trouble qualifying for one of those hunk-of-the-month calendars....

"What's so funny?" he asked, pulling the last of the curtains closed again and walking toward her.

"Nothing," Annie said, backing away.

"Look," Pete said. "I'd really feel a whole lot better if I could sleep in here tonight." He paused for a moment. "You won't even know I'm here," he added.

Oh, sure, Annie thought. And they're expecting

heavy snow this year in the Sahara desert. She forced herself to stay in control of what was rapidly becoming a ludicrous situation.

"No," she said. "Maybe I'd feel different if I thought I was in any kind of real danger. But I just don't buy it."

She walked him to the door. He hesitated before stepping out of the room, but finally he did.

"Feel free to use the spare room," Annie said. "It's across the hall. The bed's already made up."

He didn't say anything. He just watched her from behind his expressionless mask.

"See you in the morning," she finally said, closing and locking the door.

Pete stood out in the hall, listening as Annie got ready for bed. The water ran for a while in the bathroom, the toilet flushed and finally the lamp clicked off.

And still he stood there, just listening and waiting.

Chapter 4

Annie woke up at nine o'clock, before her alarm went off. Regardless of the fact that it was Saturday morning, she had work to do down in the lab. And wasn't today the day that Jerry Tillit was bringing in his latest finds from South America? *That* meant that Cara would be downstairs, despite it being a weekend. And there was that pickup she had to make at the airport....

She closed her eyes briefly. Damn, damn, damn. Six hours of sleep *used* to be enough. Five, really—she hadn't been able to fall asleep right away last night. She'd been thinking about...work. Yeah, right. Work. She was so far behind schedule, she had absolutely no time to spend thinking about anything or anyone else.

So why did Pete Taylor's dark eyes seem to penetrate her dreams?

Because his presence was a pain in the butt, Annie decided. And as soon as the sun came up in Texas, she'd give Steven Marshall a call and get this body-guard business straightened out once and for all.

Rolling out of bed, Annie tiredly pulled her pajama shirt over her head, then pushed her hair out of her face as she walked toward the bathroom.

Oh, Christmas, Taylor was sleeping on her floor.

She quickly covered herself with her flannel top, holding it against her body, slipping the fabric under her arms.

He was fast asleep, on some kind of thin sleeping bag with a blanket over him. He'd taken off his jacket and shirt, and even in repose, the hard muscles in his arms and shoulders stood out underneath his tanned skin. His face looked younger, softer, less fiercely con-trolled as he slept. Annie stared in fascination at the way his long dark eyelashes lay against his smooth cheeks.

He *was* a very good-looking man.

And he was leaving this morning, Annie reminded herself. So why the heck was she admiring his eye-lashes? She should be angry with him—God, he'd broken into her room while she was sleeping. She won-dered how long he'd stood watching *her* sleep. He had no right....

She reached out a toe to nudge him awake.

It happened so quickly. One moment she was stand-ing up—the next she was on the floor, on her back, with Pete Taylor's heavy body on top of her, his arm pressed up, hard, against her windpipe, cutting off her air.

Her first instinct was to fight, but he had her so thor-oughly pinned down, she could do little more than wig-gle against him. He was breathing hard, as if prepared to fight as he pulled his arm away from her throat.

Gratefully, she sucked in a breath of air as he stared down at her.

"Don't *ever* do that again," he said sternly, his eyes hard, his face harsh.

"Me?" Annie sputtered. "What did I do? I only woke you up. *You're* the one who tackled me and nearly choked me to death. *You're* the one who was asleep on my floor after I specifically told you I didn't want you in here, pal."

She glared up at him, straining against him, trying to get free.

Although he had taken off his shirt while he slept, he had kept his necklace on. Now it hung down between them, the pendant brushing her neck and shoulders and—

Oh, God, she'd dropped her pajama top.

Annie saw from the sudden flicker in his eyes that he realized it the same moment she did. His bare chest was against hers, skin against skin, hard against soft.

They both froze.

She could feel his heart beating against her. Or was it her own heart? Whoever's heart it was, it was starting to beat faster.

"I think you'd better get off of me," Annie whispered.

Silently Pete pulled back, sliding away from her. Man, she was beautiful, he thought, watching her grab for her pajama top and pull it over her head. Her breasts were soft and full, with large dark pink nipples that had hardened into firm buds at the tips.

Pete sat on his bedroll, leaning back against the wall, glad that he was wearing his jeans, that she couldn't see how badly he wanted her. Man, what a way to start the morning.

"I'm going to take a shower," she said, her cheeks faintly pink. "If that's all right with you."

"Yeah," he said.

"Sure you don't want to check the bathroom out first?" she asked, standing up and looking down at him, hands on her hips. "You never know—maybe there's a bad guy hiding in the toilet tank."

Pete stood up gracefully and walked past Annie into the bathroom.

"I was *kidding*," Annie said, following him, trying not to stare at the rippling muscles in his back.

The bathroom was decorated in sea greens and blues. There was a claw-footed tub in one corner. Another corner held a large shower stall. The sink had a marble countertop, and it was cluttered with Annie's makeup, lotions, soaps and shampoos.

There was a small window in the room, with frosted glass in the panes. Pete glanced at it, then tried the lock. It was secure.

He opened the door to the shower stall and looked inside.

"Oh, come on," Annie scoffed. "The window was locked. How could someone have gotten into my shower?"

Pete looked at her levelly. "Last night the door to your bedroom was locked. That didn't keep me from getting in. Hasn't it occurred to you that if I could do it, someone else could, too?"

She stared at him. Well, actually, no, it hadn't....

He went back into the bedroom. Annie followed him to the bathroom door and watched him roll up his blanket and sleeping bag. "If that's the case," she said, "why should I bother locking the door at all?"

Pete used a piece of string to tie the sleeping bag up.

"Locks on doors and windows will keep most people out," he said. He stood up then, folding his arms across his broad chest. "And as for the people determined to get in… That's what I'm here for."

"That's very good," Annie said. "You should write that down and use it on your business cards. Just the right amount of macho with a little superhero thrown in. I think it'll sell. Unfortunately, I'm not interested in buying."

She went back into the bathroom, not bothering to lock the door behind her.

The water in the teakettle had just begun to boil when Pete came into the kitchen. His hair was still wet from his shower, and he'd changed into a plain black turtleneck that hugged his muscular chest and was tucked neatly into his jeans.

Annie poured steaming water on top of the tea bag in her mug. "I don't have much to offer you in the way of breakfast," she said apologetically. "I usually don't do much more than eat some fruit myself, and even that's running low—"

"I'm eating on Mr. Marshall's expense account, remember?" Pete said, sitting down at the kitchen table. "But if it's not any trouble, would you mind if I kept some supplies in your refrigerator?"

Annie leaned against the counter, holding her mug in both hands. "In theory, I don't object," she said. "But remember? After I talk to Marshall this morning, you're going to be leaving."

"No, I don't think so," he said.

"Well, I *do* think so," she said.

"Sorry, you're wrong," Pete said, unperturbed. "Mr. Marshall is very anxious to avoid bad publicity. Did you know that he's facing racketeering charges out in Dallas?"

"Steven Marshall?"

Pete nodded. "Call him if you want," he said. "But I know he's going to insist that I stay. If something happened to you, it would be *very* bad publicity for him."

"But what about *me?*" Annie said, putting her mug on the counter. Her bangs were pulled back from her face with an Alice in Wonderland-like headband. She wore a bright white sweatshirt over her jeans, and a pair of black lace-up boots. She sat down at the table, across from Pete. "I don't *want* a bodyguard. No offense, but... I *like* being alone."

"I'll try to stay out of your way," he said. "You won't even know I'm around."

"Yes, I noticed how well you stayed out of my way this morning, particularly when you pinned me to the floor," Annie said. "I can't wait to see what the rest of the day brings. Maybe a little kick-boxing?"

She noticed that he didn't even have the grace to look embarrassed as she left the room.

She *had* to talk to Steven Marshall.

Annie hung up the phone with a crash and an oath, making Cara look up.

"Old Steven M. didn't go for your 'I can take care of myself' routine, huh?" Cara said unsympathetically.

"He is *such* a jerk!"

"Things *could* be worse," Cara said.

"Yeah," Annie muttered. "You could start telling me exactly how they could be worse."

Cara ignored the comment. "You could have been stuck with one of those no-brain, mountain-of-muscles-type bodyguards with a shaved head and equally shaved intellect. If someone told *me* that I'd have to spend the next few weeks with a guy as gorgeous as Peter Taylor watching my every move, you wouldn't hear *me* complaining."

"But I like my privacy," Annie said, sitting down at her desk for about four seconds before popping up and pacing again.

"Hey," Cara asked, "did you catch sight of his necklace?"

"Navaho," Annie said. "Looks like it dates around 1860, maybe even earlier. You see his ring?"

"And the belt buckle? Yeah. You're gonna try to buy 'em, aren't you?" Cara finished clearing the files off her desk, uncovering a paperweight made of petrified wood, three framed pictures of her nephews and nieces and a plastic Homer Simpson doll with his head attached by a spring. She looked up at her friend. "Aren't you?"

Annie shook her head.

"You're kidding. Why not?"

"Because it's none of your business," Annie said crossly, throwing herself down into her chair again. "Since when do I have to justify myself to you? You work for me, remember?"

"You're not going to try to buy it off him because you like the man," Cara said triumphantly, making Homer's head bob wildly. "You like him, I knew it. You don't want to take advantage of him."

Annie put her head down on her desk. "Oh, Mac-Leish, he's going to be here for weeks and weeks and *weeks*. What am I going to do?"

"At least he's handsome," Cara said. "Imagine if you had to stare at some guy with no neck all day and night—"

Annie stared up at her. "Yeah, terrific. Great. Wonderful. He's handsome. He's gorgeous. To tell you the truth, I'd prefer staring at some guy with no neck. Taylor's so good-looking, it's distracting as hell, and he's... standing in the door, listening to me say this," Annie said, looking over at Pete, who was leaning against the door frame, amusement in his dark eyes.

"We were talking about you," Cara said unnecessarily. She smiled happily. "How embarrassing for us."

"It's not embarrassing," Annie said to Cara. "I mean, the fact that he's gorgeous shouldn't come as big news to him. He knows what he looks like. And the fact that we were discussing him also shouldn't put him into shock. He's invading my life, and I deserve a chance to bitch and moan about it—about *him*." Annie gestured toward Pete.

Still smiling happily, Cara said, "Annie just spoke to Marshall—"

"The bastard," Annie interjected.

"—on the phone," Cara finished. "Looks like you might want to get your suitcase in from the car and put it someplace a little more permanent."

"Oh," Pete said.

"Don't gloat," Annie snapped.

His eyebrows moved a millimeter. "All I said was—"

"I'm *so* annoyed," Annie said. "Marshall—"

"The bastard," Cara supplied.

"—doesn't think a woman can take care of herself," Annie sputtered. "I asked him to hire a female bodyguard—no offense, Taylor—"

"None taken," he said.

"—and Marshall—"

"The bastard." This time Pete interjected, his lips twitching up into a smile.

"—laughed that obnoxious wheezing laugh of his." Annie demonstrated it, sounding an awful lot like a circus seal in mortal terror. "And he said that he'd *still* have to pay Taylor—to protect the female bodyguard! He said being a bodyguard is a man's job! Of all the stupid, chauvinistic things to say! *And* he topped it off by calling me 'little lady'! As if '*darlin*' weren't bad enough. So I told him I quit. I told him he could take the stupid artifact and have it authenticated by a stupid *man*."

"And?" Cara asked, grinning in anticipation.

"Marshall—"

"The bastard—" Cara and Pete said in unison.

"Laughed again and said—" Annie imitated Marshall's heavy Texan accent "—'It's typical of a woman to try to break a written, binding contract.' Then he suggested we talk again when it was a better time of month! I wanted to reach through the phone, grab his nose and twist it—hard!"

"So?" Cara asked.

"So *nothing*. I've still got a contract *and* a bodyguard," Annie muttered, with a black look in Pete's direction.

"You know—" Pete started to say.

"You might not want to be talking right now," Annie interrupted him. "I'm starting to feel the urge to vent some of my hostilities, and you're looking like an extremely attractive target."

"Extremely attractive, eh?" Cara smiled, leaning back in her chair and putting her feet up on the desk.

"That's *not* what I meant," Annie said dangerously. "You're fired, MacLeish. Go make some copies or do whatever else it is that I pay you to do."

The phone rang, and Annie swooped toward it.

"Maybe it's Marshall," she said. "Maybe he changed his mind...." She picked up the receiver hopefully. "Hello?"

She'd pulled her headband out while she was pacing, and now she pushed her hair back from her face with one hand as she used the other to hold the receiver to her ear. As Pete watched, she stared into the distance, her eyes temporarily unfocused as she concentrated on the call. He saw surprise, then shock flash across her face. Then her blue eyes narrowed.

"Who is this?" she demanded. "You want to do those things to me? I *dare* you to try. Why don't you show yourself? Come here in person, instead of hiding behind threatening phone calls and rocks thrown through windows—"

Pete leapt toward her, grabbing the telephone out of her hand, trying to activate the tape recorder the FBI had left behind. But the connection had been broken, and the line buzzed with a dial tone.

"Damn it," he swore, hanging up the phone. "What the hell is wrong with you? Why didn't you record that call? And what the hell possessed you to say those things? You really want this guy to come out here?"

She was shaking. "Don't you shout at me!" she said, her eyes blazing. "I just listened to some crackpot describe some incredibly sick fantasy of his in detail, and I happened to have a major role. You can't expect me not to tell him off—"

"I expect you *not* to goad him on," Pete said, his own eyes glittering chips of obsidian. He stood with his hands on his hips, effectively pinning Annie in against her desk.

She wanted to move, but in order to do that she'd have

to push past him, or climb over her desk. So she stayed where she was and tried to hide her shaking hands by sticking them into the back pockets of her jeans.

Pete picked up a pad and a pen from her desk. "You have to tell me what he said to you," he said brusquely. "Word for word."

Annie shook her head. "Sorry, I can't."

"If you don't remember exactly—"

"That's not it," she said. "I can remember. I just… can't repeat what he said. It was too awful."

She tried to meet his gaze challengingly, but her eyes suddenly welled with tears. She swore softly and blinked them back. "I'm having a really bad day," she said.

Pete turned away, shocked at his emotional response to the tears in her eyes. He wanted to pull her into his arms, tell her everything was going to be okay and kiss her until her hands shook for an entirely different reason. He wanted to tell her he'd take care of her, protect her.

But he couldn't tell her that, and he certainly couldn't protect her without her cooperation.

Annie took the opportunity to move around to the other side of her desk and sit down. She wished that Taylor would leave her alone. God, wasn't it bad enough that she'd been subjected to that obscene phone call? She wanted to forget about it. The thought of having to tell him exactly what that creep had said to her made her cheeks burn.

Out of the corner of her eye, she saw Taylor pull up a chair across from her desk. He sat down, then looked over her head, across the room to where Cara sat. Annie glanced at her friend, who was watching them both with unabashed interest.

"Would you mind…?" Pete said to Cara.

Cara stood up uncertainly.

"Set up the final test for that copper bowl, please, MacLeish," Annie said. "I'll be out in the lab in a minute."

Cara hated being left out of anything, but she went out of the office. Pete stood up and closed the office door behind her.

Annie looked up at him as he sat back down across from her. To her surprise, his eyes were soft, kind even.

"The reason I wanted to record this call," he said quietly, "was to help us track the caller. And I'm not just talking about locating him—most of these people call from public telephones, so that doesn't do much good. But the FBI can use their computers and try to match phrasing or word choice or even sentence structure, in the event that this is a repeat pattern offender." He pushed the pad and pen toward her. "And that's why I need to know what he said to you. As exactly as you can remember. Maybe it would be easier for you to write it down."

For a long time she didn't move. She just stared at him. Then, suddenly, she picked up the pen and paper and began to write.

Pete sat back in his chair, watching her.

Sunlight was streaming in the window, and it lit her from behind, creating an auralike glow around her. Pete remembered the words he had overheard her saying to Cara. He distracted her. *He* distracted *her*? Not half as much as she distracted him, he was willing to bet.

He was carrying around this tight feeling of need all the time now, Pete realized. It no longer was triggered only by her quick smile, or her walk, or her low, sexy laugh. All he had to do was see her…. Man, all he had to do was *think* about her and, whammo, he wanted her. And when he wasn't with her, he sure as hell was thinking about her.... This could turn out to be one hell of an uncomfortable two months.

Annie finished writing, put the pen down on top of the paper and stood up. "I'll be in the lab," she said shortly and left the room.

"Thanks," Pete called after her.

She didn't respond.

He reached across the desk and picked up the pad she'd written on. As he read the words that the phone caller had said to her, his jaw tightened. The threats had a horrific, nightmarish quality to them. They were all violently sexual and graphically explicit.

He read it over and over, each time his sense of uneasiness growing. It was entirely possible that these were not idle threats meant only to frighten Annie. It was entirely possible that her life really was in danger.

He reached for the telephone and dialed Whitley Scott's number.

"One of us has to run out to the airport," Cara said to Annie as they finished up the test on the copper bowl. "We've got that package from France coming in."

Annie looked at her blankly.

"Remember, the package coming in to Westchester Airport?" Cara said. "The job you aren't going to get to for a decade? Subject of a conversation we had two days ago?"

"Right, right," Annie said. She had put her hair back into a ponytail while they were working, but now she pulled it free, and it swung down around her shoulders. She sat down on one of the wooden stools that were scattered throughout the lab. "MacLeish, when's the last time we took a vacation?"

Cara pushed her glasses up higher on her nose and frowned. "You mean, like a trip to Easter Island and two weeks of crashing through the underbrush and staring at giant rock heads from some distant, ancient culture? Or are you talking about Thanksgiving at the parents' house? *Or* do you mean Club Med—lying on the beach in bikinis while handsome men bring us daiquiris and margaritas?"

"I mean Club Med. I *definitely* mean Club Med."

Cara chewed her lip as she thought hard. "I've worked for you for...how long now?"

"Forever," Annie answered.

"Right. And the last time we took a vacation was... Never?"

"That decides it," Annie said. "We need a vacation. When we're through with what we've got—when's that gonna be?"

Cara shrugged. "End of December, beginning of January?"

"We're taking January off," Annie said. "Don't accept any more work unless the clients can wait until February for us to start the project."

"Thank you, Lord," Cara said to the ceiling. "Club Med, here we come! Bless you, master!"

Annie stood up. "Back to work, slave," she said. "I'm heading for the airport."

She quickly ran upstairs and grabbed her jacket and car keys. "See you later," she called out to Cara as she ran lightly down the stairs.

Outside, the air was crisp and cold, and she buttoned her jacket, thinking it was time to dig her scarf out of her closet—

Pete Taylor was standing next to her car.

"Ready to go?" he asked.

She looked at him blankly.

"I'm your bodyguard," he said patiently. "That means when you go someplace, I go, too."

Annie closed her eyes. *Please, God,* she thought, *when I open my eyes, make him be gone. Make this all just be a bad dream....*

He was still there. Damn, damn, *damn.*

"I'll drive if you want," he said.

"I *like* to drive," Annie said. But her car was piled high with books and papers and empty seltzer cans. And *his* car was a sporty little Mazda Miata.... Her eyes slid toward his shiny black car.

"We can take mine if you want," Pete said, as if he could read her mind. He held out the keys. "You can drive."

Slowly she reached for them. "What's the deal? Is it rented?"

He shook his head. "No," he said with one of his rare smiles.

"You'd trust me...?" Annie asked.

"You're trusting me with your life," Pete said. "I'll trust you with my car."

Annie got in behind the steering wheel and adjusted the mirrors. She didn't realize just how little the car was until Pete got in and nearly sat down on top of her. He was so close, they were practically touching. Maybe they should've taken her car instead....

She turned the key and the engine hummed.

"I faxed the FBI your transcript of that phone call," he said.

"Oh, great," Annie said sourly. "I'll bet they get a

good laugh out of *that*." She eased the sports car out of the driveway, feeling the power in the engine.

"They're checking a number of different leads," Pete said, ignoring her sarcastic comment. "There are a couple of radical groups who have already lodged ownership claims to Stands Against the Storm's death mask. And another group has sent a formal complaint, claiming it should be returned to the Navaho people in New Mexico."

"Don't tell me. None of those groups is actually connected to the Navaho," Annie said, glancing at him, already knowing the answer.

"You're right." A white flash of teeth made her turn quickly back to the road. His smile was a killer. It was a good thing he didn't do it more often. "The Navaho don't want anything to do with the death mask. As far as they're concerned, they were happier with Stands Against the Storm's bad spirit safely across the Atlantic Ocean in England."

"How do *you* feel about it?" Annie asked. "Having the death mask in the house?"

She risked another look at him. He wasn't smiling, but his eyes were lit with humor.

"You don't really think it would bother me, do you?" he said.

"You are at least *part* Navaho," Annie said. "Aren't you?"

"Yeah," he said. "Half. Is it that obvious?"

"Actually, no. But your necklace gave you away. It's so valuable. I figured it must have sentimental value to it, that it must be an heirloom and that's why you wear it. Because if you were just a collector, you'd keep it locked in a case."

"My grandfather gave it to me," Pete said. "His

grandfather made it. My great-grandfather made the ring and the belt buckle. They were all made to be worn—not locked away."

She glanced at him again. When she met his gaze, she felt a jolt of warmth that was different from the attraction that always seemed to simmer between them. This was friendly and comfortable. Oh, brother, she was actually starting to *like* this guy.

She pushed the Miata up to seventy.

"So what do you think?" she asked. "Who's really after this death mask? If it's not the Navaho…"

Pete shrugged. "Maybe the FBI's right and it's one of these radical Friends of the Native Americans groups."

"But you don't think so." She glanced over at him. He was watching her, his eyes warm. What would he do, she wondered suddenly, if she reached over and took his hand?

He'd assume she'd fallen for him—the way every woman who'd ever crossed his path had no doubt done. But she didn't want to be just another notch on his belt. No way. If she was going to be stupid enough to fall in love with this man, she was going to make damn sure he fell in love with her, too.

Something told her she'd better work fast. She already liked him, and Lord knows she was attracted to him. Her heart was ready for some bungee jumping. It had been a long time since she'd met a man she wanted to get to know better, a man she could imagine becoming involved with. And she could imagine being involved with Pete Taylor. Oh, baby, could she imagine it.

With very little work at all, she could imagine the way his strong, hard-muscled body would feel against hers. She could imagine his mouth curling up into one of his rare, beautiful smiles before he kissed her. She could imagine him in her bed, his hair damp with perspiration, his naked body slick and locked together with hers. She could imagine his dark eyes watching, always watching, learning all of her secrets, giving away none of his own.

She glanced at him again, then quickly looked away, afraid if he gazed into her eyes too long, he might somehow read her mind.

But he managed to anyway. When she looked up at him again, there was a moment when she could see deep hunger in his intense, dark eyes. But he turned away before she did, as if he, too, were fighting the attraction.

Annie cleared her throat, focusing all her attention on the exit ramp that led to the local airport.

Pete tried to wipe his damp palms inconspicuously on his jeans. Man, this woman disturbed him. One of these days, he was going to lose the last bit of his control.

Annie was following the signs leading to the main terminal parking lot. She slid the car into an empty parking space and shut off the engine. She turned in her seat and looked at him.

"How much danger am I really in?" she asked him point-blank. "Isn't it true that most of the creeps who make crank phone calls only intend to frighten their victims?"

"Yeah," Pete said. "But even if the odds are one in a million, why take that risk?" And the transcript she'd written from the last phone call had really bothered him. His gut reaction was that there was something to worry about here. It couldn't hurt to err on the side of caution.

"There's better than a one-in-a-million chance that

I'll be killed in a traffic accident, isn't there?" Annie said. "But I take that risk every day."

Pete was silent, just watching her as they sat in the car. What was he supposed to tell her? "I got a bad feeling about this," he finally said.

She smiled. "You and Han Solo."

He blinked. "What?"

"Star Wars," she explained. "Didn't you see that movie?"

"Yeah?"

"Well, that was what Han Solo kept saying," she said, then drawled, "'I got a bad feeling about this, Chewie.'" She laughed at the expression on his face. "Lighten up, Taylor, will you?"

"If memory serves me, Solo's premonition was on the money," Pete pointed out. "His ship was tractor beamed into the death star, right?"

"Yeah, well, you win some and you lose some," Annie said with a smile. "And they won in the end, when it really mattered."

Pete was watching her, and she looked back at him, examining his face as carefully. There was a small scar interrupting the line of his left eyebrow, but other than that, his features were the closest thing to perfection Annie had ever seen. His nose was straight and just the right size for his face. His eyes were large, with thick, long lashes that would put any mascara company to shame. They were framed by cheekbones of exotic proportions, making him not merely good-looking, but stunningly, dangerously handsome. His lips were neither too thick nor too thin, and sensuously shaped. But he held them far too tightly, giving himself a serious, almost grim expression. Although his hair was cut too short, it was dark and luxuriant. If it had been another few inches longer, Annie would have been sorely tempted to run her fingers through it. As it was, its length served to remind her who he was, and why he was here.

But looking into his eyes was like staring into outer space on a moonless night. Dark, endless, mysterious, exciting. With a hope and promise for adventure, and a consuming, beckoning pull.

Annie wondered why he didn't try to kiss her. As soon as the thought popped into her mind, she berated herself. Kissing her wasn't in his job description. She was a job, not a date.

On the other hand, there was no denying this attraction between them. Annie had seen it in his eyes before, just a flash here and there, but enough to make her catch her breath. It was there now as he looked at her—a hint of slow burning embers of desire, ready to leap into flames at the slightest encouragement.

A significant part of her wanted to give him that encouragement. But she'd had a relationship based on sex before, and it hadn't lasted. Shoot, wasn't her aversion to casual sex the reason she hadn't gone to bed with God's gift to women, Nicholas York? Except, as attractive as Nick was, he couldn't hold a candle to Pete. It had nothing to do with physical appeal—Nick was as handsome as Pete, but in a golden blond, blue-eyed way. In fact, with Nick's easy smile and cheerful facade, many women would find him the more attractive of the two men. But Annie could trust Nick only about as far as she could throw him. Sometimes she wondered if deception was a sport for him, or maybe a way of life.

Pete Taylor was mysterious, but her instincts told her that the man was honest. If pressed, he might lie, but it certainly wouldn't be a game to him. Not the way it would be for Nick.

And Pete Taylor wasn't entirely selfish. Or unreliable. Or as unfaithful as they come....

Of course, she hadn't realized Nick was any of those things when she first met him. And even though her instincts told her Pete was good and kind and honest, her instincts had been wrong before.

No matter how strong the chemistry was between them, Annie wasn't going to do anything rash or stupid. At least not intentionally, she told herself with an inward smile. Pete was going to be hanging around for nearly two months. That was plenty of time for them to get to know each other, to become friends. And after they were friends, if she still felt this nearly irresistible gravitational pull toward him, well, that's when she'd do something about it.

"You know what I think?" she finally said.

Silently, still watching her, Pete shook his head.

He didn't try to speak because he wasn't sure he could utter a word. In fact, Pete wasn't sure he could move. Somehow, during the last few minutes, the interior of the car had shrunk. Without either of them moving a muscle, they were now so close that all he'd have to do was lean forward to kiss her.

Pete forced himself to look into her eyes, not at her mouth. Not at her soft moist lips...

He had to get out of this car, or he was going to do something stupid. But he couldn't get out, because just looking into her eyes had turned him on so much, he couldn't even stand up without embarrassing himself. Damn, what was *wrong* with him? He felt seventeen again, and desperately out of control.

"*I* think the FBI is behind this whole thing," Annie

was saying. She climbed out of the car, then leaned down, sticking her head through the open door. "I think they made those phone calls and threw that rock through my window. I think this is just more of their intimidation technique."

Pete's face was expressionless. "I guess you think I'm FBI, too."

"Are you?"

He met her eyes squarely. "No," he said. "No, I'm not."

She nodded, her eyes never leaving his face. "This is stupid. You know, I have no reason to, but I actually believe you." A wry smile turned up one corner of her mouth. "I guess I sound pretty paranoid, huh? Come on, Han Solo, let's go inside."

Pete slowly climbed out of the car, and stood looking at her across the roof. He felt as if he were balancing on top of eggshells. So far he was okay, but he had to take a step, and it had better be a careful one....

"It must be rough," he said, "when no one believes you."

"Damn straight," she said.

"Tell me about the whole art-theft conspiracy mess," he said. "Maybe I can help."

She was looking at him, her blue eyes wide and vulnerable. Was she involved? He didn't have a clue. But maybe she'd tell him about it. *Trust me, Annie,* Pete thought. *Trust me, trust me, trust me—*

"Can you help make the FBI believe that I'm innocent?" she asked almost wistfully. Then she shook her head. "I'm innocent, but I can't prove it, so I'm being hounded. Whatever happened to innocent until proven guilty, Taylor? *That's* what I'd like to know."

She glanced at the terminal, then at her wristwatch.

"MacLeish said air freight is only open 'til three. We better hurry."

Pete watched her walk briskly toward the low brick building. Did he believe her? He wanted to.

Slowly he followed her into the airport terminal, watching the life in her quick step, the unconscious sexiness in the sway of her slim hips.

Yeah, he wanted to believe her, because he wanted her.

Normally he didn't allow sex to complicate things. Sex was...sex.

But he liked Annie. He really, truly liked her. And, strange as it might seem, he didn't sleep with women that he liked. Unless, of course, it was a totally mutual, honest relationship.

Well, they had the mutual part covered—Pete had seen the reflection of his own desire in her eyes. But honest? Mentally, he sounded the loser buzzer. Not much honesty here, at least not on his side of the relationship.

No, there was no way on earth that he was going to sleep with her. Even if she came to him and begged, he wouldn't.

Yeah, and my mother's the queen of England, he thought morosely.

Pete watched Annie sign all the papers releasing the valuable package into her custody. He slid the box closer to the edge of the air freight counter and lifted it. It was heavier than he'd imagined, he thought, frowning, and much too ungainly to carry with only one arm.

"We're going to need someone to carry this out to the car," he said to the man behind the counter.

Annie looked at him in surprise. "It's not *that* heavy," she said.

Pete actually looked embarrassed. "Yeah, well, I have this policy of never carrying anything that ties up both my hands at once. I need to keep at least one hand free, in case I need to go for my gun."

"Good point," Annie said dryly. "You never know when you'll need it to blow away some evil spirit."

"Sam's on a break," the man behind the counter said, unfazed by neither the mention of a gun or evil spirits. "He can help you, but he won't be back for another twenty minutes."

"We can wait," Pete said.

"No we can't," Annie said, exasperated, picking up the box herself. Pete opened his mouth to protest, but she cut him off. "What do I look like?" she asked. "Some kind of weakling? I'll carry it. I would have if I'd picked it up a couple of days ago, before you started following me around."

She started for the exit, aware of Pete's discomfort. He was a gentleman, she realized as he held the door for her. It really, truly bugged him to see her straining to lug something he could have carried easily.

"Okay, look," he said when they were outside. "I'll carry it."

Annie kept walking. "Absolutely not," she said. "You should stick to your rules. You always have, haven't you?"

He nodded slowly.

"That's probably why you're so good at what you do," she said.

"Yeah, but I feel like a jerk."

"The very fact that you feel like a jerk proves that you're not," Annie said with a smile. "So relax. You're a nice guy. Don't beat yourself up for sticking to your guns—no pun intended."

She thought he was a nice guy. Pete felt warmth and pleasure spread through him at her words. Sixth grade, he thought suddenly with an inward groan. He hadn't felt like this since sixth grade.

Chapter 5

Annie let Pete drive home. She sat in the front seat with the heavy package on the floor at her feet. She opened it carefully. There were two silver statues inside, wrapped in bubble pack and newspaper, stuffed into a box filled with big foam beads.

The statues glistened, a mournful shepherd kneeling and a Virgin Mary, both faces decidedly Byzantine. They had been cast from a mold, their seams worn with age, seemingly ancient.

Her heart began to beat faster as she examined them. These could be real. Boy, she loved it when the artifacts were genuine. She loved holding the smooth metal in her hands, knowing that other hands had held these the same way over the course of hundreds, even thousands, of years. She loved wondering about the people who had poured the metal, people turned to dust centuries ago....

Annie packed them back into the box, sighing with contentment, and looked out of the car window.

Traffic on Route 684 was heavy for a Saturday afternoon. Pete had the Miata all the way to the left, moving well above the speed limit. Still, a drab gray sedan pulled up alongside them, in the middle lane of the highway. Annie glanced over at the other car's driver.

He had thick, bushy brown hair that looked as if it hadn't been combed since the late 1980s. A full, shaggy beard covered most of the lower half of his face.

Annie pulled her eyes away, afraid to be caught staring. But the sedan didn't pass or fall back. Instead, it kept pace, right next to them.

Annie looked up again, and this time the driver looked over at her and smiled.

Her mouth dropped open in shock.

His teeth had all been filed into sharp-looking fangs. And his eyes…! His eyes were an unearthly shade of yellow-green.

Like an animal's eyes. Like some kind of cat or… Or a wolf.

Wide-eyed, Annie watched with revulsion as the man made an obscene gesture with his tongue. Then he lifted a bright orange squirt gun to the window and she realized the back of his hands were covered with the same thick brown hair—or fur!—that was on his head. He squeezed the trigger.

A stream of red sprayed the inside of his window, hanging on the glass, thick and bright as fresh blood.

"God!" Annie cried, jumping back and slamming into Pete's hard shoulder. "Did you see that?"

"What?"

"That car!" Annie said. But the gray sedan was already falling back, merging into the right lane. "That guy! He had a gun—"

Suddenly she was being shoved down, hard, her head pushed into Pete's lap, her ribs pressed into the gearshift. "Which car?" he shouted.

"The gray one," Annie said, her cheek against the worn denim of his jeans. She tried to sit up, but his arm was pinning her down.

Taylor swore. "I don't see it. Are you sure it was gray?"

The muscles in his thighs flexed and tightened as he drove. He smelled good, Annie thought suddenly, like fresh air and leather, a fading remnant of smoke from an open fire, and a warm, spicy sweet smell that she already recognized as being his own. It definitely wasn't fair. A man who looked as good as Taylor shouldn't be allowed to smell so good, too.

"Gray, four-door," Annie said. "Midsize. I think it might've been a Volvo." She twisted her neck to look up at him. His eyes were narrowed in concentration, his mouth an even grimmer line than usual. She pushed against him again. "Taylor, let me up!"

"Don't fight me," he snapped.

The muscles in his legs moved again, and Annie could feel the car slow. Pete moved his hand then, to downshift as he took the exit ramp off the highway.

She pulled herself up, sweeping her hair back from her face as she looked at him. He pulled into the lot of a 7-Eleven and parked, turning toward her.

"Are you okay?"

She nodded. There was real concern in his eyes. Pete took his job seriously—that much was clear.

"Did you get a good look at him?" he asked.

Annie nodded again. "I sure did," she said. "He

could have been anywhere from twenty-five to sixty years old. His hair was brown and shaggy, he had a full beard and bushy eyebrows that grew together in the middle. He looked like he hadn't showered or shaved in about ten years, and he was skinny.... More than skinny—gaunt...you know, hollow cheeks. He had yellow eyes and black claws at the ends of his...paws."

"Paws," Taylor repeated expressionlessly.

"Did I mention the fangs?" Annie asked. "He had fangs. A complete set."

He sighed, looking away from her, out the front windshield. "Are you sure?" he finally said, turning back to look at her. But even as he asked, he knew from the set expression on her face that she meant exactly what she had said.

"I'm sure. I notice details, and I remember them," she said. "It's my job, it's what I do. And you know, pal, details like fangs and paws aren't easy to forget." She ticked off the other details on her fingers. "The outside of the car was dull gray, the inside was beige, vinyl seats. His rearview mirror had a crack on the upper-right corner, and the driver had fangs. His left lateral incisor was filed shorter than the other teeth. He had a small mole next to his left eyebrow. I didn't get a clear look at the right side of his face. Presumably it was covered with as much hair as the left side of his face."

Taylor's eyebrow had twitched a fraction of an inch upward. "Anything else?"

"His gun wasn't real."

His eyes narrowed very slightly. "That's not always easy to tell," he said. "Even for someone who's good with details."

"This detail was kind of hard to miss," Annie said. "The gun was orange."

She was grinning at him, her blue eyes sparkling with humor. "It was a water pistol, Taylor," she said. "The only danger I was in was from you—and the gearshift." She rubbed her side. "I think I've got one hell of a bruise. If I'd known you were going to go all macho on me, I would've told you about the gun a little bit differently."

She gave Pete a quick description of the bloodlike liquid the man had sprayed on the inside of his window. "It was probably just a coincidence," she said. "It's getting close to Halloween. It probably didn't have anything to do with me."

"I don't believe in coincidences," Taylor said.

"*I* don't believe in werewolves or ghosts or witches, Navaho or otherwise," Annie said. "I seriously doubt the spirit of Stands Against the Storm drives a gray Volvo. And no self-respecting Navaho witch is going to leave the Southwest, let alone cruise the highways of suburban New York City in wolf form on a Saturday afternoon. If this wasn't a coincidence, I'd say it's a sure bet that someone is trying really hard to make it look as if the Navaho are behind the death threats. But if that's the answer, it leaves an even bigger question. Why?"

Jerry Tillet was in the office, perched on the edge of Annie's desk, smiling at Cara.

His reddish hair had grown long, and he wore it pulled back into a ponytail at the nape of his neck. He had a thick beard and mustache, and he wore a battered Red Sox baseball cap on his head. His skin was sunburned on top of a deep tan, and his clothes looked as though they hadn't seen a washing machine in weeks.

"Is it safe to stand downwind of you, Professor?"

Annie asked from the doorway. "That *is* you under all that hair, isn't it, Tillet?"

"Hey, Doc," Jerry said cheerfully. "Cara was telling me about the evil spirits. Bummer. So where's your little shadow?" His gaze flickered over Annie's shoulder. "Big shadow," he corrected himself.

Annie turned to see Pete standing behind her. She introduced the two men. "Peter Taylor, Jerry Tillet." Pete leaned past her to shake Jerry's hand, and she could feel the heat radiating from his body.

Why am I fighting this? she thought suddenly. *Why do I even bother when it would be so easy to give in?* But she knew the answer. She didn't know Pete at all. And if she slept with him just because her hormones were urging her to, and he turned out to be a real yuck or some kind of Attila the Hun, she'd feel mighty stupid. But still, there was something to be said for surrendering to the animal attraction.

Annie smiled, picturing the look on Cara's face if she suddenly said, "Excuse me, guys, but Taylor and I have to go upstairs and have sex now...."

Instead, Cara had her "I'm dealing with the village idiot" look on her face. "Well?" she asked Annie.

"Well, what?" Annie said. "Were you talking to me?"

"I asked if it was all right with you if Jerry and I left now. We were hoping to catch a double feature."

"Sure, I've just about had it myself," Annie said, straightening up, reaching her arms over her head, stretching out her back. She stopped, midmotion, aware of Taylor's dark eyes on her, aware that her sweatshirt was riding up, exposing several inches of bare stomach above the waistband of her jeans. With a quick tug, she pulled the sweatshirt back down.

"It's getting late," Pete said. "We have to go upstairs."

Annie froze. Then laughed nervously. Upstairs? There was no way he could have read her mind.... Was there? "Why?" she asked.

If he noticed any suspicion or hostility in her voice, he ignored it. "I need to check out the security system on your top floors. I need to know what has to be fixed or added to make this place secure," he said.

"I've got to lock this in the safe," Annie said, motioning to the box that she'd brought in from the car.

"Well, we're outa here," Cara said, grabbing Jerry's hand and pulling him toward the door. "See you on Monday, Annie."

Annie started to lift the heavy box, but Pete was there. "I'll get it," he said, picking it up.

She raised her eyebrows and he smiled. "I think I can probably risk carrying it all the way to the safe," he said.

Pete followed Annie down the hall and into the lab. "I've got the same alarm system upstairs as I do down here," she said, returning to their conversation. "You know, the kind that doesn't work real well? It also doesn't work real well upstairs, too."

Annie opened the door to the safe and Pete put the box on the shelf next to the crate containing Stands Against the Storm's death mask. She closed the door tightly, spinning the combination lock.

"You know how the alarm system works," she said. "So why do you need to look at it?"

"I need to do a window count," Pete said. "As long as Marshall's willing to foot the bill, you might as well let him upgrade your security."

"How? By putting bars on the windows?" she asked.

"Then what? A barbed-wire fence and a pair of Dobermans? No thanks. I have no intention of turning my house into a high-security compound."

He shifted his weight, crossing his arms, still watching her steadily. *This,* Annie thought, *is what it feels like to be a specimen under a microscope.*

"Invisible bars," Pete answered. "Motion detectors to start. We can go from there."

"My neighbors are going to *love* this," Annie muttered, following him up the stairs. "Every time a moth bumps against my window, the alarm's going to go off. I won't get any sleep—except when I'm in jail for disturbing the peace."

She trailed along after him as he went from room to room, checking the windows and recording information in his little pocket notebook. He finally paused in front of two closed doors on the second-floor landing.

"What's in here?"

"A linen closet," Annie said, opening the door to reveal her haphazardly stashed collection of sheets and towels.

He pointed at the second door. "And here?"

"Stairs to the attic."

Taylor opened the door, flicking on the light.

"There's nothing up there," Annie said.

He started up the dusty stairs. They creaked and moaned noisily under his weight.

Lit only by one bare bulb, the big attic was full of shadows—and junk. An old rocking horse sat in one corner with a broken television set. A collection of cross-country skis and poles and a child's wooden sled were in another. Boxes and boxes and boxes of books and clothing and stuff were everywhere, some of their contents spilling out onto the wooden floor.

"Nothing up here?" Pete said, a glint of amusement in his eyes as he watched Annie climb the last few stairs into the attic.

She smiled sheepishly. "Nothing important," she said.

But Pete's eyebrows had dipped slightly down in the closest thing she'd seen to a frown on his face as he crossed from one window to another.

"You don't have your alarm system connected to these windows," he said, a note of disbelief in his voice. "Not a single one."

"Well, it would've cost nearly double," Annie explained. She moved toward a window, looking down through the dusk at the ground three distant stories below. "There's no way someone would climb up here. I mean, they'd be crazy—"

"I've known some cat burglars who wouldn't hesitate to scale seventeen stories for an easy target," Pete said. "This would be a cakewalk."

"No way." Annie shook her head, glancing down again. The lawn was *so* far away. She couldn't imagine climbing up this high. The shingles on the roof were slippery and some were loose. One wrong step, one misjudged placement of a foot, and there'd be nothing but air. Air and then the bone-breaking earth.

Pete reached up to lean his arms against the rough wooden rafter, the muscles moving under his trim black turtleneck as he looked down at her. "I guess you're not a climber," he said with a small smile.

"A climber?" she echoed, trying not to melt under his warm gaze.

"People are either climbers or not," he explained. "The not-climbers are more comfortable on the ground. It's not that they're afraid of heights, they just have a healthy respect for gravity. Too healthy. As a result, they doubt the very existence of climbers."

"I'm definitely a not-climber," Annie admitted.

"Climbers were born knowing about toeholds, and wanting to touch the sky," Pete said. "And climbing up to the attic of a three-story house wouldn't even get them half the way there."

"Which are you?" Annie asked.

Before he had a chance to answer, she launched herself at him, screaming like a banshee. His hands automatically came down to catch her, but he lost his footing, and he and Annie tumbled to the dusty attic floor.

His body responded instantly, his arms going around her, his fingers threading into the fine, golden-brown hair that he'd so often imagined touching. Silk. It felt like silk. Softer.... Oh, man—

"Oh, man," Annie wailed, pushing herself away from him and scrambling to the stairs.

He heard her stumble in her haste, and then the solid slam of the door.

With a groan, Pete lay back on the floor, feeling as if he'd been run over by a truck. What the hell had just happened? She'd tackled him, out of the *blue,* for crying out loud....

He saw it then.

It was a small black shadow, flitting up near the eaves.

A bat.

Annie was afraid of bats.

She had leapt on top of him not from unrestrained attraction, but out of fear.

He tried to convince himself that the feelings flooding him were relief, nothing more. But he couldn't contain the laughter that bubbled up, laughter mostly aimed at his own overinflated ego.

He pulled himself up off the floor and opened one of the attic windows. Gently he herded the tiny bat in that direction, until it noticed the obvious path of escape and disappeared into the cool night air. Pete closed the window and looked around, dusting himself off.

Annie sat at the kitchen table, her hands wrapped around her mug of tea, as if for warmth. She glanced up as Pete came into the room, meeting his eyes only briefly before looking away, embarrassed.

"You okay?" he said.

"Yeah, I'm sorry," she said. "I'm, um…a little freaked-out by bats."

"A little," he agreed, amusement lighting his eyes.

She looked up at him again as he sat down across from her. A rueful smile slowly spread across her face. "You probably didn't know what hit you," she said.

"I *was* a little confused at first," he replied with an answering smile. "I got the bat out of there and found where he must've gotten in. I stuffed a rag in the hole. It's not a permanent fix, but it should keep him from coming right back inside."

"Thanks." She paused for a moment, then said, "Don't tell anyone. Please?"

"That you're afraid of bats?" Pete asked, surprise in his voice.

"Yeah. Cara doesn't even know."

"What difference does it make?" he asked curiously.

"I'm an archaeologist," Annie said. "Bats and I tend to hang out in the same places. I would be teased mercilessly if my colleagues knew I was afraid of them. And I'm really okay around bats if I'm expecting them to be there," she said. "It's when I'm not expecting them that I suddenly become nine years old again."

He was watching her with that funny little half smile on his handsome face, and Annie had an extremely vivid memory of the way his body had felt against hers. The man was all muscles, all hard, solid strength. But his hands had been so gentle as he touched her hair....

"Promise you won't tell," she said.

Her blue eyes were wide, watching him with such hopefulness, such trust and such innocence. She actually believed that if he told her that he wouldn't tell anyone, then he wouldn't. Pete had to look away, wishing he deserved that trust, knowing he didn't. Not by a long shot.

"I'd think at least you would've told Cara," he said. "You two seem pretty tight."

She shook her head.

"Why not?" he asked.

Her eyes narrowed slightly as she met his gaze. "Can you honestly tell me that *you* don't have some deep, dark secret that no one knows—not even your best friend?"

He laughed, but there was no humor in it. "I have way too many secrets," he said.

"Well, good. You tell me one of your secrets," Annie said, "and then we'll be even. You don't tell anyone that I'm a baby when I see a bat, and I won't tell anyone that...you secretly watch old Doris Day movies whenever they're on television."

Pete raised an eyebrow. "How did you guess?"

Annie laughed. "Do you really?"

"How many secrets do you want me to give away?" he countered.

He was flirting with her, Annie thought with a sudden flash of pleasure. "Just one," she said. "You know what I'd really like to know?"

"I can't begin to guess," he said.

"I want to know your real name."

Pete stopped breathing. She knew. How the hell could she know?

"You *do* have a Navaho name, don't you?" she asked.

He understood with a flash of relief. God, for a second there, he'd actually thought she knew he was undercover.... "Yeah," he somehow managed to say.

Annie looked across the table at him. He was watching her, his face suddenly guarded, expressionless. She wondered if perhaps she was prying too deeply. "I'm sorry. You don't have to tell me if you don't want to."

"Hastin Naat'aanni," he said. His voice was so soft, it was almost a whisper as he spoke the language of his grandfather. "That's what I was called."

Intrigued, Annie leaned forward. "What does it mean?"

He stood up. "It doesn't translate well," he said, obviously hedging.

"Roughly, then," she said. She stood up, too, testing her legs, checking to see that the wobble had truly gone away.

He turned to watch her closely, making sure she was okay. When had it stopped being annoying? Annie wondered. When had his presence changed from interfering to nice, to making her feel safe and protected?

"Roughly, it means 'Man Speaking Peace,'" he said. His lips curled up into a sardonic smile; then he turned and left the kitchen.

"That's a great name," Annie said, following him down the stairs. "Who gave it to you? How old were you? Why were you named that?"

At the bottom of the stairs he stopped and faced her, bringing them nose to nose.

"That's another secret entirely," he said.

They were standing close enough for him to kiss her. It would take very little effort on his part. She wanted him to kiss her, she realized suddenly. She actually *wanted* him to. Was she crazy?

But he didn't move.

"I'm going to use your phone," he said, "to call Steven Marshall. He'll authorize me to have your security system updated and rewired to include the third floor."

Annie felt the first sparks of anger. But that was good—anger was better than whatever it was that she'd just been feeling. Wasn't it? "But I don't want my system updated," she said, turning and going back up the stairs. "I'm happy with everything exactly the way it is."

"Then you better get used to me camping out on the floor of your bedroom every night," Pete said. He followed her back into the kitchen. "Because until we get motion detectors and a laser security system installed, that's exactly where I'm going to be."

"Oh, come on, Taylor," Annie said. "You don't really think I'm in any kind of danger, do you?"

"I've been hired to protect you," he said evenly, crossing his arms and leaning against the door frame. His dark eyes watched her as she took a loaf of bread from the cabinet, and jars of peanut butter and jelly from the refrigerator. "What I think is irrelevant."

Annie pulled a clean plate out of the dishwasher and set it on the kitchen table, then selected a dinner knife from the utensil drawer. She folded one leg underneath her as she sat at the table, opening the bread bag and pulling out two slices of thick, dark whole wheat bread.

"I don't enjoy sharing my bedroom," she said, frowning down at the chunky peanut butter she spread on one of the slices of bread. "Particularly since I don't believe someone really wants to hurt me."

"Maybe not," Pete said. "But maybe you're wrong. If I were you, I wouldn't want to find out the hard way that I was wrong."

He was watching her as if he were memorizing the way she put jelly on bread. "You hungry?" she asked suddenly. "Want a sandwich?"

Pete shook his head, a small smile playing about the corners of his mouth. "No, thanks," he said. Then he added, "Is this your dinner?"

She shrugged, taking a bite. "Believe it or not, it's healthy," she said around the peanut butter in her mouth. "The peanut butter is natural—just a little salt added—and the jelly's that all-fruit stuff. I got the bread at the health food store. You sure you don't want some?"

"I'll send out for something, thanks," he said dryly.

"I still don't think anyone would be able to climb up to the third floor of this house," Annie argued after she swallowed a bite. "Even if someone managed to get up there, the neighbors would see them and call the police."

Pete stepped into the kitchen, sitting down across from her at the table. "But what if someone *could* get up there?" he said. "What if they could gain access to your house that way? Then what? Your artifacts are locked in the safe. They're secure. But the lock on your bedroom door wouldn't keep anyone out."

"I can take care of myself," Annie said. "I'm not defenseless, you know."

"So you could defend yourself," Pete said. One eyebrow went up a half a millimeter. "With that plastic gun you had in the lab—the kind that says Bang! on a little flag when you pull the trigger? Very effective."

Annie actually blushed, then couldn't keep a smile from spreading across her face. "I was improvising," she said. "Gimme a break. It was the middle of the night and the alarm system went off."

"Look, I'll make a deal with you," Pete said. "Lock me out of your house. Then give me five minutes to get back inside without triggering your alarm system. If I can do it, then you stop complaining about updating the system, and you let me sleep on the floor of your bedroom until I'm convinced the house is secure."

Annie had started to take another bite of her sandwich, but she pulled it out of her mouth. "There's no way you can get back inside in five minutes," she said. "No way." She bit down on the sandwich as if for emphasis.

"So is it a deal?"

"What do I get if you can't do it?"

His dark eyes rested warmly on hers. "You get whatever you want," he said. Even with his face expressionless, his words had a faintly suggestive quality.

I'm imagining it, Annie thought, turning away from him. *I'm reading things that aren't really there.*

Nodding, she stood up, gesturing toward the hallway. Sandwich in one hand, she followed Pete down to the front door. He opened it, and looked down at her before opening the storm door.

"Lock the door and turn on your security system," he said. "Then check the ground floor to make sure all the windows are locked."

"Can I turn on the outside lights?" Annie said, peeking out into the already dark evening.

Pete shrugged. "Whatever you like."

He pushed open the storm door.

"Hey, you better take your jacket," Annie said. "It's cold out there."

His eyes shone with that inner amusement she'd come to recognize. "I'm not going to be outside that long."

He vanished into the shadows.

Holding her peanut-butter-and-jelly sandwich in her mouth, Annie used both hands to quickly shut and lock the front door, activate the alarm system and turn on all the outside lights, including several spotlights that illuminated her stately Victorian house. She then went through the lab, and then the office, eating her sandwich and checking all the windows on the lower floor. They were all locked. There was no way he could get in that way.

Satisfied, she climbed the stairs. She would go into the kitchen, get the second half of her sandwich, then go down to the lab and— Oh, Christmas!

Pete Taylor was sitting at the kitchen table.

Annie felt her mouth drop open, and she looked at her watch. It hadn't even been three minutes, let alone five.

"How the hell did you do that?" she finally said.

"I climbed up to the attic," he said. "Came in the window."

"But—"

"I think I've proved my point," he said. "Now, can I use your phone?"

Annie was staring at him, her blue eyes troubled. "You just climbed up...that quickly?" she asked. "It was that easy?"

"Yeah," he said, all amusement gone from his eyes. "It was that easy."

She nodded, looking away and frowning thoughtfully. She met his eyes and nodded again. "Use the phone down in the office," she said.

Pete stood up.

"So you're a climber, huh?" she asked.

He nodded. "Yeah."

"You ever touch it? You know, the sky?"

He smiled then. "Not yet."

Annie lay in the darkness, listening for any sound at all from Pete Taylor.

Nothing.

No movement, no breathing, nothing.

But she knew he was there. He'd been there, lying on his bedroll, next to the wall by the bathroom when she'd turned out the light.

"Taylor—you awake?" she finally whispered.

"Yeah."

His voice was soft and resonant, thick, like the darkness that surrounded her.

"This is weird," Annie said. "Kind of like the first night of college, when my freshman roommate was still a stranger."

From where Pete lay on his bedroll, he could hear the rustling of her sheets as she sat up in bed.

"Except we didn't go to sleep," Annie's musical voice said, cutting through the darkness. "Instead, we stayed up, talking until dawn. It was my first all-nighter."

She was silent for a moment, then she asked, "You ever pull any all-nighters, Taylor?"

All the time, over in 'Nam. And twenty-four hours without sleep was a breeze. More often, it was seventy, eighty hours with nothing but caffeine and nicotine to keep him awake, to keep him alive— But Peter Taylor had supposedly gone to NYU, not Vietnam. "Yeah," Pete said softly. Still, it wasn't really lying, was it?

"I suppose in your business you still do it all the time," she said.

"Yeah," he agreed. That was closer to the truth.

"When's your birthday?" she asked.

"February 6th," he said.

"How old are you going to be?"

"Thirty-nine."

"What's your favorite color?"

Pete had to think about it. "Blue," he said finally. Yeah. Blue. The color of the sky, the color of the ocean. The color of Annie's eyes....

"Mine's red," she said. "Who's your favorite singer?"

He shook his head in the darkness. "I don't have one," he said. "I don't listen to music much these days."

"Why not?"

"I don't know," he said honestly. "I used to be into the Beatles...."

"I hate to break it to you," Annie said, "but they split up."

His laughter rolled through the darkness. "I said I didn't listen to music. I didn't say I didn't know what was going on."

"When you were a little kid," Annie said, "what did you want to be when you grew up?"

Pete was quiet for a moment. "Honestly?"

"Of course."

"I wanted to be a priest."

Annie didn't laugh, the way most people would have. "What happened?" she asked.

He sat up, leaning back against the wall. She could barely see him in the darkness, but despite that, his quiet strength seemed to radiate out into the room.

"I found out about the restrictions that went with the job," he said, laughter in his voice. "So I changed my career goals—I decided I'd be president."

"Of the United States?"

"Yep."

She saw the white flash of his teeth as he smiled, and she lay back in her bed, afraid to look at him, afraid of the reaction her body had to him.

"How about you?" he asked. "You must've always wanted to be an archaeologist, right?"

"Well, no," Annie said, lacing her fingers behind her head as she stared up at the dark ceiling. "When I was eight, we came back to New York for a few months and I realized that most kids didn't live out of suitcases, in tents. I discovered that most kids didn't speak five different languages or have a monkey for a pet, and I developed a rather strong longing for what I now call 'TV normal.' It has nothing to do with reality, but, well, to make a long story short, I wanted desperately to grow up to be Mrs. Brady."

"You mean, the mother in 'The Brady Bunch'?"

"Bingo. I wanted suburbia, lots of kids…"

"A maid named Alice," Pete said.

Annie laughed. "A tall, handsome husband who kissed me on the forehead and called me 'dear' as he left for work," she said. "Fortunately for my parents, my fascination with a 'Brady Bunch' lifestyle lasted only a few months. I think after that I wanted to be an astronaut. Yeah, that was when we moved to Greece, and I caught reruns of 'Star Trek.' You know, I can say 'Beam me up, Scotty,' in seven different languages."

"Very impressive."

"Thank you. I've always been easily influenced by television and movies. I saw so little of them, and they seemed so magical. You know, I'm still affected by movies. I just saw *A Few Good Men,* and it made me want to go back to school and become a lawyer."

Pete laughed again. "That would be a major career switch," he said.

"Not as major as trying to be a suburban housewife," Annie said.

They were both quiet for a moment; then Annie said, "It's fantasy, you know? I mean, I love what I do. I really love it. It's not work to me. It's play. But still, I can't help but wonder what it would be like to do something different."

She was silent again for a moment. "Do you like your job, Taylor?" she asked.

Pete didn't answer. He couldn't answer. Yeah, Pete Taylor liked his job. He loved his job, since it meant lying there in the dark with Annie Morrow, talking to her, finding out that he liked her and that he wanted to keep finding out more about her.

But he wasn't Pete Taylor. He was Kendall Peterson. He was sent to spy on this woman, to uncover her secrets and betray her confidences. And Kendall Peterson had never hated his job more in his entire life.

Chapter 6

The morning passed quickly. Annie stretched and, for the first time in hours, looked up from the test she was running. She caught Pete's eye and smiled at him. He didn't smile back, but that was okay—she hadn't expected him to. Instead, he pulled off the headphones of the Walkman she'd lent him, and pushed the button that stopped the tape he was listening to.

"Lunchtime," she said.

"Does this mean you're actually going to eat?" Pete asked, his eyebrows moving slightly upward. "Or is this going to be a replay of breakfast where you just wave a mug of tea in front of your face?"

Annie's smile turned into a grin. "I'm starving," she admitted. "I better get a chance to actually eat. Although, first I've got to hit the office, check the fax machine and return all the phone calls I didn't take this morning."

Pete trailed down the hallway after her.

"You must be going nuts," she said. "Sitting there watching me all morning. Not too stimulating, I'm afraid."

On the contrary, Pete thought. He'd had an entirely enjoyable morning just watching her and listening to her collection of cassette tapes. He'd heard everything from Bach to a band called the Spin Doctors, and he'd enjoyed it all. It had been a long time since he'd taken the time to listen to music. The headphones Annie had didn't cut out the room noise, so he felt secure knowing he could hear everything that was going on around him.

And watching Annie was never a chore. Even when she was sitting, she was in motion. A foot was always jiggling, a pencil tapping, fingers moving.... He'd particularly enjoyed memorizing every little worn spot in her faded jeans. There was a place on her left hip where the seam was starting to tear....

It was Sunday, and Cara was spending the day with Jerry, so the answering machine had been on all morning. Annie pushed the message button, then went to the fax machine. Something had come in. She tore the sheet of paper free and looked at it as the messages played.

There were three calls from people whose names she didn't recognize, then Nick's familiar English accent came on, reminding her of their date at the Museum of Modern Art bash. He wanted her to call him. No doubt he had some new find that needed to be authenticated with utmost haste and great urgency. And gratis, as a favor to an old friend, of course. He wasn't a client, but somehow he always brought her work. He would ask her to squeeze it in, offer to stay up late into the night with her as she ran the tests, ply her with wine and promises of dinner....

There were messages from the buyer and the seller of the copper bowl she was working on, and five other messages from other clients.

Annie dialed the first of the clients who had called, and after saying hello, spent the next ten minutes listening to questions he had about her latest report on a piece he was trying to sell.

So much for lunch.

Annie's stomach growled. "Can you hold on a sec?" she asked, and pushed the hold button.

Annie looked up at Pete. "Will you do me a big favor?" she asked. "Will you go up to the kitchen and get me the bread, the peanut butter, the jelly, a plate and a knife? I'm never going to get off this phone."

"I'll do even better than that," Pete said. "I'll make you a sandwich."

"You don't have to do that," she said, surprise in her voice.

"I know," he said and smiled. "And believe me, I wouldn't do it for just anyone."

But he'd do it for me, Annie thought, a shiver going down her spine as she looked into his dark eyes. The guy had a killer smile, on top of his being drop-dead handsome, and so far, she'd only found things to like about him. He couldn't possibly be perfect, could he? As unrealistic as it seemed, she found herself praying that he was. Peter Taylor, security consultant, a.k.a. bodyguard, had appeared in her life totally out of the blue. Was it possible to hope that he might be here to stay?

He backed out of the door, his eyes not leaving hers until the last possible moment. Annie found herself listening to his footsteps on the stairs as she reconnected the line to her client. She glanced at her watch. Quarter to one. She was actually looking forward to tonight—to locking herself in her bedroom with Pete Taylor. And talking, she reminded herself. Just talking.

Ten minutes later, Annie stared at the telephone. One down and five to go. She exhaled fully, and glanced up at the calendar on the wall. October. It was only October. Could she really keep up this pace until December?

A flash of movement at the window caught the edge of her vision, and she turned.

What the heck…?

Something was hanging from the tree right outside the window. Something red, and…

Very dead.

A carcass.

A very dead, very skinned carcass of an animal hung gruesomely from the tree, and she caught another streak of movement, as if someone were running away.

"Pete!" she shouted, rocketing out of her chair and scrambling toward the window. Whoever had been out there disappeared around the side of the house. She saw only the back of a black jacket. Or was it long black hair? "Taylor!"

She ran toward the front door, but Pete was already down the stairs, moving down the hall toward her with speed normally reserved for smaller, more compact men. He caught her in his arms to keep from plowing her down as he skidded to a stop on the slippery hardwood floor.

"What is it?" he said sharply. "Annie, what's wrong?"

"Someone was outside," she gasped. "Hurry! Maybe you can still catch him."

"Stay here," Pete ordered, then ran for the door. He drew his gun from his shoulder holster as he went out into the crisp afternoon air. Orange, yellow, brown and red leaves blanketed the wide lawn, and he could see the path the trespasser had made through them as he ran away from the house. That path led directly into one of the neighbors' yards, through a windbreak of tall bushes.

Pete raced up to the bushes, peering through them. The other yard was empty—no sign of anyone. He glanced back at the house. He didn't like leaving Annie alone, unprotected. What if this were only a diversion, designed to draw him away from the house, away from Annie?

She stepped out onto the front porch, and he felt a flash of annoyance. He trotted back toward her. "I thought I told you to stay inside," he said coldly. But his anger melted instantly as he saw the look on her face.

"I'm sorry," she said, hugging her arms across her body, trying to stay warm in the chill air. Her blue eyes looked even bigger than usual. "I, um, got spooked all alone in there."

Pete reholstered his gun. "Come on," he said, not unkindly. "It's cold out here. Let's get back inside."

But Annie was walking determinedly around to the other side of the house. "We have to cut it down," she said. "We can't leave it there."

Puzzled, Pete followed her, then stopped short at the sight of the animal hanging from the tree. He swore under his breath.

"I think it's a rabbit," Annie said, swallowing hard. "*Was* a rabbit, I mean. Do you have a knife?"

"Wait," Pete said. "We can't cut it down."

"Why not?"

"It's evidence," he said.

Annie stared at the skinned animal, blinking back the tears that suddenly appeared in her eyes. "It's hanging right outside my office window," she said, unable to keep her voice from shaking.

"I'll call the FBI," Pete said gently. "Hopefully they can send someone down to take care of it right away."

"And if they can't?"

"Annie, we've got to do this by the book."

"I don't know which is worse," she said. One tear escaped, rolling down her cheek before she brusquely wiped it away. "The fact that someone hung that thing there, or the fact that I can't cut it down when I want to."

"I'm sorry," Pete said, stepping toward her. He reached out toward her, well aware that this was exactly what he'd been so carefully avoiding—all physical contact. He wouldn't be able to hold her in his arms without wanting to kiss her. And if he kissed her, he'd be lost. He reached for her anyway, wanting only to stop her tears.

But she pushed past him, heading back into the house.

He followed her into the lab, where she ignored him completely, concentrating intently on the work at hand.

Pete went into the office and called the FBI, then brought Annie the sandwich he had made for her.

It lay on the counter, untouched, all afternoon.

Annie lay soaking in her bathtub with her eyes closed. The water turned from hot to warm to tepid, and she was considering letting some of it out and running in some more hot when a knock sounded at the bathroom door.

"You all right in there?" Pete's husky voice asked.

She sighed. "Yeah. I'll be out in a minute."

"Take your time," he said, but he heard the sound of water spilling down the drain.

Five minutes later the bathroom door opened, and Annie came out, dressed in a pair of plaid pajamas. Her face was scrubbed, and she was brushing her hair. Her eyes found Pete, who was standing by the bedroom door.

"Can I lock this?" he asked.

She nodded, sitting cross-legged on her bed, still brushing her long, shiny hair. "How long till the motion detectors are installed?" she asked.

Pete knew that what she meant was, *How long till you're out of my room?* "With any luck, they'll be up in a couple of days," he said.

She nodded.

He used the bathroom quickly, washing up with the door open, so he could hear her if she needed him. He hung his towel on the rack next to hers. Annie's towel was damp from her bath, and smelled like her. The entire bathroom smelled like her—fresh and clean and sweet.

Pete turned out the bathroom light and went into the bedroom. He sat down on his sleeping bag, leaning back against the wall.

As he watched, Annie put her hairbrush on the small table next to her bed, then turned off the light.

Darkness.

It surrounded him completely, and he waited patiently for his eyes to adjust. He took advantage of the privacy the darkness provided and pulled off his T-shirt and slipped out of his jeans. He'd slept in his clothes the night before, and woke up much too hot. He lay back against his pillow, listening to the rustling of sheets as Annie moved about, trying to get comfortable.

There was silence then for several long minutes before he heard Annie ask, "Taylor, you still awake?"

He smiled into the darkness. "Yeah."

"I was wondering…"

"Mmm?"

"When do you get a day off?" she asked.

"I don't," he said. "Not until after the job's finished."

"But that's probably going to be at least six more weeks," Annie said. "Doesn't that get a little intense? You watch me all day, *and* all night. Aren't you going to burn out?"

"No."

It was said so absolutely, Annie had to believe him. "Is your job always like this?" she asked. "You know, round-the-clock? What about your social life?"

"I don't have a social life."

"By choice?" she asked.

He was quiet for a moment. "Yeah, I guess so," he said. "How about you? You work all the time, too."

"I have a social life," Annie said defensively. "I go… places, and do…things."

Who was she trying to convince? she wondered. Pete or herself?

She frowned up at the dark ceiling. When *was* the last time she'd had a date? It was when Nick had last been in town. He took her out to a little Italian restaurant in the city and tried to convince her to come back to his hotel room afterward. She'd had too much wine, she remembered, because she'd almost given in.…

"Annie, I'm sorry about this afternoon," Pete said, the faint Western drawl of his rich voice making all thoughts of Nick vanish from her mind. "I wish it could've been handled differently."

"It wasn't your fault," Annie said tiredly.

"Yeah, well, I still wish…" His voice trailed off. Man, he wished this whole investigation had been handled differently. He wished Annie hadn't turned out to be so friendly and funny and charmingly sweet. He wished he could allow himself to care what happened to her. *Too late,* a little voice spoke in his head. *Too late, you already do care…*

On the other side of the room, he heard Annie sit up. "What?" she asked, her voice little more than a whisper. "You wish what?"

Pete pushed himself up on his elbows, sensing her sitting there in the darkness, afraid she was going to get out of bed and move toward him. Disaster. That would be a disaster. If she as much as touched him, he would go up in flames. Spontaneous combustion. A life, a solid career reduced to little more than a sensational headline on the front of the *National Enquirer*.

He remembered running down the stairs that morning, adrenaline sweeping through his system after she'd shouted his name. He'd held her in his arms then. True, it had only been for a few short seconds, but he could take that memory, play it on slow motion and… Dangerous. Man, that was way too dangerous.

"What do you wish?" Annie asked again. He heard a noise, as if she were moving down to the foot of her bed, down where she could see him if she peered through the darkness.

"Too many things," Pete said. "Go to sleep, Annie."

The noise stopped.

Pete prayed, sending a few words up to the gods of his grandfather, as well. *Please don't make this temptation worse than it already is….*

There was silence for several long minutes.

Annie swore choicely, her voice breaking through

the darkness. "I can't sleep. I'm exhausted, but my brain won't slow down. And I have to get up early tomorrow, and—"

"Are your eyes closed?" Pete asked.

"Well, not exactly—"

"Close your eyes," he said in his tone of voice that left no room for argument. "I'm going to teach you a relaxation technique, okay?"

"Okay," Annie said, doubt in her voice. "But I've tried this kind of thing before, and it doesn't work."

"This one does," Pete said. "Do you have a favorite place? Somewhere you can go and feel totally calm?"

Annie squinted up at the ceiling, thinking. "Monument Valley," she said decidedly. "I loved it there. Sunrises were *incredible*. Except… No, maybe the beach on Tahiti would win. *That* was fabulous." She sat up. "I *really* loved it there. Although, there was something about the pyramids in Egypt that made me feel like I was on another planet, which was surprisingly calming—"

"Annie."

"Yes?"

"Lie down."

She lay back against her pillow, pulling her sheet and the comforter up to her chin.

"I'm going to tell you about *my* favorite place, okay?" Pete's voice was soft but clear.

"Okay," Annie said.

"Close your eyes," Pete said, "*and* your mouth, or else it won't work."

She was obediently silent.

"My favorite place was a beach," Pete said. "It wasn't Tahiti, but it was the Pacific Ocean. Usually when I got there, I was tired and hot and dirty, so the first thing I'd do was take off my boots and walk straight into that clear blue water." He would come out from the jungles of Vietnam, and wash all the blood and death away from him in the ocean. "Picture yourself doing that. Picture yourself in the water, letting everything that happened today just get washed away. Out where you are, behind the break, the ocean's calm, with gentle swells that lift you up. You can look out toward the horizon, and it's all blue water, as far as you can see. It just goes on and on and on, almost forever."

Annie lay in the darkness with her eyes shut, letting Pete's soft voice wash over her. His twang was more pronounced as he himself relaxed and his voice grew lazy. She liked it. The drawl suited him far better than the clipped accentless voice he assumed when giving orders.

"You climb out of the water," he was saying. "And up onto the beach. The sand's fine and soft and hot under your feet. It feels real good. There's a blanket already spread out, and you lie down on it. It's warm and the sun feels great on your face. There's no one else on the entire beach—you've got the whole place to yourself— so you take off your wet clothes."

Pete paused a moment, unable to get the picture of Annie lying naked on the beach out of his mind. Damn, this was supposed to be relaxing....

"You lie back against that blanket, and feel that hot sun on your skin. The sky is the bluest you've ever seen it, and the sand is so white. You close your eyes, though, and listen to the sounds of the waves, and to the seabirds. It's like music, with its own special rhythm and rhyme. It's soothing, and soon you're so relaxed, you seem to be floating...."

He could hear Annie breathing, slow and steady as he let his voice trail off. She was asleep.

She trusted him. Another few nights like this, and he'd ask her about what she'd done in Athens—who she talked to, where she'd gone. He'd ask her if maybe she was in too deep....

Although he couldn't believe she was involved with any kind of conspiracy. He smiled to himself. She didn't seem to have the ability to lie. Another few nights and he'd know for sure....

Except the alarm system was scheduled to be updated starting tomorrow afternoon, and he'd soon be sleeping in the guest bedroom, away from her.

Pete lay awake, staring up into the darkness for a long time before he finally fell asleep.

Pete called Whitley Scott in the morning, while Annie was in the shower.

"Can you talk?" Scott asked.

"For maybe three minutes," Pete said. He stood in the office doorway, listening for Annie, and looking down the long hallway, watching the front door for Cara. "I need you to delay the installation of the motion detectors. Have the alarm installers call Annie and tell her it'll be at least a week before they can get the system out here."

"Annie, huh?" Scott said meaningfully.

Pete ignored the comment. "Will you do it?"

"Sure."

"What have you found out?" Pete asked.

"You mean about the phone calls?" Scott asked.

"And the rock through the window, and the wolf man in the car, *and* the carcass hanging—"

"Right, right," Scott interrupted him. "Not much. It's not our main concern right now—"

"Push it up a little higher on the priority list," Pete said, his tone leaving no room for argument.

But Scott argued anyway. "Come on, Captain," he said. "You know those nutball groups. This could be any one of them. We don't have the manpower to waste an investigation on a threat that's not real—"

"I think it *is* real," Pete said tersely. "Get a team working on it immediately."

Silence. Whitley Scott didn't like being ordered around. But Pete waited him out, and Scott finally sighed with exasperation. "I'll see what I can do," he said grouchily. "So what's happening up there? Are you getting somewhere with Morrow?"

"She's starting to trust me," Pete said. "She's starting to think of me as a friend."

"A friend?" the head of the FBI division scoffed. "What's this *friend* crap, Pete? Seduce her, for crying out loud. Women naturally trust the men they sleep with. She'll tell you all her secrets then."

"I've got to go," Pete said brusquely, even though he could still hear the water coursing through the house's old pipes, and there was still no sign of Cara. He hung up the phone, Scott's words echoing in his mind. *Seduce her.*

Why should Scott's nonchalant words make him so angry?

Because Annie was…well, *Annie*. She was special. Pete liked everything about her. He liked her a lot— way too much to take advantage of her that way.

He sat down heavily at Annie's desk, massaging the tense muscles in his neck and shoulders. The ironic thing was, if he really *were* Pete Taylor, if he really *were* plain and simply Annie's bodyguard, with no ulterior motives or hidden agendas, he would have been working hard to get into her bed long before this.

Life was too damn strange.

"Yo," Cara said, breaking into Annie's concentration. "You've got a phone call I figured you'd want to take. It's the burglar-alarm guy."

Annie looked up from her equipment, stretching her stiff shoulders and back, and working out the kink in her neck with one hand. "Thanks," she said to her assistant. "I'll take it in here."

She crossed to the white lab phone that hung on the wall next to the door. It was late afternoon, and the light was already starting to fade. She picked up the phone and flicked on the bright overhead lights.

"Anne Morrow speaking," she said, glancing over at Pete. He sat leaning back in a chair, his feet up on a stool. His relaxed position was only a sham, she realized. He was watching her as intently as ever, no doubt noticing the way she couldn't keep her eyes from running the long, lean lengths of his jean-clad legs. Shoot, the man was just too good-looking. She turned her back, trying to focus on the voice speaking to her over the phone.

"We gotta little problem with scheduling," the man with the heavy New York accent said, after identifying himself as being the owner of the burglar alarm installation company Pete had called to put in the motion detectors. "The earliest I'm going to be able to send a crew out is next week. End of next week. Thursday, Friday at the earliest. Maybe not even till Monday."

"Oh, shoot." Annie chewed her lip. "You were supposed to be here today."

"Sorry, miss," the man said, not sounding remotely remorseful. "It's that time of year. Halloween. You can try calling another alarm company, but it's the same all over. Everyone's backlogged."

Annie stared out the window into the deepening twilight. Another week and a half of Pete sleeping in her room at night. Now, why didn't that news bother her the way it would have a day or two ago?

"You still wanna keep your name on our list?" the man asked.

"Yes," Annie said. "Yeah, thanks. Thanks for calling."

Slowly she hung up the phone and told Pete about the call. He took the news with his normal lack of expression. Was he disappointed? Pleased? She couldn't begin to tell.

"Is this an official break?" Cara asked cheerfully, coming back into the lab. "It's time. You've been hard at it all afternoon. I, for one, have finished inputting all that data from the dread phony copper bowl, so I'm ready to celebrate."

"You're always ready to celebrate." Annie smiled.

"Yes, but this time I have an excuse," Cara said. "Jerry's coming over in a little while. What do you say we all go out and have Chinese food?"

"I don't know," Annie said.

"Oh, come on," Cara urged. "You know how weird you get when you don't leave the house for days on end. A little fresh air and some moo goo gai pan'll be good for you."

Annie glanced at Pete. "Whaddaya say, Taylor? Do you want to go?"

"I go where you go," he said.

"I know that," she said impatiently. "I asked you if you *wanted* to go."

He pulled his worn-out cowboy boots off the stool and stood up. "I would love to," he said, a smile breaking across his face as he steadily met her eyes.

Annie watched Pete as Jerry talked about his latest exploits in South America, telling stories across a table that was littered with the remains of their dinner. As the busboys began to clear away the dishes, Pete looked over at Annie and smiled. She felt the now-familiar warm rush of attraction and had to look away.

This was not a date, she reminded herself for the hundredth time that evening. Pete was her bodyguard. He was there only to protect her, despite the fact that his eyes sometimes burned with an intensity that could take her breath away.

In the few short days that he'd been protecting her, he'd done nothing to make her think she meant anything to him besides a reason for employment. True, he was friendly, kind even, generally polite, but in short, he wasn't acting like a man who was going crazy, longing for her touch.

The way she was longing for him to touch her.

Damn, damn, damn, Annie thought. When had she crossed the line between *This is a guy I'd like to get to know,* and *This is a guy I must have?* When had it happened?

Last night, probably, when she'd drifted off to sleep listening to his soft, husky voice. Or it might've been earlier that day, when he'd offered to make lunch for her. Or maybe it was the night before, when they first lay awake, talking....

"You're awfully quiet tonight," Jerry said to Annie. "And you barely ate anything. What gives?"

Annie could tell from the way he and Cara were sitting that they were holding hands underneath the table. Cara looked so happy.

"She's had a bad week," Cara answered for her. "She lost a couple of days' work by going to England to pick up old Stands Against the Storm's death mask, and then when she came back, she got hassled by the feds while she was going through Customs. They detained her *six* hours."

"Why?" Jerry asked. "Whatd'ya do this time, Morrow?"

Annie glanced at Pete, who was watching her intently. "After I picked up the artifact from the English Gallery, the place was bombed and robbed," she said.

"You're kidding," Jerry said with shock.

"I wouldn't kid about something like that," Annie said ruefully.

"God, you have the worst luck," Jerry said, shaking his head. "Maybe you should stay stateside for a while. I mean, another coincidence like that and—"

"No thank you," Annie said with a flash of anger in her eyes. "My job requires international travel. I'm not going to let myself get bullied into changing my life."

"Maybe you should've been more cooperative with the Athens thing," he said, frowning.

"How much more cooperative, Tillet?" Annie said tartly. "You mean, like giving them a signed confession? Because that's what they want." She turned to look at Pete. "We better get going. I've got more work to do tonight."

"Does she ever not work?" Jerry asked Pete. He turned to Annie. "You must be disgustingly rich.

Maybe I should be hitting *you* up for funding for my latest project. See, I found a site in Mexico—"

"I know, I know!" Annie said, rolling her eyes. "I've heard it…what? Five thousand times this week already."

"You know that you're interested," Jerry said. "You could come along." He shot a sideways glance at Cara. "You, too," he added. He looked back at Annie. "When was the last time you participated in a dig?"

"It would be fun," Annie said, "but I *really* don't have the money."

The waiter brought the dinner check, and she reached for it, but Pete grabbed it first. "This one's courtesy of Mr. Marshall," he said with a smile.

"I'll drink to that." Jerry grinned.

Annie watched Pete bring the check to the cashier. She stood up, pulling on her jacket. Pete's leather jacket was on the back of his chair, and she picked it up. God, it was heavy. "See you guys tomorrow," she said, giving Cara an overobvious "have fun" wink.

Pete met her at the door and took his jacket. "Thanks," he said.

"What are you carrying in your pockets?" Annie said, leaving the warmth of the restaurant and going out onto the sidewalk. "Your jacket weighs a ton."

Zipping her own jacket up, she shivered slightly in the cold autumn night.

"It's armor," Pete said. "In case I have to throw myself in front of any speeding bullets."

Annie laughed.

"I'm serious," he said. "It's bulletproof."

He was watching her in the dim light from the street lamp on the corner. His dark eyes were soft and warm, luminescent. If any other man had looked at her like that, she would have bet her life savings that he was going to kiss her. But not Pete Taylor. He broke the eye contact, looked down at the ground and took two solid steps backward, away from her.

Hiding her exasperation, Annie turned, and they walked to his car in silence.

Chapter 7

Annie threw her jacket over the back of her chair in the office and pressed the playback button on her answering machine.

The first voice on the tape was Nick. He didn't even bother to identify himself, assuming that she'd recognize his voice. Which, of course, she did.

"Sweet Annie," he said in his proper English accent. "I'm beginning to consider taking your answering machine to the party at the museum instead of you. I've spoken to it more often in the past few weeks. Where are you? MacLeish says you're busy, but you've never been too busy for me before. What's going on? Call me."

Pete had assumed his regular position, leaning in the doorway.

"That was Nick York," she told him.

"I know," he said. "Why don't you call him back?"

Annie sighed, temporarily stopping the tape. "Because he's going to ask me to authenticate some very tiny, but *very* important, archaeological find for him. It'll be really easy, he'll tell me, it'll only take a few hours of my time, I can surely squeeze him in. Except something will go amazingly wrong—there'll be some glitch in the test, and I'll end up working until dawn four nights in a row." She sighed again. "Somehow Nick always talks me into doing things. This time I really *don't* have the time, so it's easier to avoid him." She met Pete's eyes and smiled ruefully. "I know it's the coward's way out. I also know that he's going to catch up with me sooner or later. At the fund-raiser at the Museum of Modern Art, at the very least."

Pete kept his face expressionless, afraid that the flash of jealousy he'd felt at the sound of York's voice would still somehow show. Jealousy? Man, what the hell was he doing feeling *jealous?* He had no right. No right at all. So just stop it, he ordered himself.

He cleared his throat. "What other messages are on there?" he asked, motioning toward the answering machine with his head.

Annie started the tape rolling again.

Another message was from the Westchester Archaeological Society, asking if Dr. Morrow had any free time in the next few months to come and give a lecture at one of the group's monthly meetings.

"Free time," Annie laughed. "If they only knew.…"

There were four hang-ups in a row, then a voice spoke.

"I am calling on behalf of Stands Against the Storm." Annie looked sharply up at Pete. He hadn't moved a muscle, but he was instantly a picture of intensity, his dark eyes burning into hers as they both listened. The voice belonged to a man and was accentless and soft.

"You must surrender the death mask," he said, almost mildly. "Return it to the Navaho people. It is for your own good that I tell you this. The evil spirit within the mask will awaken if you disturb it. Do not touch it, do not hold it—or be ready to face the spirit's wrath. Your life as you know it will crumble. Await further instructions."

There was a click, and the answering machine beeped twice, signaling that there were no more messages, and shut off.

Annie sat so still at her desk that Pete could hear the wall clock ticking as its second hand jerked around the dial. But as if her energy couldn't be contained, she stood up suddenly, pushing past him out of the room and down the hallway. He followed her into the lab, where she switched on the bright overhead lights and crossed directly to the big safe.

It only took several quick spins to the combination lock, and the heavy door swung open. Without a word, Annie took out the heavy crate from England and carried it to the wide lab counter. She set it down and got a hammer from one of the cabinet drawers.

Pete didn't ask what she was doing—he already knew.

"You know," Annie said evenly, "this thing is such a pain in the butt, and I haven't even taken a good look at it yet."

She used the forked end of the hammer to pry the top of the crate up and off.

The crate was filled with large foam peanuts. Annie dug through them, finding the top of the heavy artifact about six inches down. She pulled it out, careful to keep the foam chips in the box.

The death mask had been wrapped in layers of bubble pack. She peeled them back to find the artifact surrounded by a soft cloth. Carefully she unwrapped it, setting it on the counter on top of that same piece of fabric.

It was amazing. The gleaming, golden face of Stands Against the Storm sat in front of her, every wrinkle, every sagging muscle in the old man's face recorded forever by the casting that had been done shortly after his death. His eyes were closed, and he looked so tired, so sad. Annie wondered what his eyes had been like, wondered if he'd had eyes like Pete's—dark and burning with intensity and life.

Annie glanced up at Pete. "Curses, shmurses," she said, and picked the death mask up, holding the cool metal in her hands. Nothing happened. She wasn't immediately struck by lightning or attacked by a flock of screaming evil spirits. And as far as her life crumbling…well, it couldn't really get *that* much worse. Could it?

She carried the death mask to the other side of the lab, to a big magnifying glass that was clamped to the counter with an accordion-like arm. She turned on another, even brighter, light and held the artifact under the glass, looking at it closely.

Pete pulled up a stool and watched.

Annie examined the casting marks, moving slowly across the piece for several long minutes. Finally she looked up at Pete.

"Is it real?" he asked.

She didn't answer at first. Instead, she brought the artifact up to her mouth and licked it. She grinned at the way his eyebrows moved upward. "Well, it's real gold, at the very least," she said.

"You can tell that by tasting it?"

Annie nodded. "Yes."

"That doesn't seem too scientific," he said. "All these high-tech instruments in this lab, and you end up using your tongue."

"That was just a preliminary test," she said. "I'll get a full metal content when I have more time. But I think the final outcome is going to have to be decided by carbon dating."

"Why?" asked Pete, watching her.

She had put the death mask down on the counter, and now she gathered her long hair away from her face, pulling it easily into a ponytail and using a rubber band to hold it back. She was wearing her worn-out jeans and a red sweater that was textured, designed to be touched. Pete hooked his thumbs through his belt loops and tried to concentrate on what she was saying.

"Well, it certainly passes a quick inspection," Annie said. "The casting marks all look comparable to what was being done in England in the nineteenth century. But without written records—you know, receipts or bills of sale, something to document it—the only way to be sure it wasn't cast last month in Liverpool is to carbon-date it."

Pete leaned in for a closer look. "So, how long will that test take?"

She turned and found herself nearly nose to nose with him. Up close, his eyes were beautiful. They were exquisitely shaped and surrounded by thick, black lashes. But his expression was so closed, so guarded, he might have been a statue. He didn't seem to notice that he had long since invaded her personal space, that he was sitting at a distance more appropriate for an embrace than a conversation.

She swallowed, moistening her dry lips with the tip of her tongue. "Even if I start the tests now, it will probably be weeks before I get the results. I have to contract out for carbon dating."

There was a flash of relief in his dark eyes, and Annie's heart leapt. He was glad. He wanted to stick around for a while. More than ever, she wanted him to kiss her. *Kiss me,* she thought, staring into his eyes, hoping he could read her mind.

But he didn't move.

She was going to have to do it, she realized. She was going to have to kiss him. She looked away, gathering her courage. The worst he could do was laugh at her, right? So she should just do it—

Pete straightened up, pushing his stool back, out of range.

Damn, Annie thought. The moment had passed. What was wrong with her? she wondered. Wasn't she making her interest in him obvious enough? Or maybe it was Pete, she thought glumly. Maybe he had a reason to fight the attraction that sparked between them every time they were together in a room. Maybe he was in love with someone else. Shoot, maybe he was married....

She sat at the lab counter for a long time, pretending to study the death mask, but in truth thinking long and hard about Peter Taylor.

Annie turned off the light on her bedside table, determined to follow the resolution she had made while she was brushing her teeth in the bathroom just a few moments ago. She was not going to chase this man. She had let him know—subtly, of course, but Pete Taylor was a smart man—that she was interested in him. It had been up to him to do something about it. Or not.

Obviously, he'd chosen "or not."

Well, okay. That was fine. She was a grown-up; she could deal with that.

But it wouldn't do her any good to lie in the dark, talking to him until the early hours of the morning. It wouldn't do her any good at all to share more secrets with him. And it certainly wouldn't do her any good to fall in love with him.

She lay in the dark, in silence, hoping that it wasn't already too late.

Minutes passed. Long, endless minutes, during which she tried to organize and prioritize the work she had to do tomorrow. Then she tried to think of all the songs she knew that started with the word *I*. "I Think I Love You," "I Wanna Hold Your Hand," "I Had the Craziest Dream," "I Do," "I'm Dreaming of a White Christmas"—no, that was the first line, not the name of the song.

She gave up. "Taylor, are you awake?"

"Yeah."

On the other side of the room, Pete closed his eyes briefly. Annie had been quiet for so long, he had been afraid that she had broken her pattern and was already asleep.

"Do you think that guy on the phone meant he's going to call again and tell me to bring the death mask someplace, when he said, 'Await further instructions'?"

Pete knew exactly which guy she was talking about. "Probably," he said. "But first I think he and his buddies are going to try to scare you badly enough so you won't want to get the police involved."

"The police are already involved," Annie said. "What do these guys think I'm going to do? Simply hand them a piece of gold that's worth tens of thousands of dollars? And that's ignoring any possible historical value. Even if I do hand it over, then what? I call up Ben Sullivan and say, 'Oops. Lost your artifact. Sorry'?"

"*I* know you're not about to do that," Pete said. "But these people don't know you. They don't realize you don't scare easily."

"Maybe you don't know me, either, Taylor." Annie's voice was soft. "Sometimes I think I'm scared of everything."

"It's one thing to be scared," he said, "and another thing entirely to let it affect you."

"Like my fear of bats," Annie said wryly.

"Obviously you've dealt with that pretty damn well," he said, "since I'm the only one who knows about it."

"Aren't you afraid of anything, Taylor?" Annie asked.

Pete stared at the outline of the windows for a long time before he answered. "Yeah," he finally said. "I get afraid when the line between right and wrong isn't clear. Lately it seems it never is. It's been scaring the hell out of me."

There was silence for a moment, then he laughed, but there was no humor in it. "I'm also afraid I haven't lived up to the name my grandfather gave me."

Pete hadn't wanted to go to Vietnam and had seriously considered losing himself up in the Rocky Mountains, much in the way his ancestors had when they'd received orders from the federal government that they hadn't liked.

But he obeyed the draft, and he went to Vietnam. At first he wondered what the hell someone named Man

Speaking Peace was doing stalking through a foreign jungle with an automatic weapon in his hands and camouflage gear on his back. But it didn't take him long to realize that he was good at staying alive, and especially good at keeping the men around him alive, too. And somehow, when the real war was over and the American troops were shipping out of Saigon, he'd remained behind, part of the exclusive force assigned to locate and rescue the massive numbers of POWs and MIAs still in the jungles.

Ever since the summer that he was drafted, when he was barely eighteen years old, not even old enough to drink in Colorado, he'd always carried at least one gun. He felt it now, a hard lump, tucked under his bedroll where he could reach it easily if he needed it.

"A man of peace needs no weapon," he could remember his grandfather telling him. "Only a conscience, a will and a voice loud enough to carry."

"Man Speaking Peace." Annie's voice cut into his thoughts. "Why were you named that?"

He was silent for so long, she thought maybe he wasn't going to answer.

"I haven't thought about any of this in a really long time," Pete finally said. "I'm not sure I want to…."

"I'm sorry," Annie said. "I was just— I shouldn't have—"

"I was thirteen years old," he said, interrupting her. "It was the summer that my aunt died—my mother's sister. It really messed my cousins up. They came to stay with us at the ranch. There were five of them— Jack was the oldest, he was twelve. Then there was Wil, Thomas, Eddie and Chris, who was just a baby really. He couldn't have been more than five. He missed his mother something fierce. They all did, but Chris was the only one who would cry. He would cry, and Tom would taunt him, saying boys didn't cry, only babies cried. Then Jack would beat the hell out of Tom, and soon they'd all be fighting.

"Well, I spent all of July being a mediator, keeping the peace between those five boys. I was older than them, and they looked up to me. But more often than not, as soon as my back was turned, *wham,* someone would end up with a fist in his eye.

"After a few weeks, I began to realize that there was a pattern to when little Chris would cry about his mother. He usually cried first thing in the morning, and at a certain time in the afternoon—about one o'clock, I think it was—because that was the time his mom had set aside a half an hour every day to read to him and play with him—with *just* him, giving him her full attention, while the other boys were off at school.

"So I started distracting him. I'd be the one to wake him up in the morning, and I'd keep him so busy, he'd never really notice the emptiness. And I did the same thing in the afternoon, and his bouts of crying happened less and less often."

Annie listened, realizing she was almost holding her breath. Pete had never spoken at such length in the entire time she'd known him, and certainly never about himself, about his childhood.

"Unfortunately, the same couldn't be said about the fighting," he said, with a low laugh. "Even when Chris's crying stopped, the older boys found other reasons to set themselves off. I couldn't figure out what had gotten into them. They'd never fought before—not like this."

He paused. *Don't stop,* Annie thought. She could picture him as a thirteen-year-old boy, tall and serious, with those same intense, dark eyes. "So what happened?" she asked softly.

"I went and talked to my grandfather," Pete said. "I asked him why my cousins were fighting. He told me it was their way of grieving for their mother. Well, I thought about that for a couple of days. But after I watched Wil give Jack a broken nose, and after Jack damn near broke Tom's arm, I decided that those boys needed to find a different way to deal with their mother's death.

"I took the whole pack of them out on a hike, up into the mountains, to a place I knew about where you could see down into the whole valley," Pete said quietly. "It was like heaven up there. You could look out across my father's ranch, at the fields laid out like squares on a patchwork quilt. Everything was alive and growing. There were so many different shades of green, and the sky was so blue, it hurt to look at it.

"We sat down on some rocks, and the boys were quiet for once, just taking it all in," he said. "I sat there, thinking about my aunt Peg, their mother. I thought about her, and it didn't take me long to start to cry. So I sat there, with tears running down my face, and one by one those boys noticed I was crying. They were shocked, really shocked, because, as Tom was so fond of pointing out, boys weren't supposed to cry.

"Wil asked me why I was crying, and I told him it was because I missed his mother. I told them that sometimes even men had to cry, and if it was okay for a man to cry, then it was surely okay for a boy to cry. And they believed me, you know, because I was older than them. Soon Chris started in—it never took much to set him off—but then Tom broke down, and Wil and Eddie, and finally even Jack was crying. We all just sat

there and cried for about an hour. Then I told them that
this place that we had climbed to was my special place,
but that they could use it whenever they needed it.

"We went back down that mountain, and from that
day on almost all the fighting stopped," Pete said. "It
was at the end of that summer my grandfather gave me
the name Hastin Naat'aanni, Man Speaking Peace. It
was the name of a great Navaho leader, back more than
a hundred years ago."

He had been so proud, so young and full of hopes
and dreams. Pete didn't have to wonder what had happened, what had changed him. He knew damn well.
Vietnam.

"That's a great story," Annie said, her voice soft in
the darkness. "Thanks for telling me. Your grandfather sounds like he was really cool."

"Yeah," Pete said, closing his eyes, remembering.
"He was a full Navaho. He must've been in his sixties
back then, but he still had long, black hair that he kept
out of his face with a headband. He was a silversmith
and he traveled all the time, selling his jewelry at fairs
and rodeos. When he was visiting, he'd set up a work-
shop in the barn. He didn't want me to go."

"Go where?"

To Vietnam. His eyes snapped open. Oh, man, what
was he doing? Had he actually forgotten who he was,
why he was here? Peter Taylor hadn't gone to Vietnam.
"To New York University," he said, glad he had a ready
answer.

"Why *did* you go?" she asked, her voice slipping
through the dark of the room as if it were something
he could reach out and touch.

"I had to," he said simply.

"You didn't *have* to," she said. "Nobody *has* to do something if he doesn't want to."

"Not true," he said. "There are some things that you have no choice about."

He had to get back on track, Pete thought. They had to stop talking about him, and focus the conversation on her. He had to get her talking about Athens, about England and about the people she had met with there. But how?

"Annie."

She closed her eyes, loving the way he said her name, and knowing that she shouldn't. "Mmm-hmm?"

"If you ever find yourself in any kind of trouble," he said slowly, searching for the right words to say, "I hope that you'll come to me and let me help you."

The room was suddenly silent. The little sounds Annie made—all the restless movement, the whisper of sheets, even the sound of her breathing—all stopped. Fifteen seconds, twenty seconds, the silence stretched on and on....

"Taylor, I can't figure out what you're trying to say," Annie finally said. "Why don't you do me a favor and just say it?"

Pete laughed, unable to hold it in. Man, this woman was too much.... "Okay," he said. "I guess what I'm trying to say is, if you're somehow involved with this art robbery thing, and you're in too deep, I wish you would tell me, because I can help you."

There were another few seconds of silence. Then Annie said, "Thanks, Taylor, that's really sweet. Good night."

Chapter 8

Waffles. Annie woke up wanting waffles. It didn't happen too often—only about twice a year—but when the urge came upon her, she'd get the waffle iron down from the top shelf of the kitchen cabinet, pull out the one-hundred-percent pure maple syrup and actually spend more than her usual five minutes in the kitchen.

She climbed out of bed, pulled her bathrobe on over her pajamas, found her slippers and shuffled into the kitchen.

A short time later, the batter was nearly entirely blended, and the waffle iron was heating and Annie was rummaging through the refrigerator, looking for the maple syrup. She spotted the glass bottle way, way in the back. Almost diving in headfirst, she triumphantly pulled it out, only to discover it was nearly empty.

"Oh, shoot," she said crossly. She turned the waffle

iron down to the very lowest setting, and went back into her bedroom.

Pete was in the bathroom. Annie could hear the sound of the shower running, so she quickly pulled on her jeans and a sweatshirt and slipped her feet into her sneakers. She ran her brush quickly through her hair, and pulled it back into a ponytail, then grabbed her purse and her car keys.

She was nearly out the front door when she realized she should probably leave a note for Pete. She quickly scrawled one on the back of an envelope, and left it at the bottom of the stairs.

Her car started grouchily in the cold morning air, and Annie found herself wishing that she'd taken the time to grab her jacket from where she had left it in the office. It was only a few minutes' ride to the grocery store, though, so she didn't go back for it.

She parked in a space close to the store, and ran to get inside quickly. The automatic doors opened with a mechanical swish, then closed behind her. She didn't bother to get a shopping cart or even a basket, going straight to the aisle that held the boxed pancake mixes and the syrup. There were shelves and shelves of the cheap, imitation syrup, but only one brand of the real stuff. It was from Vermont, no less. She took the glass bottle to the express line and was standing there, cheerfully reading the headlines on the sensational gossip newspapers, when she was roughly grabbed.

Startled, she let out a yelp before she realized who had grabbed her.

Pete.

He was barefoot, wearing only his jeans and an unbuttoned shirt. His hair was wet and he brushed a drop of water from his nose as he glared angrily at her.

"What the hell did you think you were doing?" he said, his voice getting steadily louder until the very last word was practically roared.

The cashier looked at him curiously, and rang up Annie's maple syrup.

"I had to get this," Annie said, wide-eyed, motioning to the syrup. "You were in the shower, so—"

He was holding her tightly, his fingers encircling her upper arm. "So you should've waited until I got out, dammit," he spat out.

He was furious, and he wasn't trying to hide it. She could see the muscles in his jaw working, the force of his anger in his eyes. She had never seen such emotion on his usually carefully controlled face.

"Four dollars and seventy-nine cents," the cashier said, snapping her gum and watching them with unconcealed interest.

Before Annie could take her wallet from her purse, Pete threw a five dollar bill down on the counter and snatched up the bottle of maple syrup. He pulled her toward the door with him. "You are to go *no*where without me," he said, his voice harsh. The mechanical door didn't open fast enough for him, and he slammed it with the palm of his hand, pushing it, accentuating his words. "*No*where."

As they stepped out into the parking lot, out into the cold, crisp air, Annie pulled free of him, taking the maple syrup possessively and stashing it in her purse. "Oh, come on, Taylor," she said, getting angry herself. What gave him the right to drag her out of the store and shout at her in front of the entire town? What gave him the right to tell her what to do, anyway?

"No. *You* come on, Annie. You're a smart lady." Pete made a tremendous effort to lower his voice, and his words were clipped, spoken through tightly clenched teeth with a quietness that sounded far more dangerous than his outburst. "Nowhere means *no*where. I don't want you stepping outside of the *house* without me, do you understand?"

When he couldn't find her in the house, he had been so scared, he could barely breathe. There was some kind of electric frying pan in the kitchen, and the power had been left on. There was a mixing bowl filled with something on the counter, eggs and flour all over the place. The first thing he thought was that somehow she'd been snatched right out from underneath his nose. Her car keys and purse were missing, but her jacket was right where she'd thrown it last night. He had been damn close to calling the FBI when he found her little scribbled note at the foot of the stairs.

And the fear that had tightened his chest had turned instantly to anger. White-hot, burning, seething anger.

But fear gripped him again as he raced to the grocery store without even taking time to pull on his boots. What if someone had been watching, waiting for the moment when she was alone, unprotected...?

"Aren't you getting a little carried away, Taylor?" Annie said, her own eyes flashing with anger now, her breath making a white mist in the cold air. "I only went to the grocery store, for crying out loud."

She turned on her heel and started toward her car. But Pete caught her arm, spinning her around, hard, to face him.

"What, you think you can't get killed in a grocery store?" he said roughly. "Think again, Annie. I've seen more victims of assassins' bullets than I care to remember—every one of them killed because they were careless, because they didn't think they needed protection while they ran to the bank or the pharmacy. *Or* the grocery store."

She tried to pull free, but his hands were on her shoulders, and he wouldn't let go.

"You can *not* go out by yourself," he said, his eyes burning with intensity as he tried to make her understand how important this was. "Annie, there's someone out there who says that he wants you *dead*." His voice broke with emotion. "Damn it—"

She was staring up at him, her lips slightly parted. Her long hair had come free of its restraint, and it hung down around her face, moving slightly in the chill wind. Pete didn't notice the cold air blowing against the bare muscles of his chest. He was unaware of the cold, sharp pebbles of the parking lot underneath his bootless feet. All he could see, all he could feel, was Annie. He was drowning. Drowning in the shimmering blue ocean of her eyes…

He wasn't sure how it happened, but suddenly she wasn't trying to pull away from him anymore. Suddenly she was in his arms and he was kissing her.

He wasn't supposed to be doing this.

Her lips opened under his, and he plundered the sweetness of her mouth desperately. He wanted more than just a taste, he wanted to consume her, totally, absolutely, utterly.

Her mouth was softer and sweeter than he'd ever dreamed, so soft, yet meeting the fierceness of his kisses with an equally wild hunger. She clung to him, one hand in his hair, pulling his head down toward her, the other up underneath his shirt, exploring his muscular back, driving him insane.

He shouldn't be doing this.

He groaned, pulling her even closer to him, pressing her hips in tightly against him, kissing her harder, deeper, longer. He kissed her with all the frustration, all the pent-up passion of the past few weeks. Man, he'd wanted to kiss this woman since he first set eyes on her from behind the one-way mirror in the airport interrogation room.

He shouldn't be doing this.

She moved, rubbing against his arousal, and he heard himself make a sound—a low, animal-like growl in the back of his throat. Oh, man, he wanted her more than he'd ever wanted anything in his life. He wanted to bury himself deep in her heat, deep inside of her. He wanted to make love to her and never stop, never stop, never...

Stop.

He shouldn't be doing this.

It wasn't right.

He couldn't do this.

Kendall Peterson, a.k.a. Pete Taylor, was a strong man, but he didn't know how strong he was until he pulled away from that kiss.

Annie stared up at him, her eyes molten with desire, her cheeks flushed and her lips swollen from the force of his mouth on hers. He watched her chest rise and fall rapidly with each breath she took, saw the pebbled outline of her taut nipples even underneath the thick material of her sweatshirt.

"Pete," she breathed, reaching for him.

Somehow he kept her at arm's length. "Get in your car," he said hoarsely. "I'll follow you home."

For the hundredth time that afternoon, Annie found herself staring sightlessly at her lab equipment, unable to concentrate. She looked across the room to where

Pete was sitting and pretending to read a newspaper. He had to be pretending—he hadn't turned the page in over an hour.

As she watched him, he glanced up, meeting her eyes. His expression was so guarded, he might have been carved from stone. In a flash, she remembered the way his face had looked after he had kissed her. She'd read so many things in his eyes. She'd seen desire, but no, it was more than mere desire. It was hunger—a burning, scorching need. But she'd also seen confusion and uncertainty. And fear.

Annie sighed, glancing over to the other side of the room, where Cara was working. Cara had been in the office when they'd come back from the grocery store.

Pete had just kissed Annie like no other man in her life had ever kissed her, and she had a million things to say to him, only they had no chance to talk, no privacy to continue what they'd started. And she got the feeling that he was relieved about that.

That feeling turned to certainty as the day wore on and Pete made a point to keep Cara around, like a chaperon at a high school dance. And those rare times when Cara was out of the room, he managed to be on the telephone.

Annie restarted the test she was running, a test to check the purity of a bronze knife blade, and sighed again. He'd kissed her, and suddenly it all seemed so clear to her, so obvious. Sure, they were friends. It was true that she liked him on that level. But there was no way she would've reacted the way she had to a kiss from a mere friend. That kiss had been more disturbingly intimate, more earth-shatteringly intoxicating than anything she had ever felt before.

No, there was more than mere friendship here.

Truth was, she was falling in love with this man. And he was scared to death of her.

Annie looked at Cara across the office. "Well, shoot," she finally said with a smile. "It's about time."

Cara nervously fiddled with the toys on her desk. "It still seems so sudden to me," she said. "I mean, marriage..."

"MacLeish, you've known the man for three years." Annie shook her head.

"But as friends," Cara said. "We were just friends."

"I can't think of a better way to start," Annie said quietly. "Have you set a wedding date?"

Cara grinned. "Jerry wants us to fly to Las Vegas this weekend."

"Good old Jerry," Annie said, rolling her eyes. "Always the romantic."

They both were quiet for a moment, then Annie asked, "So, are you trying to work up the courage to give me notice?"

Cara looked up, shocked. "No!" she said. "I mean, I don't know.... You know, Jerry's trying to get funding to go to Mexico in February...."

"You're irreplaceable, MacLeish," Annie told her. "But don't worry, somehow I'll muddle through."

"I'll definitely stay until the end of December," Cara said. "Remember, we were going to take January off anyway...."

Annie turned away, not wanting her friend to see the sadness that she knew must be on her face. January was looking to be a very cold, very lonely month, with both MacLeish and Taylor leaving for good.... She managed to smile at Cara as she left the room, though. "Congratulate Tillet for me, will you?"

Chapter 9

From the lab, Annie heard the sound of the door closing as Cara left for the evening. She heard Pete slide the bolt home and turn on the alarm system.

This was it. They were finally alone in the house, just the two of them.

She heard the sound of Pete's cowboy boots on the hardwood floor of the entryway, and her heart went into her throat. Turning, she saw him standing in the doorway. His face was carefully expressionless, but there was a tenseness about the way he was standing, an infinitesimal tightness in his shoulders. He was as nervous as she, Annie realized.

"I'm sending out for a pizza," he said.

It was the first full sentence he'd spoken to her since they'd gotten home from the grocery store, since that kiss.

"Want to split it?" he asked. "There's a place in

town that delivers. Tony's. Unless you know some-place better...."

He was trying to pretend nothing had happened, Annie thought. He was standing there talking about the best place in town to get a pizza, when they should have been addressing the fact that that morning he had taken her into his arms and nearly kissed the living daylights out of her.

His casualness didn't come as a surprise—not after the way he'd avoided her all day. He was telling her, not in so many words of course, but he *was* telling her that he regretted the kiss, that it had been a mistake.

Disappointment shot through her, and she turned away, not wanting him to see it in her eyes.

"You know, if you're not done working, I can wait to call," Pete offered. "'Course, it'll be about forty-five minutes before the pizza's delivered even if I call now."

Her composure regained, Annie looked at him. From the tips of his boots to the top of his short, dark hair, the man was extremely easy on the eyes. Faded blue jeans cut loose, but not loose enough to hide the taut muscles of his legs—long, strong legs—stretched way up over narrow hips. His plain brown leather belt with the shining buckle encircled his trim waist. He was wearing a heavy white canvas shirt, the kind with snap fasteners instead of buttons, open at the throat, sleeves rolled up to just below his elbows. He drove his hands deep into the pockets of his jeans, and the tanned, sinewy muscles of his forearms strained the fabric of his shirt. His shoulders were broad, his chest powerful.

And that was just his body.

Inside that perfectly shaped head, behind those intense dark eyes, underneath that thick, black hair, beneath the movie-star features, was a mind and a soul that Annie couldn't help but like, couldn't help but fall in love with.

But he didn't want her. Not the way she wanted him. If he did, he wouldn't be acting so business-as-usual, would he?

"Pizza sounds great, Taylor," she said, keeping her tone light. "Forty-five minutes'll give me just enough time to finish up in here."

He turned so that his face was in the shadows. "I'll call from the office," he said, and disappeared.

It was clear, Annie thought later as they ate their pizza, that to Pete, the morning's kiss had been an aberration, a slipup, a mistake. Their conversation wasn't as stilted or awkward as Annie had feared it would be, but Pete's face never lost its carefully guarded expression. And his eyes never even once lit with the heat she'd seen that morning—not even when they accidentally collided in the small kitchen as they prepared a salad to go with the pizza. He'd reached out to steady her, and she'd looked up into his face. But his eyes were distant, emotionless.

After dinner, Annie spent several restless hours in her office, putting little more than a small dent in the paperwork that sat on her desk. As she sat there, buried in files, Pete's eyes seemed to haunt her. Even though he wasn't in the room, she could still see his eyes, so detached, almost cold.

Oh, Christmas, she thought suddenly, sitting up straight in her chair. *What if it was me? What if I threw myself at him this morning?*

How exactly had it happened? Who kissed who first? She closed her eyes, trying to think back.

Pete had been so angry, holding her arms tightly

enough to bruise her. She'd been trying to pull away from him, hadn't she? But he just held on to her; he wouldn't let go. She remembered staring up at him, intrigued by the sparks of anger that seemed to fly from his eyes, startled by the raw emotion displayed on his face. She remembered seeing the fire in his eyes change to a heat of an entirely different kind. And then she remembered him bending to kiss her.

He kissed her. Yes, she thought with relief, he definitely kissed her. Thank goodness she could remember. It wasn't that she necessarily minded making a fool of herself. But she hated the thought of not being aware she'd made a fool of herself. *That* was too much to take. But it was okay. She *hadn't*—

"You working or sleeping?" Pete's husky voice cut into her thoughts and her eyes flew open. He was leaning in the doorway, with his arms crossed in front of him, watching her.

Annie grinned wryly. "Would you believe neither?" she said.

"It's nearly midnight," he said quietly, his eyes following her movements as she shut off the computer and restacked the files, putting them into her in basket. As she pushed her shining hair back behind one ear. As she unconsciously moistened her lips with the tip of her tongue…

Oh, damn, thought Pete. He'd spent the entire day and evening trying to fool himself into believing he was unaffected by that kiss. He'd tried to ignore the fact that when he kissed her, she'd kissed him, too. She wanted him. Even now, even though she was trying to hide it, he could see it in her eyes.

All he had to do was say the word, and he could have her.

But while making love to her would certainly solve tonight's immediate and pressing problem, it would generate a vast array of other, even more difficult future problems. If he slept with her without telling her who he really was, she would hate him. On the other hand, if he told her who he was *before* he slept with her, she wouldn't sleep with him, *and* she would still probably hate him.

But maybe not as much.

Pete followed Annie up the stairs and checked the windows in the bedroom while she went into the bathroom and got ready for bed.

Maybe if she didn't hate him quite so much, he'd still have a chance....

To what?

To have a future with her?

Ruthlessly, he crushed that thought, pushing it away, out of sight.

Pete refocused his attention on the sound of water running in the bathroom. Annie was brushing her teeth. She'd be out any minute now.

He locked the door to the bedroom and sat down heavily on his bedroll.

Tomorrow would be easier, he thought. All he had to do was get through tonight. He closed his eyes, hoping, praying to whatever gods were listening, that Annie wouldn't try to talk about that kiss.

He'd been waiting for her to say something all through dinner. He'd never even tasted the pizza, he'd been wound so tight. He'd half expected her to reach out for him, to touch him, to try to finish what they'd begun.

Expected? Or hoped?

No, he couldn't hope for it. As much as he wanted

to kiss her again, he couldn't even allow that much to happen.

Because if she touched him, she'd know. And how the hell was he going to explain why he wouldn't make love to her when he wanted her so badly, it was making him shake?

The bathroom door opened and Annie came out.

She was wearing her oversize plaid flannel pajamas, and she was brushing her hair.

Pete couldn't watch. He lay back against his pillow and closed his eyes.

It didn't help.

Annie set the brush on her bedside table, the same way she did every night, and turned off the light. She pulled the covers up over her and curled onto her side.

"Good night, Taylor," she whispered, but Pete didn't answer.

For once she could hear his breathing. It was slow and steady, as if he already were asleep.

She sighed, flipping onto her back, trying to get comfortable. She stared up at the dark ceiling, willing herself to relax.

Picture yourself on a tropical beach, she told herself, closing her eyes. Remembering the way Pete had talked her through it just a few nights ago, Annie pictured herself wading out into the warm Pacific Ocean. She imagined the clear water washing all her problems away. She imagined herself coming out of the water, taking off her silly plaid pajamas as she walked up to a beach blanket that had been spread out upon the sand. She imagined Peter Taylor lying on it, as naked as she was. He smiled up at her, reaching for her hand and pulling her down next to him, covering her mouth with his own—

Annie's eyes opened. What the heck was she doing? This was supposed to be a relaxation technique, not self-torture. How could she possibly rub salt into her own wounds by fantasizing about a man whom she *knew* wasn't interested in her?

But...

Annie squinted up through the darkness at the ceiling. Wait a minute.

She didn't really *know* he wasn't interested in her. She was only assuming it. He never actually *said* that he only wanted to be friends. He never actually *said* that he didn't want their relationship to progress any further.

Shoot, she was supposed to be some kind of brilliant scientist, and here she was *assuming* a whole hell of a lot of unproven facts....

"Taylor, you awake?"

The sound of Annie's voice came slicing through the darkness. Pete almost jumped. Almost. Instead he continued to breathe slowly and deeply, pretending to be asleep.

Coward, he silently accused himself.

"Taylor?" she said again. Then, "Pete?"

The sound of her voice saying his first name nearly did him in. But somehow he didn't move, and he didn't answer.

Come on, Annie, he thought. *Roll on over and go to sleep.*

The sheets rustled, but she wasn't pulling them up. She was pushing them back. He heard the sound of her bare feet on the hardwood floor. Oh, damn, she was out of bed. She was walking toward him—

"Pete, wake up," she said, her voice next to him in the darkness.

He opened his eyes to see her crouched down beside him. He could just barely make out her features in the dim light from the windows.

"Go back to bed," he said. But he didn't sound very convincing, even to his own ears.

Annie sat down, cross-legged, next to him. It was obvious that she wasn't planning on going anywhere. At least not real soon. "We have to talk," she said.

Pete pushed himself up so that he was sitting, his bare back against the coolness of the wall, putting several more inches between them. Man, she was still sitting much too close. He could smell her gentle fragrance, see the pulse beating at the delicate juncture of her neck and collarbone. His gaze was drawn to the deep-V neckline of her pajama top. He made himself look away.

"Annie, go back to bed," he said, louder this time. His eyes met hers and locked. "Please," he added, but it was little more than a whisper.

He turned his head away, but not before Annie saw it. It was only a flash, only a glimmer in his dark eyes, but it was there. The same deep hunger she'd seen that morning before he'd kissed her....

"Pete, why did you kiss me?" she asked, her voice husky.

"I shouldn't have," he said. "I was out of line." He braced himself to look up at her, steeling himself to remain expressionless. "I'm sorry."

"But I'm not," she said. She frowned very slightly. "You didn't answer my question. See, I just can't seem to figure out why you'd go and kiss me, and then act like I've got the plague. What's the problem? Are you married?"

"No."

"Involved?"

He was involved more than he wanted to be, and it was getting worse every second. "No. Annie, please—"

"So why did you kiss me, Taylor?"

"Let's just drop this—"

"I don't want to *drop* this," she said fiercely. He was saying one thing with his words, but his eyes were telling her something entirely different. "If there's a problem, tell me what it is. If there's not a problem—" She waited until he looked up at her. "Kiss me again."

Pete drew in a long, shaky breath. "You don't know me—who I really am," he said, caught in the depths of her eyes.

"I know enough," she said. Her hair was shining in the pale light from the windows, her eyes colorless and mysterious. She reached up to touch the side of his face, but he caught her wrist.

"You wouldn't like me," he rasped.

"Isn't that for me to decide?" Annie asked.

It would have been so easy to kiss her. She was leaning toward him, inviting him....

"I can't get involved with you," he said harshly, releasing her wrist as if it burned him. "It's not possible. It's not smart—"

He saw the flash of hurt in her eyes, and it did him in. "Annie, believe me, I have no choice," he said, his voice gentler. "It's damn near killing me, but I care too much about you to start a relationship that I know won't go anywhere." He reached out, turning her chin so that she looked up at him. "You'll see, it's better if we just stay friends."

This time Annie moved toward him first, thinking that if he still told her he only wanted to be friends after she kissed him, then she'd believe him. So she kissed him.

He groaned, his voice a note of despair, as his lips and then his tongue met hers in a long, deep kiss that sent fire racing through his body.

His arms went around her, pulling her toward him, closer, closer, until she was on his lap, pressed against him, and still that wasn't close enough.

He kissed her, again and again, almost frantically now as his need for her increased with each pounding beat of his heart. She received him feverishly, her hands sweeping down his back, over his chest and arms, as if she couldn't get enough of touching him.

And still he kissed her.

So much for his words. So much for his good intentions.

She was straddling him now, and his hands explored the strong muscles of her thighs. Moving upward, he found the soft flannel edge of her pajama shirt and swept one hand underneath it. Annie shuddered with pleasure as his roughly callused hand caressed her back. His fingers moved down, slipping under the elastic waistband of her pajama pants, stroking the soft, smooth skin of her buttocks.

Slowly, so slowly, he tightened his grip on her, pulling her hips forward until she was positioned directly on top of him. It was exactly what he knew he shouldn't do, but he couldn't seem to stop. It was an invitation, a silent question. Did she want more?

She gave him her answer by pressing herself down against the hardness in his jeans, by moving against him.

Yes, she wanted him.

And despite his resolve, despite knowing that he

shouldn't, he was going to take her. He knew now that all along he'd been fooling himself. He had no choice— that much had been true. He was aching for her, dying for her. He reached for her, and she was there, her sweet mouth against his.

You're weak, a small voice in his head accused. But he had to protest. The odds weren't exactly in his favor. It was two against one—his body and her body against his resolve to stay away from her. He didn't stand a chance.

But it wasn't right. She didn't know the truth about him.

He kissed her, determined to ignore the tiny disapproving voice that chastised him. *Don't think,* he told himself. *Don't think....*

Annie pulled her pajama top over her head, and Pete stopped thinking.

In one movement, he flipped them both over, so that he was on top of her. Her blue eyes sparkled as she smiled up at him, and he kissed her again. He started at her mouth and moved down her long, slender neck. He traveled slowly across her collarbone and kissed his way down to her breasts, taking first one and then the other firm nipple into his mouth, caressing it with his tongue until she cried out.

He lifted his head then, gazing down at her. The sparkle in her eyes had been replaced by liquid fire. Man, he'd fantasized about her looking at him like that. He'd fantasized about having sex with her. What he *hadn't* fantasized was that sex with Annie would be the best he'd ever had in his life. But it was. He'd never felt like this before. Never. And he still had his pants on....

She smiled at him again and lifted her mouth to be

kissed. He met her lips slowly, a gentle, lingering kiss that grew into an earth-shattering touching of souls.

Suddenly Pete knew what was different. Shaken, he pulled back. He rolled off her and scrambled to his feet.

Annie sat up. "Pete?"

He'd done something really stupid. Outrageously stupid. He ran his fingers through his hair. When had it happened? How could he have let it happen?

"Pete?" Annie said again. She got to her feet and took a tentative step toward him. "Are you all right?"

He'd gone and fallen in love with her.

That's what was so different. Sex with Annie wasn't simply sex, it was making love. Oh, man, he *loved* her....

She took another step toward him, concern on her beautiful face.

He had to get out of here. He had to think. He had to figure out what the hell he was going to do.

"I'm sorry," he whispered to Annie. "I'm—"

He spun on his heels, nearly leaping for the door to the hallway, leaving Annie alone in her bedroom for the first time in a week.

Pete leaned his head back against the wall and stared at the closed door that led to Annie's bedroom. This was crazy. This was ridiculous. He had never even believed in love before. He thought it didn't exist. But all the symptoms were undeniably there. He was in love with Annie, no doubt about it. It felt so much like what was described in all those silly songs he'd scoffed at for so many years, it was almost laughable. Except he didn't feel very much like laughing right now.

For the first time since he was a kid, he knew exactly what he wanted. He wanted Annie. He wanted her to fall in love with him. He wanted a chance at a future together. He wanted…forever.

Forever. Now *there* was a good joke. What were the chances that she'd want to spend forever with him after she found out he was a government agent sent to gather evidence against her?

Pete ran his fingers through his hair for the hundredth time and looked at his watch. Three-fifteen. Man, was this night never going to end?

He swore under his breath, knowing that he was in too deep. He was emotionally involved. He should be on the phone with Whitley Scott right now, making arrangements to be taken off this case.

But if he were removed from the case, who knew who they'd assign to take his place? What if the replacement agent wasn't able to protect her? There was no way he was going to trust her life to someone else. No way.

He closed his eyes for a moment. Damn, he ached all over.

He put his head in his hands, remembering the look on Annie's face as he bolted for the door. Talk about coitus interruptus, he thought with a strangled groan. She must think he was nuts, the way he jumped up like that, right in the middle of such serious foreplay.

He groaned again. She must not be very happy with him right now. He doubted if Miss Manners had a book on sexual etiquette, but he was willing to bet if she did, she would frown heavily upon a gentleman heating a lady up and then leaving her out in the cold.

But if Pete had made love to Annie, if they'd gone all the way, he'd have blown his chance at a future with her. When she found out he was CIA, she would assume he'd been assigned to seduce the art robbery information out of her. Which he had. Which was why he couldn't... This was *way* too complicated.

Annie woke up to the clock radio, and lay in bed for at least half an hour, listening to the country station and wishing that Pete was lying next to her.

But Pete didn't want her.

A tear slipped out and slid down her cheek, and she wiped it quickly away.

Why hadn't she listened to him? It was the same question that had kept her tossing and turning all night long, and the only answer she could come up with was that she was a fool. He had told her in no uncertain terms that he only wanted to be friends. But no, she had to go and throw herself at him. She had to go and try to show him how wrong he was. But she was the one who had been wrong.

It wasn't fair, but love never was. There was never a guarantee that two people would feel the same way about each other. In fact, it seemed like happy, mutual love was the exception rather than the rule. Why else would there be so many songs about unrequited love? Four out of seven of the country songs she'd heard that morning had that age old "you-don't-love-me-as-much-as-I-love-you" theme.

Another tear escaped, and Annie brushed it away. What was it Cara always said? Look on the bright side.

She stared up at the ceiling, trying to find the bright side as another song started. Look on the bright side, she thought. At least this had happened before she let herself fall in love with him.

But deep down inside, she knew that was a lie.

* * *

That night, Pete lay on his bedroll in the dark, waiting for Annie to ask him if he was awake.

The day had seemed endless, with Annie avoiding him when she could and being distantly polite when she couldn't.

He'd apologized, and she'd shrugged it off, telling him to forget it, it was her fault.

Pete frowned. She'd seemed so flip, so casual. Was it possible she didn't care? Was it possible that all she'd wanted was a quick roll in the hay?

No. He'd seen the hurt in her eyes, hurt that she couldn't hide. He closed his eyes, flooded by a wave of shame and remorse. His only comfort was knowing that he would be feeling equal amounts of shame and remorse if he *had* made love to her. Not to mention an additional dose of guilt.

Come on, Annie, he thought, lying there on the floor of her room. *Talk to me.*

But she didn't say a word.

Chapter 10

Cara looked at Annie speculatively. "Why?"

"Does it really matter why?" Annie asked.

"You're asking me to spend all my waking hours over the next three days virtually locked in the lab," Cara said, crossing her arms. "Is it so strange for me to want to know why?"

With a sigh, Annie got up and closed the office door. "If we work overtime, we can get a sample of Marshall's death mask ready to go to the carbon-dating lab by the end of the week. Then it'll only be another week, maybe two before we get the results. *Then* both the death mask *and* the people making those threats will be out of my hair."

"Pete Taylor will be out of your hair, too," Cara commented.

"Yes," Annie agreed. "Taylor, too."

Cara leaned back in her desk chair, eyes narrowing. "I thought you were starting to really like this guy."

"Yeah," Annie said, looking away. "I was."

"So why do you suddenly want to get rid of him?" Cara asked, lazily reaching out to bob the spring-attached head of her Homer Simpson doll. "What happened?"

"Nothing," Annie said.

"What, did he put the moves on you?" Cara asked, grinning. "Did he come on too strong, too fast?"

Annie put her head down on her desk.

"Give the guy a break," Cara said. "You should see the way he looks at you. It's like he's been struck by lightning—"

"He's just embarrassed," Annie said, looking up at Cara, her own cheeks flushing slightly from the memory. "I...well, I sort of... I tried to seduce him. But he just wants to be friends."

"You're kidding," Cara said, looking very shocked. "You mean you...? And he *didn't*...?"

Annie buried her face in her hands. "You got it."

"But I've seen him look at you like he's totally in love with you," Cara protested.

"Well, you're wrong," Annie said sadly. "He's not."

The front doorbell rang, and Pete put down his book. He went out into the foyer, checking the gun in his shoulder holster before opening the door.

Three men stood on the front porch. A van was in the driveway behind them; a colorful sign on the side read Mt. Kisco Security Systems.

"Dr. Morrow?" the older of the three men said.

"No," Pete said.

"We're here to install a burglar alarm," the man said, glancing at his clipboard, checking the address.

"Wait here," Pete said, and closed and locked the door, leaving them outside.

He swore silently to himself as he walked down the hall to Annie's office. This was really going to mess things up. With the system upgraded, he'd have no reason to sleep in Annie's room. And if he didn't sleep in her room, they'd never get back to the same friendly, easygoing relationship they'd had before.

He knocked on the office door.

"Come in," Annie's musical voice called.

He opened the door.

She was sitting at her desk, wearing a long-sleeved, flower-print T-shirt and her faded jeans. Her long hair was pulled back into a ponytail, making her look more like a college coed than a Ph.D. As she looked up at him, there was apprehension on her face.

Pete swore to himself again, but for an entirely different reason. "There are some guys at the door," he managed to say expressionlessly. "From Mt. Kisco Security. Did you call them?"

She stood up. "Yeah," she said. "I thought it would be a good idea to get the new system installed as soon as possible." Her cheeks flushed slightly, but she met his eyes solidly. "I thought it would make it easier... for both of us."

"What kind of system are they going to put in?" Pete asked, following her down the hallway.

He wasn't happy about this. Annie wasn't sure how she knew since his face betrayed nothing. But she did know. "The same kind you wanted that other company to install," she answered. "I wrote down the model number and the manufacturer's name. This company had the equipment in stock, and the manpower to do it today...."

"All right." Pete nodded and turned to open the door.

Later that afternoon, he called Scott to inform him of the setback to the investigation. Scott told Pete to get what he needed, and then get out. When he hung up the phone, Pete cursed softly.

The days sped past with Annie and Cara spending nearly three straight days and nights in the lab. Cara often didn't leave before midnight, and Annie frequently worked until two or two-thirty in the morning.

With the new alarm system installed, Pete slept in the guest bedroom. He moved the bed so that he could clearly see the new secondary burglar alarm control panel that had been installed next to Annie's bedroom door. If he woke up in the night, he could look over across the hall and be reassured. A red light meant the system was on-line and working. Green would mean it had been shut off.

Regardless of the new security system, Pete insisted that both bedroom doors be left open. But despite the fact that Annie was just across the hall, it seemed as if she were miles away.

He was no closer to finding out about her involvement in the art robberies than he'd been before. And he was slowly going crazy, wanting to hold her, wanting to make love to her....

Pete was plagued by the notion that if he *had* made love to her that night, she probably would have opened up to him by now and told him if she was involved in anything illegal. And if he had made love to her, he wouldn't have to face that flash of hurt confusion that even now still sometimes crossed her face. And, if he had made love to her that night, he probably would have made love to her the next night, and the next, and the night after....

Instead, he sat with her as she ate her lunch and dinner, telling her stories about his grandfather, about his childhood. They were pieces of himself he hadn't shared with anyone, secrets he'd kept locked away since Vietnam. In Vietnam, he hadn't talked about himself; he never got personal, he hadn't made friends. In Vietnam, if you made friends, you had to watch those friends die.

And after the war, when he'd joined the agency, he was always on assignment, always undercover. His past was fictional, part of an assigned bio.

Pete Taylor hadn't grown up on a ranch in Colorado. But Kendall Peterson had, and despite knowing better, despite being unable to tell her his real name, Pete wanted Annie to know who he was, who he *really* was.

And he wanted to make her smile again.

On Thursday, the doorbell rang, and Annie peeked through the window to see a stranger on the front porch. She pushed the button on the intercom that had been installed with the new security system and buzzed Pete, who was up in the kitchen.

"Yeah," he said, his voice sounding surprisingly clear over the cheap speaker. "What's up?"

"There's an unidentified male Caucasian outside the door," she reported. "He's approximately forty-five years old, wearing a dark business suit and a black overcoat. He hasn't smiled yet, but he doesn't quite seem the fanged wolfman type...."

The doorbell rang again.

"Just the facts, ma'am," Pete said, coming down the stairs and smiling at her. "No speculation, please."

Annie's heart flipped until she remembered that his smile was only a smile. He wanted to be friends, nothing more. "He *does* look like a thug," she said. "And *that's* a fact."

Pete's tweed jacket had been casually draped over the end of the banister, and he picked it up and slipped it on over his T-shirt, hiding the brown leather straps of his shoulder holster.

"Stay back, okay?" Pete said, and Annie nodded. He pushed the override button that would allow them to open the front door without shutting down the entire system. The light on the control panel still glowed red, but now there was an additional orange light signaling that the front door could be opened without triggering the alarm.

He opened the door. "Can I help you?" he asked the man politely, but with no nonsense in his tone. He adjusted the lapels of his jacket, pulling it back slightly on the left side so that his gun was briefly, but quite clearly revealed. It was no accident, Annie knew.

If the man standing on the porch was at all disturbed by the sight of the gun, he didn't show it. "You must be the butler," he said dryly.

"Something like that," Pete said.

The man held out a business card. "I'm looking for Dr. Anne Morrow," he said. "She at home?"

Pete took the card. He glanced down at it, then handed it back, behind the door, to Annie. "Joseph James," it said. "Antiquities Broker." There was a New York City address and telephone number.

"What's this in reference to?" Pete asked.

"I'm afraid I can discuss that only with Dr. Morrow," James replied smoothly.

Pete's gaze flicked back to James's face. The man's

nose was flat, as if it had been broken many times. There were several small scars up by his eyebrows, and a longer one on the left side of his jaw. Antiquities broker and knee breaker, he thought.

"So. May I come in?" James asked.

"No," Pete said pleasantly. "We're not inviting anyone inside these days." He leaned closer and added almost conspiratorially, "We're having a little problem with evil spirits."

"Lookit, I have a business matter to discuss with Dr. Morrow," James said. "So if you don't mind…?"

Pete looked back at Annie, who told him with a shrug that she didn't recognize the name on the card.

"If you want to talk to her, I'm going to have to search you first," Pete explained in that same pleasant tone.

James stared at him. "You're kidding, right?"

Pete stepped out onto the porch, pulling the door most of the way shut behind him. "Hands on the top of your head, legs spread," he said. "Please."

"Lookit," James said. "I'm carrying. But I've got a license, it's legal."

"Hands on your head, legs spread," Pete said again.

James crossed his arms, his patience obviously flagging. "I know you're just doing your job, buddy, but why don't you let it go. I didn't come out here to shoot Dr. Morrow. I came to talk."

"Hands on your—"

"Will you give me a break?" he said. Annoyed, James moved past Pete, reaching for the door.

It happened so fast, Annie realized that if she had blinked she would have missed it. One second James was heading toward the door, and the next, Pete had him backed up against the porch's sturdy wooden pillar, his gun dangerously close to the broker's face, his other arm pressed up under the man's chin. Annie rubbed her neck, remembering how unpleasant that felt.

"Taylor, is everything okay?" she called out, stepping into the doorway.

"Hey, lady," James squeaked. "Call off Fido, will you?"

Pete released James, but still held his gun trained unwaveringly at the center of the man's chest. "Please keep your hands on your head," he said calmly.

"You wanted to talk to me, Mr. James?" Annie asked.

James rested his hands reluctantly on the top of his thinning hair. "This wasn't exactly what I had in mind," he said crossly.

"I'm sorry," Annie apologized. "There've been a number of threats to my life recently. Taylor likes to err on the side of caution."

"Does he do this to all your customers?" James asked. "It must be great for business."

"Please get to the point," Pete said. "Dr. Morrow is very busy."

James gave Pete a black look, then turned toward Annie. "In that case, I'll be as brief as I possibly can. I have a client, Dr. Morrow, who is interested in purchasing the gold death mask owned by one Benjamin Sullivan that is currently in your possession. This client will pay four million, sight unseen, uncertified."

Annie's mouth fell open. "You can't be serious."

"I'm quite serious," James said. "My client is willing to give you a broker's fee of ten percent if you submit this offer to Mr. Sullivan and convince him to sell."

With great difficulty, Annie closed her mouth. "But I haven't authenticated it yet," she said. "It may not be genuine."

"My client wants this artifact, authentic or not," James said. "In fact, my client has a personal relationship with another authenticator, and would prefer that authenticator check the piece out instead of you."

Annie nodded slowly. "What's so special about this death mask?" she asked.

James smiled. Annie was reminded of a shark. "My client is…shall we say, eccentric? I'm afraid I'm not at liberty to discuss his motives any further."

"Ten percent of four million, huh?" Annie asked. "I'm assuming the transaction will be legal, with contracts and taxes paid…."

"Of course," James said, sounding affronted.

"Why can't you broker this yourself?" she asked, direct as usual.

James shrugged. "I've tried. Mr. Sullivan won't take my calls."

"What makes you think he'll take mine?"

"My *client* thinks he'll take your call," James said. "I think it's a gamble, just like anything else. Except this is one sweet gamble for you. You stand to lose nothing, or gain four hundred G's."

Annie thought about that for several long moments. "All right," she finally said. "I'll talk to Sullivan, and get back to you."

Annie and Pete watched in silence as Joseph James got into his Cadillac and pulled out of the driveway.

"Four hundred thousand dollars," Annie said wistfully as Pete closed and locked the door, and turned off the override to the alarm. The control panel glowed with a single red light.

"That's a lot of peanut butter and jelly," he said.

She smiled. "I could finance one hell of a field project with that much money," she said, warming to the subject. "I could back Tillet's dig in Mexico. I could cohead the excavation, get my hands dirty for a year or so, learn something new.... Do you know how long it's been since I've been camping?"

Pete shook his head, smiling at her excitement. "No."

"*Too* long," she said with a grin and disappeared into the office.

Benjamin Sullivan was back in town, and he greeted Annie warmly when he picked up the phone. "You know," he said, in his upper-crust Bostonian accent, "I had dinner with your parents two evenings ago."

"How are they?" Annie asked. "*Where* are they?"

"Fine and Paris." Sullivan chuckled. "I was on a stopover, they were on their way to Rome. Their book is coming along quite nicely. They've finished a first draft."

"Now *that's* good news," Annie said. She took a deep breath and plunged right in. "Mr. Sullivan—"

"Please, call me Ben," he interrupted. "Mr. Sullivan makes me feel so old, and I'm only in my seventies."

"Okay, Ben." Annie briefly outlined the offer for the death mask.

Ben didn't answer right away. "Well," he finally said. "This is a bit unfortunate, isn't it? The contract with Mr. Marshall has been signed. Even though it's only for a tenth of what the other collector is offering." He sighed. "I suppose we might be able to try to wriggle out of the deal," he said, "but that's just not for me. I guess being honest costs a bit of money, but in the long run, it's worth it. At least I hope it is." The old man laughed, then went on. "Strange, though, that this offer didn't come until now—I had put the word out that the piece was for sale some time ago." He paused for a moment. "No matter. I can't do it."

"I see," Annie said.

Ben chuckled. "You sound disappointed, Annie. What was your take going to be? Ten percent?"

Annie laughed. "Yeah. The money could have come in handy. I have a friend who's looking for funding for a project in Mexico, and ten percent of four million would've been perfect."

"Anyone I know?" Ben asked, interest evident in his voice.

"Do you know Jerry Tillet?" Annie said.

"Haven't met him," Ben said. "But I've heard only good things. Mayan specialist, if I remember correctly."

"That's him. He's found a site that he believes was a major trading center. The dig's scheduled to start in February, if he can find the backing."

"Sounds exciting," Ben said. "I'll have my accountant look into it, see what I can do to help out."

Annie laughed. "Oh, that's terrific."

"I've got to get back to work," he said. "I'm sorry I can't accept Mr. James's client's offer."

"Let me know if you change your mind," Annie said and hung up the phone.

She looked up to find Pete standing in the doorway, watching her. She made a face at him. "Sullivan won't sell," she explained, "but he's thinking about backing Tillet's project, so it wasn't an entire washout."

She shuffled the papers around on her desk, searching for Joseph James's business card. She quickly dialed his number and left a brief message on his answering machine, then tossed the business card into the top drawer of her desk.

Pete came into the office and sat down across from

her. Annie looked up to find his dark eyes on her. She couldn't look away, trapped by his gaze. He was looking at her as if he wanted...what? She knew he didn't want her, so what did that heat in his eyes mean? Damn, damn, *damn*—she couldn't figure this guy out for the life of her.

The phone rang, loud and shrill.

Annie jumped. "Excuse me," she said to Pete, then picked up the receiver.

Pete watched her glance up at him, then swivel her chair so that she turned slightly away. "I haven't been avoiding you," he heard her say. She was talking to Nick York. It had to be him. Pete resisted the urge to clench his teeth.

"All right," Annie said, laughter in her voice. "Yeah, you're right. Okay! I give in. I *have* been avoiding you." She paused, then laughed. "Yeah, but if you bring anything with you, it had better be flowers, not some archaeological find you want me to test." She laughed again. "Don't count on it, pal."

Pete stood up, unwilling to listen to Annie being flirted with over the telephone. Particularly not by someone who was probably far better suited for her than he was....

Annie watched Pete leave the room. Before he closed the door, he glanced back at her, briefly meeting her eyes.

It was that look again, Annie realized. He wanted something, and he wanted it badly. Too bad it wasn't her.

Chapter 11

Friday morning dawned bright and clear—a perfect autumn day. Despite working late the night before, Annie woke up early and pulled on her rattiest pair of jeans, an old sleeveless T-shirt and a sweater whose collar was starting to come undone. She rummaged in her closet, searching for a moment before she located several pairs of work gloves.

Whistling, she crossed the hall to Pete's room.

The door was open as usual, but he was still in bed. His hair was getting longer, and it was rumpled. He needed a shave, and his night's growth of beard made him look dangerous, particularly with his shirt off and so much hard muscle showing.

Annie steeled herself against the attraction that threatened to overpower her whenever they were together. She tossed the larger pair of gloves onto his chest.

Pete stared down at them for a moment, then up at

Annie, one eyebrow quirked. "If you're challenging me to a duel," he said, "you missed."

Annie grinned. "It's leaf-raking day," she said.

Pete rolled over to look at his alarm clock. "Didn't we just go to sleep?" he asked.

Annie crossed to the window and pulled up the shade. Sunlight flooded the room. "How can you sleep on a day like today?"

Pete squinted from the brightness. "Leaf-raking day, huh?"

"Hurry up and get dressed," Annie said. "I want to go outside. If we work fast, we can get most of the lawn done before Cara even gets here."

She turned to leave, but Pete's voice stopped her. "Annie."

He was pulling on his jeans, and her eyes were drawn to his hands as he fastened the button and pulled up the zipper. *Oh, Christmas, stare, why don't you,* she chastised herself, feeling her cheeks flush.

"I'm not sure if this is such a good idea," Pete said, gracefully ignoring her discomfort. "You're much safer inside the house. Out in the yard, you're a target. It's harder for me to protect you."

"You know, Taylor," Annie said, "a perfect day like this doesn't come along all that often. I'm sorry, but I can't let it pass me by. I'll wait for you downstairs."

When Cara's car finally pulled into the driveway, Annie and Pete hadn't finished raking half of the big yard. The day was unusually warm, and Annie had long since stripped off her sweater. Even with only her old T-shirt on, she had sweat running down her back and trickling between her breasts.

"Darn," Annie said. "Guess I miscalculated how long this would take."

Pete leaned on his rake and looked at her. It was that look again, Annie thought, nervously tucking a loose strand of hair behind her ear. Why did he watch her that way? With his shirt off, and his upper body glistening with perspiration, she couldn't bear to look at him. Instead, she turned and watched Cara climb out of her car.

"If you promise to keep the alarm on after you go inside," Pete said, "I'll finish up."

"Oh," Annie said, glancing back at him. "No…"

"I don't mind," he insisted. "In fact, it feels good to be out here. But you've got to promise to let the answering machine pick up all the phone calls. And if anything strange happens—anything at all—you call me. Immediately. Is that clear?"

She smiled. "Yeah."

He reached out, and for one heart-stopping moment, Annie thought he was going to touch her, to pull her in close to him. But he only plucked a leaf from her hair and tossed it to the ground. She turned quickly then, and nearly ran back to the house, hoping that he hadn't seen the hope that she knew had briefly flared in her eyes.

She tried to comfort herself by counting the days until the carbon-dating test results on Stands Against the Storm's death mask would come in. Eight more days at the most, maybe even less. Eight more days, and then he would be gone.

Now, why didn't that make her feel any better?

Annie took a gallon of ice tea and a pile of peanut-butter-and-jelly sandwiches out to Pete at lunchtime. She sat and ate with him, then closed her eyes and let the sun warm her face.

She'd showered and changed earlier that morning, and she now wore a bright yellow T-shirt with her jeans. Her hair was down loose around her shoulders, shining as it moved slightly in the gentle breeze.

Pete lay on his back in the grass, pretending to watch the clouds, but in truth watching Annie. Just when he thought he'd memorized every angle and plane of her face, he'd see her in a different light. With her eyes closed, her face held as if in worship up toward the sun, she looked angelic and serene—two characteristics Pete didn't normally associate with Annie Morrow.

He ached from wanting her. But every time Annie called him Taylor, he was slapped in the face with the magnitude of the lies he had told her—was continuing to tell her.

And the worst part of the situation was that he no longer doubted her innocence. Annie Morrow was not involved in an art conspiracy. Pete would bet his life on that. He'd been with her every moment for weeks now, and she'd neither received nor made one single suspicious phone call. No one had tried to contact her any other way. She left her mail opened and out on her desk—there was nothing she was trying to hide.

Except her feelings for him.

Pete knew that it was only a matter of time before he gave in to his own feelings, his own needs. Man, when she looked at him, when he saw that longing in her eyes—

Annie opened her eyes slowly and caught him staring at her.

Embarrassed, she looked away. When she glanced back at him, he'd sat up and was scraping some dirt off the well-worn toes of his cowboy boots.

"I have a date tonight," she said.

His dark eyes flashed toward her, and for an instant, Annie thought she saw surprise on Pete's face. But it was quickly covered up, if it was ever even there.

"Tonight's the fund-raiser at the Museum of Modern Art in the city," Annie said. "All kinds of backers and grants people and just plain rich folk are going to be there." She smiled wryly. "Along with every museum and university and private researcher vying for any extra cash that might be lying around. It'll be a real schmoozefest."

"Who's the lucky guy?" Pete asked.

Annie looked at him blankly.

"Your date," he said. "Who is he?"

"Nick York," Annie said.

Pete nodded slowly.

Annie fought a wave of disappointment. But what did she expect? she scolded herself. Did she really expect Pete to be jealous? In all likelihood, he was probably relieved. If she was with Nick, she wouldn't be at home, mooning over Pete like a star-struck teeny-bopper.

"I'd better get back to work," she said, standing up and brushing off the seat of her jeans. She started toward the house.

"Annie."

She stopped, turning slowly back around.

Pete was standing there, looking like an ad for Levi's, with his snug jeans riding low on his hips, and his tan muscles gleaming in the sunshine.

"Thanks for the lunch," he said.

His eyes seemed to drill into her, burning with that same, unmistakable intensity. It was that look again.

Annie shook her head, letting all the air out of her

lungs with an exasperated laugh. "Taylor, what do you want from me?"

He blinked. "What?"

"Why do you look at me that way?"

Pete looked down at the ground. "What way?" he asked, knowing damn well exactly what she was talking about.

"Oh, forget it," she muttered and stalked back to the house.

"Keep the alarm system on," he called after her, and without turning around, she held up one hand, signaling that she'd heard him.

He watched as she went inside, then picked up the rake and went back to work.

What did he want from her?

He should have told her. What would she have said, he wondered, if he'd told her the truth?

At one-thirty in the afternoon, the phone rang. Annie was in the office, and she answered it without thinking, remembering only after she said hello that Pete had told her not to answer the phone.

"Sweet Annie!" came a familiar voice. It was Nick York. "What are you wearing?"

"Jeans," Annie said. "Why?"

"No, not right now, you darling idiot." Nick laughed. "Tonight. What are you wearing tonight?"

Outside the office window, Pete carried a bundle of leaves toward the compost pile. Annie followed him with her eyes, trying not to crane her neck too obviously as he passed out of view. "I don't know," she said. "I haven't thought about it yet."

"Go all out tonight, will you, love?" Nick said. "Wear something tiny, with lots of leg and cleavage.

Maybe something blue, to match your eyes. I want 'em drooling."

"And *I* want to preserve my reputation as a legitimate scientist," Annie protested.

"You're the best in your field," Nick murmured. "Everyone knows that. Promise me you'll wear high heels?"

"I promise I'll wear blue," Annie said. "Tiny or high heels I can't guarantee."

"Fair enough," Nick said cheerfully, "though if you love me, even just the teeniest little bit, you'll wear high heels tonight. I'll pick you up at seven."

Annie hung up the phone, mentally reviewing the clothes that hung in her closet. Blue, she thought. What did she have that was blue? She had a new pair of blue jeans. She snickered, imagining the look on Nick's face if he came to pick her up and she was wearing jeans—and her navy-blue high-top sneakers. *That* would be perfect.

But how often did she get a chance to dress up? She wore jeans all the time.

Outside the window, Pete was almost finished raking the leaves. Annie imagined coming down the stairs, wearing something tiny, with high heels showing off her long legs. She imagined breezing past Pete to kiss Nick fondly on the cheek. She and Nick would get into his sports car and drive off, leaving Pete openmouthed and jealous.

Well, probably not openmouthed, Annie thought. She sighed. And probably not jealous. Pete wouldn't even notice.

She stood up. Pete might not notice what she was wearing, but Nick sure as heck would. And maybe that would give her bruised ego a well-needed boost.

Annie took the stairs up to her apartment two at a time. Somewhere, in the back of her closet, was the perfect little dress for this particular occasion.

The door to her bedroom was closed, and Annie hesitated, her hand on the doorknob. That was funny, she thought. She hadn't closed the door. It had been open a few hours ago when she brought the plates back from lunch....

Maybe Cara had been up here.

She retraced her steps back down the stairs, and went into the lab where Cara was painstakingly cleaning the rust from an ancient iron pot.

"MacLeish, have you been upstairs?" Annie asked.

Cara looked up, thinking for a moment. "Nope," she said. "Not today."

"How about Jerry?" Annie prodded. "When he was here at lunchtime, did he go up?"

"No," Cara said, putting down her brush. "Why? Is something wrong?"

But Annie had already gone into the foyer. She overrode the alarm system, allowing the front door to be opened, and went outside.

Pete was by the toolshed, folding the tarp. He still wasn't wearing his shirt, and he still was gorgeous. He looked up as she approached. "What's the matter?" he asked, dropping the tarp immediately and crossing toward her.

He'd picked up on her tension, Annie realized. His dark eyes raked her face, narrowing slightly, trying to read her mind.

She swallowed, and smiled weakly. "This is probably silly," she said, "but my bedroom door is closed, and I'm sure I left it open. Cara didn't close it, Jerry wasn't even upstairs when he was here, and…" She shrugged. "It was probably just the wind."

Pete looked up at the house, his sharp eyes quickly locating Annie's bedroom. "Your windows are closed," he said. He gave her a quick, fierce smile. "I'm proud of you. You didn't open the door. You came and told me. That was the right thing to do."

He took her by the arm and hustled her around the side of the house to the front door. He had already pulled his gun from its holster in his back pocket, Annie realized, and held it in front of them as they went inside.

Pete looked up the long staircase, then back at Annie. If an intruder was in the house, it didn't necessarily mean he was behind that closed door. She would be safer if she was near him.

"Stay right behind me," he said quietly.

Annie nodded, and Pete started up the stairs. He glanced at her over his shoulder. "Closer," he whispered, reaching back with his left hand to pull her in toward him, almost pressing her against his back.

She put her hand out to keep her nose from bumping into his solid shoulder blades. Her fingers touched the heat of his back and the hard smoothness of skin stretched tightly over his well-defined muscles. She resisted the urge to press her lips against him, to taste the saltiness of his skin with her tongue.

Pete positioned them against the wall next to her door, out of any possible line of fire. Slowly he reached out and turned the doorknob. He gave a push, and the door swung open.

The bedroom was dark inside, all the curtains drawn. There was no sound, no movement.

"I left the shades up after my shower," Annie breathed, her mouth close to Pete's ear.

He nodded once. "Stay back," he whispered, checking his gun, making sure the safety was off.

She caught his arm. "Be careful, Pete," she said softly.

His eyes moved down to her mouth, and for a heart-quickening instant, Annie thought he was going to kiss her. Instead he smiled, touching her cheek briefly with his work-roughened fingers.

Without warning, he leapt in front of the open door. His arms were outstretched, his left hand supporting the gun he held in his right. Startled by his sudden movement, a cloud of bats erupted from Annie's room.

Bats!

Pete swore, ducking as the bats fluttered and screeched around him.

Annie was flat against the wall, panic in her eyes. He grabbed her and pulled her down to the floor, covering her with his body. With one hand he reached out and caught the bottom edge of the door, yanking it shut.

"Cara, close the door to the lab!" he shouted.

He heard the thump of the downstairs door slamming closed, then Cara's voice raised in a plaintive wail, "Oh, yuck, are those *bats* out there?"

There were hundreds of them. They fluttered and swooped, dazed and confused by the bright sunlight.

Pete pulled Annie toward the stairs, half carrying, half dragging her down with him. He had to get her out of there, more than just her fear motivating him. Bats carried rabies. He couldn't let her get bitten, but there were so many of them, and they were *every*where....

He pulled her toward the front door, pulling it open.

As if sensing the freedom, a bevy of the bats rushed toward the open door.

Annie ducked, desperately trying to get out of their way. But she wasn't quick enough. Its radar off kilter, one of the bats swooped too low.

Annie felt the tug as the bat became entangled in her hair. Panic engulfed her, and she swatted at it, breaking free from Pete and running for the open air of the front yard. The bat struggled, equally frightened, but only became more firmly ensnarled.

"Pete!" Annie screamed, and he was instantly at her side. His strong fingers plucked the bat from her hair, throwing it onto the ground. Rabies, he thought. What if the bat had rabies? He crushed it with the heel of his boot.

Annie's knees buckled. But Pete's arms were around her, holding her. Gently he lowered them both down, so that he was sitting on the ground with Annie on his lap. He could feel her trembling as she clung tightly to his neck.

He held her close for several long minutes, until he felt her heartbeat start to slow. Then gently he tried to pry her fingers loose. But she wouldn't let go of him. "Come on, sweetheart," he murmured. "I've got to make sure it didn't bite you."

Annie released him and sat quietly with her eyes closed, letting Pete run his fingers through her hair, meticulously checking every square millimeter of her scalp and neck.

By the time he was done, the paramedics Cara had called had arrived, followed closely by the police and a fire truck. The FBI even pulled up, glaringly obvious in their big, unmarked car and dark suits. Last but not least to make the scene was a pest control van. As the paramedics checked Annie, a man and a woman dressed in sturdy protective gear went into the house and rounded up the rest of the bats. Pete pulled on the T-shirt he had discarded on the lawn while he was working.

The police bagged the dead bat that had been in Annie's hair, to send it to the county lab to test for rabies. As far as anyone could tell, Annie hadn't been bitten. But if the bat turned out to be rabid, the police officer told her, she'd probably still want to look into having a series of rabies shots—better safe than sorry.

It was after five by the time the pest control folks finished locating and removing all the stray bats. By then the burglar alarm company van had appeared in the driveway. The same man who had installed the system was in the foyer, deep in argument with Pete, insisting that if the motion detectors had been operational and on-line, there was simply no way an intruder could have gotten into the house without triggering the alarm.

"Maybe the bats made their way into the house through a hole in the roof," Annie heard the alarm specialist suggest as she approached the two men.

"Did they also close my bedroom door and pull down the shades?" she asked tartly.

Pete glanced at her. Her face was still a shade or two too pale, but she'd bounced almost all the way back, and the fire had returned to her eyes.

"The system was on all day," Pete added, crossing his arms as he brought his attention back to the man. "Occasionally we bypassed the front door, but I was in sight of that door each time, and believe me, no one unauthorized entered or exited that way."

The alarm specialist shrugged. "I'll check the system again," he said, returning to the control panel.

Pete turned to Annie. "I'm so sorry about this," he said, emotion in his voice.

"I have to wash my hair," she said, then shuddered. "Lord, I hate bats."

Pete's face darkened. "*I* hate knowing that someone was in here with you while I was out in the yard." He rubbed his forehead, then ran his hand through his hair as if he had a headache. "If they'd wanted to kill you," he said, his voice harsh, "they could've. And I wouldn't have been able to do a damned thing. Annie, I wouldn't have even *known*."

She put her hand on his arm. "It didn't happen," she said. "It's all right."

"It's *not* all right," Pete said. He looked down at her hand, her fingers pale and smooth against his tanned skin. He took a step back, and her hand fell away from him. "We can't stay here tonight. It's not safe."

"It was a prank," she protested. "They only wanted to scare me." She smiled ruefully. "They succeeded."

"If they got in once, they can get in again," Pete said.

"You said yourself that if they wanted to kill me, they could've," Annie said. "Obviously, they don't want to."

"Yet." Pete shook his head. "I'm authorizing a further upgrade of your security system. Until it's installed, we're not going to stay here. We're going to a hotel. I've already talked to the FBI team about additional protection."

Annie crossed her arms. "What about the artifacts? I've got over two million dollars' worth of antiquities in my safe. I'm not just going to leave them here."

"I'll post a guard," Pete said. "Round-the-clock, outside the house. I've also made arrangements to have all your locks changed."

Annie stared at him. "Did it occur to you to ask me if I *wanted* my locks changed?" she asked, annoyance in her voice. This was just too much....

"I assumed you'd want to stay alive," Pete said.

Annie glanced at her watch. It was nearly six o'clock. She had only an hour to get all these people out of her house, shower and change. "Where's Cara?" she said suddenly, noticing that the front lab was empty.

"She's in the office, being questioned by the FBI," Pete said.

"Questioned?"

"She's a suspect, Annie," he said. "She and Tillet are the only ones who have keys to this house besides you and me. If Tillet's as desperate for money as he says he is—"

Annie's eyes were shooting fire. She took an angry step toward him. "You go in there," she said, "and you tell them that Cara is *not* a suspect."

Pete held up his hands as if to placate her. It didn't work. "Annie, you've got to admit, Cara had access to your bedroom all day. There's no proof that she's not somehow involved—"

"I don't need proof," Annie said hotly. "Now, are you going to tell them to stop harassing her, or am I?"

Before Pete had a chance to reply, the office door opened, and Cara came out, looking dazed.

"Are you okay?" Annie asked, her eyes filled with concern for her friend.

Cara's lower lip trembled. "Annie, *you* don't think I had anything to do with putting those bats in your room, do you?"

"I know you didn't, MacLeish," Annie said, forcing herself to make light. "I just can't picture you handling two hundred bats."

"Yuck," Cara said, smiling shakily.

"I'm giving you two weeks' paid vacation," Annie said.

Cara frowned. "You can't afford that right now—"

"Courtesy of Mr. Marshall," Annie said with a grin. Her smile faded. "MacLeish, I'm not going to let you get blamed for everything that goes wrong around here. Do us both a favor. Leave tonight and don't come back for two weeks."

"I'll feel like I'm deserting you," Cara protested.

"You're not," Annie said. "I'll see you at the museum tonight, all right?"

"What?" Pete asked.

"Oh, no, look at the time," Cara said. "I should've been home an hour ago. Jerry wanted to get there early...." She hugged Annie. "See you later."

Pete's jaw tightened as he watched Cara let herself out of the house. He turned to Annie. "You're not going to that fund-raiser."

Annie raised her chin. "Oh, yes, I am."

Pete ran both hands down his face, and took a deep breath, trying to calm himself. "Annie." He shook his head. "We're both exhausted. This isn't the best time to go out into a crowd. It's too dangerous."

Maybe if he had talked to her before changing the locks, maybe if he had stood up for Cara, maybe then she would have agreed with him. She *was* exhausted. But she was angry—angry that things had gotten out of control, angry that her life seemed to be no longer her own, angry at Pete...

"I've got a date," Annie said coolly. "I've got to go get ready."

She started up the stairs. When she reached the top, she turned and looked back at Pete. He was standing where she had left him, looking up at her. His jeans were dirty, his T-shirt was stained with sweat and grass and he hadn't shaved or showered all day. "Please tell the FBI agents to leave," she said. "I don't want them here when Nick shows up."

Annie was putting on her stockings when she heard a soft knock at her bedroom door. She slipped into her bathrobe and opened the door. Pete stood in the hall.

"York's here," he said expressionlessly. "He's waiting in the living room."

Annie nodded, unable to meet his eyes. "Thanks."

She started to close the door, but he stopped it with his hand. "I'm going to take a shower," Pete said. "Don't leave without me."

Annie crossed her arms. "Taylor, I'm going on a date. Somehow I don't think Nick's going to appreciate it if you tag along."

Pete smiled, and Annie had to look away. "Understandable," he said, watching her study the floorboards. "But I'm going to protect you. From Nick York, at the very least."

Annie looked up sharply. "What if I don't *want* to be protected from Nick?"

Pete didn't say anything; he just looked at her. "Don't forget to pack a change of clothes," he finally said. "We might as well spend the night at a hotel in the city."

Annie felt a stab of annoyance. "What if I decide to go home with Nick?" she said, then instantly regretted saying it.

Pete looked stunned. He covered it almost immediately, but he couldn't hide the hurt that lingered in

his eyes. "I'm sorry," he said. He shook his head. "I...
didn't know you and York were..."

"No," Annie said quickly. "We're...*not*. I don't know
why I said that. It was stupid. I—" She looked away
from him, embarrassed. "I was just trying to make
you jealous," she admitted in a low voice. "I'm sorry."

"It worked," he said.

She met his eyes, and shook her head. "I still don't
know what you want from me, Pete. It would've been
really nice if things had worked out between us, but,
look, they didn't, and tonight I'm going out with Nick.
If you've got to come along, be inconspicuous, okay?
Do you have something to wear? This is a formal
event...."

"I can handle it," Pete said, releasing the door.

Great, thought Annie, closing the door tightly. *But
can I?*

Chapter 12

It was twenty after seven before Annie, walking carefully in her high heels, went into her living room.

Nick, resplendent in his tux and black tie, got to his feet. The gleam in his blue eyes was almost as bright as the light reflecting off his golden hair as he came toward her, arms outstretched. He kissed her, first on one cheek, and then on the other, before he nuzzled her neck.

"Perfect," he said, his quick grin showing off a white flash of teeth. "I couldn't have dreamed up a better dress. You look good enough to devour, sweet Annie. All of New York City will be salivating. I love it when you wear your hair up, darling—you look like a little girl playing dress-up."

Pete stood quietly in the doorway, looking at Annie. York was right, he realized. With her hair elegantly swept up off her neck, with those wispy bangs in the front, with her wide blue eyes and generous mouth,

Annie actually looked younger than when she wore her hair down. But her dress revealed a body that was all grown-up. It was blue velvet with an off-the-shoulder neckline that plunged down between her breasts. Short stand-away sleeves further framed her long neck and smooth shoulders. The bodice of the dress was tightly fitted, sweeping down into a short skirt that hugged her every curve. Sheer stockings covered elegantly shaped legs that went on and on and on, tucked into a pair of black-velvet high-heeled pumps. Her only jewelry was a pair of dangling coin-silver earrings. They were Navaho, Pete noticed.

"Hel-lo." Nick had spotted him. "Who's this?"

Annie's eyes widened at the sight of Pete. His tuxedo was perfectly tailored, fitting his trim body exactly. With his hair slicked back and his cheeks freshly shaven, the only similarity between him and the dangerous-looking man who'd so recently raked her yard without a shirt was his dark, glittering eyes.

Pete couldn't help himself. Involuntarily, his gaze swept down and then back up her body, lingering on her long legs and the soft, exposed tops of her breasts and throat. His eyes met hers, and he knew from the look on her face that he wasn't able to hide his desire, his need from her any longer. Hell, he'd given himself away. Turning, he tore his gaze away from her, staring blindly down at the Persian rug that covered the floor.

Annie had to work to catch her breath, wondering if she'd only imagined the raw desire she'd seen in Pete's eyes. But no, she knew what she had seen. She just couldn't begin to explain it.

"Nick, this is Pete Taylor," Annie said, trying to cover her sudden breathlessness. "He let you in, remember? Pete, Dr. Nicholas York."

The two men shook hands. Annie could see Pete quietly sizing Nick up. Nick was a little less subtle, giving Pete an obvious once-over.

"I thought you were the gardener," Nick said. "Apparently I was mistaken." He turned to Annie. "Darling, you didn't tell me you'd gotten a new research assistant."

"Taylor's my bodyguard," Annie explained.

"A bodyguard," Nick said, turning to look at Pete again. "You're kidding."

"Annie's been getting death threats," Pete said, his gentle Western drawl a sharp contrast to Nick's clipped English accent. His eyes met Annie's again for only the briefest of instances before he looked away.

"*Annie* has, has she?" Nick said, exaggerating Pete's use of her first name. He looked at Annie. "You know, that's the problem with you Americans. You're so focused on equality, you let the servants call you by your first names." He turned back to Pete. "Take the night off, old boy. I can protect her just as well as you can. Better, no doubt—my IQ's probably twice as high as yours."

"Don't be a jerk, Nick," Annie said sharply.

Nick put his arms around her waist, pulling her in close to him. "I had a *very* romantic evening planned," he whispered. "I intended to seduce you in the back of the limo on the way into the city."

Pete clenched his teeth. It wasn't hard to squelch the urge to grab Nick York by the front of his white tuxedo shirt and rearrange his perfect, golden-tanned features, but the fact that Pete had had the urge in the first place was alarming. Pete had no claim on Annie. He'd had his chance, but he'd declined, he'd passed, and now, God help him, he had no right to do or say anything at all.

"A *limo?*" Annie said, pulling away from Nick.

Nick grinned. "I'm in desperate need of funding," he said. "Down to my last nickels and dimes. But there's going to be quite a bit of money floating around tonight. And I figured, people like to back a winner, right? And winners arrive in limos. Speaking of arriving, we should get going. We don't want to miss the buffet—it may be my one square meal all week."

"I'll be right there. I just want to check to make sure everything's locked up." Annie headed down to the lab with Pete and Nick trailing after her.

As Nick went toward the front door, Annie went into the office and turned off the lights. She then checked the lab. The instruments were put away, the sinks were clean, the counters were cleared off. Everything was in order, the safe was securely locked. She turned back to the door, coming face-to-face with Pete.

Their eyes met and again she saw heat. This time he didn't look away.

"You look beautiful," he said softly.

Annie stared up at him, hypnotized by the look in his eyes. "Thank you," she murmured.

Pete couldn't stop himself. He took a step toward her, and another step. As he watched, she nervously moistened her lips, and he felt desire slice through him, hot and sharp and very painful.

God help him, he had to kiss her——

Nick's voice floated in from outside. "Darling, I hate to be a nag, but we really must be on our way."

Pete turned abruptly away, nearly consumed by a wave of anger and frustration. He wasn't sure who he was angrier at—York, for interrupting them, or himself for nearly giving in to his weakness.

Annie turned off the lights in the lab, then hurried past Pete, heading out the door.

"Ready then, are we?" Nick smiled, taking her arm and leading her toward the waiting limo.

Pete carried out Annie's overnight bag and his backpack and put them in the trunk. He was about to join Annie in the main body of the car when Nick stopped him.

"Servants go up front," Nick said, his eyes cool. "You can sit with the driver."

Pete kept his expression carefully neutral. "Not this time," he said and climbed into the back. He sat down across from Annie, sinking into the soft leather seat.

As Nick climbed in beside Annie and the limo rolled slowly out of the driveway, Pete stared out the window, steeling himself for the long night ahead. He could feel Annie's eyes watching him. Her confusion was nearly palpable, and he knew he shouldn't look into her eyes again—it would only make things worse.

But he couldn't help himself. He looked up. He'd meant only to glance in Annie's direction, but her gaze caught and held him.

As he stared into the bottomless blue depths of her eyes, he knew for damn certain he was out of control.

Inside the Museum of Modern Art, the party was in full swing. An orchestra played music in the main lobby, and people were dancing. A buffet table had been set up, and it was loaded with wonderfully aromatic food.

Pete left Annie's jacket and their two bags at the coat check, keeping a careful eye on her the entire time.

Nick had whisked her out onto the dance floor where

they moved gracefully to an old song. "Stardust," Pete thought. It was called "Stardust." He moved to the edge of the crowd, where he could see Annie and Nick clearly.

Annie stood out in the crowd. With her gleaming hair, her long, graceful neck, those creamy white shoulders contrasted by the deep blue of the dress… She looked as if she belonged here, amid the glitter of New York society. And Nick York looked as if he belonged at her side.

Pete watched York bend down and say something in Annie's ear. She smiled distractedly. She was looking around, searching the crowd…. Her eyes landed on Pete, and he realized with a sudden breathlessness that she'd been looking for him.

Even across the room, the charge that their locked gaze generated seemed to spark and crackle with heat. But then York spun Annie around, turning her so that her back was to Pete.

Pete took a deep breath and glanced around the room, looking for any sign of trouble, anything out of the ordinary. It wouldn't be too difficult in a crowd like this for an assassin to get up close and do some real damage with a knife. One quick thrust, and the victim wouldn't even fall, held up by the crush of people. Man, what he wouldn't give to be next to Annie, to be able to shield her with his own body. What he wouldn't give to be able to dance with her, to hold her in his arms….

The orchestra ended the song, and the dancers applauded. Pete watched York lean close to Annie's ear again and gesture toward the food.

Annie let Nick lead her by the hand to the buffet table. She glanced back through the crowd to where she'd last seen Pete, but he was gone.

He'd been standing there through the entire dance, watching her, looking at her the way he had back at the house, and for most of the limo ride. What was going on? By running out of her room that night, Pete couldn't have told her any more clearly that he didn't want her. So why was he suddenly looking at her as if he did? Was this some kind of macho possessive thing? Annie wondered, frowning slightly. Maybe even though Pete didn't want her, he simply didn't want Nick to have her, either. Or maybe he just liked the idea of jerking her around. Maybe he liked having her panting after him. Maybe—

Pete was standing by the buffet table, looking at her as if *she* were the main course. His dark eyes swept her face, lingering on her mouth a heartbeat or two longer than necessary. Silently, he offered her a plate, but she shook her head.

"No, thank you," she said. "I'm not very hungry."

Through the throng of party-goers, she spotted Jerry Tillet. "Excuse me," she murmured to Nick, and slipped her hand out from his arm. As she approached Tillet, she saw that he was talking earnestly to a tall, broad-shouldered man who was wearing a cowboy hat. It wasn't until she was closer that she realized it was none other than Steven Marshall—the buyer of Stands Against the Storm's death mask, and Pete's employer. She greeted both men with a smile.

"Dr. Tillet, I didn't realize you knew Mr. Marshall," she said.

Despite his smile, Jerry looked uncomfortable. "Yeah, well," he said, "in this business, everyone knows everyone else. You know how it is…."

Marshall shook Annie's hand, then brought it up to his lips. "How's it goin', darlin'?" he asked. "Everything okay?"

Annie extracted her fingers from his grip. "To be perfectly honest, things are getting a little out of hand."

Marshall's light brown eyes sparkled in amusement. "Dr. Tillet told me about the bats," he said. "That musta really shook things up."

A waiter with a tray of champagne glasses passed, and Marshall deftly removed two, handing one to Annie with a flourish. She took a sip, glancing around the room—and directly into Pete's eyes. He stood about fifteen feet away, leaning against the wall, watching her. Deliberately, she turned her back to him.

"I bumped the death mask up on my list," Annie told Marshall. "I should be getting carbon-dating results back any day now."

Marshall's smile broadened. "Well, all right," he said. "Your rainy day makes my garden grow. But that's the way life is, isn't it?"

"Yeah, that's life," Annie agreed.

Tillet looked positively antsy, and Annie realized she'd broken into the conversation before he'd had a chance to hit Marshall up for funding. "Has Dr. Tillet told you about his latest Mayan project?" she asked him. "It's fascinating."

With a grateful smile, Tillet launched into his well-rehearsed patter. Annie had heard it too many times before, so she let her attention wander, sipping her champagne and looking around the room.

Pete Taylor had moved, planting himself once again directly in her line of sight.

Annie tried to stare him down, but the heat in his eyes only intensified. *It's a mind game,* she told herself. *He's just toying with me.* She held on to her anger, trying not to give in to the molten feeling of desire that was forming in the pit of her stomach.

She turned away abruptly, heading back to the buffet table in search of Nick and safety. She had to laugh at the thought of that. Nick would be highly offended to find out she considered him safe.

But he was deep in conversation with three wealthy-looking women, no doubt trying to charm them into making a sizable donation to the Nick York fund.

Annie frowned down at the table that held the food, wishing that she had stayed home, thinking sourly about the way her colleagues had to scrape and grovel for money to support their scientific research. Ever since government funding had virtually disappeared, brilliant scientists were forced to spend nearly all their free time begging and scratching for money to keep their projects alive. And not just their free time, Annie realized, but also much of the valuable time they should have been spending doing research.

Still frowning, she stabbed a black olive with a toothpick, popped it into her mouth and turned away from the table.

"Don't tell me that's all you're going to eat."

Startled, Annie looked up, directly into Pete's obsidian eyes. He was standing much too close, only inches from her.

She backed away. "You're not being very inconspicuous," she accused him.

He moved closer. "Do you want me to get you a plate?" he asked. "There are some tables free, if you want to sit down."

Annie was staring up at him, an odd mixture of disbelief and longing on her face. Still, he moved toward her, stopping when there was only a hint of space between them. If she took a deep breath, he realized, her breasts would brush his chest.

"Pete, why are you doing this?" she asked softly.

It was a good question. Why *was* he doing this? He knew damn well that if he made love to her tonight, the way he wanted to, he would be risking everything. For one brief moment, he thought crazily, fleetingly, of taking Annie and running away. They could leave the country, leave behind the art conspiracy charges, leave behind Captain Kendall Peterson. He could spend the rest of his life as Pete Taylor. Annie would never have to know; he would never have to tell her who he really was, tell her that he'd lied to her.

"What do you want from me?" she whispered.

"Dance with me, Annie," he said, his voice husky.

Annie felt her throat tighten, and she steeled herself, ordering herself not to cry. "Don't do this," she said, her voice shaking slightly despite her attempts to keep it steady. "Don't play with my feelings, Taylor. You know full well that I..." She closed her eyes, and took a deep breath. "...want you. There. I admitted it. You win. Now leave me alone."

She turned, nearly diving for the other side of the room. She could feel the sting of unshed tears on the backs of her eyelids, but she forced herself to smile brightly at the faces she recognized in the crowd. How she wanted to go home. But home was off-limits, unsafe until a new, more elaborate security system could be installed.

She caught sight of the bar, stretching across one entire end of the gaudily decorated lobby, and headed for it. She'd get a tall, cool glass of seltzer, then hunt for Cara. They could hang out in the ladies' room together, away from Pete Taylor....

"Dr. Morrow! What a pleasant surprise!"

Annie turned to find a small man with brown wavy

hair standing before her. He wore a thick gold chain around his wrist and a white carnation in the lapel of his tux. It was Alistair Golden, her chief competitor.

"Dr. Golden," she said, taking the hand he had extended.

"How's work?" he asked, his startling green eyes probing.

Talking to this man was a lot like being interrogated, Annie thought. It wasn't his words, but rather the penetrating way he had of staring. He reminded her of a frog eyeing a fly it was going to eat for dinner. And she was the fly.

"Fine," she lied. "And how are things with you?"

"Fine," he said, and she wondered if he was lying, too. "I heard you're having some security problems lately. Something about…evil spirits?"

"News does travel," Annie murmured, looking longingly at the bar.

The man's gaze focused over Annie's right shoulder, and she turned to find Pete standing there.

"I don't believe we've met," Dr. Golden said.

"Dr. Alistair Golden, Pete Taylor," Annie said briefly. The two men shook hands.

"Taylor works for me," she said, intentionally labeling him as mere hired help. "He's a security guard." She didn't call him a bodyguard, not wanting to make their relationship even that personal. "Excuse me," she added, taking the opportunity to escape both from Golden's inquisitive eyes and Pete's presence.

She was still twenty feet from the bar when a hand caught her arm. She froze, knowing without turning around that it was Pete.

"Annie, we have to talk," he said, his soft drawl somehow cutting through the noise of a thousand people talking and laughing, through the sound of a twenty-piece orchestra playing an old romantic song.

She turned, then. "No, we don't," she said. "Give me a break, Taylor. Please? I don't feel like talking."

"Then dance with me."

Her eyes flashed with anger. "Read my lips, pal. No. Get it? *No*—"

She turned away, but he caught her wrist and pulled her back. "Then *listen* to me," he said. "You don't have to talk, you don't have to say anything."

"I don't want to listen—"

"Annie, have mercy on me—"

"Sweet Annie!" Nick York bounded up, startling them both. "They're playing our song!"

Nick pulled her out onto the dance floor and wrapped his arms around her. Annie looked over his shoulder. She could see Pete shake his head slightly with frustration. When he looked up and met her eyes, Annie caught her breath, recognizing that same look, the one that had been confusing her for weeks now.

Why now, out of the blue like this, did Pete suddenly want to dance with her? It didn't make sense. *None* of this made any sense at all.

A wave of fatigue washed over her and she stumbled. Only Nick's arms around her kept her from falling.

"Nick, I'm exhausted," she said, looking up into her friend's eyes. "I'd like to leave."

"Shall I call you a cab?" he asked, then, realizing how callous he sounded, added, "I can't leave now, Annie." His eyes were serious and he actually had the decency to look ashamed. "I'm sorry, darling, but I've got a few leads on some backers and—"

"It's all right," she said. And it was. She hadn't really expected Nick to leave this party three hours early. She'd hoped, but not expected. "I'll get a cab my—"

"Oh, Lord, there's Mr. and Mrs. Hampton-Hayes," Nick said. "And they're heading for the door. Annie, they're richer than God and I've *got* to talk to them. Call me, darling."

He was gone, leaving her standing alone in the midst of all the dancers. Good old Nick. If there was one thing you could count on, it was that you couldn't count on him.

"I was going to ask if I could cut in, but it looks like your partner already cut out."

Pete.

Annie turned to find him standing behind her, and before she could say anything, before she could move, he'd taken her into his arms.

It was heaven.

He held her so close, she could feel his heart beating. His arms were strong, yet he held her gently, one hand at her waist, the other holding her hand.

Annie closed her eyes, leaning against him. This had to be a dream. Certainly she'd dreamed about Pete holding her like this often enough. In a heartbeat, all her resistance had vanished. She pulled her hand free and slipped it up around his neck, pulling him even closer, running her fingers through the softness of his hair.

His arms tightened around her waist, and she looked up to see desire growing in his eyes. He slid one hand up to the deep-V back of her dress, letting his fingers trail lightly across her bare skin, up to her smooth shoulders, and back down again.

Pete felt, more than heard, the small sound she made

as he touched her, and it was almost too much for him to take.

"Annie," he breathed. "Annie…"

He'd lost his mind—there was no doubt about it. He'd told her that they had to talk, but really, what was he going to say to her? He couldn't tell her he was CIA; he couldn't do that.

He could tell her that he loved her.

He could pray that she loved him, too—enough to forgive him for all the lies, all the half-truths, all the deception.

His thighs pressed against her as they rocked back and forth, pretending to dance, and Annie looked up at him again, losing herself in the bottomless depths of his eyes.

Why didn't he kiss her?

She couldn't stand it another second. Standing on her toes, she pulled his head toward her and brushed his lips with hers. "Kiss me, Taylor," she said, her lips parted invitingly.

He gave a sound that was half like a laugh, half like a groan. "I can't."

She pulled back, as far as she could with his arms still around her. "Why not?"

Pete could see frustration in her eyes, frustration and questions and a shadow of hurt. She didn't understand. She thought he didn't want to kiss her. Man, if she only knew…

He reached up and touched the side of her face, gently tracing her lips with his thumb. "Annie, I want to," he said softly. "But I'm supposed to be protecting you. How can I watch for trouble if I'm kissing you?"

He could feel her trembling in his arms. "Kiss me with your eyes open."

"Not a chance." Pete shook his head. "When I kiss you, I'm going to do it right."

Their eyes locked and for several long seconds, Annie couldn't breathe. *Why now?* The question kept popping into her head. He'd run away from her the night she'd offered herself to him. He could have had her, but he'd turned her down. So why did he want her now?

Don't think, she ordered herself. *Don't wonder, don't ask questions, don't ruin this. And maybe whatever "this" is could last forever....*

She nervously wet her lips. "If you won't kiss me with your eyes open, then we should go someplace you feel is safe enough to close your eyes."

His fingers were at the nape of her neck, gently stroking her soft skin. "That sounds like a great idea to me," he said.

He took Annie's hand and led her off the dance floor, knowing full well that leaving the lights and the crowd was a mistake. Tonight they would share a hotel room, and unless he got a sudden burst of self-control, he'd share her bed.

Pete looked at the woman following him, looked at her soft, smooth skin, her beautiful face, her blue eyes, so wide and trusting— He swore, silently, harshly, knowing his self-control was long gone, and praying she'd forgive him when she found out the truth.

Chapter 13

The city streets were crowded even though the night air was cold.

Pete had his backpack and Annie's overnight bag slung over his right shoulder. His other arm was wrapped tightly around her shoulders. She looked up at him and tried to smile. Pete realized she was as nervous as he was.

"Where are we going?" she asked.

"I know a place over on the west side," he said, looking casually over his shoulder. But his eyes were sharp, his swift gaze missing no detail of the people and cars around them.

"Are we going to walk? Usually I don't mind walking. It's just these shoes aren't exactly cut out for— Hey!"

In a flash, Pete scooped her up in his arms.

"I was thinking more along the lines of a cab," she said, looping her arms around his neck. "But this is nice." She closed her eyes, leaning her head against his shoulder. "Yeah, I could get real used to this."

"We're going to get a cab," Pete said, carrying her across the street. "I didn't want to find one too close to the museum. We'll be harder to trace this way."

He gently set Annie down on the sidewalk, but she kept her arms around his neck. "I feel very safe," she said. "Are you sure you can't kiss me yet?"

"Definitely not yet." He glanced down at her, a smile softening the lines of his face. "I feel like we're targets at a shooting range. If I kiss you now, it would have to be over quick," he said, looking boldly into her sweet blue eyes. "And, Annie, when I finally do kiss you, it's going to last a long, long time."

Annie smiled. "I like the sound of that, Taylor."

Taylor. Right. Pete had to look away. Would she still smile at him that way after he told her who he really was, and why he'd been sent to play the part of her bodyguard? *Please,* he prayed to his vast collection of deities. *Please let her forgive me....*

When he glanced back, she was still smiling at him. "Think maybe it'll be safe enough in the cab for you to kiss me?" she asked softly.

Pete's arms went around her, and he pulled her in tightly. "It better be," he murmured into her soft hair.

He reluctantly detached Annie's hands from his neck and stepped toward the curb. Down the block, the light turned green, and a wall of headlights approached. They were too far away for Pete to distinguish the cabs from the regular vehicles, but there was one car traveling faster than the others. It moved to the right lane, as if the driver had spotted them. Pete lifted his hand, signaling that they needed a cab.

He saw that there was no taxi roof light at the same instant that he realized the car was speeding up, not slowing down. Something was wrong. Something was really wrong....

He turned, and fear hit him like a solid punch to the gut. Annie wasn't next to him! God, where was she?

Searching wildly, he spotted her several yards away, leaning against an open-air telephone booth. She stood on one foot, serenely unaware of any danger. Her shoe was in her hand as she gracefully bent her leg to examine a rubbed spot on her heel.

Pete dropped her overnight bag, and went for Annie at a dead run, catching her around the waist as the speeding car jumped the curb and came onto the sidewalk. Around him, everything switched into slow motion. Out of the corner of his eye, he could see the startled look on Annie's face, and her shoe pinwheeling from her hand. There was a storefront ahead of him, with a door set back from the sidewalk. If he could make it there, they'd be safe. But the distance he'd have to cross, the actual sidewalk itself, seemed to stretch, to lengthen into an impossibly unattainable goal.

As the car came closer, he could see the face of the driver. The man's teeth were bared in a grimace of concentrated rage; his eyes were wild. Pete's training kicked in, and he glanced down at the car's license plate, instantly committing the three numbers and three letters to memory. Memory, yeah, right. As if he'd even have a memory after this was over....

Pete had been faced with his own probable death before, but it had never angered him the way this did. No way was he going to let Annie die. And no way was *he* going to end up dead, either. Not now. Now when he'd finally found the best reason he'd ever had for staying alive.

With herculean effort he pushed his straining muscles harder, and threw both Annie and himself into the storefront. The car missed them by mere inches, but hit the phone booth, knocking it down and dragging it several hundred feet before driving away, tires squealing.

Pete turned instinctively into the fall, to cradle and protect Annie. With a tearing sound, the left sleeve was torn off of his tuxedo jacket as he skidded on the rough concrete. His shoulder was badly scraped, but he felt nothing but relief as he pulled Annie onto his lap.

He ran his hands quickly down her arms and legs to reassure himself that she was still in one piece. Her right knee was scraped, the stocking destroyed, but other than that she was all right.

"Pete, you're bleeding," she said, her voice remarkably clear.

As he looked up, he realized she was checking him over as carefully as he had checked her. His elbow was a mess, along with his left knee, and blood stained the fine fabric of his tux. He couldn't see his shoulder—didn't want to see it.

"Still feel safe?" he asked her hoarsely.

To his surprise, she smiled. It was shaky, but it was definitely a smile. "If you're with me," she said, "then I'm safe."

Man, she was giving him an awful lot to live up to. Painfully, he stood up, pulling Annie to her feet. There was a crowd gathering, and he wanted to get away from all the curious eyes.

"We've got to get out of here before he comes back," he said. His pack was still on his back, but he'd dropped Annie's bag on the sidewalk. Miraculously, it hadn't been stolen; it still lay where it had fallen. Wincing, he bent to pick it up. There was a distinct tire track on the soft leather.

Someone in the crowd handed Annie her missing shoe.

She thanked them politely, calmly, as if this sort of thing happened every day.

Several cars had stopped at the accident scene, one of them a cab. Its off-duty light was lit, but Pete pulled several twenty-dollar bills from his wallet, and the driver was happy to get back to work.

"Where you heading?" the cabbie asked as they got in.

"Madison Square Garden," Pete said. "And I'll give you another fifty bucks if you keep the off-duty light on."

"But that's illegal—"

"A hundred."

"You're the boss."

As the cab pulled away from the curb, Pete pulled Annie down with him so that they were both lying on the seat, hidden from view. Her face was illuminated in spurts by the streetlights they passed under, and she stared up at him, her eyes wide.

"You okay?" he asked.

She nodded, looking into his eyes as if he were a lifeline. "That was no accident," she said. "Someone tried to kill us, didn't they?"

"Yeah."

Annie nodded again, still looking into his eyes. "Are *you* okay?" she asked him.

"I'm fine."

"Really?"

The cab's suspension system squeaked as it hit a pothole. Annie's hair had all but fallen down around her shoulders, and he pushed a lock off her face. "Ask me that same question in a minute," he murmured. "Something tells me I'm going to be even better than fine."

He kissed her gently, just a slight brushing of his lips against hers. She smiled, then lifted her mouth to his for more. He kissed her again, a long, slow, sweet kiss that made his heart pound and sent his blood racing through his veins.

"Madison Square Garden," the cabbie announced. "Uh, you folks want me to go around the block a few more times?"

Annie grinned. "What does he think we're doing back here?" she whispered into Pete's ear.

"Probably exactly what we *are* doing," he whispered back, kissing her neck. "Yeah, keep going," he said in a louder voice to the driver. He lifted himself up slightly, so he could peek out the back window.

After the cab made three right turns with no cars following them, Pete had the driver pull over, and he and Annie climbed out.

The cab had no sooner pulled away from the curb when Pete flagged down another taxi. They quickly climbed in.

"La Guardia Airport," Pete directed the driver.

An hour and a half later, they ended up in an expensive hotel overlooking Central Park. The room was large and elegant, decorated in hushed shades of rose and burgundy, with a beautiful floral-printed wallpaper that reminded Annie of an English garden. A table and chairs sat in the corner by the window, a couch and several overstuffed chairs were positioned around a cold fireplace and a big bed was against the wall. One bed. Annie pulled her eyes away from it and looked at Pete.

"You know, when you told that cabdriver to take us to the airport," she said, "for a while there, I thought you wanted to catch the next flight out of town."

Pete slipped the chain on the door and fastened a deadbolt. "Would you have gone?" he asked.

"Yes," she said without hesitating even a second. "If that's what you wanted."

She trusted him. It was clear from her eyes and her voice. Perfect, Pete thought grimly. She trusted him absolutely, yet he'd told her nothing but lies and half-truths. She would have every right to be furious with him when she found out the real story, every right never to trust him again.

Annie watched as he pulled the desk chair over and wedged it tightly underneath the doorknob. He seemed more silent and expressionless than ever, as if he were hiding something. Were they really safe here? Maybe they *should* have taken a flight out of New York, away from the city....

"Does that work?" she asked, gesturing to the chair.

"It's not going to stop anybody who's determined to get in here," Pete said. "But it makes me feel better."

"Are we safe?" she asked.

His eyes met hers, and electricity seemed to crackle between them.

Safe.

If they were safe, Pete could relax. He could close his eyes and kiss her. And if he could close his eyes and kiss her...

"Yeah," he said. "For now."

His gaze was so intense, Annie had to look away. Her overnight bag was on the floor, and she looked at it, seeing for the first time the tire mark that marred its leather surface. Her eyes were very wide and very blue as she looked back up at Pete. "I nearly got you killed. Didn't I?"

Pete shook his head. "*You* didn't try to run me over," he said, painfully shrugging out of what was left of his tuxedo jacket, depositing onto the table a small gun that he'd somehow concealed up his sleeve. "Don't go doing the guilt thing on me, Annie. I knew exactly what I was getting myself into when I took this job."

He pulled another gun out from where it had been tucked into the back of his pants.

"Did you really?"

He turned to glance at her, and froze. Annie had taken off her evening jacket, too, and she stood in front of him, her sexy blue dress wrinkled, her stockings torn, her makeup smudged, her hair disheveled and down around her smooth shoulders. She was gorgeous, perfectly, mind-numbingly gorgeous. Desire slammed into him, running him down and crushing him so that he could barely breathe.

"No," he managed to say, his voice sounding raw. "I didn't have a clue."

He couldn't hide how badly he wanted her—he knew it was written clearly across his face. He turned away abruptly, unfastening his shoulder holster and putting that gun with the others. He knew he should wash the scrape on Annie's knee, and maybe take a look at his shoulder in the bathroom mirror....

Annie walked slowly toward him, hoping for another glimpse of that exhilarating fire she'd seen burning in his eyes. "Do me a favor, Taylor," she said, her voice even lower and huskier than usual. "Unzip me?"

She turned, sweeping her hair in front of one shoulder, exposing her slender neck and smooth back, waiting. For several long seconds, she was afraid he wasn't going to do it. Then his big, gentle fingers found the tiny zipper pull and tugged it slowly down. Annie heard Pete take a deep breath.

"You should take a shower," he said on the exhale. Pete briefly closed his eyes, willing her to walk away from him. But she didn't. When he looked again, she was still standing in front of him. And he couldn't resist.

Annie sighed with pleasure as she felt Pete touch her shoulders, his callused fingers stroking her soft skin.

"Annie," he breathed close to her ear. "*I* should take a shower—a cold one."

"I have a better idea," she said, turning to face him. The heat in her eyes left him no doubt as to what she had in mind.

He knew that he should stop touching her, he should stop tracing the line of her delicate collarbone, he should keep his fingers out of her silky hair....

She took a step toward him, closing the shrinking gap between them, and suddenly his arms were around her and he was kissing her.

This was not like the sweet kisses they'd shared in the back seat of the taxi. This was an explosion, a scorching, turbulent eruption of emotion and desire held far too long in check. He molded her body against his as their mouths met hungrily, frantically. He welcomed her tongue into his mouth, pulling her inside him, as if he wanted to devour her whole. She moaned, a soft, sensual sound that nearly brought him to his knees, and he swept his tongue past her lips, piercing her, possessing her, claiming her as his own.

Annie heard herself moan again, as Pete's hands moved down to her buttocks, pressing her tightly to the ironlike hardness of his arousal. Feeling herself flood with even more heat, Annie wrapped one leg up around him, fitting herself against him. She could feel his hand slide up the silky nylon that covered her thigh, slipping underneath her dress.

Suddenly, violently, Pete pulled away from her. He crossed to the other side of the room, as if to put as much distance between them as possible. Not again, Annie thought with frustration, watching him lean against the far wall, pressing his palms to his forehead. She took a deep breath, trying to calm her ragged breathing. At least he didn't run away, she told herself. This was definitely a step in the right direction....

"Annie, I'm dying to make love to you," he said. "But we have to talk first. You need to understand that there are things I can't tell you—"

Annie slipped out of her dress, kicking her shoes into the corner of the room. She wore a black bustier that ended in a point just above the black silk of her panties. Pete watched, almost hypnotized, as she peeled off her tattered stockings and tossed them into the wastebasket.

She walked toward him then, saying, "We were attacked by a flock of bats *and* nearly run over by some maniac, all in the space of a few hours. Maybe this is just a day's work for you, pal, but I've had it. I don't want to talk. I don't want to deal with any problems. And I don't want to have to wonder if I'm going to get killed before I get a chance to make love to you."

"Annie—"

She pressed her fingers to his lips. "Tell me tomorrow," she said, her blue eyes beseeching him. "Please?"

The last time Pete had seen her dressed in only her underwear, she'd stood this close to him, but she'd been on the other side of a thick pane of glass. This time, with no barrier between them, he couldn't help himself, and he reached out for her.

She went into his arms willingly, thankfully, kissing him as his hands swept over her body, stroking, touching, exploring. Her fingers fumbled as she unbuttoned his shirt, but finally it was open, and she ran the palms of her hands up and down the hard, smooth muscles of his chest. "Make love to me, Pete," she whispered.

In one sudden movement, he scooped her into his arms and carried her to the big bed. Still holding her with one arm, he grabbed the covers and wrenched them back. He sank down onto the clean white sheets, pressing himself on top of her, kissing her eyes, her mouth, her neck, sliding lower and lower until his mouth found her breast. Her nipples were already hard with desire, and he took one into his mouth, sucking and pulling through the delicate lace of her bra. His hands found a hook and eye at her back and he undid it, but it was just one of a whole long row of fasteners. Growling with frustration, he rolled her onto her stomach. With his fingers and eyes working together, the bra was easy to remove, and he quickly tossed it onto the floor.

He sat back to pull his shirt off, uncaring of the pain in his scraped shoulder and elbow, knowing only that he had to feel his body against hers with no barriers in between. He watched Annie sit up, her breasts round and full, her nipples invitingly taut.

He knew that it was a mistake to make love to her like this, before she knew the truth about him. But he also knew that mistake or not, it was too late to turn back—his need for her possessed him. The only way he'd be able to turn away from her now was if she begged him to stop. Pete groaned as her slender fingers unfastened the button at the waist of his pants. No, she definitely didn't want to stop.

He took her hand, pulling it down and pressing it against the hard bulge in his pants. Their gazes locked, and they both smiled, quick, fiery grins of recognition at the need for haste that they saw in each other's eyes. Pete pushed off his shoes as Annie tugged at his pants.

He lifted his hips and yanked both his pants and his shorts down, then groaned with pleasure as her hand closed around his shaft. He rolled on top of her, pinning her with his body as he kissed her almost feverishly.

His hand slipped underneath the thin black silk of her panties, finding the heat between her legs, finding her moist and ready for him. He slid his fingers into her tightness, and she moaned, lifting her hips and pressing against him.

"Pete," she whispered huskily, looking up at him with passion in her eyes. "Please..."

Her soft words ignited him, and the black panties joined her bra on the floor. He scrambled for his pants, searching the pockets for the condom he'd put in his wallet weeks ago, back when Annie was only a suspect to be investigated. He'd put that condom there in anticipation of good sex—nothing more than physical pleasure with a beautiful adversary. But it was more than sexual desire that made his hands shake as he put it on now. It was knowing that he wanted Annie in ways that he'd never wanted anyone before. It was love, pure and simple, and oh, so complicated. Too complicated for words....

Pete turned back to Annie and kissed her as if the world were coming to an end. His body covered hers, and she put her arms around his sleek, strong back, pulling him even closer to her, opening herself to receive him. But he paused, his muscles tight in his arms and chest as he looked down at her.

"I love you," he breathed. "Annie, I love you so much—"

Beads of sweat stood out on his forehead and he was breathing hard, as if holding back was a test of endurance. But while his eyes blazed with the intensity of his desire, they also held another flame, the softer, smoldering fire of love that promised to burn forever.

Annie felt her eyes fill with tears. He loved her....

"Promise me you'll never forget that," he said, his voice husky with emotion.

"How could I ever forget?" she asked, pulling his head down, meeting his mouth with her lips. She kissed him, drinking in his sweetness, pulling him toward her, wanting more, more. She lifted her hips up, pressing against his hardness, wanting him, needing him, now and for all time.

He entered her with one smooth thrust and they both cried out, their voices intertwined in the hushed stillness of the room.

Harmony. There was perfect harmony in the way their bodies moved together, harmony in the emotions that seemed to charge the very air around them, harmony in the love Pete felt for her, a love he knew she felt, too, just from looking into her beautiful eyes. It was like the sonorous consonance of nature, the perfectness of marriage between a Colorado mountain peak and the blue sky above it. Two bodies, two hearts, two souls joined in the ultimate collaboration. They were one, part of each other forever.

Annie exploded, swirling in a barrage of colors and sounds and sensations that focused on the man in her arms, this man she held so tightly, this man who had stolen her heart. Through the waves of her pleasure, she heard him call out her name, felt the shudder of his own tremendous release.

She held on to him tightly, feeling the pounding of both their hearts begin to slow. Spent, he lay on top of her, and still she clasped him to her, holding his body against hers, wanting to freeze time, keep them in this special place forever.

Pete's breathing became slow and steady, deep and relaxed.

"Taylor, are you awake?" Annie whispered.

He lifted his head to find himself staring directly into Annie's blue eyes. "Yeah," he said, then smiled, a slow, satisfied smile that made Annie's heart turn a quick somersault.

"I love you, too, you know," she said, and Pete closed his eyes briefly, feeling the warmth of her words surround his heart. She loved him.

"Pete, why did you leave my room that night?" she asked softly. "You know, I wanted you to stay."

"I couldn't," he said, tracing her eyebrows with one finger. "I wanted to, but I couldn't."

"Why not?"

He shook his head, uncertain of the best way to explain. "I wanted—I *still* want—more than just a sexual relationship," he finally said. "I want more than just a night or two or even two months of nights. I want forever, Annie. I want you to marry me—"

"Yes," she said, interrupting him.

Pete laughed. "But I wasn't— That wasn't—" He took a deep breath and started over. "There are things you need to know about me before I can even ask you to marry me."

He was looking at her with such love in his eyes, such emotion on his face. Annie shook her head. "I love you, Pete," she said simply. "And there's nothing you can tell me that will make me stop loving you."

He rolled onto his back, pulling her with him and holding her close. "I hope so," he said. "I hope so."

Chapter 14

Morning dawned cold and gray, but Annie was warm and secure, wrapped in Pete's arms in the hotel bed. She slept soundly, her long hair fanned out against the pillow, her legs comfortably intertwined with Pete's.

Pete watched her as she slept. He'd watched her sleep before, but this was the first time he'd watched her as he held her in his arms.

She loved him.

She'd told him that over and over last night, with more than just words.

Pete studied the freckles on her nose and the way her eyelashes lay against her cheek, hoping against hope that she loved him enough to handle the truth, to understand why he'd intentionally misled her.

What he couldn't figure out was how the hell he was going to find the right time, the right moment to tell her who he really was. He had to wait until the investigation was over, of course. But that wouldn't be long—not after Whitley Scott received Pete's report, which stated that, in his opinion, Annie Morrow was not involved in any kind of conspiracy.

How long would it take to get the report filed and the investigation dropped? A week, maybe two. By then they'd have this death mask mess cleared up, too. They'd track down whoever it was who had tried to kill them—

He'd come so close to losing her last night. Pete stared at the ceiling, holding Annie tighter. He couldn't bear the thought of losing her.

But when he imagined himself telling Annie he was CIA, it was so easy to picture her anger, to picture her storming out the door.

But she loves you, he reminded himself. Or did she? She loved Peter Taylor. Maybe she wouldn't feel the same about Kendall Peterson.

He closed his eyes, willing himself to stop thinking, letting sleep wash over him.

"Annie." Pete's lazy drawl whispered in her ear. "Wake up."

She awoke to the sensation of his roughly callused hands sweeping across her body. His thumb gently flicked her nipples to life, as his other hand moved lower, starting that now familiar surge of fire through her body. He pulled her hips toward him, entering her slowly.

She opened her eyes to find him watching her, his eyelids half-closed, a small smile on his handsome face. He moved languorously, unhurriedly, deliciously.

"Morning," he said.

"Well, this sure beats an alarm clock," Annie said

with a smile. She stretched, lifting her hips and join-ing his rhythmic movements. "I could get used to this."

"You and me both," Pete said, rolling onto his back, pulling her on top of him. She leaned forward to kiss him, and the telephone rang.

Annie froze. "Nobody knows we're here," she said. "Do they?"

She moved to get off him, but he held her in place, reaching with his right hand to answer the phone. "Yeah," he said into the receiver, tucking it between his ear and shoulder. He looked up into Annie's eyes and pushed himself more deeply inside of her. She swallowed a sound of pleasure that almost escaped, and glared at Pete in mock outrage. He grinned at her. *Oh, yeah?* thought Annie. *Well, two can play this game.*

She began to move on top of him. His eyelids slid halfway down again and he smiled, his dark eyes mol-ten with desire.

"Yeah, that's fine," he said into the telephone. His gaze strayed downward, caressing Annie's body. "Re-ally fine," he said to her.

But she wanted to see him squirm. She leaned for-ward, leaving a trail of light, feathery kisses up his neck to a little extrasensitive spot she'd found right underneath his ear—

"Uh!" Pete said, then covered it with a cough. He wiggled away, pushing her back up, keeping her at arm's length. "No, no, I'm all right," he said into the telephone, flashing Annie a look of surrender. "Okay, but we need an hour." There was a pause, then he said, "Tough. Go eat a doughnut. I'll see you in an hour."

He hung up the phone, then pulled Annie down, kissing her hard on the mouth.

They made love slowly, tenderly, in the morning light.

"Who was on the phone?" she asked later, lying back, satisfied, in his arms.

He kissed the top of her head. "A guy named Scott, from the bureau."

Annie sat up, turning to look at him. "Bureau? As in Federal Bureau of Investigations? As in the FBI?"

Pete nodded. "Yeah. I called them last night while you were in the shower. I thought they might like to know the plate number of the car that tried to flatten us. At the same time, I figured we could use 'em for a safe ride up to Westchester this morning. That was what they were calling me about. They've got a car ready, down on parking level one."

"You actually got a look at the license plate of that car last night?" Annie said, her eyes wide. "*And* you remembered it? I'm impressed."

"Just doing my job, ma'am," Pete said a little too modestly. He swung Annie up, pushing her out of the bed. "In about twenty-five minutes, there's going to be a swarm of FBI agents knocking at the door, ready to escort us down to the car. I recommend taking a shower now, because when we get back to your house, we're going to have to give them a detailed account of the hit and run attempt. It could take some time."

"Don't I know," Annie muttered under her breath.

She took a quick shower, then eased her blue jeans on over the scrape on her knee. She sat on the bedroom floor and rummaged in her overnight bag, pulling out a well-worn T-shirt and a pair of socks and her sneakers, and quickly got dressed.

There was a pile of weaponry on the table—Pete's

guns. Bemused, she counted three different guns. Why so many? she wondered. In case he dropped one?

A loud hammering at the door made her jump. Startled, she scrambled to her feet, backing toward the bathroom door.

Pete was still in the shower; she could hear it running. But the water shut off as the pounding was repeated.

The door to the bathroom was ajar, and Annie pushed it open. "Pete?"

Steam swirled in the small room, fogging the mirrors, curling around Pete as he stood naked on the bath mat, drying his lean, athletic body. He looked up at her, reading her face swiftly and accurately as usual. "What's wrong?"

"Someone's at the door."

He swore under his breath, giving himself a few more swipes with his towel before he wrapped it around his waist. Annie followed him out into the bedroom, and Pete motioned for her to move to one side as he grabbed one of his guns and approached the door. Obediently hanging back, Annie watched as he looked out into the hallway through the door's peephole. The tension in his shoulders and neck visibly decreased, and he pulled the chair away from under the doorknob and opened the door a crack.

"You're early," Annie heard him say.

"Brought ya breakfast," she heard a man's voice say. "A bag of doughnuts and coffee. Figured you could probably use the extra energy more than I could."

"Give me ten minutes," Pete said, "and we'll be ready to go."

"Take all the minutes you need," the man said. "No one's going anywhere for a long time."

The tightness returned to Pete's shoulders. "What's going on?"

"You'd better open the door, Captain," another, different voice said.

Captain, thought Annie. *Now why the heck would they call Pete that?*

He shot a quick look over his shoulder at her, then moved closer to the door, saying something in a low voice.

"To hell with your cover, Captain Peterson," the first man said. He pushed his way through the door, into the room, his eyes falling on Annie. "This entire investigation's over," he said, waving a folded document in the air. "I'm holding a warrant for the arrest of Dr. Anne Morrow."

Annie stared. "What?" she said. She looked at Pete. "Pete, what's going on? Who is this man?"

"It's simple, lady." The man smiled at her from behind a thick pair of glasses. "I'm Whitley Scott, with the FBI. You're already familiar with Captain Peterson, here. He's CIA."

Pete had taken the paper from Scott's hand and was reading it, his eyes quickly skimming down the pages. He looked up to meet Annie's shocked gaze.

"No," Annie breathed. But she knew it was true. She could see the guilt in Pete's dark eyes.

"And you," Scott continued, "are busted. We're charging you with five different felonies, including robbery, conspiracy, felony murder." He turned to Pete. "You wanna Miranda her?"

"Oh, God," Annie said. Pete was CIA....

"No," Pete said, his voice low.

"Collins," Scott addressed one of the other men who

had come into the room with him. "Read her her rights and frisk her."

"No," Pete said, his voice sharp. "She's clean."

"You know it's gotta be done," Scott said.

"You have the right to remain silent," Collins began to drone.

"I'll frisk her," Pete said.

"Anything you say can and will be used against you in a court of law."

"Nice room," said Scott. He looked at the unmade bed, at the condom wrappers that still lay scattered on the floor. He smirked. "Must've been one hell of a night, eh, Peterson?"

"Oh, *God*," Annie said. Pete was *CIA*....

Pete took her arm, and she looked up at him, startled by his touch. "You son of a bitch," she said, pulling away from him.

"You have the right to an attorney," Collins said.

"Annie, I don't know what this is all about," Pete said, talking low and fast, "but I'm going to find out. Right now you need to stay calm."

"If you cannot afford an attorney," Collins said, "one will be appointed for you at no cost."

On the other side of the room, Scott opened the curtains and the gray light of a rainy October morning did little to illuminate the room. "Nice view of the park," he said.

"This has to be done," Pete told Annie, "and I'll do it as quickly as I can, but you've got to help me."

"Do you understand these rights as I have read them to you?" Collins said.

"Spread your legs apart and put your hands on your head," Pete said.

Woodenly, Annie obeyed him.

"Dr. Morrow," Collins said. "Do you understand these rights?"

"Yes," Annie whispered. She closed her eyes as Pete's hands moved methodically and impersonally over her body. Oh, *God...*

"She's clean," she heard him say, his voice tight, clipped.

Everything he had told her was a lie. His name was Peterson, not Pete Taylor. He wasn't a bodyguard. He probably wasn't even half-Navaho, probably had never even been to Colorado. He'd only been using her to get information.

He didn't love her.

It was all a lie. He didn't love her....

"I'm going to be sick," Annie said, lunging for the bathroom.

Collins and the other FBI agent moved to follow, but Pete blocked the door. "I'll handle it," he said.

He went into the bathroom, closing and locking the door behind him.

Annie knelt on the floor in front of the commode. Her face was pale. Taking a washcloth from the towel rack, Pete ran it under cool water and handed it to her.

"Pete, how could you?" she asked, reproach in her eyes. "How could you use me this way?"

His clothes lay in a pile near the shower. He pulled his shorts on under his towel, then used the towel to dry his hair. "There's something really wrong here," he said, almost to himself.

"Captain Peterson," she said, looking at him with new horror in her eyes as he pulled on his jeans. "You're that horrible man who was behind the mirror window at the airport, aren't you? And I *slept* with you. You *bastard*—"

"Annie, I meant it when I said that I loved you," he said. "You've got to believe that. And you've got to trust me until I figure out what's going on."

She laughed, a dull, hollow sound. "You're kidding, right?"

He grabbed her by the shoulders, pulling her up to her feet. "You made me a promise," he said, shaking her slightly. "You promised not to forget that I love you, so don't forget, damn it."

She pulled away from him. "I made that promise to Pete Taylor, and you're obviously not him." Her eyes filled with tears, and she fought them back. "You can go to hell, Captain Peterson."

She turned and walked out of the bathroom, closing the door tightly behind her.

Chapter 15

The interrogation room held one table and some stiff-backed wooden chairs. The walls were a dull, ugly shade of beige, and the floor was cheap, industrial linoleum tile. *This is what hell looks like,* Annie thought, fatigue washing over her as she looked around the table at the myriad of FBI agents that sat looking back at her. She was even willing to bet that Satan wore a dark suit exactly like the ones these men had on.

She clasped her hands tightly in front of her on the table. "If you can't get more specific with your charges," she said tightly, "then you better release me."

Scott leaned back in his chair. "So you're saying that you've never been in possession of these artifacts, and you don't know how they got into your house."

Annie glanced down at the pictures for the hundredth time in the past few hours. They were antiquities—some she recognized, most she didn't. But none had ever been near her house, much less in her possession. "I told you I don't know how any of this happened," she said, not for the first time.

Scott nodded, obviously not believing her.

She leaned forward. "Tell me, Scott," she said. "Why in God's name would I become involved in some idiotic art robbery? Why would I bomb museums? I've got an impeccable reputation, I make a decent living, I'm respected by my peers—why would I risk all that?"

"You tell me."

The door opened and Pete came in. Captain Peterson, Annie corrected herself, trying to numb the pain that seeing him brought. He was wearing a conservative dark suit exactly like all the other agents, and Annie almost didn't recognize him. Almost. He looked around the room, and one eyebrow went down very slightly in his version of a frown. Annie's stomach hurt. She could read his face so well, even now. How was it that she hadn't picked up on his lies?

"Where's your lawyer?" he asked Annie.

Scott answered for her. "She's waived her right." He grinned. "She says she's not guilty, so she doesn't need an attorney."

"Get her one," Peterson said coldly.

"She doesn't want one," Scott said. "I can't force one down her damned throat."

Annie was looking at Pete as if he were something that had crawled out from under a rock. "I don't want him in here," she said to Scott. "Make him leave."

Scott shrugged, obviously enjoying her discomfort. "Can't do that," he said. "Captain Peterson's as much in charge here as I am."

Pete set a file down in front of Scott and sat down across from her. Annie turned away, not looking at him.

"All right," Scott said to Annie, opening the file

and shuffling through the papers. "You want to get specific?" He pulled out a piece of paper, and began to read it.

"'Two packages were observed on a counter in the laboratory of the suspect's house. They were open, and contained articles numbered one through eight. The articles, in plain view of the investigating officers, matched the description of those articles missing from the English Gallery. The packages were seized in accordance with the warrant blah blah blah.'" He pushed the report across the table to her. "Read it and weep," he said.

The room was spinning. Annie leafed through the pages of the report, describing the room-by-room search, the description of the artifacts...

"What gave you the right to search my home?" she asked quietly.

"The warrant was obtained as a result of evidence gathered over the course of this investigation, and a tip—"

"Who?" Annie demanded. "Who gave you this *tip?*"

"This information came to us anonymously," Scott said.

"Oh, terrific!" Annie threw up her hands. "Obviously a reliable source—"

"It certainly turned out to be, didn't it?" Scott said, leaning across the table. "Especially when we found materials to construct explosives in a desk drawer in your office."

"What?" Annie gasped. Her eyes moved involuntarily to Pete's face. He was expressionless, his dark eyes watching her steadily. "This is some kind of setup," she said. The enormity of the situation crashed down around her, and she realized for the first time that she was in serious trouble. The stolen artifacts, the explosives… "I want a lawyer."

She looked back at the report in front of her. "Two packages were observed on a counter in the laboratory of the suspect's house."

On a counter in the laboratory of the suspect's house.

In the laboratory!

Yes!

Pete had been in the lab with her before they left for New York City. He'd seen that the counters were clean, everything put away. He had locked the place up as they left the house, and had been with her ever since. He could confirm her story. He would tell them she had nothing to do with this!

Yes!

"Pete," she said, excitement vibrating through her voice. She handed him the report. "You were with me when I went into the lab to turn off the lights before we went out last night, remember? The lab was all cleaned up—the counters were clear. You were right there in the doorway."

Pete glanced up from the report. His eyes were expressionless, his face guarded.

"Remember?"

He had to remember. Of course he'd remember.

"Nick was waiting for us outside. You told me I looked beautiful." Suddenly she looked down at her hands, and blushed at the memory. But she had to go on; she desperately needed him to stand with her now, no matter how humiliating. "You were looking at me—" she swallowed and looked up at him "—like you wanted to kiss me."

Pete met her gaze for only a second before looking

back at the report, his eyes narrowing as if in concentration.

"Remember?"

He handed the paper back to Scott, glancing briefly at Annie, his eyes cold, detached. "No."

She stared at him, shock draining the blood from her face, leaving her pale. Oh, God, he was part of it, part of the setup....

Pete stood up, careful not to meet her eyes. "I'll go make arrangements for a lawyer," he said, leaving the room.

Annie stared down at the table, forcing herself not to cry as what was left of her heart shattered into a billion tiny pieces.

Annie walked up the driveway to her house. Her thin formal jacket was wrapped tightly around her, but it did little to keep out the rain on the long, cold walk from the train station. There were no lights burning in her windows, nothing to welcome her home.

Home. Lord, she couldn't believe she was actually here. Once her attorney had arrived, the endless interrogation had stopped and bail was set. She'd been ready to call her parents to ask for help in posting the quarter-million-dollar bail when she found out that bail had already been paid by an anonymous source. Her father, she thought gratefully. Somehow he had found out she was in trouble even before her call, and he'd come to her rescue.

The trial date was set for three months from now, and her license was revoked until that time. She couldn't work, couldn't even finish the work she'd started.

With a disparaging laugh, she remembered the phone call that had told her not to touch the golden death mask, warning her that Stands Against the Storm's evil spirit would harm her if she did. As a result, her life would crumble.

You win, Stands Against the Storm, she thought. Her life had indeed crumbled.

Keying her authorization code into the outside alarm control panel, she waited for the light to go from red to green. Unlocking the front door, she sighed. First thing in the morning, she'd have to pack up everything in her safe, ship it back to all the owners....

She turned the alarm back on and climbed the stairs in the dark and went into her bedroom. Was it only last night that she'd been so happy? Dancing with Pete, making love to him— How could she have been so stupid? He must be laughing at her now.

She dumped her bag on the floor. Shivering, she went into the bathroom, turned on the light and quickly stripped off her wet clothes.

Steam from her hot shower soon fogged the mirror, and she washed herself, washed off the very last trace of Pete's scent. Closing her eyes, she let the water run over her face, disguising the tears that she couldn't hold back any longer.

"Annie, wake up."

She opened her eyes to find Peterson sitting on her bed, looking down at her. She didn't move, she just stared.

"Are you awake?" he asked. The morning light coming in behind the curtains dimly lit his face. He looked tired, his eyes red and bleary, as if he hadn't slept. He had changed out of that dreadful dark suit and back into his familiar blue jeans and T-shirt.

"No," she said. "I better not be. I better be dreaming. You better not be sitting here in my room like this."

He tried to smile, but it came out as a wry twist of his lips. "Sorry," he said. "I'm really sitting here."

A host of different emotions flew across her face, but anger won. Her eyes blazed. "Get out."

"Annie, I had to—"

"I don't want to hear it, *Captain Peterson*." She said his name sarcastically, her teeth clenched in barely controlled rage. "You son of a bitch. You set me up. Get out of my house!"

"I didn't know about—"

"You really expect me to believe that?" she seethed. "I know damn well you remember coming into the lab with me when I turned off the lights that night. You *know* that stuff from the English Gallery wasn't there."

"Annie—"

She kicked him, hard, her foot against his back, but the bed covers broke the force of the blow, and he didn't even flinch. "You bastard," she shouted. "The FBI decided that I was guilty five months ago. But they couldn't prove it, so they had to frame me. And you're just going to go along with it, aren't you? Because you're one of them, you creep!"

He gave up trying to explain. He sat there, watching her quietly, letting her vent her anger.

"Tell me," she said, her voice biting, "do you get extra points for sleeping with me, Captain? Four times in one night! You probably got stud points from the other guys for that. Oh, yeah, and once in the morning. A nice touch. Make your buddies wait out in the hall while you make it with the suspect one last time before you arrest her—"

He couldn't hold it in. "I didn't know they had a warrant—"

"Do you *really* expect me to believe *any*thing you say?" she said, as her eyes accused him of terrible crimes.

He looked down at the floor, knowing that he was guilty. He'd kept the truth about his identity from her for all those weeks, even after he knew he was in love with her, even after he knew she couldn't possibly be involved in any kind of crime. He *was* guilty. "No," he said quietly. "No, I don't."

"You were so good," she said, her voice breaking. "All those stories you told about when you were a kid, living out in Colorado, about your Indian grandfather— You probably grew up in the Bronx, right?"

"Not everything I told you was a lie," he said, meeting her gaze. "Those stories were all true. And I was telling you the truth when I said that I love you." He looked down at his hands, clenched tightly into fists on his lap. "I know you don't believe me...."

"Yeah, you're right. I don't," Annie said, watching him close his eyes against the harshness of her words. "What do you want from me? Why are you here?"

Pete stood up and walked across the room. "You're being framed," he said, his back to her as he composed himself.

She laughed, a harsh exhale of air. "Tell me something new, Captain America."

"I want to help you," he said, turning to look at her.

"*Now* you want to help me?" she said, tight anger in her voice. "Yesterday, you could have told them that those things weren't in the lab—"

"Annie, I'm here because you're not safe," he interrupted. "Someone on the inside is in on this frame, and I don't know who it is."

Annie stared at him.

He smiled, a tight, satisfied smile. "Yeah, I *was* there that night, Annie. And I *do* remember. I saw the lab. I know you're being set up."

She kept staring at him, the tiniest seed of hope fluttering in her stomach.

"Why didn't you say something yesterday?" she asked, her voice low. "You could have saved my reputation."

"I thought it was more important to save your life." His dark eyes held her captive. "Until I know how many people are in on this thing, you're safer if they think no one believes you."

"But the FBI? How—"

"All I know is too many things don't add up. How did someone get into the house to put those bats in your room? How did they get in to plant that stolen art? Nobody had the codes to the security system except you, me and Cara...*and* anyone who had access to your case file."

"But what about all those fringe groups the FBI was going to investigate?"

He shook his head. "There's no way one of those groups is responsible for bombing and robbing two European art galleries—or disarming a professional alarm system to plant bats in your bedroom and stolen art in your lab."

Pete was pacing now. "There's just too much that's wrong about this." He stopped in the middle of the room and faced Annie again. "Why would someone want to kill you? Or why would they want you arrested, in jail, out of the picture?"

Annie stared at him and Pete smiled grimly. "There's a lot of things we don't know. And it's about time we started finding out."

Pete sifted through the pile of file folders that were out on Annie's desk. He ran his fingers through his hair, then leaned back and stretched. Man, they were getting nowhere....

"*Here* it is," Annie called from the floor in front of her file cabinet. "June 4, 1989. Back before I started using my computer system. That was the last time I tested anything for the English Gallery. It was a gold ring from ninth-century Wales. Wanna see the file?"

"Sure, why not?" Pete said. He spun in his chair to face her as she brought the folder to the desk. "How come it's been such a long time? Recession hitting them, too?"

Annie shook her head. "No. Alistair Golden's pretty much got that gallery locked up for sales coming into the United States. They use him exclusively. If it hadn't been for Ben Sullivan, I never would have gotten this job."

Pete frowned. Then reached for the telephone. As Annie watched, he dialed a number. "Yeah," he said, into the phone. "This is Peterson. I need access to a list of all sales of artwork and other artifacts brought into the U.S. via the English Gallery."

"But I've got that information," Annie said.

He looked at her in surprise. "Let me call you back," he said into the phone. He hung up and looked at her questioningly.

"I'm tied into a computer network that keeps track of current sales of artwork and artifacts—anything from a Picasso to a Stone Age ax," Annie said. She came around to his side of the desk and turned on her personal computer and her modem. "It's useful information for art brokers to have. Using this list, I can track down and access a buyer for just about anything. Take your necklace, for instance. If you wanted to sell it, I could find a buyer simply by calling up the names of all the people who have made multiple purchases of Navaho jewelry over the past several months."

Pete leaned back in his chair to give her better access to the keyboard. She narrowed her eyes slightly in concentration as she keyed in the commands to sign on to the network.

"All we have to do is request a specific list where the gallery was the English, and point of shipping equals U.S.A...."

She was close enough for him to reach out and touch her, but Pete didn't dare. Just over twenty-four hours ago, she'd told him that she loved him. But he could still see the look on her face when she found out he was a government agent, sent to investigate her. He remembered her eyes as her love for him died. His heart ached. It was his own damned fault....

"Here we go," she said.

A list of dates and items scrolled down the computer screen. Pete forced his thoughts back to the task at hand and leaned forward for a closer look.

"It's chronological," Annie said, turning toward him. They were nearly nose to nose, and she quickly straightened up. "The most current shipments are at the very bottom."

She sat on the edge of the desk and watched Pete from a safe distance as he moved the cursor down the long list. His handsome face was lit by the amber light from the computer screen. He looked exhausted, over-tired, but there was a glint of determination in his eyes. He glanced up, feeling her watching him.

"Why are you doing this?" she asked.

"Because I know you're not guilty," he said, looking back at the computer.

"You paid my bail, didn't you?"

"Yeah."

"Where did you get that kind of money?" Annie asked.

"I borrowed it. If you skip town, I lose everything. My car, my condo…" He looked up at her again, and the familiar glint of humor in his eyes made her heart twist. "Who knows? The guys I borrowed it from would probably even break my legs."

"Why would you risk all that for me?" she asked.

"I'd risk everything," he said simply, squinting at the computer screen. "Even my life…."

"Why?"

Pete looked up at her. "It's not that hard to figure out," he said. "I'm in love with you, Annie."

She stared down at him for several long moments, wishing that he hadn't turned into this stranger sitting before her—a stranger she somehow knew so well. But that was just an illusion. She only thought she knew him. Pete Taylor had been only a cover, a charade. He was gone as absolutely as if he had died. Annie felt a stab of grief so sharp and painful that she almost cried out.

"Is there…" Pete said, then cleared his throat and started again. "Do I have any chance at all? With you?"

He looked like Pete Taylor. He sounded like Pete Taylor. He even acted like Pete Taylor. But he wasn't Pete Taylor. He wasn't—

Annie pushed herself off the desk, unable to meet his eyes. "No."

Pete nodded, as if that were the answer he had been expecting. With the muscle in his jaw working, he turned his attention back to the computer, as though his last hopes hadn't been dashed to bits.

Chapter 16

When Annie went back into the office, Pete was on the phone again.

He had printed out a list of names, dates and transactions from the computer, and she glanced over his shoulder, trying to make some sense of it.

He hung up the phone and turned toward her.

"Any luck?" she asked.

"You know this guy Steadman?" he asked, pointing to the list. He was a buyer, and his name appeared repeatedly.

Annie shook her head.

"He buys things from the English Gallery like it's a K mart end-of-the-season sale," Pete said. "There are also a couple of other partnerships and corporations whose names come up frequently."

"But these were all legitimate transactions," Annie protested, looking at the list again. "Some of these pieces are well-known, and these prices are all fair...."

Pete spent the rest of the morning and most of the afternoon on the telephone, trying to gather more information.

Annie went upstairs and cleaned the last of the mess the bats had made out of her bedroom and tried not to think about Peterson. But as she scrubbed the floor, she kept hearing his voice as he asked her if he still had a chance with her. No, she told herself over and over. Absolutely not. She didn't love him. She refused to love him. Sure, she still found him physically attractive....

She closed her eyes for a moment, remembering the night they'd spent together, the night they'd made love. Had it been only two nights ago? It seemed as if a million years had passed since he'd held her in his arms....

"Are you all right?"

Startled, Annie opened her eyes to find Pete standing in the doorway. "Yeah," she said, attacking the floor with renewed vigor. "What did you find out? Anything?"

Pete squatted down next to the bucket, pulling out a second sponge and going to work beside her. "Something," he said. "I'm waiting for a few more calls that should give me the rest of the information I need. Apparently, Mr. J. J. Steadman is buying most of the stuff that comes out of the English Gallery one way or the other. He's an owner or a partner in every single one of the companies on that list of buyers."

Annie stopped scrubbing the floor. "Quite the busy little collector."

Pete smiled and Annie had to look away. "Quite. And quite the mediocre one, too, it seems. He rarely holds on to the pieces for more than a couple of months after he buys them, and he often sells them at a small loss."

"Big deal," Annie said. "There's no law that says that rich people can't be stupid."

"Yeah," Pete said. The muscles in his back and arms rippled as he rubbed the sponge across the dirty floor. "But get a load of this." He smiled at her as he rinsed the sponge in the bucket. "Guess who else owns a piece of J. J. Steadman's companies. Give you a hint. Funny green eyes, gold bracelet, kind of like a rattlesnake in a tux?"

Annie had to smile at him. "Let's see... Could it be Alistair Golden?"

They smiled into each other's eyes; then Annie looked away, her expression suddenly guarded, distant.

They scrubbed for several minutes in silence; then she leaned back on her heels. "You know, Peterson, I don't even know your first name."

Pete looked up. "Kendall," he said. "But nobody calls me that. Everyone calls me Pete."

"Even your mother?" Annie asked.

"She calls me Hastin Naat'aanni."

Man Speaking Peace, his Navaho name.

"That really happened?" Annie said. "It was true, that story you told me, about your cousins, when your aunt died?"

Pete threw his sponge in the bucket and sat cross-legged on the floor, his elbows around his knees. "With the exception of my name, my career and my college, I lied to you only by omission," he said. "Everything else I told you was the truth. I just didn't tell you enough."

Annie was quiet for a moment. "Why did you lie to me about going to New York University? Where *did* you go to school?"

"I didn't," Pete said. "I went to Vietnam. I was drafted when I turned eighteen."

"*That's* where your grandfather didn't want you to go," Annie said, sudden comprehension lighting her eyes.

Pete nodded, looking into the bucket of soapy water. "He didn't understand why a kid named Man Speaking Peace had to go fight a war on the other side of the ocean. He didn't like war," he said. "I didn't, either." But he smiled, and Annie was chilled by the hardness in his eyes. "I was good at it, though. I was good at staying alive, too. And I was good at search-and-rescue raids. I spent most of my time in enemy territory, finding the guys who'd been shot down and bringing them out of the jungle. In '75, after they pulled the troops out, I was asked to stay behind."

"Stay behind," Annie repeated, horror in her voice. "Why on earth would you want to do that?"

"I didn't *want* to. But they asked me to become part of an agency team that was working to locate and free POWs and MIAs," Pete said quietly.

"So you stayed."

"I stayed. I spent about four more years in southeast Asia, doing what I did best," he said. "Making war."

"You were saving lives," Annie protested. "How many men did you help set free?"

Pete looked at her in surprise. She was actually defending him. His heart skipped a beat and he tried to control it. It didn't mean a thing.... "I never knew the exact figures," he said. "But it was in the hundreds."

"After that you joined the CIA?" she asked.

She wanted to know about him. Was it mere curiosity, or... Pete couldn't dare to hope. He nodded. "As a field operative."

"So you've spent most of the past two decades risking your life," she said, shaking her head.

"Not all the time—"

"Oh, I suppose you get a weekend off every few years or so," she said. "How can you live that way, with your life always in danger...?"

"Look at it from my perspective," Pete said. "If I'd stayed in Colorado, I would never have met you."

Annie's eyes narrowed. "Then you definitely should have stayed in Colorado," she said sharply. She stood up suddenly and carried the bucket into the bathroom, flushing the dirty water down the toilet, watching it swirl away.

Pete followed her. "In my life, with my job, I have to get things right the first time around," he said, his voice low and intense. "If I don't, I'm dead. Every now and then I'll blow it, though. I'll make a really bad decision, make a major mistake. After I get over the surprise that I'm still alive, I grab that second chance and I don't let go. And I'm damn sure I don't mess up the second time around."

She was looking at him, her eyes so wide, so blue. He couldn't help himself—he took a step toward her, and then another and another. Before he could stop himself, he'd taken her into his arms. She was shaking, but at least she didn't pull away. "Annie, give me a second chance," he whispered. "I love you— God, please, I need you in my life...."

And still she didn't pull away. Her breasts were rising and falling with each breath she took, as if she had just run a mile. Pete felt his own pulse pounding as his fear of driving her away wrestled with his need. Need won, and he kissed her.

Her mouth was soft, warm and as sweet as he remembered. He felt her arms tighten around him as she responded to him, and he prayed—hell, he *begged* the gods for that second chance.

She opened her mouth under his, and he nearly wept—until she struggled to break free. He released her immediately, and she stared at him, her eyes accusing.

"No," she breathed. "I can't."

Annie ran from the room, leaving Pete alone.

The phone rang shrilly, quickly pulling Annie out of a restless, uneasy sleep. The clock on her bedside table said it was after 2:00 a.m., but there was a light on in the kitchen, shining in through her bedroom door. She could hear Pete talking on the phone, his voice lowered so as not to disturb her.

He was on the phone, sitting at the kitchen table, writing in his little notebook. His T-shirt was off and his hair was rumpled. His eyes were rimmed with red, as if he still hadn't gotten any sleep.

"Yeah, I got it all," he said into the telephone, looking up at Annie. She stood in the doorway, squinting at him, letting her eyes adjust to the bright light. "Thanks, I owe you one."

Pete stood to hang up the phone, and Annie saw that he wore only a tight pair of white briefs. She looked away, embarrassed at her body's instant reaction to his masculinity, afraid to be caught staring.

He immediately noticed her discomfort. "I'm sorry," he apologized quietly. "I was lying down when the phone rang. I wanted to answer it before it woke you."

Annie went to the stove, putting on a kettle of hot water for tea. "What did you find out?" she asked, her back to him.

"Let me put on my jeans," he said. "Then I'll tell you."

"Do you want a cup of tea?" Annie asked as Pete came back into the kitchen, tucking his T-shirt into the waistband of his jeans. Now *she* felt underdressed, standing there in her flannel pajamas.

"Thanks," Pete said gratefully.

She got a second mug down from the cabinet and dropped a tea bag into it, then leaned against the counter, arms folded across her chest, waiting for the water to boil.

Pete took a lemon from the refrigerator, grabbed the cutting board from the shelf and opened the knife drawer. He was at home here in her kitchen, Annie realized. He knew where everything was; he knew where to find the plates and the glasses, he even knew where she hid a chocolate bar for those times when nothing else would substitute. *He* knew all those things. Captain Kendall Peterson, formerly of the U.S. Army, currently of the CIA, knew all sorts of private and personal things about her. Because everything that Peter Taylor had seen and heard, Kendall Peterson remembered.

"How do you do it?" Annie asked.

He glanced up at her, then finished cutting the lemon neatly into eighths. "Do what?"

"How can you take on someone else's identity for such a long period of time?" Annie asked. "Don't you start to lose your own self?"

Pete shook his head. "Annie, it's not like I'm an actor," he said. He turned toward her, trying to make her understand. "I just take a different name, a different label. It doesn't matter whether you call me Captain or Peterson or Taylor or Hastin Naat'aanni, or whether my driver's license says I'm from Colorado or New York City. I am always the same man. I am me—I'm Pete."

"You think of yourself as Pete," Annie said, "not Hastin Naat'aanni, Man Speaking Peace?"

Pete was silent for a moment, looking down at his bare feet against the black-and-white tile floor. "I *am* Hastin Naat'aanni. I always will be. But in Vietnam, the men in my platoon called me Machine—short for War Machine. I'm that, too."

The teakettle whistled, and Annie turned toward the stove, shutting off the gas. She filled both mugs with steaming water, then set them down on the table. Pete brought the plate of lemons over and sat down across from her.

Annie bobbed her tea bag up and down in her mug, watching as the hot water was slowly stained brown.

"Want to hear what I found out?" he asked.

"Is it good news or bad news?" she countered.

"It's strange," Pete said.

"Fire away."

"Okay. So far, we've got J. J. Steadman—whoever he is—and Alistair Golden as partners in some pretty lame art-collecting companies. And we already know Golden authenticates everything that comes out of the English Gallery—everything except for this one artifact, the death mask." Pete thought for a moment, and then asked, "Does it make any sense that Golden should fly to England *before* every single transaction?"

"Hardly," Annie said, taking a sip of her tea, testing to see if it was strong enough. "But Golden isn't exactly what I'd call sensible. Apparently he insists on packing the artwork or artifacts himself. I think he's kind of anal retentive."

She was silent as she fished the tea bag out of her mug and put it in the garbage. She squeezed a piece of lemon into her tea, then took another sip. "I called Ben

Sullivan and told him about this mess I'm in," she said, taking a sip. "I told him I'd be shipping the death mask back to him, and he asked me to recommend another authenticator besides Golden. Seems Golden threw a little bit of a fit when he found out he wasn't going to do the work, and he called up Ben and screamed in his ear. Ben was not impressed."

Shipping the death mask back.

The death mask.

Somehow it was connected to Annie's being framed.

And although Pete couldn't say why, returning the death mask to Sullivan seemed even more dangerous than keeping it.

Chapter 17

The next day, Alistair Golden called.

"He said that he wants to come by and discuss taking over some of my work," Annie said. "Since my license has been revoked, *some*one has to do the jobs. And suddenly he's my best friend…."

Pete listened silently.

"He says he'll pay me a referral fee," Annie continued, "and, of course, he'll get all the necessary approvals."

Pete nodded. "Squeaky-clean."

Annie shrugged. "I told him it was okay with me. I mean, I've got to do something with all this work I'm supposed to be doing. I can't just sit on it until my trial."

"Yeah, I know." Pete stood up. "When's he coming?"

"Sometime around three this afternoon."

"I'd like to talk with him when he gets here," Pete said. "On the record."

* * *

At around noon, Annie watched as Pete carefully taped the tiny microphone to his chest, just under his collarbone. Then he buttoned his shirt back up and shrugged on his heavy leather jacket. He picked up the set of headphones he had placed on the desk in the office and handed them to Annie. "This whole surveillance unit is mobile. You can hook the recorder to your belt and carry it with you wherever you go. If you want to hear what's going on, just listen in on the headphones."

"What do you expect him to do, confess to framing me?" Annie said. "We don't even know he's involved."

"Maybe he's not, but maybe he is," Pete replied. He headed downstairs, and Annie followed. "I'm going to go outside and walk around the house to check the range on this thing. When he comes, I want to meet him outdoors and see if I can find out anything before we let him in."

He accessed the alarm system bypass and opened the front door.

"I'll keep talking as I walk around outside," Pete said. "You keep the headphones on, and if you can hear me, flick the outside floodlights on and off."

She looked up at him and said, "I know it's silly, and Alistair Golden is probably about as dangerous as a worm, but this cloak-and-dagger stuff really gets me nervous."

Annie stared into Pete's bottomless dark eyes, searching for what, she wasn't sure. Dishonesty, maybe. Or deceit. But all she could see was love. He loved her. He really, truly loved her. He looked away, as if embarrassed by her scrutiny.

"I'd better get out there," he said.

"Pete," she said.

He stopped and turned back, his face carefully revealing no emotion. "Yeah?"

"No matter what happens, you're going to be careful, right?"

He didn't answer right away, but his heart showed in his eyes as a seed of hope took root and bloomed all in the space of a few short seconds. "Yeah," he finally said, his voice huskier than usual. "You bet I'm going to be careful."

She looked so worried, her blue eyes darkened with anxiety. He reached out and pushed a lock of hair back from her face, stroking her soft cheek with his thumb. "Everything's going to work out," he said gently.

Annie's blue eyes filled with tears. "Everything but us," she said. "I just can't forgive you, Pete."

"Have you really tried?" he asked softly.

Annie slipped the headphones over her ears.

"Okay, I'm out here," Pete said as he stepped off the porch. He turned to see the floodlights switch on and then off again. "I'm heading around to the side of the house now."

The lights flicked on and off steadily as he made his way around the house, talking all the while. When he got to the front of the house he went onto the lawn and said, "I'm in the front yard now, and believe it or not, it looks like the lawn could use another raking." He looked back at the house, and for a moment, the lights did not come on. Then they did, and quickly went off again. He then spoke softly. "And I'd very much like to help you rake it, Annie." And again the lights stayed unlit for several moments, finally flashing on for a brief second before being extinguished again.

Finally Pete squared his shoulders in the middle of the yard and faced the house head-on. Looking directly into the darkened floodlights, he tried to speak, but his voice broke. He bowed his head, looked up again at the big house he had come to think of as his home, took a deep breath and said, "I'm talking really quietly now, I can barely hear my own voice. Can you hear me? I love you, Annie. And I'm going to win you back if it's the last thing I do."

The floodlights never came on.

Annie brusquely wiped at the tear that had escaped and was running down her cheek. She was about to pull the headphones off when she heard Pete curse under his breath, and then say, "Annie, our guest has arrived three hours early. How rude of him. Of *them*."

At that, Annie hurried to the front of the house to look out the window. Golden, impeccably dressed in a dark blue suit and a maroon tie with accent handkerchief, was getting out of his car, and that broker, Joseph James, or James Joseph, or whoever he was, wearing jeans and a light jacket, was getting out of the other side of the car. Pete was running across the lawn toward them as they came up the porch steps. Pete was whispering to her as he ran.

"Annie, lock the door and don't open it, *no matter what happens*. Turn on the alarm, get the death mask out of the safe and hide it in the attic somewhere. Then get out the back door, and get to a safe place. Do you understand me?"

Even as he said the words, she was locking the door, turning on the alarm. As she ran to the safe, got the death mask and hauled the heavy box up to the attic, she muttered under her breath, while another tear ran down her cheek, unchecked, "You be careful, do you understand *me*?"

* * *

"Well, lookee here, if it isn't Fido," Joseph James said to Pete, an unpleasant smile on his unpleasant face.

"You gentlemen might want to get someone to check your watches. You appear to be a little early." Pete smiled. "What's the rush?"

"We decided to come for lunch," Joseph James said, folding his arms across his broad chest with a smirk. "On account of our busy schedules."

Joseph James.

It came to him in a flash.

Pete eyed the two men and decided to take a chance. If he was right, he had to keep them talking and out of the house. If he could get them to say something stupid, the tape would prove Annie was innocent, even if he messed up and they killed him.

Pete smiled broadly at the taller of the two men. "Well. We were expecting only Dr. Golden, not you, Mr. James. Or is it Mr. Joseph? Or maybe…Mr. Steadman?"

At that, the man took a step toward Pete, until his face was inches away. "Maybe you should shut up," he snarled.

Jackpot.

Pete looked steadily at Steadman, unperturbed. "My mistake. Your name is undoubtedly Grumpy." He turned to Golden. "And that must make you Sleazy."

Pete was banking on Steadman's anger. He knew that Joseph James Steadman wanted to take a swing at him, to get back at Pete for having been roughed up the last time he was out here. That was good. Angry people didn't think clearly. Angry people weren't careful about what they said, and the mike inside Pete's jacket was ready to pick it all up….

"We're here to see Dr. Morrow," Dr. Golden said, his green eyes a little too bright in his face. "I'd like to get this over with."

"That's a pity," said Pete. "She just went into town. She said she wouldn't be back for a few hours."

Golden smiled, and Pete was reminded of a lizard. "I don't think so," he said. "Her car is still in the driveway."

Inside the house, Annie had called Whitley Scott at the FBI. Scott had said they were on their way. They'd arrive in twenty minutes, maybe less. She now stood at the top of the stairs, listening through the headphones to the conversation outside.

"In fact, I'll bet she's standing on the other side of these windows, listening to us talk," she heard Golden say.

"Maybe," she heard Pete drawl, his Western accent more pronounced than usual. "Maybe not. Why don't you just tell me what you want, and then maybe I can help you." He paused. "Maybe."

Outside, Steadman was starting to lose his cool. "Maybe you'd better be quiet before I use this to blow your head off your neck, smartass," he said as he reached into his jacket pocket and pulled out a huge automatic pistol. He jammed it under Pete's chin.

A vein bulged in Golden's forehead, and Pete thought the man was going to have a stroke.

"It's certainly big enough," Pete said with a cocky smile. "Fire this sucker, and the entire neighborhood will come running to see what happened."

"Keep the gun under your coat," Golden snapped nervously at Steadman.

Inside the house, Annie's fingers clutched the banister. They were threatening Pete with a gun! *Where* was the FBI? According to her watch, they were still over fifteen minutes away. For the first time in a long time, she found herself wishing they would show up early. Slowly she crept down the stairs, closer to the front door.

"Why don't you tell me what you want," Pete offered. "I'm listening." Me and the FBI, he thought. "Maybe we can make a deal."

"You give us the death mask," Steadman said, "and we don't kill you. How's *that* for a deal?"

Pete pretended to think about it. "I guess you're going to have to try to kill me," he finally said. "Though, I've got to warn you, I don't die very easily."

Oh, Pete, what are you doing? thought Annie.

"Or, you guys could crawl into whatever hole you came out of," Pete said. "And come back when you're ready to make a real deal."

Steadman pulled the gun away from Pete's head. With an angry look, he began to attach a large silencer to the barrel.

Unconcerned, Pete sat down on the top of the porch steps and looked up at the two men. "Using a silencer is illegal, you know," he said. "Shame on you."

"Tell Morrow to open the door," Golden said.

"Tell me," Pete said pleasantly. "Do I look that stupid?"

"I would really like to shoot you," Steadman snarled.

"Gee, what a coincidence. I'd like to shoot you, too," Pete said to Steadman, still in the same pleasant tone.

"Put your hands on your head," Steadman snapped, a touch of panic in his voice. He glanced at Golden. "Check his pockets. He's carrying."

Golden was nervous as hell, but he pulled Pete's gun out of his jacket pocket, holding it like a dead mouse.

"I'm not cut out for this," Golden said. "Let's get that crate and go."

"Dr. Morrow," Steadman called, his voice angry. "Open the damned door."

"Annie, I know you're not even in there, but if you are, don't open the door," Pete said calmly.

From inside the house, Annie watched as Steadman backhanded Pete across the face. With a gasp, she saw Pete skid along the porch, hitting the side of the house with a solid thud.

"Open the door, Annie," Steadman called. "Or I'm gonna kill this bastard."

Pete came up smiling. "I hate to break it to you guys," he said, "but I'm Navaho. And you know what happens when a Navaho dies. Sure you do—you did your research before you made those threatening phone calls to Annie. But in case you need a refresher course, I'll tell you. A dead Navaho returns to avenge the wrongs made against him in life. Kill me, and my evil spirit will kick you straight to hell."

Steadman didn't look worried. "I'm gonna count to three, *Annie,*" he said, "and then I'm going to shoot him. One..."

"She's not going to open the door," Pete said. "She knows that you're bluffing."

Annie stood at the door, her hands on the deadbolt. His leather jacket was lined with a bulletproof vest, she reminded herself, trying to force back the panic that threatened to overpower her. Even if they shot him, he'd be okay, wouldn't he? Oh, God, unless they shot him in the head. If they shot him in the head, he'd die. The panic was back full-force. If she didn't open the door, and Pete died, she'd never be able to live with herself, knowing that she could have saved him.

"Two," shouted Steadman. "I'm not bluffing."

She didn't want Pete to die. She desperately didn't want him to die....

"Yes, he is," Pete said. "Annie, don't open the door!"

Because, dammit, she loved him. She yanked the headphones off her and pushed the alarm system's front door override.

"Three!"

Annie jerked the door open.

"No!" Pete shouted. God, no! He'd told her to keep the door shut no matter what!

Steadman's gun swung toward Annie.

Pete moved fast, letting his backup gun drop from his sleeve into his hand. He blocked Annie with his body, shooting Steadman cleanly in the right arm and in the leg. Steadman's shots went wild, hitting the roof of the porch, the side of the house.

Then three more gunshots rang out. Bullets from the gun Golden was holding hit Pete, the force knocking him back into the house and slamming him into the foyer wall. He fell like a stone onto the floor.

Annie slammed the door shut and threw the deadbolt, leaving Golden and Joseph James Steadman out on the porch. They pounded on the door, and it strained beneath their combined weight. Much more of this, and they were going to break through, taking the old door right off its hinges.

Pete didn't move.

"Pete," Annie said. "Get up!"

She'd seen the bullets hit him in the chest. That meant he was all right, because his jacket was bulletproof.

But he still didn't move.

"Pete!" she shouted. It was only natural that he be

dazed. He probably had the air knocked out of him. He probably needed to lie there a minute and catch his breath. But she was starting to get scared. Golden and Steadman were going to bust through the door any second....

"Pete, come *on!*" she yelled, turning to look at him. Blood.

Pete's blood.

Bright and red, it seeped out from underneath him, running in the cracks on the hardwood floor....

With a cry, she ran toward him. Oh, God, he was bleeding. "Please don't be dead. Please, God, don't let him be dead!"

She turned him over onto his back, oblivious to the door breaking open, oblivious to Golden and Steadman as they shouted and waved their guns at her. Annie was only aware of Pete, of the blood.

There was so much blood, leaking out from underneath the waistband of his jacket, staining the front of his jeans.

He wasn't breathing. God, he wasn't breathing....

"Pete," Annie cried, touching his face, his hair, his arms. Arms that had held her, lips that had kissed her... "No! God, no! Pete, I love you, don't be dead—"

Rough hands pulled her up, off the floor, away from Pete's body. She struggled, sobbing his name, trying to get back to him, uncaring of her safety. Golden hit her, and she fell to the ground, not feeling the pain, not feeling anything but grief. Oh, God, Pete was dead....

He was lying sprawled on the floor, one arm trapped underneath the weight of his body, the other flung out, his fingers spread wide as if he were reaching for something, reaching for her....

"He's dead," Golden said, nudging Pete with his

foot. His green eyes looked almost feverish in his white face. He looked frighteningly inhuman, his nervousness frozen away by whatever coldness now inhabited him. "Open the safe, or you will be, too."

Annie sat very still. She didn't care. By killing Pete, Golden had already killed her.

Swearing, Golden began to drag her into the laboratory.

"For crying out loud, give me a hand," he finally said to Steadman.

"Which hand do you want, Al?" Steadman said, his voice pinched with pain. "I got a bullet in my right arm, and I think it's broken, and I'm bleeding like a stuck pig from this gash in my leg—"

"Shut up," Golden said, finally pushing Annie down in front of the safe. He held the gun to her head. "Open it."

Woodenly, she pulled herself up and began to open the safe. He was going to kill her. She knew he would, as soon as she gave him the death mask. He'd killed Pete, and he was going to kill her.

But he wasn't going to get away with it. If she stalled, Whitley Scott and the FBI would come. If she stalled long enough, she might even live to see Golden and Steadman rot in prison....

"You set me up, Golden," she said, suddenly feeling almost deadly calm, turning to look at him. "Didn't you?"

"Open the safe," he hissed.

"The death mask isn't in there," she said.

Steadman cursed loudly.

The panic in Golden's eyes deepened. "Where is it?"

"Tell me why you set me up," Annie said.

"Because it was so easy to do," he said. "The FBI

was already investigating you. I just played into their hands."

"What are you talking about?"

"Do we really have to get into the details? The incident at Athens was just your bad luck. We didn't have anything to do with that—you came under suspicion because they couldn't find anyone else. So we staged a similar little event in England after you left. And then we planted the stuff in your lab. Are you satisfied? We gave the FBI what they needed, and now you're gonna give me what I need. Then I'm gonna burn this place down." Golden cocked his gun, pressing it against Annie's head. "Now, where is that crate?"

"Upstairs," she said, curiously unafraid of the gun, its cold metal barrel bruising her temple. "In the attic." Something still wasn't clear. What was the big deal about this artifact? Why did they have to frame her? She'd probably never know....

"I can't handle the stairs," Steadman complained. "You take her. And leave her up there, will you?"

Golden forced Annie's arm back behind her, twisting it upward so that she should have cried out from the pain. But the numbness was surrounding her so completely, she didn't make a sound.

Pete's body lay in the foyer with all that blood, and the grief tore through, slicing into her, cutting her in two. He never knew that she loved him. He had died before she had a chance to tell him. No, that wasn't true. She'd had plenty of chances, she had just been too pigheaded, too stubborn, too *selfish,* and now he was dead and he would never know.

Tears spilled down her face, and she stumbled on the stairs, looking back at him. His face was probably already growing cold to the touch. The puddle of blood had grown. There was even blood on the knees of his jeans....

Annie froze. Outwardly, she made herself keep going, but inwardly, even her heart had stopped beating.

Pete's fingers had been spread, reaching, but now they were clenched, his hand in a tight fist.

Breathe, she told herself. *Breathe.*

Around her, everything snapped into tight focus. She tried to appear to move at a normal speed, and still stall their inevitable climb up to the attic. They were walking up the stairs in slow motion. The light was on in the kitchen, and the black-and-white tiled floor became almost three-dimensional. There was a cobweb hanging from the light fixture in the hall. The banister at the edge of the second-floor landing was in serious need of dusting. And the secondary burglar alarm control panel that had been installed next to Annie's bedroom door was flashing green.

Green. The system had been shut down.

The motion detectors had been turned off. But when she opened the front door, she'd activated only the override, leaving the rest of the system on-line. If *she* hadn't turned off the alarm system, then...

Pete.

Pete was alive.

She started to shake, and Golden pushed her harder. "Scared?" he taunted her. "You better be. If that crate isn't up here, you're dead."

But she wasn't scared. She was happy, thunderously, joyfully happy. Pete was alive! God was giving her a second chance....

His clenched fist had been some sort of signal to

her. He knew that she would notice—he knew she always noticed details.

He was trying to tell her something. But what?

They reached the top of the stairs and she pointed to the attic door, unable to speak. Golden motioned for her to open it.

The attic stairs creaked as they went up, up to the attic, up where Golden intended to leave her. Permanently.

Annie's heart was pounding.

She strained her ears, but she heard no sounds from downstairs. No struggle, no scuffle, nothing.

What was Pete trying to tell her?

Golden released her arm as they stepped up into the attic. He held his gun steady with both hands as he aimed it at her. "Get it."

Behind the old TV. She had put the crate behind the...

The crate!

In a flash she remembered picking up a similar heavy package at the airport. Pete had lifted it up, realized he would need both hands to carry it and refused. *She* had ended up lugging it all the way out to the car because, he said, if something threatening happened while he was carrying it, he wouldn't be able to properly protect her. He wouldn't be able to go for his gun.

He couldn't carry the package and hold a gun at the same time!

And if *Pete* couldn't...

With a silent heave, Annie picked up the crate and placed it solidly in Alistair Golden's outstretched left hand. And she watched as he brought his right hand, his gun hand, over to support the bottom of the heavy crate.

Annie wasn't sure if the look of surprise on Golden's
face was from the unexpected weight of the crate, or
from the sight of Pete, covered with blood and looking as if he'd risen from the dead, crashing through the
attic window, a gun in each hand.

"Freeze," Pete shouted. "Annie, get down!"

Annie dove for cover as Golden lunged toward Pete,
futilely throwing the crate at him. She heard the sound
of gunshots.

Then there was silence.

"You stupid son of a bitch," Annie heard Pete say.
"I *told* you to freeze."

Slowly she poked her head out. Golden lay on the
floor, his sightless eyes staring up at the rafters, but
Annie could see only Pete.

Pete!

Standing in front of her, breathing, living. . . .

"You're alive," she said, unaware of the tears that
coursed down her face. "My God, you *are* alive."

She moved toward him, held by a gaze she'd thought
she'd never see again, beautiful dark eyes filled with
life. And pain.

"Careful," he said, "I'm covered with glass."

"I don't care," she said, touching his face, wrapping
her arms around him. "I love you. I'm never going to
let go of you again."

He kissed her, sweetly, softly.

Downstairs, a team of federal agents poured into
the house.

"Well, if it isn't the cavalry," Pete said, swaying
slightly in her arms. "About time." And then his knees
gave out.

The next few seconds blurred together as Annie
caught him, shouting, screaming for help. She didn't

have the strength to hold him up, but she kept him from hitting the floor with force, lowering him gently down.

Whitley Scott was there in an instant. "Agent down!" he shouted. "We have an agent down! Get those paramedics up here—"

Someone unzipped Pete's jacket. There was a huge stain of bright red blood on his lower left side.

"The bullet went in under his jacket," Scott's voice said, "and angled up...."

Pete looked up at Scott. "Steadman—" he croaked.

Scott nodded. "We found where you left him," he said. "He hasn't come to yet, but he's cuffed."

"What's this on the floor?" someone asked. "Whoa, these aren't your everyday, average foam chips...."

"Peterson's lost an awful lot of blood," someone said.

Another voice swore softly. "How the hell did he manage to climb up the outside of the house in this condition? It's unreal...."

"Had to," Pete whispered. "Stairs creak...."

"Cocaine," Annie heard someone say. "This entire crate is *filled* with cocaine...."

"Hang in there, Captain," another man's voice said. "Paramedics are on their way."

"Get him downstairs," Scott ordered. "Lift him up and get him down and into a car. There's no time to wait. We can meet the ambulance halfway—"

This couldn't be happening, Annie thought, letting go of Pete's hand as five men lifted him. She couldn't get him back only to lose him again.

Miraculously, the ambulance had arrived, and the paramedics were in the foyer with their stretcher. The other agents laid Pete gently on it.

"Annie," he whispered.

She leaned over him, touching his face. His skin felt so clammy. "Don't you dare die on me, Peterson," she said fiercely. "Not twice in one day. I won't let you!"

"I have no intention of dying," he said, his voice little more than a rasp. His eyes were glazed with pain, his fingers gripping hers. "No way...."

"I love you," Annie told him. "You better not forget that."

Somehow he managed to smile. "I won't."

Chapter 18

Pete woke up.

Intensive care, he thought, staring at the massive array of monitors and machines that surrounded his hospital bed.

He was alive.

Yes, he was definitely alive. The pain in his gut was proof of that.

His throat was dry, his mouth was gluey and tasted like old socks. He tried to swallow, but it was a lost cause.

He had an IV tube in the back of his right hand.

His left hand was stuck in some kind of vise....

No, that was no vise grip, that was Annie! She held his hand tightly as she sat next to his bed, her head resting on the edge of the mattress, her eyes closed, her breathing even. She was asleep.

Gently he pulled his hand free, then touched the silky smoothness of her hair.

Her eyes opened slowly, and she sat up, looking at him. "I was starting to wonder if you were ever going to wake up," she said, her eyes filling with tears. One escaped and slid down her cheek.

"Don't cry." Pete couldn't make his voice any louder than a whisper. "Everything's gonna be all right—"

Her eyes blazed with anger. "You should have told me that you were going to try to provoke Golden and Steadman. I had no idea what you were doing— I thought you'd lost your mind. And when Whitley Scott told me that you had intentionally been making them angry, that you wanted them to try for you, that you were fast enough to disarm them both by winging them and that *I* was responsible for your getting shot because I opened the door and distracted you—"

Huge tears fell from Annie's eyes, faster and faster. Pete reached out to touch her hand, but she jerked away. But then, as if on second thought, she took his hand, bringing it up to her lips, then pressing it against the side of her face.

"I'm really mad at you," she said.

"It wasn't your fault," he whispered. "I underestimated Golden, didn't think he would have the guts to shoot me—"

"If I hadn't opened the door, he *wouldn't* have," Annie said, "but, God, Pete, I was so afraid you were going to die."

"I didn't," he said.

"I love you," she said.

"I remember."

Pete rode in the wheelchair down to the lobby. Outside the big double doors, he could see the flash of Annie's shining hair in the bright autumn sunshine.

The nurse pushed him through the doors and out onto the sidewalk. The morning air was cold, bracing. He took a deep breath, then smiled up into Annie's dancing blue eyes.

"Okay, Captain," the nurse said. "You can take it from here."

Pete stood up, still moving slowly, carefully. It would be a few more weeks before he was running any laps.

Annie was watching him carefully. "You talked to Whitley Scott this morning?" she asked.

"Yeah."

"Did they find out who was the inside contact?"

"Collins," Pete said. "He had access to the security codes—he got Steadman and Golden into your house."

"So this whole thing was about smuggling drugs?"

"That's it," Pete said. "Steadman put up the money to buy the art, and Golden would take on the task of authenticating it. But what he really did was fly out to England and pack the piece using special foam packing peanuts that he'd picked up wholesale in Colombia. The peanuts were loaded with cocaine, sometimes tens of millions of dollars' worth. Golden would bring the cocaine into the U.S. via England. He figured—correctly—that anything brought in from Colombia would be carefully searched, whereas England's not particularly known for its drug trafficking, so Customs tends to be more lax. As for the artifact, Steadman would turn right around and sell it—usually at a loss. He didn't care if he lost a few dollars on the art, he was making a bundle distributing the coke.

"When Ben Sullivan specifically called for you to authenticate the death mask, Golden had already packed it—gotten it ready to ship," he said. "He and

Steadman stood to lose the whole shipment of cocaine."
They had reached the car. Pete looked at the woman he
had risked his life for, the woman he would gladly risk
his life for a hundred times more. "They stood to lose
millions. Or worse. You could have found the coke.
So they made those threatening phone calls, trying to
set up a Navaho group as the fall guy when they stole
the piece from you. When *I* made the scene and security got too tight, they got desperate. They tried to kill
you, and when that didn't work, they resorted to their
back-up plan—they framed you. They were willing to
do *any*thing to get Golden named as the authenticator
again. Because then the crate—with the coke—would
go back into his possession."

Annie shuddered. "I'm just glad the whole mess
is over."

Pete let her help him into the car, then watched as
she slid behind the wheel.

"Ready?" she asked.

"Very ready." Pete leaned over, pulled her toward
him and kissed her, long and hard. They were both
breathing heavily when he finally let her go. "Guess
what I want to do first thing when we get home?"

Annie frowned in mock seriousness. "You promised
the doctor no strenuous exercise."

"Who said anything about strenuous?" He smiled,
tugging on her earlobe with his teeth.

She pulled away. "No, Pete, really," she said, all teasing gone. "You better ask the doctor first, make sure
it's okay...."

"It's okay," he said, playing with her long, brown
hair, running it through his fingers. "And I didn't even
have to ask. The doctor brought it up himself. I think
he noticed the way I look at you."

The way Pete was looking at her right now... It was heat, steam, fire, his eyes glowing with flames. He bent to kiss her again, and Annie closed her eyes, losing herself in the conflagration....

"Let's go home," he whispered.

Heart pounding, Annie pulled out of the driveway and onto the main road. After a mile or two, her pulse had finally returned to near normal, and she glanced over at Pete. "Jerry Tillet got funding for his Mexico project," she said. "Ben Sullivan came through."

"That's great news," Pete said. "Can't you drive any faster?"

Annie laughed. "We're five minutes from home," she said.

Pete's eyes told her that five minutes was five minutes too many.

"Cara's going to Mexico with Tillet," she said, trying to distract him—trying to distract herself. Would this traffic light *never* change? "Now I've got to find another research assistant."

"I thought you were thinking about going along," Pete said as the car moved forward. "You know, get your hands dirty for a change, do a little camping...."

Annie didn't answer, didn't even look up from the road. *What are your plans?* she wanted to ask. *When do you have to return to work?* But she didn't. She couldn't get the words out.

"I have a great idea," Pete was saying. "We can go out to Colorado first, then head down to Mexico—"

"We?" She couldn't hide her surprise.

Pete smiled at her. "Yeah. We. You. Me. You know. We could make it our honeymoon."

Annie pulled sharply off to the right, into a department store parking lot. She stopped the car, then turned to look at him. "Are you asking me to marry you?"

There was a spark of uncertainty in his eyes. "I thought I already did," he said slowly. "In the ambulance. On the way to the hospital?"

"You remember that?" Annie said in disbelief. "Pete, you were delirious."

"Well, yeah." He grinned. "Because you said yes...." His eyes were intense and his smile disappeared as he watched her. "*Will* you marry me, Annie?"

She moistened her lips. "I'm not sure I want to be married to someone who works for the CIA," she said softly. "I'm not sure I could handle it...."

The silence in the car stretched on.

Who was she fooling? Annie thought. It wouldn't be easy; she'd spend all her time worrying that he would be hurt, shot, killed even. She'd hate the long hours, the weeks away. But she loved him, and she was willing to take whatever he was willing to give.

"Yes," she said, at the exact same moment he turned to her and said, "I'll retire."

They stared at each other for a long time, then Pete said again, "I *will* retire."

"You don't have to," Annie said quietly. "I'll marry you anyway."

"But I want to," he said, taking her hand in his and kissing the tips of her fingers. "I've been thinking about it for a while. I just never had a good enough reason to retire before this."

"But what will you do?" Annie said. "You're awfully young to retire."

Pete smiled. "I've been thinking about a career change," he said. "I heard there's this really terrific position open—someone's looking for a research assistant. I don't have a whole hell of a lot of experience in a lab, but I'm really good at camping and digging in the dirt, or whatever it is you archaeologists do."

Laughing, Annie kissed him. And kissed him, and kissed him.

When they drew apart, her hands were shaking. "Well," she said. "I'm glad *that's* settled."

But Pete touched her chin, tugging her face toward him. "Wait," he said. His eyes were serious. "I need to ask you…" He looked down for a moment as if gathering his courage. "I know you love me." His eyes met hers. "But have you forgiven me?"

"Forgiven? Yes," she said. "Forgotten? Never. I'm not going to make *that* mistake twice."

His eyebrow moved slightly in the tiniest of frowns. He didn't understand….

"I'm *never* going to forget that you love me," she said, and put the car into gear. "Let's go home."

* * * * *

Elle James, a *New York Times* bestselling author, started writing when her sister challenged her to write a romance novel. She has managed a full-time job and raised three wonderful children, and she and her husband even tried ranching exotic birds (ostriches, emus and rheas). Ask her, and she'll tell you what it's like to go toe-to-toe with an angry 350-pound bird! Elle loves to hear from fans at ellejames@earthlink.net or ellejames.com.

Books by Elle James

Harlequin Intrigue

Mission: Six

One Intrepid SEAL
Two Dauntless Hearts
Three Courageous Words
Four Relentless Days
Five Ways to Surrender
Six Minutes to Midnight

Ballistic Cowboys

Hot Combat
Hot Target
Hot Zone
Hot Velocity

SEAL of My Own

Navy SEAL Survival
Navy SEAL Captive
Navy SEAL to Die For
Navy SEAL Six Pack

Visit the Author Profile page at
Harlequin.com.

HOT COMBAT

Elle James

This book is dedicated to my three lovely writing friends who encouraged me to write like my fingers were on fire during our annual writing retreat. If not for them and the timing of the retreat, this book might not have been written! Thank you, Cynthia D'Alba, Parker Kincade and Mandy Harbin.

Chapter 1

Charlie McClain pinched the bridge of her nose and rubbed her eyes. Fifteen more minutes, and she'd call it a night. The computer screen was the only light shining in her house at eleven o'clock. She'd kissed her six-year-old daughter good-night nearly three hours ago, and made it a rule not to work past midnight. She was closing in on breaking that rule and knew she would pay for it in the morning.

She looked forward to the day when her student loans were paid off and a little money was socked away in the bank. Until then, she telecommuted developing software during the day and at night she moonlighted, earning additional money surfing the internet for the Department of Homeland Security.

Fortunately, she didn't have to use her own internet provider to do the DHS surfing. She lived on the edge of town, beside Grizzly Pass's small library with free Wi-Fi service.

Since she lived so close, she was able to tap in without any great difficulty. It had been one of the reasons she'd agreed to take on the task. As long as a hacker couldn't trace her searches back to her home address, she could surf with relative anonymity. She didn't know how sophisticated her targets were, but she didn't want to take any more chances than she had to. She refused to put her daughter at risk, should some terrorist she might root out decide to come after her.

Charlie had just about reached her limit when her search sent her to a social media group with some disturbing messages. The particular site was one the DHS had her monitor on a regular basis. Comprised of antigovernment supporters with axes to grind about local and national policy, it was cluttered with chatter tonight. The group called themselves Free America.

Charlie skimmed through the messages sent back and forth between the members of the group, searching for anything the DHS would be concerned about.

She'd just about decided there wasn't anything of interest when she found a conversation thread that made her page back to read through the entire communication.

Preparations are underway for TO of gov fac.

Citizen soldiers of WY be ready. Our time draws near.

A cold chill slid down Charlie's spine. TO could mean anything, but her gut told her TO stood for *takeover*. As a citizen of the US and the great state of Wyoming, she didn't like the idea of an antigovernment revolt taking place anywhere in the United States, especially in her home state.

Granted, Wyoming stretched across hundreds of miles of prairie, rugged canyons and mountains. But there weren't that many large cities with government facilities providing prime targets. Cheyenne, the state capital, was on the other side of the state from where Charlie and her daughter lived.

Charlie backed up to earlier posts on the site. She needed to understand what their grievances were and maybe find a clue as to what government facility they were planning to take over. The more information she could provide, the more ammunition DHS would have to stop a full-scale attack. What government facility? What city? Who would be involved in the takeover? Hell, for that matter, what constituted a takeover?

Several of the members of the group complained about the government confiscating their cattle herds when they refused to pay the increase in fees for grazing rights on federal land. Others were angry that the oil pipeline work had been brought to a complete halt. They blamed the tree huggers and the politicians in Washington.

Still others posted links to gun dealer sites and local gun ranges providing training on tactical fire and maneuver techniques used by the military.

The more she dug, the less she liked what she was finding. So far, nothing indicated a specific date or location for the government facility takeover. Without hard facts, she wasn't sure she had anything to hand over to DHS. But her woman's intuition was telling her she had something here. She tried to follow the post back to its orgin, but didn't get very far.

A message popped up in Charlie's personal message box.

Who is this?

Shocked at being caught, Charlie lifted her hands off the computer keyboard.

I can see you. Come, pretty lady, tell me your name.

Charlie's breath lodged in her lungs. Could he see her? Her laptop had a built-in webcam. Had he hacked into it? She slammed the laptop shut and stared at the device as if it was a snake poised to bite. Her pulse raced and her hands shook.

Had he really seen her?

Pushing back her office chair, Charlie stood. If he had seen her, so what? She could be anyone who just stumbled onto the site. No harm, no foul. She shoved a hand through her thick hair and walked out of her office and down the hallway to the little bedroom where her six-year-old daughter lay peacefully sleeping.

The message had shaken her and left her rethinking her promise to help DHS monitor for terrorists.

Charlie tucked the blankets up around her daughter's chin and straightened. She shouldn't let the message bother her. It wasn't as if just anyone could trace her efforts at snooping back to her laptop. To track her down would require the skills of a master hacker. And they'd only get as far as the library's free Wi-Fi.

Too wound up to sleep, Charlie walked around her small cottage, checking the locks on the windows and doors, wishing she had a big bruiser of a dog to protect her if someone was to breach the locks.

Charlie grabbed a piece of masking tape, opened the laptop and covered the lens of the webcam. Feeling a little better, she took a seat at her desk and drafted an email to Kevin Garner, her handler at DHS. She'd typed This might not be anything, but check it out. Then she went back to the social media site and was in the middle of copying the site's location URL where she'd found the damning call to arms when another message popped up on her screen.

You're trespassing on a private group. Cease and desist.

Charlie closed the message and went back to pasting the URL into her email.

Another message popped up.

I know what you look like and it won't take long to trace your location. Pass on any information from this group and we'll find you.

The next thing to pop up was an image of herself, staring down at her laptop.

A horrible feeling pooled in the pit of Charlie's belly. Could he find her? Would he really come after her?

Suddenly the dead bolt locks didn't seem to be enough protection against whoever was at the other end of the computer messaging.

Charlie grabbed her phone and dialed Kevin's number. Yeah, it was after eleven o'clock, but she needed to hear the sound of someone's voice.

"I got it," Kevin's wife, Misty, answered with a groggy voice. "Hello."

"Misty, it's Charlie."

"Charlie. Good to hear from you. But what time is it? Oh, my, it's almost midnight. Is anything wrong?"

Charlie hesitated, feeling foolish, but unwilling to

end the call now. She squared her shoulders. "I need to talk to Kevin."

A moment later, Kevin's voice sounded in her ear. "Charlie, what's up?"

She drew in a deep breath and let it out, willing her voice to quit shaking as she relayed the information. "I was surfing the Free America social media site and found something. I'm not sure it's anything, but it set off alarm bells in my head."

"Shoot."

She told him about the message and waited for his response.

"Doesn't sound good. Got anything else?"

"I looked, but couldn't find anything detailing a specific location or government facility."

"I don't like it, but I can't get a search warrant if I don't have a name or location."

"That's what I figured, but that isn't all."

"What else have you got for me?"

"While I was searching through the social media site, a message popped up."

"A message?" he asked.

Charlie read the messages verbatim from her laptop. "He has my picture."

"Hmm. That he was able to determine you were looking at the site and then able to take command of your laptop long enough to snap a picture has me concerned."

"You're not the only one." She scrubbed a hand down her face, tired, but too agitated to go to sleep. "I was using the library's Wi-Fi. He won't be able to trace back to my computer."

"That's good. More than likely he's near the state capital."

"Are you willing to bet your life on that?" she asked.

"My life, yes."

"What about the life of your son or daughter?" Charlie asked. She knew he had two kids, both under the age of four. "Would you be able to sleep knowing someone is threatening you? And by threatening you, they threaten your family."

"Look, can you make it through the night?" Kevin asked. "It'll be tomorrow before I can do anything."

"I'll manage."

"Do you want me to come over?"

She shook her head, then remembered she was on the phone. "No. I have a gun. I know how to use it. And I really don't think he'll trace me to my home address so quickly. We don't even know if he has that ability."

"He snapped a picture of you," Kevin reminded her. "I'd say he's internet savvy and probably pretty good at hacking."

"Great." Charlie sighed. "I'll do okay tonight with my H&K .40 caliber pistol. But tomorrow, I might want some help protecting my daughter."

"On it. I'm expecting reinforcements this week. As soon as they arrive, I'll send someone over to assess the situation."

"Thanks." Charlie gripped the phone, not in a hurry to hang up. As if by so doing, she'd sever her contact permanently with the outside world and be exposed to the potential terrorist on the other end of the computer network.

"Look, Charlie, I can be there in fifteen minutes."

"No, really. I'll be fine." And she would be, as soon as she pulled herself together. "Sorry to bother you so late."

"Call me in the morning. Or call me anytime you need to," Kevin urged.

She ended the call and continued to hold the phone so tightly her fingers hurt.

What was supposed to have been an easy way to make a little extra cash had just become a problem. Or she was overreacting.

Just to be safe, she entered her bedroom and opened her nightstand where she kept the pistol her father had purchased for her when she'd graduated college. She could call her parents, but they were on a river cruise in Europe. Why bother them if this turned out to be nothing?

She found her pistol beneath a bottle of hand lotion and a romance novel. The safety lock was in place from the last time she'd taken it to Deputy Frazier's ranch for target practice six months ago. She removed the lock, dropped the magazine full of bullets and slid back the bolt. Everything appeared to be in working order. She released the bolt, slammed the magazine into the handle and left the lock on. She'd sleep in the lounge chair in the living room so that she would be ready for anything. She settled in the chair, her gun in her hand, hoping she didn't fall asleep, have a bad dream and shoot a hole in her leg.

She positioned herself in the chair, her gaze on the front door, her ears tuned in to the slightest sound. Not that she expected anyone to find her that night, but, if they did, she'd be ready.

Jon "Ghost" Caspar woke to the sun glaring through his windshield on its early morning rise from the horizon. He'd arrived in Grizzly Pass sometime around two o'clock. The town had so little to offer in the way of amenities, he didn't bother looking for a hotel, instead parking his truck in the empty parking lot of a small grocery store.

Not ten minutes after he'd reclined his seat and closed his eyes, a sheriff's deputy had rolled up beside him and shone a flashlight through his window.

Ghost had sat up, rolled down his window and explained to the deputy he'd arrived later than he'd expected and would find a hotel the next day. He just needed a few hours of sleep.

The deputy had nodded, warned him not to do any monkey business and left him alone. To make certain Ghost didn't perform any unsavory acts, the deputy made it his sole mission to circle the parking lot every half hour like clockwork until shift change around six in the morning.

Ghost was too tired to care. He opened his eyes briefly for every pass, but dropped back into the troubled sleep of the recently reassigned.

He resented being shuffled off to Wyoming when he'd rather be back with his SEAL team. But if he had to spend his convalescence as a loaner to the Department of Homeland Security, it might as well be in his home state of Wyoming, and the hometown he hadn't visited in a long time.

Seven years had passed since the last time he'd come back. He didn't have much reason to return. His parents had moved to a Florida retirement community after his father had served as ranch foreman for a major cattle ranch for the better part of forty years. Ranching was a young man's work, hard on a body and unforgiving when it came to accidents. The man deserved the life of leisure, soaking up the warm winter sunrays and playing golf to his heart's content.

Ghost adjusted his seat to the upright position and ran a hand through his hair. He needed a shower and a toothbrush. But a cup of coffee would have to do. He was supposed to report in to his contact, Kevin Garner, that morning to receive instructions. He hoped like hell he'd clarify just what would be entailed in the Safe Haven Task Force. To Ghost, it sounded like a quick path to boredom.

Ghost didn't do boredom well. It nearly got him kicked out of the Navy while in rehab in Bethesda, Maryland, at the Walter Reed National Military Medical Center. He was a SEAL, damn it. They had their own set of rules.

Not according to Joe, his physical therapist. He'd nearly come to blows with the man several times. Now that Ghost was back on his own feet without need of crutches, he regretted the idiot he'd been and had gone back to the therapy center to apologize.

Joe had laughed it off, saying he'd been threatened with far worse.

A smile curled Ghost's lips at the memory. Then the smile faded. He could get around without crutches or a cane, but the Navy hadn't seen fit to assign him back to his team at the Naval Special Warfare Group, or DEVGRU, in Virginia. Instead he'd been given Temporary Duty assignment in Wyoming, having been personally requested by a DHS task force leader.

What could possibly be so hot that a DHS task force leader could pull enough strings to get a highly trained Navy SEAL to play in his homeland security game? All Ghost could think was that man had some major strings to pull in DC. As soon as he met with the DHS guy, he hoped to make it clear he wanted off the assignment and back to his unit.

The sooner the better.

He'd left Grizzly Pass as a teen, fresh out of high school. Though his father loved the life of a ranch foreman, Ghost had wanted to get out of Wyoming and see the world. He'd returned several times, the last to help his parents pack up their things to move to Florida. He'd taken a month of leave to guide his parents through the biggest change in their lives and to say goodbye to his childhood home one last time.

With his parents leaving Wyoming, he had no reason to return. Having recently graduated from the Basic Underwater Demolition/SEAL training and having just completed his first deployment in his new role, Ghost was on a path to being exactly what he wanted—the best Navy SEAL he could be. A month on leave in Grizzly Pass reminded him why he couldn't live there anymore. At the same time, it reminded him of why he'd loved it so much.

He'd been home for two weeks when he'd run into a girl he'd known since grade school, one who'd been his friend through high school, whom he'd lost touch with when he'd joined the Navy. She'd been the tagalong friend he couldn't quite get rid of, who'd listened to all of his dreams and jokes. She was as quirky and lovable as her name, never asking anything of him but a chance to hang around.

With no intention of starting a lasting relationship, he'd asked her out. He'd told her up front he wasn't there to stay and he wouldn't be calling her after he left. She'd been okay with that, stating she had no intention of leaving Wyoming and she wouldn't be happy with a man who would be gone for eleven months of the year. But she wouldn't mind having someone to go out with while he was there.

No strings attached. No hearts broken.

Her words.

Looking back, Ghost realized those two weeks had been the best of his life. He'd recaptured the beauty of his home and his love of the mountains and prairies.

Charlie had taken him back to his old haunts in her Jeep, on horseback and on foot. They'd hiked, camped and explored everywhere they'd been as kids, topping it off by skinny-dipping in Bear Paw Creek.

That was when the magic multiplied exponentially. Their fun-loving romp as friends changed in an instant. Gone was the gangly girl with the braid hanging down her back. Naked, with nothing but the sun touching her pale skin, she'd walked into the water and changed his life forever.

He wondered if she still lived in Grizzly Pass. Hell, for the past seven years, he'd wanted to call her and ask her how she was doing and if she still thought about that incredible summer.

He supposed in the past seven years, she'd gone on to marry a local rancher and had two or three kids by now.

Ghost sighed. Since they'd made love in the fresh mountain air, he'd thought of her often. He still carried a picture of the two of them together. A shot his father had taken of them riding double on horseback at the ranch. He remembered that day the most. That was the day they'd gone to the creek. The day they'd first made love. The first day of the last week of his leave.

Having just graduated from college, she'd started work with a small business in town. She worked half days and spent every hour she wasn't working with Ghost. When he worried about her lack of sleep, she'd laughed and said she could sleep when he was gone.

She wanted to enjoy every minute she could with him. Again, no strings attached. No hearts broken.

Now, back in the same town, Ghost glanced around the early morning streets. A couple of trucks rumbled past the grocery parking lot and stopped at the local diner, pulling in between several other weathered ranch trucks.

Apparently the food was still good there.

A Jeep zipped into the diner's parking lot and parked between two of the trucks.

As his gaze fixed on the driver's door as it opened, Ghost's heartbeat stuttered, stopped and raced on.

A man in dark jeans and a dark polo shirt climbed out and entered the diner.

His pulse slowing, Ghost let out a sigh, squared his shoulders and twisted the key in the ignition. He was there to work, not rekindle an old flame, not when he was going to meet a man about his new assignment and promptly ask to be released to go back to his unit. The diner was the designated meeting place and it was nearing seven o'clock—the hour they'd agreed on.

Feeling grungy and road-weary, Ghost promised himself he'd find a hotel for a shower, catch some real sleep and then drive back to Virginia over the next couple of days.

He drove out of the parking lot and onto Main Street. He could have walked to the diner, but he wanted to leave straight from there to find that hotel and the shower he so desperately needed. Thirty minutes max before he could leave and get some rest.

Ghost parked in an empty space in the lot, cut the engine, climbed out of his truck and nearly crumpled to the ground before he got his leg straight. Pain shot through his thigh and kneecap. The therapist said that would happen if he didn't keep it moving. After his marathon drive from Virginia to Wyoming in under two days, what did he expect? He held on to the door until the pain subsided and his leg straightened to the point it could hold his weight.

Once he was confident he wouldn't fall flat on his face, he closed the truck door and walked slowly into the diner, trying hard not to limp. Even the DHS wouldn't want a man who couldn't go the distance because of an injury. Not that he wanted to keep the job with DHS. No. He wanted to be back with his unit. The sooner the better. They'd get him in shape better than any physical therapist. The competition and camaraderie kept them going and made them better, stronger men.

Once inside the diner, he glanced around at the men seated at the tables. Most wore jeans and cowboy boots. Their faces were deeply tanned and leathery from years of riding the range in all sorts of weather.

One man stood out among the others. He was tall and broad-shouldered, certainly capable of hard work, but his jeans and cowboy boots appeared new. His face, though tanned, wasn't rugged or hardened by the elements. He sat in a corner booth, his gaze narrowing on Ghost.

Figuring the guy was the one who didn't belong, Ghost ambled toward him. "DHS?" he asked, his tone low, barely carrying to the next booth.

The man stood and held out his hand. "Kevin Garner. You must be Jon Caspar."

Ghost shook the man's hand. "Most folks call me Ghost."

"Nice to meet you, Ghost." Garner had a firm grip,

belying his fresh-from-the-Western-store look. "Have a seat."

Not really wanting to stay, Ghost took the chair indicated.

The DHS man remained standing long enough to wave to a waitress. Once he got her attention, he sat opposite Ghost.

On close inspection, his contact appeared to be in his early thirties, trim and fit. "I was expecting someone older," Ghost commented.

Garner snorted. "Trust me, I get a lot of push-back for what I'm attempting. Most think I'm too young and inexperienced to lead this effort."

Ghost leaned back in his seat and crossed his arms over his chest. "And just what effort is that?"

Before the DHS representative could respond, the waitress arrived bearing a pot of coffee and an empty mug. She poured a cup and slapped a laminated menu on the table. "I'll be back."

As soon as she left, Garner leaned forward, resting his elbows on the table. "Safe Haven Task Force was my idea. If it works, great. If it fails, I'll be looking for another job. I'm just lucky they gave me a chance to experiment."

"Frankly, I'm not much on experiments, but I'll give you the benefit of a doubt. What's the experiment?"

"The team you will be part of will consist of some of the best of the best from whatever branch of service. They will be the best tacticians, the most skilled snipers and the smartest men our military has produced."

"Sorry." Ghost shook his head. "How do I fit into that team?"

Garner slid a file across the table and opened it to display a dossier on Ghost.

Ghost frowned. SEALs kept a low profile, their records available to only a very few. "How did you get that file?"

He sat back, his lips forming a hint of a smile. "I asked for it."

"Who the hell are you? Better still, what politician is in your pocket to pull me out of my unit for this boondoggle gig?" Ghost leaned toward Garner, anger simmering barely below the surface. "Look, I didn't ask for this assignment. I don't even want to be here. I have a job with the Navy. I don't need this."

Garner's eyes narrowed into slits. "Like it or not, you're on loan to me until I can prove out my theory. Call it a Temporary Duty assignment. I don't care what you call it. I just need you until I don't need you anymore."

"There are much bigger fish to fry in the world than in Grizzly Pass, Wyoming."

"Are you sure of that?" Garner's brow rose. "While you and your teammates are out fighting on foreign soil, we've had a few homegrown terrorists surface. Is fighting on foreign soil more important than defending your home turf?"

"I might fall for your line of reasoning if we were in New York, or DC." Ghost shook his head. "We're in Grizzly Pass. We're far away from politicians, presidents and wealthy billionaires. We're in the backside of the backwoods. What could possibly be of interest here?"

"You realize there's a significant amount of oil running through this state at any given time. Not to mention, it's also the state with the most active volcano."

"Not buying it." Ghost sat back again, unimpressed. "It would take a hell of an explosion to get things stirred up with the volcano at Yellowstone."

"Well, this area is a hotbed for antigovernment movements. There are enough weapons being stashed and men being trained to form a sizable army. And we're getting chatter on the social media sites indicating something's about to go down."

"Can you be more specific?"

Garner sighed. "Unfortunately, not yet."

"If you're done speculating, I have a two-day drive ahead of me to get back to my unit." Ghost started to rise, but the waitress arrived at that time, blocking his exit from the booth.

"Are you ready to order?"

"I'm not hungry."

Garner gave the waitress a tight smile. "I'd like the Cowboy Special, Marta."

Marta faced Ghost. "It's not too late to change your mind."

"The coffee will hold me." Until he could get to Cheyenne where he'd stop for food.

After Marta left, Garner leaned toward Ghost. "Give me a week. That's all I ask. One week. If you think we're still tilting at windmills, you can go back to your unit."

"How did I get the privilege of being your star guinea pig?"

Garner's face turned a ruddy shade of red and he pressed his lips together. "I got you because you weren't cleared for active duty." He raised his hand. "Don't get me wrong. You have a remarkable record and I would have chosen you anyway, once you'd fully recovered."

That hurt. The Navy had thrown the DHS a bone by sending a Navy SEAL with a bummed-up leg. Great. So they didn't think he was ready to return to duty either. The anger surged inside him, making him mad enough to prove them wrong. "All right. I'll give you a week. If we can't prove your theory about something about to go down, I'm heading back to Virginia."

Garner let out a long breath. "That's all I can ask."

Ghost smacked his hand on the table. "So, what exactly am I supposed to do?"

"One of our operatives was threatened last night. I need you to work with her while she tries to figure out who exactly it is and why they would feel the need to harass her." He handed Ghost his business card, flipping it over to the backside where he'd written an address. "This is her home address here in Grizzly Pass."

"I know where that is." Orva Davis lived there back when he was a kid. She used to chase the kids out of her yard, waving a switch. She'd been ancient back then, she couldn't possibly be alive now. "She's expecting me this morning?"

"She'll be happy to see anyone this morning. The sooner the better."

"Who is she?"

At that exact moment Garner's cell phone buzzed. He glanced down at the caller ID, his brows pulling together. "Sorry, I have to take this. If you have any questions, you can call me at the number on the front of that card." He pushed to his feet and walked out of the building, pressing the phone to his ear.

After tossing back the last of his coffee, Ghost pulled a couple of bills from his wallet and laid them on the table. He took the card and left, passing Garner on his way to his truck.

The DHS man was deep in conversation, turned completely away from Ghost.

Ghost shrugged. He'd had enough time off that he was feeling next to useless and antsy. But he could handle one more week. He might even get in some fly-fishing.

He slid behind the wheel of his pickup and glanced down at the address. Old Orva Davis couldn't possibly still be alive, could she? If not her, who was the woman who'd felt threatened in this backwater town? Probably some nervous Nellie.

He'd find out soon enough.

And then…one week.

Chapter 2

Charlie had nodded off once or twice during the night, waking with a jerk every time. Thankfully, she hadn't pulled the trigger and blown a hole in the door, her leg or her foot.

She was up and doing laundry when Lolly padded barefoot out of her bedroom, dragging her giant teddy bear. "I'm hungry."

"Waffles or cereal?" Charlie asked, forcing a cheerful smile to her tired face.

"Waffles," Lolly said. "With blueberry syrup."

"I'll start cooking, while you get dressed." Charlie plugged in her waffle iron, mixed the batter and had a waffle cooking in no time. She cleaned off the small dinette table that looked like a throwback to the fifties, with its speckled Formica top and chrome legs. In actuality, the table did date back to the fifties. It was one of the items of furniture that had come with the house when she'd bought it. She'd been fortunate enough to find the bright red vinyl fabric to recover the seats, making them look like new.

On a tight budget, with only one income-producing person in the family, a car payment and student loans to pay, she couldn't afford to be extravagant.

She was rinsing fresh blueberries in the sink when a dark figure suddenly appeared in the window in front of her. Charlie jumped, her heart knocking against her ribs. She laughed when she realized it was Shadow, the stray she and Lolly had fed through the winter. Charlie was far too jumpy that morning. The messages from the night before were probably all bluster, no substance, and she'd wasted a night she could have been sleeping, worrying about nothing.

The cat rubbed her fur against the window screen. When that didn't get enough attention, she stretched out her claws and sank them into the screen netting.

"Hey! Get down." Charlie tapped her knuckles against the glass and the cat jumped down from the ledge. "Lolly! Shadow's hungry and my hands are full."

Lolly entered the room dressed in jeans, a pink T-shirt and the pink cowboy boots she loved so much. The boots had been a great find on one of their rare trips to the thrift shop in Bozeman, Montana. "I'll get the bowl." She started for the back door.

I'll find you.

The message echoed in Charlie's head and she dropped the strainer of blueberries into the sink and hurried toward her daughter. "Wait, Lolly. I'll get the cat bowl. Tell you what, you grab a brush, and we'll braid your hair this morning."

Charlie waited until her daughter had left the kitchen, then she unlocked the dead bolt and glanced out at the fresh green landscape of early summer in the Rockies. The sun rose in the east and a few puffy clouds skittered across the sky. Snow still capped the higher peaks in stunning contrast to the lush greenery. How could anything be wrong on such a beautiful day?

A loud ringing made her jump and then grab for the telephone mounted on the wall beside her.

"Hello," she said, her voice cracking, her body trembling from being startled.

"Charlie, it's me, Kevin."

"Thank goodness." She laughed, the sound even shakier than her knees.

"Any more trouble last night?"

She shook her head and then remembered he couldn't see her. "No. I'm beginning to think I'm paranoid."

"Not at all. In fact, I'm sending someone over to check things out. He should be there in a few minutes."

"Oh. Okay. Thanks, Kevin."

"The guy I'm sending is one hundred percent trustworthy. I'd only send the best to you and Lolly." He broke off suddenly. "Sorry. I have an incoming call. We'll talk later."

"Thanks, Kevin." Feeling only slightly better, Charlie returned the phone to its charger and stepped out onto the porch.

Shadow rubbed against her legs and trotted to the empty bowl on the back porch steps.

"Impatient, are we?" Charlie walked out onto the porch, shaking off the feeling of being watched, calling herself all kinds of a fool for being so paranoid. She dropped to her haunches to rub the cat behind the ears.

Shadow nipped at her fingers, preferring food to fondling. Charlie smiled. "Greedy thing." She bent to grab the dish. When she rose, she caught movement in the corner of her eyes and then there were jean-clad legs standing in front of her.

She gasped and backed up so fast, she forgot she was still squatting and fell on her bottom. A scream lodged in her throat and she couldn't get a sound to emerge.

The man looming over her was huge. He stood with his back to the sun, his face in the shadows, and he had hands big enough to snap her bones like twigs. He extended one of those hands.

Charlie slapped it away and crab-walked backward toward the door. "Wh-who are you? What do you want?" she whispered, her gaze darting to the left and the right, searching for anything she could use as a weapon.

"Geez, Charlie, you'd think you'd remember me." He climbed the steps and, for the second time, reached for her hand. Before she could jerk hers away, he yanked her to her feet. A little harder than either of them expected.

Charlie slammed against a wall of muscle, the air knocked from her chest. Or had her lungs seized at his words? She knew that voice. Her pulse pounded against her eardrums, making it difficult for her to hear. "Jon?"

He brushed a strand of her hair from her face. "Hey, Charlie, I didn't know you were my assignment." He chuckled, that low, sexy sound that made her knees melt like butter.

Her heart burst with joy. He'd come back. Then as quickly as her joy spread, anger and fear followed. She flattened her palms against his chest and pushed herself far enough way, Jon was forced to drop his hands from around her waist. "What are you doing here?" she demanded.

"I'm on assignment." He grinned. "And it appears you're it."

She shook her head. "I don't understand."

"Kevin Garner sent me. The Navy loaned me to the Department of Homeland Security for a special task force. I thought it was going to be a boondoggle, and actually asked to be released from the assignment. But it looks like it won't be nearly as bad as I'd anticipated."

Charlie straightened her shirt, her heartbeat hammering, her ears perked to the sound of little footsteps. "You were right. Get Kevin to release you. Go back to the Navy. They need you more there."

"Whoa. Wait a minute. I promised Kevin I'd give it a week." Jon gripped her arms. "Why the hurry to get rid of me? As I recall, we used to have chemistry."

She shrugged off his hand. "That was a long time ago. A lot has changed since then. Please. Just go. I can handle the situation myself."

"If you're in trouble, let me help."

"No." God, why did he have to come back now? And why was it so hard to get rid of him? He'd certainly left without a care, never looking back or contacting her. Well, he could stay gone, for all she gave a damn. "I'm pretty sure I don't need you. Ask Kevin to assign you elsewhere."

"Mommy, I found the brush." Lolly pushed through the back door, waving a purple-handled hairbrush. "You can braid my hair now." Charlie's daughter, with her clear blue eyes and fiery auburn hair tumbling down her back, stepped through the door and stopped. Her mouth dropped open and her head tilted way back as she stared up at the big man standing on her porch. "Mommy?" she whispered. "Who is the big man?"

Charlie's heart tightened in her chest. If only her daughter knew. But she couldn't tell her and she couldn't tell Jon. Not after all these years. Not when he'd be gone again as soon as he could get Kevin to release him. "This is Mr. Caspar. He was just leaving." Thankfully, her daughter looked like a miniature replica of herself, but for the eyes. No one had guessed who the father was, except for her parents, and they'd been very discreet about the knowledge, never throwing it up in her face or giving her a hard time for sleeping with him without a wedding ring.

Jon dropped to his haunches and held out his hand. "Would you like for me to brush your hair? I used to do it for your mother."

The memory of Jon brushing the hay and tangles out of her hair brought back a rush of memories Charlie would rather not have resurrected. Not now. Not when it had taken seven years to push those memories to the back of her mind. She had too much at stake.

Charlie laid a hand on her daughter's shoulder. "Mr. Caspar was leaving."

He shook his head and crossed his arms over his chest. "Sorry. I promised to stay for a week. I don't go back on my word."

No, he didn't. He'd told her he wasn't looking for a long-term relationship when he'd last been in town. He'd lived up to his word then, leaving without once looking back. "Well, you'll have to keep your promise somewhere else besides my back porch."

Her daughter tugged on the hem of her T-shirt. "Mommy, are you mad at the man?"

With a sigh, Charlie shook her head. "No, sweetie, I'm not mad at him." Well, maybe a little angry that he'd bothered to come back after seven years. Or more that he'd waited seven years to return. Hell, she didn't know what to feel. Her emotions seemed to be out of control at the moment, bouncing between happiness at seeing him again and terror that he would discover her secret.

Since Jon seemed in no hurry to leave, she'd have to get tougher. Charlie turned her little girl and gave her a nudge toward the door. "Go back inside, Lolly. We adults need to have a talk."

Lolly grabbed her hand and clung to it. "I don't want to go." She frowned at Jon. "What if the big man hurts you?"

Lord, he'd already done that by breaking her heart. How could he hurt her worse?

Ghost watched as the little girl, who looked so much like her mother that it made his chest hurt, turned and entered the house, the screen door closing behind her.

Charlie hadn't waited around for him to come back. She'd gone on with her life, had a kid and probably had a husband lurking around somewhere. "Are you married?" He glanced over her shoulder, trying to see through the screen of the back door.

"Since you're not staying, does it matter?" She walked past him and down the stairs, grabbed a bowl from the ground and nearly tripped over a dark gray cat twisting around her ankles.

When Charlie stepped over the animal and started up the steps, the feline ran ahead and stopped in front of Ghost. She touched her nose to his leg as if testing him.

Ghost grew up on a ranch with barn cats. His father made sure they had two or three at any given time, but had them spayed and neutered to keep from populating the countryside with too many feral animals with the potential for carrying disease or rabies around the family and livestock.

He bent to let the cat sniff his hand and then scratched the animal's neck. "You didn't answer my question," he said. Why would she avoid the simple yes or no question?

"I don't feel like I owe you an explanation for what I've been doing for the past seven years." Her tone was tight, her shoulders stiff.

When he'd first seen her on the deck, he hadn't immediately recognized her. Her hair was longer and loose around her shoulders. When they'd been together, all those years ago, she'd worn her hair in a perpetual braid to keep it out of her face.

Her hips and breasts were fuller, even more enticing than before. Motherhood suited her. If possible, she was more beautiful and sexier than ever.

His gut twisted. But who was the father? Lolly was small. Maybe five? Though he didn't have a claim on Charlie, he never could stomach the idea of another man touching her the way he'd touched her.

The fact was babies didn't come from storks. So Charlie wasn't the open, straightforward woman she'd been all those years ago. She probably had a reason for being more reserved. Having a child might have factored into her current stance.

He straightened. "So, tell me about the threats."

"You're not going away, are you?" Her brows drew together, the lines a little deeper than when she'd been twenty-two. She sighed. "I really wish you would just go. I have enough going on."

"Without me getting in the way?" He shook his head. "I'm only going to be here a week. Unless you have a husband who is willing to take care of you, let me help you and your family for the week." He smiled, hoping to ease the frown from her brow. "Show me a husband and I'll leave." He cocked his brows.

She stared at him for a long, and what appeared to be wary, moment before she shook her head. "There isn't a husband to take care of us."

"Is he out of town?" He wasn't going to let it go. The thought of Charlie and her little girl being threatened didn't sit well with him. Who would do that to a lone woman and child? "I could stay until he returns."

"I told you. There isn't a husband. Never has been."

He couldn't help a little thrill at the news. But if no husband, who was the jerk who'd gotten her pregnant and left her to raise the child alone?

His heart stood still and his breath lodged in his lungs. Everything around him seemed to freeze. *No. It couldn't be.* "How old is Lolly?"

"Does it matter?" Charlie spun and walked toward the door. "If you want to see the threats, follow me."

He caught her arm and pulled her around to face him, his fingers digging into her skin. "How old is she?" he demanded, his lips tight, a thousand thoughts spinning in his head, zeroing in on one.

For a long moment, she met his gaze, refusing to back down. Finally, she tilted her chin upward a fraction and answered, "Six."

"Just six?" His gut clenched.

"Six and a few months."

Her words hit him like a punch in the gut. Ghost fought to remain upright when he wanted to double over with the impact. Instead, he dropped his hands to his sides and balled his fists. "Is she—"

"Yours?" She shrugged. "Does it matter? Will it change anything?"

"My God, Charlie!" He grabbed her arms wanting to shake her like a rag doll. But he didn't. "I have a daughter, and you never told me?"

"You were going places. You had a plan, and a family wasn't part of it. What did you expect me to do? Get an abortion? Give her up for adoption?"

"Hell, no." He choked on the words and shoved a hand through his hair. "I can't believe it." His knees wobbled and his eyes stung.

He turned toward the back door. The little auburn-haired girl-child stood watching them, her features muted by the screen.

That little human with the beautiful red hair, curling around her face was his daughter.

Chapter 3

Charlie walked toward the house. As she reached for the doorknob, her hands shook. Now that Jon knew about his daughter, what would he do? Would he fight for custody? Would he take her away for long periods of time? Would he hate her forever for keeping Lolly from him?

Questions spiraled out of control in Charlie's mind.

Lolly stood in the doorway, watching the two adults. Had she heard what had passed between them? Did she now know the big man was her father?

Up until Lolly had started school, she hadn't asked why she didn't have a father. Her world had revolved around Charlie. She didn't know enough about having a father to miss it.

Charlie pulled open the screen door, gathered her daughter in her arms and lifted her. "Hey, sweetie. Do you still have that brush?"

Her daughter held up the brush. "Is the big man

going to stay?" She shot a glare at Jon. "I don't like him."

"Oh, baby, he's a nice man. How can you say you don't like him when you don't know him yet?"

That stubborn frown that reminded Charlie so much of Jon grew deeper. "I don't want to know him."

Charlie cringed and shot a glance over her shoulder at the father of her child. Had she been wrong to keep news of his daughter from him? Would he have wanted to be a part of her life from birth?

Jon's expression was inscrutable. If he was angry, he wasn't showing it. If Lolly's words hurt...again, he wasn't letting on.

Then he smiled. Though the effort appeared forced to Charlie, it had no less of an impact on her. She remembered how he'd smiled and laughed and played with her when he'd been there seven years ago.

She still had a picture they'd taken together. He'd been laughing at something she said when she'd snapped the photo of them together.

Her heart pinched in her chest. No matter how much she might want it, they couldn't go back in time. What they had was gone. They had to move on with their lives. How Jon would fit into Lolly's world had yet to be determined, if he chose to see her again. Now that Jon knew about her, Charlie couldn't keep him from being with her. She just hoped he didn't break Lolly's heart like he'd broken Charlie's all those years ago.

"Lolly, Mr. Caspar is going to be visiting for the next week. I think you'll like him." She stared into her daughter's eyes. "Please, give him a chance."

Lolly stared over Charlie's shoulder at the man standing behind her. She didn't say anything for a few seconds and then nodded. "Okay." Then she extended the hand with the brush toward Jon. "You can brush my hair."

A burst of laughter erupted from Charlie. She clapped her hand over her mouth, realizing it sounded more hysterical than filled with humor. Trust her daughter to put the man to the test first thing.

Charlie set her daughter on her feet.

Jon nodded, his face set, his gaze connecting with Lolly's. "I'd be honored." He took the brush from her and glanced around.

"You can have a seat in the kitchen," Charlie said. "I'll make some coffee. Have you had breakfast? I'm making blueberry waffles."

She went through the motions of being a good hostess when all she wanted to do was run out of the room screaming, lock herself in her room and cry until she had no more tears left. With a daughter watching her every move, Charlie couldn't give in to hysterics.

She'd cried more than enough tears over this man. No longer a young woman on the verge of life, she was a mother with responsibilities. Her number one priority was the well-being of her little girl.

Charlie rinsed the bowl in the sink, poured cat food into it and set it aside. Shadow jumped into the window again, startling her. "Cat, you're going to give me a heart attack," she muttered. "I'll be back."

As she left the kitchen with the cat food, she watched Jon and Lolly.

Jon had taken a seat at the kitchen table and stood Lolly with her back to him between his knees.

Charlie swallowed hard on the lump forming in her throat.

The Navy SEAL, with his broad shoulders and rugged good looks, eased the brush through Lolly's hair with a gentleness no one would expect from a man conditioned for combat.

Once outside, Charlie stood for a moment on the porch, reminding herself how to breathe. What was happening? She didn't know which was worse, being threatened by a potential domestic terrorist, or facing the man she'd fallen so deeply in love with all those years ago. Her life couldn't be more of a mess.

An insistent pressure on her ankles brought her out of her own overwhelming thoughts and back to a hungry cat, purring at her feet.

"Sorry, Shadow. I keep forgetting that I'm not the only one in this world." She set the bowl on the porch, straightened and was about to turn when she saw movement in the brush near the edge of the tree line behind her house.

Narrowing her eyes, she stared into the shadows. Sometimes deer and coyotes made their way into her backyard. An occasional black bear wandered into town, causing a little excitement among residents. Nothing emerged and nothing stirred. Yet awareness rippled across her skin, raising gooseflesh.

Charlie rubbed her hands over her arms, the chill she felt having nothing to do with the temperature of the mountain air. She retreated behind the screen door where she stood just out of view from an outside observer. A minute passed, then another.

A rabbit hopped out of the shadows and sniffed the air, then bent to nibble on the clover.

Releasing the breath she'd been holding, Charlie turned toward the kitchen. Out of the corner of her eye, she saw the rabbit dart across the yard, away from the underbrush of the tree line.

Charlie shook off that creepy feeling and told herself not to be paranoid. Just because someone threatened her on the internet didn't mean someone would follow through on his threat.

She closed the back door and twisted the dead bolt. It didn't hurt to be careful. Walking back into the kitchen, she couldn't help feeling safer with Jon there. He had Lolly's hair brushed and braided into two matching plaits.

Her daughter leaned against Jon's knee, showing him her favorite doll.

Jon glanced up, his eyes narrowing slightly.

Oh, yeah. He was angry.

Charlie didn't doubt in the least he'd have a few choice words for her when Lolly wasn't in the room. And he had every right to be mad. He'd missed the first six years of his daughter's life.

Glad she had a bit of respite from a much-deserved verbal flogging, Charlie rescued a waffle from burning, poured batter into the iron and mixed up more in order to make enough for a grown man. Flavorful scents filled the air as the waffles rose.

Milking the excuse of giving her full attention to the production of the waffles, Charlie kept her back to Lolly and Jon. Yes, she was avoiding looking at Jon, afraid he'd see in her gaze that she wasn't totally over him. Afraid he'd aim that accusing glance at her and she'd feel even worse than she already did about not telling him.

"Here. Let me." A hand curled around hers and removed the fork from her fingers. "You're burning the waffles."

Charlie couldn't move—couldn't breathe. Jon stood so close he almost touched her. If she backed even a fraction of a step, her body would press against his.

God, she could smell that all too familiar scent that belonged to Jon, and only Jon—that outdoorsy, fresh mountain scent. She closed her eyes and swayed, bumping her back into his chest.

With his empty hand, he gripped her elbow, steadying her. Then he reached around her with the fork, opened the waffle iron and lifted out a perfect waffle. "Plates?" he said.

His mouth was so close to her ear, she could feel the warmth of his breath, causing uncontrollable shivers to skitter across her body.

Plates. Oh, yeah. She reached up to her right and started to pluck two plates from a cabinet. Then she remembered there were three of them now. After setting the plates on the counter, she turned away from the stove, desperate to put distance between her and Jon. Her body was on fire, her senses on alert for even the slightest of touches.

"Come on, Lolly, let's set the table while Mr. Caspar cooks." She grabbed the plates and started around Jon.

He shifted, blocking her path. "We *will* talk."

She stared at his chest, refusing to make eye contact. "Of course."

He stepped aside, allowing her to pass.

Charlie wanted to run from the room, but she knew she couldn't. Her daughter was a very observant child. She'd already figured out something wasn't right between her and Jon. Besides, running away would solve nothing.

Lolly gathered flatware from the drawer beside the sink.

Charlie set the plates on the table and went back to the cabinets for glasses. While she filled them with orange juice, she took the opportunity to study Jon while his back was to her.

The Navy SEALs had shaped him into even more of a man than he'd been before. His body was a finely honed weapon, his bulging muscles rippling with every movement. He'd been in great shape when he'd come home on leave seven years ago, but he was somehow more rugged, with a few new tattoos and scars on his exposed surfaces.

Charlie yearned to go to him, slip her arms around his waist and lean her cheek against his back like she had those weeks they'd been together. She longed to explore the new scars and tattoos, running her fingers across every inch of him.

He slipped waffles onto a platter and turned toward her, catching her gaze before she could look away.

Charlie froze, her eyes widening. Shoot, he'd caught her staring. Could he see the longing in her eyes?

She dragged her gaze away and darted for the stove and the pan of blueberry syrup simmering on the back burner. Her hand trembled as she poured the hot syrup into a small pitcher.

"Careful, you might get burned." Jon took the pan from her and set it on the stove.

You're telling me? She'd been burned by him before. She had no intention of falling for him again. Her life was hectic enough as a single parent trying to make a living in a small town.

She hurried away from Jon and set the syrup in front of her daughter.

Lolly pointed to the end of the table. "Mr. Caspar, you can sit there." She climbed into her chair and waited for the adults to take their seats.

Charlie felt like she and Jon were two predatory cats

circling the kill. She eased into her chair, her knees bent, ready to launch if things got too intense.

Jon frowned. "Are you sure you don't want your mother to sit here?"

Lolly shook her head. "She always sits across from me so we can talk."

Jon glanced at Charlie.

Charlie gave half of a smile. "That's the way we roll."

"Before we got our house, we sat on the couch to eat," Lolly offered.

"How long have you been in your house?" Jon asked.

"We moved in on my birthday." Lolly grinned. "I had my first birthday party here."

"What a special way to celebrate." Jon reached for the syrup and poured it over his stack of waffles. "Where did you live before?"

Charlie tensed.

Lolly shrugged. "Somewhere else." Her face brightened. "Did you know mommies go to school, too?"

Jon smiled. "Is that so?"

Lolly nodded. "Mommy went to school."

His brows hiked as he glanced toward Charlie.

Heat rose up her cheeks. She didn't want to talk about herself. They didn't need to go into all the details of their lives for the past seven years.

Jon didn't need to know that the years before they'd moved into the little house in Grizzly Pass had been lean. Too many times, Charlie had skipped a meal to have enough money to feed Lolly and pay for the babysitter. Working as a waitress during the day kept a roof over their heads and school at night didn't leave much time for her to be with her daughter. But they'd made their time together special. Now that she worked from home, Charlie was making up for all the times she couldn't be home.

Her daughter shoved a bite of waffle into her mouth and sighed. "Mmm."

Charlie almost laughed at the pure satisfaction on Lolly's face. They hadn't always eaten this well, and it hadn't been that long since she'd landed a job paying enough money that she could afford to buy a small house in her hometown.

Jon took a bite of the waffle, closed his eyes and echoed Lolly's approval. "Mmm. Your mother makes good waffles."

"You helped," Lolly pointed out.

"So he did." Charlie pushed her food around on her plate, her stomach too knotted to handle anything. Not with Jon Caspar sitting at her table.

Hell, Jon Caspar, the man she'd dreamed about for years, was sitting at her table. She pushed her chair back. "If you'll excuse me, I just remembered something."

She took her plate to the sink and was about to scrape the waffles into the garbage disposal when Jon's voice spoke up. "If you aren't going to eat them, I will."

She stopped with her fork poised over the sink. Walking back to the table, she set her plate down beside Jon's and then ran from the room.

So, I'm a big fat chicken. Sue me.

In an attempt to take her mind off the man in the kitchen, Charlie entered the guest bedroom she'd converted into an office. A futon doubled as a couch and a guest bed. The small desk in the corner that she'd purchased from a resale shop was just the right size for her. She spent most of her day in her office, working for a software developer she'd interned with during the pursuit of her second degree in Information Systems.

The shiny new business degree she'd finished right before that summer with Jon had landed her nothing in the way of a decent job. She'd stayed in Grizzly Pass with her parents through Lolly's birth, making plans and taking online courses.

She'd moved to Bozeman to return to school for a degree in Information Systems, looking for skills that wouldn't require her to move to a big city to make a living. She'd chosen that degree because of the opportunities available to telecommute. It had been a terrific choice, giving her the flexibility she needed to raise Lolly where she wanted and provide the family support her daughter needed. She had no regrets over her decision and now had the time to dedicate to her work and her small family of two.

She booted up her laptop and waited for the screen to come to life. As she waited, she glanced around the small room, wondering if Jon could fit his six-foot-three-inch frame on the futon. Ha! Fat chance. But he wasn't going to sleep in her room. Seven years apart changed everything.

Everything but the way her body reacted to his nearness.

Hell, he'd probably had a dozen other women.

Her heart stopped for a moment as another thought occurred. An image of Jon standing beside a woman wearing a wedding dress popped into her head and a led weight settled in her belly. He might have a wife somewhere. He'd said he was there for only a week. He might have someone waiting for him back home.

And kids.

Charlie pressed her hand to her mouth, her heart

aching for Lolly. How would she feel about sharing her father with other children? Would she get along with a stepmother?

Her eyes stung and her throat tightened. Lolly's life had just gotten a lot more complicated.

The screen on her laptop blinked to life. No sooner had she opened her browser than a message popped up on her screen.

You told.
Beware retribution.

"Damn." She shut the laptop and laid her head on top of it. If only wishing could fix everything, she'd wish her problems away.

"Are you okay?" A large hand descended on her shoulder.

For a moment Charlie let the warmth chase away the chill inside her. Jon had always had a knack for making everything all right. He would help her figure out this problem. In one week, they'd solve the mystery of who was threatening her and possibly a government facility in the state of Wyoming. Just one week. And then she could get back to life as usual.

Who was she kidding? Jon wouldn't leave for good. He'd be back. For Lolly.

Charlie shrugged Jon's hand off her shoulder and sat straight, opening her laptop again. "I've had another message." When the screen lit, she leaned back, allowing Jon to read the message.

"Do you think it's some kid yanking your chain?" Jon asked.

"I wish it was." Charlie pushed her hair back from her forehead. She clicked the keyboard until she found the URL she'd bookmarked and brought it up. Scrolling through the messages, she searched for the one that had started it all. She backed up through the messages from around the date and time the call to arms had been made. It was gone.

"What the hell?" Charlie scrolled farther back. "It was here last night."

"Whoever posted it could have come back in and erased the message."

Charlie snorted. "That's fine. I saved a screenshot, just in case." She pulled up the picture and sat back, giving Jon a moment to read and digest the words. "Do you think I was overreacting by reporting it to DHS?"

Jon shook his head. "With everything happening in the country and around the world, you can't be too cautious." He reached around her and brought up the social media site and scrolled through the messages again.

"Yesterday, there were a lot more messages expressing dissatisfaction with the way the government was handling the grazing rights and pipeline work."

"Apparently, someone scrubbed the messages. These all appear to be regular chatter."

Charlie sighed. "I'm beginning to think I imagined it."

"You did the right thing by alerting DHS." He straightened and crossed his arms over his chest. "Let them handle it. They have access to people who can trace sites like this back to the IP address."

The phone on her desk rang, making Charlie jump. She grabbed the receiver and hit the talk button. "Hello."

"Charlie, Kevin here. I take it you've met Ghost?"

"Ghost?" She glanced up at Jon.

He nodded and whispered, "My call sign."

Heat rose in her chest and up into her cheeks. "Yes, I've met him." She'd met him a long time ago, but she didn't want to go into the details with her DHS handler. Kevin wasn't from Grizzly Pass, and there were certain things he didn't need to know.

"Is he there now?" Kevin asked.

"Yes."

"Let me talk to him."

Charlie handed the phone to Jon. "It's Kevin."

Jon took the phone.

When their fingers touched, that same electric shock she'd experienced the first time he'd touched her shot up her arm and into her chest. She couldn't do this. Being close to him brought up all the same physical reactions she'd felt when she was a young and impressionable twenty-two-year-old.

She pushed back in her chair and rose, putting distance between them. It wasn't enough. Being in the same room as Jon, aka Ghost, made her ultra aware of him. She wasn't sure how long she could handle being this close and not touching him.

"Ghost here." He held the receiver to his ear, unused to using landlines. But then cell phones were practically useless in the remote towns of Wyoming.

"The rest of the team has arrived. I'd like you to meet them and talk through a game plan for the security of the area."

"I thought you wanted me to stay with Ms. Mc-Clain."

"I wanted you to assess the situation and give me feedback. I think she'll be okay in broad daylight. For now, you need to come to my digs above the Blue Moose Tavern and meet the rest of the men."

Ghost glanced at Charlie.

She paced the length of the small office, chewing on her fingernail.

"I'll bring her and the child with me." His gaze locked on her.

Charlie's head shot up and she met his glance with a frown. "Wherever you're going, you'll have to go by yourself. I had plans to take Lolly with me to the grocery store and the library. You don't need to come with me. We can take care of ourselves."

"Is that Charlie talking?" Kevin asked.

Ghost nodded. "It is."

"Tell her I only need you for about an hour. Then she can have you back."

Ghost covered the mouthpiece with his hand. "Garner said he only needs me for an hour. Are you sure you and Lolly will be okay for that time?"

She nodded. "Nobody will attack us in broad daylight."

Ghost snorted. Too many people assumed that same sentiment and were dead because of it. "Stay out of the open and report in every time you come and go from a location."

"I really think we might be paranoid, but okay." She raised her hands. "I'll stay out of the open, and I'll report my comings and goings." Charlie crossed her arms over her chest and tilted her head back. "Happy?"

"Not really," he said, his lips pressing together. "I'd rather drop you where you want to go and pick you up later."

Her lips pressed into a thin line.

Ghost decided it was better not to argue while Garner waited on the phone.

"Everything set?" Garner asked.

Ghost stared at Charlie, not sure he was happy with the arrangement, but Charlie wasn't budging. "Yes. I'll see you in twenty minutes. That will give me time to take a shower."

"Will do." Garner ended the call.

"I have to meet with DHS and the team Garner is assimilating. Are you sure you'll be okay?"

She gave a firm nod. "Positive."

How she could be so certain was unfathomable to Ghost. He wasn't sure *he* was okay. Being near Charlie brought back too many memories and a resurgence of the passion he'd felt for the woman seven years ago.

When he met with Garner, he'd have to tell him that he might not be the right man for the job. They had a huge conflict of interest. He and Charlie had slept together. Hell, they had a child together.

Tired and grungy, he couldn't think straight. "I need a shower."

"What do you want me to do about it?" She stood with her arms crossed, a semibelligerent frown on her face.

The corners of his lips twitched. Ghost stepped up to her and tipped her chin with his finger. "There was a time when you would have offered to shower with me."

"I was young and stupid."

He chuckled. "And you don't want to get stupid together? There's a lot to be said for being stupid. Especially when you do this—" Before he could talk sense into his own head, he bent and touched his lips to her forehead. "And this." He moved from her forehead to the tip of her nose.

She closed her eyes and her chest rose on a deep, indrawn breath. She unwound her arms and laid her hands on his chest.

At first he thought she would push away, but her fingers curled into his shirt, giving him just enough encouragement.

"And this." Ghost pressed his lips to hers, tasting what he'd missed for all those years, drinking in her sweetness. Sweet ecstasy, he couldn't get enough. He slid his hands to her lower back and pressed her closer. Why had he stayed away so long?

He skimmed the seam of her lips with his tongue. When she opened her mouth on a gasp, he dived in, caressing her tongue with his in a long, slick slide, re-establishing his claim on her mouth.

She felt different, her curves fuller, her arms stronger, her hair longer, but she was the same inside. This woman was the only one who'd stayed with him over the years, her image tucked in the recesses of his mind as he prepared for combat. She was the reason he'd dedicated his life to serving his country. To protect her and all the other people who depended on him to secure their freedom. He risked his life so that others could live free and safe.

For a long moment, he pushed every reason he'd had for leaving her out of his mind and reveled in the warm wetness of her kiss, the sweet taste of blueberry syrup on her lips and the heat of her body pressed to his. His groin tightened, the fly of his jeans pressing into her belly.

"Mommy?"

Ghost leaped back as if he'd been splashed with ice water.

"What do you need, Lolly?" Charlie pressed one hand to her swollen lips and the other smoothed her hair before she turned to face her daughter standing in the doorway.

"Why were you kissing Mr. Caspar?"

Ghost half turned away from the child, his lips twitching. He'd leave that answer for Charlie. Although, he'd like to know the answer to that question, too.

Chapter 4

"Sweetheart, let's get your shoes on. We're going to get groceries. After that, we're going to the library. So gather your books." Charlie didn't answer her daughter's question, choosing to hustle her daughter out of her office and away from the man who'd just kissed her socks off. She called over her shoulder, "Help yourself to the shower. There are towels in the linen closet and plenty of soap and shampoo."

Her lips tingled, and she could still taste the sweetness of his mouth. Dear, sweet heaven, how was she going to keep her hands off the man if he was around all the time?

She needed air. She needed space. What she wanted was another kiss just like that one. With her knees wobbling, Charlie left Lolly in her room and hurried into the master bedroom where the bed was still neatly made. She jammed her feet into her cowboy boots and yanked a brush through her hair, securing it at the nape of her neck in a ponytail. After checking that the safety switch was set on her handgun, she slid it into her purse, hooked the strap over her shoulder, braced herself and stepped into the hallway.

Thankfully, Jon wasn't anywhere in sight.

Charlie released the breath she'd held.

Lolly emerged from her room carrying a stack of children's books.

"Let's put those in a bag." She gathered the books and carried them back into Lolly's room where she found her book backpack and slid them inside.

Lolly slipped the backpack over her shoulders and led the way from the room.

She ran ahead to the living room.

Charlie shook her purse, listening for the jingle of keys. When she didn't hear it, she returned to her bedroom and grabbed them from the nightstand.

Hurrying into the hallway, with her head down, tucking the keys into her purse, she ran into a wall of muscles.

Big, coarse hands gripped her arms, steadying her.

"Are you all right?"

Hell no, she wasn't. Her pulse raced and she was out of breath before she'd even begun her day. "I'm fine," she said, studying her hands resting on his chest.

And boy, was he fine, too. Charlie couldn't help but stare at the expanse of skin peeking through his unbuttoned shirt. She remembered the smattering of hair on his chest and how she used to run her fingers through the curls. Her fingers curled into his skin, wanting to slide upward to test the springiness of those hairs.

"Are you ready?"

More than you'll ever know. Charlie shook herself

and pushed way. "I'm taking my car since I have to stock up on groceries."

"I'll follow you there."

"No need. It's only a block from Kevin's office. If I run into any trouble, you won't be far away." She shook her head. "We'll be fine."

He stared at her for a long moment.

Charlie met his gaze and held it, refusing to back down. He'd been gone seven years. He couldn't just walk back into her life and take over.

"Okay." He started buttoning his shirt. "Let's go."

Charlie's glance dropped to where his fingers worked the buttons through the holes. Seven years ago, she would have helped him button up, and then undo them one at a time, kissing a path down his chest.

Ghost's fingers paused halfway up. "I remember, too," he said, his voice low and gravelly.

Shivers rippled through her body and Charlie swayed toward him. Then she stopped, mentally pulled herself together and said, "I don't know what you're talking about. And I don't care. Let's go."

She pushed past him, her arm bumping into his, the jolt of electricity generated in that slight touch turning her knees to jelly.

The sooner she got away from him, the sooner she'd get her mind back. What was it about the man that scrambled her brain and left her defenseless against his magnetism?

Lolly stood by the door, her thumbs hooked through the straps of her backpack.

Charlie grabbed her hand and stepped out. She waited for Ghost to exit as well before she turned to lock the door. Her hand shook as she tried to slide the key into the dead bolt lock. She fumbled and dropped them to the porch.

Ghost scooped them up, locked the door and dropped the keys into her open palm. "You sure you don't want me to come with you?"

Lolly looked up, a happy smile on her face. "Could he, Mommy?"

"Sweetheart, Mr. Caspar has to go to a meeting."

Ghost touched his daughter's chin and gave her a brief smile. "I'll see you in about an hour."

"Mommy, can we get ice cream at the Blue Moose?"

"Why don't we get ice cream at the grocery store and bring it home to eat?"

"Okay." Lolly skipped down the steps toward the Jeep.

Charlie followed, not wanting to prolong her time or conversation with Ghost. The more she was with him, the more she wanted to be with him, and the harder it would be when he left again.

The drive to the grocery store took less than three minutes. She could have walked the five blocks, but she didn't want Lolly to be exposed to the nutcase who was threatening her. And carrying enough groceries for them for the week would be difficult, especially since she planned to purchase enough for Ghost, if he stayed for the full week. A man that big had to have an appetite to match. If it was anything like it had been when he'd gotten back from BUD/S training, he could put away some groceries.

He'd looked thin and a little gaunt after his SEAL training. She'd read about BUD/S to understand a little more of what he'd gone through. They'd put him through hell. And those who stuck it out came out tougher and ready to take on anything.

He'd been tired but exhilarated at making it through.

Now, he appeared more battle weary than anything. And he limped. Had he been injured? Charlie pressed a hand to her belly. The thought of Ghost going into battle, being shot at and explosions going off around him, made her stomach twist. When he'd left her, she'd done her best to push him as far to the back of her mind as she could. But she couldn't turn off the television when she'd seen reports of Navy SEALs dying in a helicopter crash or risking their lives to save hostages in Africa or some other place halfway around the world.

Now that he was back and larger than life, all those fears would be even harder to suppress.

Despite her assurance they'd be all right, Ghost followed Charlie all the way to the grocery store in his truck. He waited in the parking lot until they were safely inside the store. Then he drove the additional block to the Blue Moose Tavern. As he pulled into a parking space on Main Street, a disturbance in front of the feed store two blocks down caught his attention.

He climbed out of his truck and studied the gathering crowd.

"Ghost, glad you could make it." Kevin Garner stepped out of the tavern, followed by three other men. He stuck out his hand.

Ghost shook it. "Charlie and Lolly are getting groceries. What's going on at the feed store?"

"Some of the local ranchers are gathering to protest the Bureau of Land Management's increase in fees for grazing livestock on government land."

He'd read about the issues the ranchers were having and how BLM had confiscated entire herds of cattle from ranchers who refused to pay the fees in protest.

As the crowd got louder, a van rolled into town with antennas attached to the top. A cameraman and reporter leaped out and positioned themselves with a view of the angry ranchers behind them.

"Is this part of the problem we're here to help with?" one of the men standing near Kevin asked. He stuck out his hand to Ghost. "Name's Max Decker. My Delta team calls me Caveman."

Ghost gripped the man's hand. "Jon Caspar. Navy SEAL. Call me Ghost."

The next man stepped up and gripped Ghost's hand. "Trace Walsh. Marine. Expert marksman, earned the nickname Hawkeye."

A tall man with a crooked nose stepped up. "Rex Trainor. Army Airborne Ranger. They call me T-Rex."

Kevin turned back to the group. "Now that you've all met, let's take it to the loft." He led the way up the stairs on the side of the tavern and entered a combination office-apartment.

Ghost followed and entered a large room with a fold-up table stretched across the center. A bank of computers stretched across one wall, the screens lit. A wiry young man sat in front of a keyboard, his gaze shifting between three monitors.

"That's Clive Jameson. We call him Hack. He's the brains behind the computer we're using to track movement and data."

"Movement of what?" Caveman asked.

"What data?" T-Rex stepped up behind Hack.

"Grab a seat, I'll explain." Garner waved his hand at the metal folding chairs leaning against the wall. "It's not the ideal location and can get pretty noisy on Friday and Saturday nights, but it gives me the space I need to run the operation."

"What operation?" Hawkeye asked.

Kevin pointed to a large monitor hung on the wall. "Hack, could you bring up the map?"

The computer guy behind them clicked several keys and a digital map came up on the monitor.

"This is the tristate area of Wyoming, Montana and Idaho. There's been a lot of rumbling going on for various reasons in the area. Between the pipeline layoffs and the cattle-grazing rights, things are getting pretty hot. We're afraid sleeper cells of terrorists are embedding in the groups and stirring them up even more and providing them with the funding and weaponry to create havoc."

"This is a hot area, anyway. Haven't there been rumblings from the Yellowstone Caldera?" T-Rex asked.

Garner nodded. "That's another reason why you four were brought into this effort. The scientists at the Yellowstone Volcano Observatory have been tracking specific trembles. They think there might be an eruption in the near future. They don't think it will be a catastrophic event, but it has generated a lot of interest and tourists are pouring into Yellowstone National Park."

"So, what specifically makes you think something big is about to happen?" Ghost asked.

"Last week, we had two men go missing from the BLM. They had been out riding four-wheelers in grizzly country near some of the park's active hot springs." Garner stared at each of the men, one at a time, then said, "They didn't come back.

"Because they were armed with GPS capability we were able to find their ATVs hidden in the brush near a particularly deadly spring. There was no sign of a bear attack, which was the rescue team's first inclination. But they did find a shoe near the spring and skid marks as if someone was either dragging or pushing a body toward the toxic water. If the BLM men found their way into that pool, either on their own, or by other more forceful means, there would be absolutely nothing left for a family member to claim. Their tissue and bones would have dissolved."

"The perfect place to hide the bodies," T-Rex said, his tone low, his eyes narrowed.

"Why bring in the military?" Ghost asked.

"DHS is spread thin, monitoring our boarders and the entrance and exit points of airports and ports. We don't have the manpower to provide assistance to a potentially volatile situation here. And frankly, I don't think we have sufficient combat training as afforded to active duty military." Kevin lifted his chin, his chest swelling. "I do know what our country is capable of, and what the best of the best could do to help the situation. You see, I'm prior military. Eight years as a Black Hawk helicopter pilot. I ferried troops in and out of combat as a member of the 160th Night Stalkers."

Ghost sat back in his chair. "So you've seen as much battle as any one of us."

"Not as intensely as you four have. But I've seen what you can do when the time comes. You're smart and you act instinctively when you need to."

Hawkeye tapped his fingers on the table. "We've been fighting in a war environment. That's not what this is."

"No? You saw that mob out there. It could escalate into a shooting match in seconds."

"Still, it's not up to us to police civilians," Caveman said. "That's why we have law enforcement."

"The law enforcement is either tapped out or worse."

Garner shook his head. "We think some might be working with the people stirring things up."

Ghost leaned forward. "What exactly are you asking us to do here?"

"I need you to do several things. We have hot spots in the tristate area." Garner pointed to the map. "One is a survivalist group on the edge of Yellowstone National Park. With all the tourists flooding the park, I'm afraid they'll use it as an excuse to stage something big. I need someone to get inside the group, spy and report back."

"I'll take that one." T-Rex raised his hand. "I can infiltrate the survivalists' group."

"All I'm looking for now is information. If they do anything, you are not to engage." One by one, Garner looked each man in the eye. "Repeat, you are not to engage."

Caveman scratched the back of his head, his brows twisting. "We're combat veterans. Why involve us if we're not to engage?"

"We want to reserve engagement until it's the last resort." The DHS task force leader placed both hands on the table and leaned toward the men. "Think of it as a reconnaissance mission. You infiltrate wherever I need you to go, assess the situation and report back."

Ghost studied Kevin, his gut telling him the man wasn't giving it to them straight. "What else are you not telling us?"

Kevin straightened, his eyes narrowing, his lips thinning into a thin line. "One of the folks we employ who monitors the internet for anything that could be construed as a potential attack, ran across a message last night. More or less, it was a call to arms to take over a government facility."

The Marine, Army Ranger and Delta Force man leaned forward.

Because he'd already heard this story, Ghost sat back in his chair and waited for the rest of whatever Kevin had to say.

"Where?" T-Rex asked.

"When?" Hawkeye wanted to know.

"We don't have that information. I need you all to keep an ear to the ground. If you hear anything, no matter how inconsequential it might sound, relay it to me."

Ghost shook his head. "The disappearing BLM men and a poorly worded message can't be all that has you calling in the cavalry. What else?"

Kevin met Ghost's gaze. "We've also been concerned about message traffic from some of the people we've been monitoring for the past six months. Men who are connected with ISIS. We intercepted a message we decoded indicating a weapons movement to this area. Enough guns and ammunition to stage a significant takeover of a state capital. Enough ammunition for a standoff. Or the murder of a great number of people."

Ghost's gut clenched. His daughter was in the area in question. If something went down, she could be caught in the cross fire. He'd just found his daughter. He'd be damned if he lost her so soon.

He couldn't wait to get out of the meeting and back to his family.

His family. Ha! If Charlie had her way, he wouldn't be anywhere near them. He'd just have to convince her she'd be better off with him sticking around.

Chapter 5

Once inside the grocery store, Charlie whirled the cart around the narrow aisles, hurrying through the tiny store, gathering only what she needed for the week. The shelves appeared barer than usual. When she got to the counter, Mrs. Penders, one of the owners of the mom-and-pop store checked her items.

"Why are the shelves so empty, Mrs. P?" Charlie asked, setting her items on the counter, one at a time. "Are you expecting a delivery today?"

She snorted and rang up a loaf of bread, the last one on the shelf. "I got a shipment this morning. We had a run on the store earlier. Did you see the crowd gathering in front of the feed store?"

She hadn't. Charlie had been more concerned about Ghost following her that she hadn't glanced farther down the street. "I'm sorry. I didn't see the crowd. What's going on?"

"A group of ranchers are taking a stand against the Bureau of Land Management over what they did."

"What did they do?"

"They confiscated half of LeRoy Vanders's herd. He refused to pay his fees for grazing rights on federal land in protest of the increase."

"Confiscated a herd of cattle?" Charlie set the jug of milk on the counter. "Can they do that?"

Mrs. Penders nodded. "Can and did. Got all the local ranchers up in arms. Sheriff's talking to them now out front of the feed store.

"I hear Jon Caspar is back in town." Mrs. Penders rang up the milk and slid it into a bag, before she raised her gaze to capture Charlie's. "You two were a thing way back in the day, weren't you?"

Charlie shrugged. "We dated."

"If he needs a place to stay, I have a room over my garage," the store owner offered.

"Mr. Caspar is staying with us." Lolly tugged on her mother's shirt. "Isn't he, Mommy?"

Heat filled Charlie's cheeks. "Just for the week while he's in town. Then he'll have to go back to his job with the Navy."

"Can't he stay forever?" Lolly asked. "I like the way he brushes my hair."

"We'll discuss this later," Charlie said, hurriedly placing the last items on the counter.

Mrs. Penders was one of the worst gossips in town. By the time Charlie reached home, the older woman would have word spread across the county that Charlie and Ghost were shacking up. She wouldn't be surprised if she got a call from her parents all the way in Europe asking about the man sleeping in her little house.

Mrs. Penders gave her a total, Charlie paid and

pushed the cart out into the parking lot. Lolly helped her load the items into the back of her Jeep.

As she pulled out of the parking lot of the store, she glanced down the street toward the feed store. Just as Mrs. Penders had said, a crowd gathered, some of the men raised their hands, shaking fists in the air.

"This can't be good," Charlie muttered, turning the opposite direction, heading for her little house on the edge of town. She passed the library.

"Aren't we going to the library?" Lolly asked.

"After we unload and put the groceries away. It won't take long, and we can walk next door."

"Okay." Lolly helped her unload the groceries, carrying in the lighter bags.

Charlie put away the items, grabbed her own bag of books and Lolly's backpack. "Let's go see Ms. Florence. She might have some new books for you today."

Grizzly Pass was a very small town, but the residents were proud of the little library they'd helped to fund. Rebecca Florence was the preacher's daughter, with a fresh degree in library science. A quiet soul, she'd returned to her hometown, glad to escape the hustle and bustle of Denver, where she'd attended her father's alma mater.

Happy to take over duties of town librarian from her aging mother, she slipped into the role with ease. Though shy and quiet, she managed to bring the library up to twenty-first century standards, writing for grant money to have computers installed and providing Wi-Fi internet for those who couldn't afford their own satellite internet.

Charlie enjoyed talking with Rebecca about the latest books. The woman was a wealth of knowledge and read extensively in fiction and nonfiction.

Before Charlie left the house, she placed a call to Kevin. His computer guy, Hack, answered the call. "He stepped out front. Is this an emergency? Do you want me to run out and catch him?"

"No. Just have him relay to Mr. Caspar that Charlie made it home and is now taking Lolly to the library. Thank you." She ended the call, grabbed Lolly's hand and left the house.

Less than twenty steps brought them to the front of the old colonial house that had been converted into the library. The wide front porch had several rocking chairs for patrons to use when they just wanted to sit outside and read a book.

Charlie and Lolly had spent a few beautiful summer days reading on that front porch. Now, they pushed through the front door with the open sign hanging in the window.

"Ms. Florence?" Charlie called out.

When she got no answer, she didn't worry. Rebecca sometimes was in the back kitchen making tea.

Charlie and Lolly laid their books on the return counter and went in search of some they hadn't read.

After a few minutes, Charlie went in search of Rebecca. She hoped the librarian could help her find more information on grazing rights and what it meant to the ranchers in the area.

She understood many of the ranchers had grazed their cattle on government land for years. Some families had been grazing cattle on government land for several generations. Paying a grazing fee wasn't the only expense they incurred. They were responsible for maintaining the fences on the land where they grazed their cattle and providing for the water, if it wasn't readily available.

"Rebecca?" Charlie pushed through a swinging door leading into the back of the house where the kitchen was. As soon as she passed through the door, she heard a soft moan, coming from the other side of an island.

Her heart slammed hard against her ribs and she ran forward.

Rebecca lay on the floor, her strawberry blond hair tangled and matted with blood. A gash on her forehead dripped blood into her eyes and onto the floor.

"Rebecca?" Charlie leaned down and grabbed the woman's hand. "What happened to you?"

"Charlie?" she said, though her voice sounded muffled. She tried to open her eyes, but couldn't seem to. Instead she gripped Charlie's hand. "Get out."

"What?" Charlie shook her head. "I'm not leaving until I get you some help."

"Go," she said. "Not safe." She coughed and spit up blood.

"Is the man who attacked you still here?"

She lay still for a moment before answering. "I don't think so." Her words ended on a moan.

Anger burned in Charlie's gut. How could anyone do this to as gentle a soul as Rebecca?

Charlie smoothed a lock of her reddish-blond hair from her face. "I'm calling the sheriff and an ambulance." She started to rise, but Rebecca tightened her hold on her hand.

"Angry. Said I told."

"Who was it?"

"Don't know." She coughed, her body tensing. "Wore a mask. Said I…was ruining…everything…" Her grip loosened and her hand dropped to the floor.

Her throat constricting, Charlie pressed her fingers to the base of Rebecca's throat, hoping to find a pulse and nearly crying when she felt the reassuring thump against her fingertips. She stood and feverishly searched the kitchen for a telephone. Thankfully, there was one on the wall near the back door.

Charlie grabbed the phone and dialed 911. After passing the information to the dispatcher, she hung up and dialed Kevin's number.

Kevin answered the phone on the first ring. "Garner speaking."

"Kevin. Thank God. It's Charlie."

"What's wrong?"

"Rebecca Florence was attacked here in the library. I've notified 911. But she was more worried about me than herself. She said the guy who attacked her was angry. She said he was mad because she told. Is Ghost with you?"

"He just left to go to your house. He should be there about now."

Charlie dropped the phone as the sound of a siren wailed toward the little house. She pushed through the swinging door, suddenly afraid for her daughter she'd left in the children's section of the library.

"Lolly!" she shouted.

Lolly emerged from the front room, carrying a colorful book, her brow pressed into a frown. "What's wrong?"

Charlie gathered her into her arms and hugged her close.

Ghost slammed through the front entrance, his eyes wide and his face tense until he spotted Charlie and Lolly. "Are you two okay?"

Charlie nodded and then tipped her head toward the kitchen door. "But Rebecca isn't. Could you take Lolly while I help her?"

"You stay with Lolly. I've had training in first aid." He stepped past her and entered the kitchen.

A few minutes later, a young sheriff's deputy entered the library, his gun drawn.

"I don't think you'll need that," Charlie said. They didn't need some rookie deputy shooting a man who was only attempting to render aid. "Jon Caspar is in the kitchen with Ms. Florence. He's one of the good guys."

The deputy didn't lower his weapon, instead, he entered the kitchen. Voices sounded through the wood paneling of the door.

Moments later the fire department paramedics entered. Charlie directed them to the kitchen and then pulled Lolly into the front parlor of the old house that Rebecca had designated as the children's room.

While she waited for Ghost to emerge from the kitchen, she read a story to Lolly.

"Mommy, you're not doing a very good job," Lolly said.

"Then *you* read it to *me*," she said, too tired to argue with her daughter.

Lolly read the story, slowing over some words, but far advanced for her age.

Charlie only half listened, her chest tight, her stomach knotted. When she saw the paramedic wheel Rebecca through the house on a stretcher, she stood.

Ghost followed, stopping in the doorway.

Charlie ran into his arms and hugged him around the middle. "Is she going to be all right?"

Ghost smoothed the hair on the back of her head. "I believe so. She took a pretty hard hit to the forehead. They'll keep her in the hospital to observe for concussion. Before she passed out, did she say who did it?"

"She didn't know. Apparently he wore a mask."

Charlie wrung her hands. "I think she was attacked because of me." She stared up into Ghost's eyes, her own filling with tears. "I couldn't live with myself if something happened to her because of me."

"Why because of you?"

Her stomach roiled. "She said he attacked her because she told."

"Why would he attack *her*, if he was looking for *you*?"

"He might have thought she was me. I was tapped into the library Wi-Fi when I was looking at the social media site. I have auburn hair, Rebecca has strawberry blond. The picture he sent was not absolutely clear, he could have mistaken her for me."

"That's it. I'm staying with you and Lolly."

"Okay."

He went off as if she'd never spoken. "Until we know what's going on, you and I need to stick together. No argument."

Her lips twitched as she touched a hand to his chest. "I said okay."

Ghost stopped talking and stared down into her eyes. "About time we agreed on something." He bent to capture her lips in a soul-defining, earth-shattering kiss that left her boneless. She leaned against him, completely dependent on his strength to hold her up.

He glanced down at Lolly staring up at them. "Yes, Lolly, I kissed your mother."

Ghost kept it together all the way back to Charlie's house. He couldn't tell her that hearing her crying out Lolly's name with a touch of panic in her voice had made his heart practically explode out of his chest. Then seeing what had happened to Rebecca and knowing it could have been Charlie made him nearly crumple to his knees.

He'd been back only a day and already he was as deeply in love with Charlie as he'd been seven years ago. The connection they'd shared had never quite gone away, instead it was there and stronger than before. The things he knew, the places he'd been and the experiences he'd survived made him even more aware of how fleeting life could be. One day a man could be on the earth, alive and healthy. The next, he could be six feet under or in the case of the two BLM men, they could have fallen into a toxic pit, leaving nothing left to identify.

He'd had friends die in his arms. He carried the pain with him every day of his life, never quite able to erase the images of them. They seemed to line up at night and dare him to sleep.

Knowing that could have been Charlie on the floor of the library left him feeling more panicked and uncertain than ever. He hadn't come back to find her, but fate placed her directly in his path and revealed to him the fact he had a child. How could he not stay and protect the two women who meant the most to him?

"You two stay here." Before he could allow them to go much farther than the front entryway, Ghost thoroughly searched the entire house. As soon as the guy who had attacked Rebecca discovered she wasn't the one he was after, he'd come back.

Ghost had to be ready.

When he returned, he found Charlie holding Lolly in her arms. The little girl was sobbing on her mother's shoulder.

Ghost's heart broke at the sound of the child's sobs. "Hey, what's all this?" he said softly.

"Ms. Florence is hurt." She sniffed and leaned back to look at Ghost. Her eyes were red-rimmed and puffy and tears stained her cheeks.

"Come here." He held out his arms. When Lolly went to him, his chest swelled two times bigger. She trusted him enough to come to him when she was distressed. That meant a lot.

Charlie stood with her hand on her daughter's back, her own eyes suspiciously glassy.

Holding Lolly in one arm, he opened the other.

Charlie stepped in and wrapped her arms around him and Lolly. For a long moment, the three of them remained in the tight hug.

Ghost had no desire to break it off anytime soon. The scent of Lolly's hair filled his nostrils. Baby shampoo and fresh air. He inhaled deeply and kissed the top of her head. Then he dropped a kiss on Charlie's temple, wishing he hadn't been such an idiot when he'd been there last. If he hadn't told her he wasn't interested in a long-term relationship, she might have let him in on the secret of his child. He wouldn't have missed all of her firsts. The first tooth, the first time she giggled. Her first step.

As he stood with his arms full of the two women he loved, he came to the conclusion he had to give up something. His career as a Navy SEAL or the family he'd just discovered.

He didn't want to give up either, but he had no right to ask Charlie and Lolly to wait around for him when he went out on missions. So many SEALs were divorced or never married. The waiting killed relationships. Most women wanted their man at home at night. Every night. And the worry of whether or not he'd come home alive, not in a body bag, was real and destructive to a spouse's peace of mind.

When his leg started aching and he couldn't stand still another minute longer, he asked, "Who wants hot cocoa?"

Lolly lifted her head from his shoulder. "Me."

"Me," Charlie agreed. "I'll fix it."

"No. Let me. Just point me in the right direction." He handed Lolly to her mother. "I can make a great cup of cocoa."

"We can all help." Charlie set Lolly on her feet and took her hand.

Lolly slipped her free hand in Ghost's and they entered the kitchen together. In a few short minutes, Ghost had the hot cocoa ready and Charlie made hot dogs for lunch.

"I know I bought ketchup," she said, sorting through the bottles of condiments in the refrigerator. When she didn't find it there, she went to the pantry. After a moment, she came back to the table with mustard. "I'm sorry. I must have forgotten it at the store."

"I put it in the refrigerator," Lolly said. She jumped up and went to the appliance and yanked open the door. "I put it right here." She pointed to an empty spot in the door.

"Well, it's not there," Charlie said. "You'll have to have mustard or eat your hot dog plain."

Lolly's bottom lip stuck out and she frowned. "I guess I'll eat mine plain." She sat at the table, and nibbled at the naked hot dog and drank the hot cocoa, gaining a white melted-marshmallow mustache on her upper lip.

Charlie slathered mustard on her hot dog and ate.

Ghost filled his bun with mustard and sweet relish and savored every bite. "That was delicious."

"Sweetheart," Charlie said softly to Lolly. "If you're done with your lunch, you can take your plate to the sink and go play in your room."

"Okay." She slid out of her chair and carried the plate to the sink.

As the child left the room, Charlie grimaced. "She usually won't eat a hot dog without the requisite ketchup."

Ghost smiled. "A girl who knows what she likes. We'll have to ease her into mustard and relish. It's an acquired taste. But so good."

Charlie stared at him for a moment, her brows pinched lightly.

Ghost tried to think of what he'd said that would make her stare at him with that look of concern.

"Now that you know about Lolly, what are you going to do?"

He glanced in the direction Lolly had gone, not wanting to discuss the future of their daughter in front of her. "If you're finished with your meal, let's take this discussion out on the back porch."

He gathered her plate and his and carried them to the sink.

"Leave them. I'll take care of them later." She led the way to the back door and waited for him to follow before she opened it wide, stopped dead in her tracks and gasped.

Ghost nearly bumped into her, she stopped so fast.

There on the porch was the bottle of ketchup and written in bright red tomato sauce were the words *I KNOW WHERE YOU LIVE.*

Chapter 6

Charlie staggered backward into Ghost's arms. He pulled her away from the door and closed it between them and the damning writing on the porch.

"How did he get in?" Charlie turned and buried her face in Ghost's chest. "I'm positive I locked the doors."

"I double-checked the windows, as well as the doors." He smoothed his hand over the back of her head, his voice low and steady. "He must have picked the lock."

"He knows who I am, and he knows now where I live. He must have figured out Rebecca wasn't the one who tapped into his messages. We're not safe. I should pack up, take Lolly and leave."

"Then he wins."

"Good God, Ghost!" She slapped her palms on his chest. "This isn't a game."

"To him, it might be." He held her arms and stared

down into her face. "He might follow you wherever you go."

"Or not. He might be trying to scare me away from Grizzly Pass until he and his following do whatever dastardly deed they have planned." She shook her head and stared at the closest button on his shirt. "I can't risk Lolly's life on a game some psycho is playing with me."

"You forget something."

"What?" She stared up at him, her eyes a little wild, scared.

"You forget that you have me."

"I could have been in the library when he attacked Rebecca," she said, a shiver slithering down the back of her neck. "You weren't there."

"I will be from now on. And you can't go anywhere without me until we catch the bastard."

"Then he wins by making me a prisoner in my own home." Charlie spun out of Ghost's grip and walked across the kitchen and back. "Look, you can stay until we figure this out. But you have to sleep on the couch. We're not picking up where we left off seven years ago. I'm a different person than the naive girl I was back then."

He nodded. "Agreed." He grinned. "About the couch and about being different. You're a much more beautiful woman, you're more independent and an incredible mother."

"And…" Her chin lifted and she captured his gaze with a cool steady one of her own. "I don't need anyone else in my life to make me happy," she insisted, if not to convince him, to convince herself.

"And you don't need anyone else in your life to make you happy," he repeated. "I get that. But when you're ready to talk, I want to discuss who Lolly needs in *her* life."

Charlie pinched the bridge of her nose and shook her head. "Can we postpone that one for another day? I have ketchup bleeding in my mind. And I'm not ready to start a custody battle."

He stepped toward her, his hand outstretched. "It doesn't have to be a battle."

She backed up. "No? I can't see anything but a battle in our future." When he opened his mouth, she held up both hands. "Please. For now, let's not go there. I can't deal with everything and a terrorist out to kill me." She looked at the floor, seeing Rebecca's limp body lying in her own blood. "I can't believe he attacked Rebecca. She wouldn't hurt a fly." She glanced up. "And it's my fault. If I hadn't been snooping on the internet for a few measly dollars extra, none of this would have happened."

"Darlin', you can't blame yourself. You didn't hurt Rebecca. *He* did. We'll deal with this together."

Though her heart warmed when he referred to her as darlin', she couldn't ignore the most important part of the equation. "What about Lolly? I don't want her to be collateral damage. She's just a child." God, what had she done? This was supposed to be an easy gig. She was supposed to be anonymous. No one would know she was the one surfing, searching for terrorist activities.

"Tell you what," Ghost said. "I'll have Garner bring new locks and keys. I can install them today."

She shook her head. "What good will that do? He'll just pick those, too."

Ghost shrugged. "It'll make *me* feel better."

She flipped her hand. "Fine. And I can get online

and see if I can find the IP address of the social media group. Maybe we can chase down the leader through it."

"Garner will have Hack working on that, as well."

She nodded. "I did give him the URL. I would think Hack could find it before I can, but two heads are better than one."

Ghost clapped his hands together. "Good. You have a plan. I have a plan. Let's get to it."

Charlie went back to work in her office, searching through the internet, looking for the IP address that the Free America group occupied.

She could hear Ghost placing a call to Kevin, explaining what had happened with the ketchup. Half an hour later, a man she didn't know arrived at her door.

Apparently, Ghost did, calling him by an unusual nickname. "Hey, Caveman. Thanks for bringing these."

"I'm staying to help install them," Caveman said.

"That'll get it done faster," Ghost agreed. "Thanks."

They didn't ask her opinion or assistance, which was perfectly okay with her. Charlie didn't leave her office, except to check on Lolly. She spent the afternoon trying everything she knew, and searching the internet for techniques she didn't know that could help her find the man who'd threatened her online.

About the time Caveman left, Charlie could hear the two men talking softly near the front door, their voices carrying down the hallway, but not clearly enough to make out their words.

Charlie didn't care. She trusted Ghost to keep her and Lolly safe. She had to get to the bottom of who was threatening her, or she'd have no peace.

Ghost appeared in the doorway a few minutes later, carrying a cup of hot tea. "Any luck?"

"I wish I could say yes, but I'm no computer forensics expert. That's not what I studied in my Information Systems degree."

"So you've been in school again?"

She nodded.

"You had just completed a degree when we met seven years ago."

"In business. It was pretty general. When I realized I was pregnant, I knew I had to get something with more of a skill I could work with at home. So I went into Information Systems and learned about databases, data management, design and programming."

"I'm impressed."

She shrugged. "My goal was to work from home so that I could live wherever I wanted." And she'd wanted to come home to Grizzly Pass to raise Lolly. It was a more laid-back and safe environment. Until now.

"I'm impressed. You've been busy."

"What about you?" She'd been dying to ask, but hadn't wanted to know more about him that would make her fall more deeply in love with the man. Still she couldn't resist knowing what he'd gone through in the past seven years. "Are you still based out of California?"

"I'm out of Virginia, now. I completed some training in riverine ops with SEAL Boat Team 22 out of Stennis Space Center in Mississippi. I've had over forty deployments since last we saw each other. But I've also managed to complete my online degree in financial management. Since I'm rarely in town, I don't have time to spend the money I make. I invest it."

She smiled up at him. "You've been busy, too."

He nodded. "Anything I can do to help?"

Her lips twisted and she shook her head. "Not unless you're an experienced hacker, along with being a trained SEAL."

He disappeared, leaving her to her work.

Charlie's senses were tuned into his movements. She could tell when he'd gone into Lolly's bedroom. Their voices drifted to her, making her want to give up on her search and join them. Normally, she would break from her work for the Bozeman software company to spend time with her daughter. But what she was doing was more important. She couldn't let the man threatening her get away with it. And since he'd attacked Rebecca, apparently he would follow through on his threat.

Charlie shivered and dug deeper, following leads on the computer, searching through videos on how to find an IP address. Everything she tried ran her into a brick wall.

The smell of cooking onions drifted into her office and brought her out of her focused concentration.

Ghost was in the kitchen and, by the sound of it, Lolly was helping. Charlie smiled. At least her daughter had a chance to get to know the man who was her father.

Ghost was a good man. Charlie shouldn't have kept the news of his daughter from him. He'd missed so much of her life already and it wouldn't be fair of her to keep him from seeing her in the future. They'd have to come up with a plan to trade off on weekends and holidays.

The thought saddened her. Charlie had grown up with parents who had been married for more than thirty years. They were still as in love with each other as the day they'd met. Their marriage was the standard by which Charlie measured all other relationships.

Perhaps theirs was the exception, not the rule. Wasn't having a part-time father who loved her better than no father at all? She had a lot of thinking to do, and perhaps this wasn't the time to do it. Her problems were more immediate than setting up a visitation schedule.

Lolly appeared in the doorway with a hand-folded paper hat on her head and a towel over her shoulder. She stood straight, her lips twitching. "Your dinner is served," she said in her most formal tone. She spoiled the effect by giggling. "Come on, Mommy. Mr. Caspar and I set the table. We made a lasagna for dinner."

"Lasagna?" Charlie's stomach rumbled. "It smells wonderful."

"It is wonderful." The child grabbed her hand and pulled Charlie to her feet. "Hurry. I'm hungry."

Charlie chuckled and let her daughter practically drag her down the hallway to the kitchen.

Ghost stood at the sink, an apron looped around his neck and tied around his narrow waist. He glanced over his shoulders. "Have a seat. Dinner is just about done."

"Can I do anything?" Charlie asked.

"You can sit down and look beautiful with Lolly." He winked at the little girl. "She even brushed her own hair and changed into that dress."

Lolly nodded. "All by myself."

Charlie stood back, studying her daughter's clothes and hair. "Good job." She gave her a high five and pulled out a chair for her daughter to slide into.

Dinner was perfect. The lasagna tasted so good, Charlie accepted a second helping and ate until she was so full, she couldn't form a coherent thought. "What did you put into that pasta? I suspect it was some kind of sleeping potion." A yawn slipped out and she covered her mouth. "I think I'll get a shower and go to bed." She glanced at Lolly. "Are you about done?"

"Don't worry about Lolly. She and I have a date with

her favorite book tonight. I'll help her through bath time and pajamas. Go. Get your shower and sleep."

Charlie didn't argue. The stress of the day and not being able to sleep the night before had left her exhausted. She trudged her way to the bathroom, stripped down and stepped beneath the spray. If she wasn't so tired, she'd be tempted to invite Ghost to join her.

Her eyes widened. What was she thinking? Invite Ghost in the shower with her? She wasn't a twenty-two-year-old anymore. Ghost wasn't going to be around forever, and she refused to put herself and Lolly through the heartbreak of a man entering and leaving her life with no commitment to return.

He might be okay with that lifestyle, but she couldn't take that yo-yo effect. Lord forbid if he should bring back a wife on one of his visits to Lolly.

Her hands clenched and heat burned through her body. She twisted the knob on the faucet to cold and stood beneath the showerhead, letting the water chill her until she shivered.

Then she remembered she hadn't grabbed a towel from the hall linen closet. She stepped out of the shower onto the bath mat, dripping wet and chilled to the bone. Grabbing her shirt, she held it up to her chest and opened the door a crack. No one was in the hallway. She could hear voices in the kitchen. With the coast clear, she darted across the hall to the closet, flung open the door and snatched a towel. She had just turned to dash back into the bathroom when the wood floor squeaked at the other end of the hallway and she heard Ghost say, "I'm going to check to see if your mother is finished in the shower. I'll be right back."

She didn't make it across the hall. Her feet froze to

the floor. Holding the towel in front of her, she couldn't think, couldn't move and only stared at Ghost.

His gaze slipped over her, traveling slowly downward from her face to her breasts, where she'd pressed the towel to the swells. Lower still, his gaze moved to the flare of her hips, clearly visible with the towel draped down only the middle of her torso.

His eyes flared and his body stiffened.

Heat rose from Charlie's core and spread throughout her body. The moisture from that short, cold shower steamed off her body as passion flared and burned a path outward, making her ache for him in every part of her existence.

"Charlie." The word came out in a low, sexy tone. He stepped toward her, his hand reaching out.

Charlie was caught in the spell, the temptation to run into his arms so strong, her arm relaxed, the towel inching downward.

"Mr. Caspar?" Lolly called out from the kitchen.

And snap. Just like that, the spell was broken.

Charlie flung herself into the bathroom, closed the door and leaned her back against it, breathing hard as if she'd run a marathon instead of three feet across the hallway.

From sleepy to wide-awake in two seconds flat. She scrubbed her body with the towel, hoping the added abrasion would push Ghost out of her mind. It had the opposite effect. Her skin tingled from the heated gaze he'd spread over her body. Her nipples were tight, puckered for his touch.

She moaned, threw the towel onto the floor and stomped it. "No. No. No. I will not make love to that man."

"Everything all right in there?" Ghost's voice sounded through the door. Was that a chuckle she heard?

Charlie channeled her desire into something just as heated. Anger. Shoving her head into her nightgown, she pulled it down over her body and slipped her arms into the matching robe. Then she frowned, fearing the garment was a little too revealing. Since she didn't have anything else with her in the bathroom, she sighed. It would have to do. She reached for her panties, but the counter was bare.

Damn. Had she forgotten them? She opened the door and peered out.

Ghost stood in the hallway, dangling a pair of soft blue bikini panties from his index finger. "Missing something?"

Her eyes widened and she reached for the panties.

He pulled them back at the last minute.

Charlie's forward momentum carried her toward him and she slammed into his chest.

Ghost clamped an arm around her waist and held her tight against him. "You felt it, too, didn't you?"

"I don't know what you're talking about." She reached for the panties again, her breasts rubbing against his chest through the thin fabric of her nightgown. "Let me have those."

He raised his eyebrows. "Say *please*."

She gritted her teeth, her core tightening, the ache building the longer she stood with her nearly naked body pressed to his. Instead of arguing over underwear, she wanted to wrap her legs around his waist. Hell, she wanted him inside her, filling that space that had been empty for so long. God, she'd missed him. And she'd miss him when he was gone.

Charlie slumped in his arms. "Fine. You can keep

them. But let me go. There really can't be anything between us."

His arm tightened around her. "Why?"

"You have your responsibilities. I have mine. I gave you my heart once. I'm not willing to do it again."

For a long moment, he held her in his arms, his gaze locked on hers.

She refused to look away first. Losing him the first time had been so hard. Carrying his baby, knowing he wouldn't be a part of their lives had nearly killed her. She couldn't let him back into her life, only to have him leave again and break not only her heart, but Lolly's, too.

Finally, Ghost loosened his hold. He could see the hurt in Charlie's eyes and he wanted to take it all away. He'd caused that. He'd been the one to break her heart. If he wanted her back, he'd have to earn her trust.

He released her, but he didn't hand back her panties. Instead, he wadded them up and shoved them into his pocket. Yeah, it might be juvenile, but he wanted something that belonged to her, should she end up kicking him out of her life. "Lolly's ready for her bath and bedtime story."

"I can take care of her."

"Get her through her bath. I'll take it from there."

"You don't need to. I'm awake now."

"I don't care if you're awake. I want to read to my daughter—to get to know her." His mouth formed a thin line, his brows dipping low. "At least give me that."

She nodded. "Fair enough." Charlie stepped away from him, spun on her heels and walked into her bedroom.

Knowing she wasn't wearing panties nearly made

Ghost come undone. The sway of her hips and the way she flung her damp hair over her shoulder was so enticing, he almost went after her. The way her nipples puckered, making little tents in her silky nightgown, was proof she wasn't immune to him.

Yeah, he had a long way to go to convince her he was worth a second chance.

You broke my heart once...

Was he selfish to want her back? He adjusted his jeans to accommodate his natural reaction to her bare-bottom state. Hell, yeah, it was selfish. What he needed to consider was if he was the man for her. Charlie was special. She deserved someone who could be there for her always.

As a Navy SEAL, he couldn't be in Wyoming except when he took leave. If she and Lolly wanted to be with him, they'd have to leave Wyoming and join him at Little Creek, Virginia. Even then, they'd only see him when he wasn't deployed. The advantage to living on or near a Navy base was the support network of the military and other military spouses.

God, she deserved so much more.

After his last deployment and being injured, Ghost had worried he wouldn't get the medical clearance to return to his unit. Now he wondered if it wasn't time for him to step down. Take a medical retirement, find a less dangerous job that allowed him to be home more often.

He walked back into the kitchen to find Lolly drying the last plate.

"I couldn't reach the cabinet." She pointed upward.

Ghost opened the cabinet and set the cleaned and dried plates inside. Then he dropped his hand to the top of Lolly's soft, red hair. He wanted the chance to be with his daughter. To get to know her, and for her to get to know him. Dragging them around the nation was selfish. But, damn it. He wanted to be a part of Lolly's life, even if Charlie didn't want anything else to do with him.

"Come on, it's time for your bath and a bedtime story." He held out his hand.

Lolly laid hers in his, so trusting. Would she be better off with a stepdad who could be there for her? Would he be kind to her and treat her like she was his own daughter?

Ghost couldn't imagine Lolly with any other father, any more than he could imagine Charlie with another man.

"You get your pjs while I run the water."

"Roger," she said and grinned up at him. "I said that right, didn't I?"

He'd been teaching her how SEALs talked to each other. The child picked up quickly. Smart as a whip. Just like her mother.

"Roger." He gave her a nudge toward her bedroom. "Go. Get those pjs." Ghost entered the bathroom. It still smelled like Charlie's shampoo, making him want to skip Lolly's bath and go straight into her mother's bedroom, climb into her bed and make crazy, passionate love to her.

Instead, he sat on the side of the bathtub, turned the handles on the faucet and adjusted the temperature to just right for a six-year-old.

Lolly entered carrying her colorful pjs, tossed them on the counter and stuck her hand in the water. "Just right."

"Need any help here? If not, I'll find the perfect book for us to read together."

"I can take my own bath. Mommy thinks I need

help, but I don't." She puffed out her chest and lifted her chin, just like Charlie did when she was standing up for herself or someone else. Lolly was so much like her mother, it made Ghost's chest hurt just looking at her.

"Okay, then." He dropped a kiss on top of her head and left her to do her thing, propping the bathroom door open so he could listen for her.

He walked back to the living room, found the phone and dialed the number for Garner.

"Charlie, how's it going?"

"It's Ghost," he said. "So far we're okay. What's the status on the librarian?"

"She's holding her own. Minor swelling on the brain. They're watching her closely and keeping her sedated. By all indications, she'll live."

"I also wanted to know if Hack found anything in those messages that would lead us to whoever has targeted Charlie."

"Nothing so far. He's close to finding the IP address. As soon as he does, I'll send one of the guys out to recon."

"I'd like to be the one to corner that man."

"You and me both. He's a slick bastard. But I find it hard to believe a rancher or pipeliner is crafty enough to pull off a takeover without some help from outside."

Ghost's fists clenched. "You think the ranchers and pipeliners are too dumb to pull this off?"

"No, no. Don't get me wrong. I think they're plenty smart. I just don't know that they could pull it off without some tactical training and influence from outside the ranching and pipeline community."

"So far, all I've seen in the way of an uprising was the ranchers protesting the confiscation of a herd of cattle. Was anyone arrested?"

"No. As long as there was no harm to anyone and no property damage, they were free to protest."

"Did you or one of the others get some names of the primary instigators?"

"Hawkeye spoke with one rancher who had twenty-eight hundred head of cattle confiscated, LeRoy Vanders," Garner said. "He was hopping mad and ready to rip into the BLM."

"And?"

"The sheriff managed to calm him. The crowd has since dissipated, but there are a lot of angry ranchers. Hack's checking online records for some of the names Hawkeye came up with from the protesters. T-Rex will be positioning himself at the County Line Bar tonight to make some new friends among the survivalist groups."

"What about Hawkeye?"

"He'll be downstairs in the Tavern striking up conversations with the ranchers and unemployed pipeline workers who come in each night to get a drink and commiserate."

"Mr. Caspar?" Lolly called out from down the hall.

Ghost lowered his voice. "I have to go. Let us know anything you might find out about the man stalking Ms. McClain. As *soon* as you find out. Even if it's in the middle of the night."

"Roger," Garner said. "I'll have Caveman swing by a couple of times during the night."

"Thanks," Ghost said. "Out here." He ended the call and hurried down the hall to the bathroom.

Lolly was out of the tub, wearing her panties, her nightgown pulled over her head, but stuck halfway down.

Ghost untangled the gown and dragged the hem downward to her knees.

She smiled up at him. "Thank you." Then she skipped past him to her bedroom and selected a book from her shelf. "Read this," she demanded.

Ghost took the book from her. "Did you brush your teeth?"

She clapped a hand to her mouth and darted for the door. "I'll be right back."

He grinned and waited for her, thumbing through the book she'd chosen about a little girl pretending to be a beauty shop lady. He chuckled at some of the descriptions. Then he turned down the comforter on Lolly's bed and sat on the edge.

Lolly was back in two minutes, smiling wide. "Clean. See?"

He frowned down at her. "You sure you brushed long enough?"

She nodded. "I sang 'Happy Birthday' all the way through twice."

"Okay. Let's find out what's going on in this book." Ghost opened the book and started reading, getting as caught up in the character's plight as Lolly by the end of the story.

"Now, this one," Lolly insisted, opening another book and handing it to him.

After reading two more books, Ghost told Lolly it was time to close her eyes and go to sleep.

Lolly pouted for a brief moment and then flopped down on her back and burrowed into the sheets and comforter, until all Ghost could make out was Lolly's cute little head poking out of the big bed. "Aren't you going to stay?" She patted the bed beside her.

Ghost sat on the edge of the bed and bent to kiss her good-night. She captured his head between her palms and kissed him soundly on the cheek.

He laughed and kissed the top of her head. "Good night, princess."

"Good night, Mr. Caspar." She yawned, stretched and closed her eyes. "I love you."

Ghost's heart squeezed hard in his chest. Those three little words practically brought him to his knees. The child hardly knew him, but she trusted him to take care of her and to be there when she woke up.

He wanted to gather her in his arms and hold her tight. Forever. His little girl.

In less than five minutes she was asleep, her breathing slow and steady. But Ghost remained perched on the side of her bed, watching her angelic face as she slept, and his heart grew fuller by the minute.

If anyone tried to hurt her… His fists clenched. He'd rip the attacker apart, one limb at a time. No one messed with his family.

"No one," he whispered.

Chapter 7

Charlie woke with a start and stared into the darkness. She'd had a dream about someone chasing her through the rooms of the library next door. He'd almost captured her, when she'd forced herself to wake.

Her heart thundered against her ribs and perspiration beaded on her forehead. A glance at the clock indicated she'd been asleep for four hours. She hadn't even heard when Lolly went to bed. That was a first in the six years she'd been a mother. Going to sleep before her daughter wasn't something she ever did. It was a testament to the trust she had in Ghost.

Which reminded her. Though she trusted him to keep her and her daughter safe through the night, she shouldn't trust him with her heart. She wasn't sure she would survive a second time around of a broken heart.

Shoving aside the covers she got out of bed and padded barefoot down the hallway to Lolly's bedroom.

Her daughter lay curled on her side, an arm wrapped

around her favorite teddy bear and sleeping peacefully with a smile curling her lips. A few books lay on the nightstand beside her bed.

Charlie smiled, imagining Ghost reading them to her daughter. She'd have him reading more than that if he let her talk him into it.

Tucking the blanket around Lolly's chin, she bent to kiss her daughter's cheek.

Lolly rolled over and whispered, "I love you, Mr. Caspar."

Charlie's breath caught at the constriction in her throat. Her daughter was already falling in love with the man who'd broken Charlie's heart seven years ago. Would Lolly's little heart be broken as well when Ghost left to return to his SEAL team?

On silent feet, she tiptoed down the hallway where she peered into the living room.

Ghost lay in the lounge chair, shirtless, wearing boxer shorts and nothing else. He leaned back, his arms crossed over his chest, his eyes closed and his breathing deep and regular. Asleep.

Charlie took the opportunity to drink her fill of him, studying his face, chest, arms and thick, muscular thighs. How she wished she could go to him, straddle his waist and press her hot center to him. She had yet to find another pair of panties. She wondered what he'd done with the ones he'd taken.

That he wanted to keep them must mean something. But what? That he wanted to make love to her? She had no doubt about that. When he'd held her close, the ridge beneath his jeans had been firm and insistent, pressing against her belly.

Warmth spread through her body, igniting the flames at her center. She burned uncontrollably, want-

ing the man more than she'd wanted anyone or anything in her life. If she gave in to her carnal lust, he
wouldn't resist. Hell, he'd welcome her with the same
level of passion. Their sex life had never been the problem between them.

Yeah, Charlie had told Ghost she didn't care if a relationship with him was only temporary. But that had
been before she'd discovered she was in love with him.
When he'd left, she'd held it together until that night
when she'd been alone in her bed. Then she'd cried.
And cried some more. Two weeks later, she was crying even harder when she discovered she'd missed her
period and the early pregnancy test proved positive.

Seven years ago, she'd given her heart to this man.
And based on the way she felt at that moment, she still
loved him. If not as much, then even more.

Her eyes stinging, Charlie backed away from the
living room and escaped into the kitchen. She peered
through the curtain over the window on the back door.
Moonlight shone onto the porch, bathing everything
in a dark blue glow.

The ketchup had been cleaned off the wooden planks.
She'd have to thank Ghost in the morning. It was one
fewer thing she had to face on her own. Though the
message was gone, it remained seared into her mind.

Unable to face going back to her lonely bed, Charlie tiptoed into her office, half closing the door. She
booted her computer and went to work, trying to find
the man responsible for the attack on Rebecca and the
ketchup message on her back porch. The threats had
to stop. Both to herself and to whatever government
facility he had in mind by his call to arms.

She returned to the site with the entries from people
who had legitimate gripes with the way they'd been

treated by local and national authorities. One by one, she followed each posting, tracking them back to their own social media pages. Each had pictures of their families posted. These were real people with loved ones. All they wanted was to be treated fairly. They were all upset about the confiscation of LeRoy Vanders's herd, wanting the authorities to return the man's animals as they were his livelihood. If he couldn't get them back, he wouldn't have the means to provide for his family. He'd posted, You might as well shoot me now. I'm worth more to my family dead than alive.

She followed LeRoy to his page. There he had posted messages from Bible scripture, praying for a peaceful resolution to the current crisis. It didn't sound like a man crazy enough to threaten someone for spying on his messages.

But then Charlie didn't know what set a man like that off. If desperate enough, he might go off the deep end and come out fighting.

She tried scanning the internet for other terrorist threats that could be tied to the state of Wyoming. At one point she found a message from a man claiming to be a member of ISIS. His threat was to all American infidels. He was coming. Be prepared to convert or die.

A shiver rippled across her as she stared into the eyes of a man who looked like he could kill without it impacting him in the least. His brown eyes had that intense crazy look that burned into her, even from a computer screen.

Charlie pushed her chair away from the monitor and keyboard. She stood, stretched and walked to the window overlooking the street in front of her house. Moonlight streamed through the window, bathing her in its pale, blue glow.

Why did something so beautiful three nights ago seem so sinister now? She'd always loved nighttime in Wyoming. She'd loved staring up at the stars with her father, identifying constellations and planets.

The night she'd spent in the back of Ghost's pickup, they'd had fun naming different stars as if they were the scientists who'd discovered them. They laughed and rolled into each other's arms. A kiss led to a caress. The caress moved from outside their clothes to bare skin. Soon, they were naked, bathed in starlight, making love.

Charlie wrapped her arms around her middle and sighed. Why couldn't things have remained the same? That had been their last night together. The next day, he'd driven to his new assignment in California and she'd stayed in Wyoming, nursing a broken heart.

She raised her hand to push her hair back from her forehead.

Seven years later, he was in her living room, wearing nothing but boxer shorts, sexier than ever, and she was staring out at the night sky wishing for something that would only bring her more heartache.

"Hey." Ghost's voice echoed in her head, like a memory she couldn't forget. Why had she never been able to forget him? Why couldn't she ignore him now?

"Charlie, darlin'." That voice again, made the ache in her belly grow.

Big hands descended on her arms, turning her to face the man she'd never stopped loving.

Ghost had remained in the doorway to Charlie's office for a long time before he'd made a sound.

She'd stood by the window, her body swathed in a

pale glow turning her into an ethereal blue image of lush, unaffected beauty.

She was sexy, but appeared sad, staring out into the darkness. He wanted to tell her to step away from the window in case someone decided to take a shot at her. As still as she was, she'd make an easy target.

When she raised her arm to push her hair back the moonlight shone through the thin fabric of her nightgown, exposing the silhouette of her naked body beneath.

His breath lodged in his lungs, or he would have moaned aloud. Every cell in his body burned for her. His pulse sped through his veins carrying red-hot blood angling south to his groin. He had to have her, to hold her in his arms. To feel her skin against his.

"Hey," he managed to say.

When she didn't turn to face him, he eased into the room. Perhaps she'd been sleepwalking and wasn't hearing him through her dream.

"Charlie, darlin'," he whispered. Gripping her arms, he turned her toward him.

She glanced up at him, recognition in her gaze and something else. Longing. Pure, unrestricted passion.

Charlie pressed her hands to his chest and slid them up to lock around the back of his neck. Then she stood on her toes, pulling his head down to hers. "Call me all kinds of a fool, for making the same mistake twice, but I want you."

"If wanting you is a mistake, I don't care what you call me. Just let me have you for a moment," he said, drawing her into his arms. He wrapped his hands around her waist and pressed her hips against his. His erection swelled, pressing into her belly, when he'd rather be pressing it into her.

He claimed her mouth in a long, hard kiss. When he traced the seam of her lips, she opened to him, meeting his tongue with hers in a twisting tangle of urgency.

She drew her arms down his chest and around to his backside, sliding her fingers beneath the elastic of his boxers. Slim, warm hands cupped his buttocks and squeezed gently.

He broke the kiss, dragging in a deep breath, barely able to hold back, when wave after wave of lust washed over him, urging him to take her now. In the office, on the desk, against the wall. Anywhere he could get inside her. Now.

He bunched her nightgown in his hands, pulling it up over her bottom and groaned.

She hadn't found another pair of panties. Her sex was bared to him, there for the taking.

Ghost slid his hands down the backs of her thighs and lifted her, wrapping her legs around his waist.

She locked her ankles behind him and captured his face between her palms. "This is for now. Nothing has changed between us. Don't expect anything from me tomorrow."

His heart tightened in his chest. He understood why she said these things. She didn't trust him. Didn't expect him to stay and she had to guard her heart and Lolly's from the hurt she expected him to inflict when he left.

He knew all of this as the truth, but he couldn't stop. He had to have her. He'd work on the trust later. When he wasn't consumed by his need to feel her against him. The need to lose himself inside her.

He carried her down the hallway to her bedroom, careful not to make enough noise that would wake the little one. Once inside, he pushed the door half-closed with his foot and carried Charlie to the bed. "Protection?"

"I'm on birth control and I'm clean."

"I'm clean, too."

She kissed his lips and whispered against his mouth, "Then what are you waiting for?"

He sat her on the edge of the bed, grabbed the hem of her nightgown and pulled it slowly over her head.

She raised her arms to accommodate the removal of her only garment. Charlie leaned back on her elbow in the glow of a night-light and spread her knees wide. She ran one hand down her belly to the triangle of curls covering her sex and threaded her fingers through them. She tipped her head toward his boxers. "Are you going to wear those all night?"

"Oh, hell no." Ghost shucked the shorts and stood before her, his shaft jutting out, his body on fire for her. His first inclination was to take her, hard and fast, to thrust deep inside her glistening entrance. But he didn't want to scare her away. He wanted her to know the depth of need and passion he was experiencing. Hell, he wanted to bring her to the very edge and make her beg for him to take her.

Ghost dropped to his knees in front of her and draped her legs over his shoulders.

Her eyes widened and her breathing became more labored. She threaded her fingers through the fluff of hair over her sex to the folds beneath.

Ghost stroked her hand and her fingers and brushed them aside to take over. He parted her folds, exposing the narrow strip of flesh between. Leaning in, he flicked her with the tip of his tongue.

She moved her hands, weaving them into his hair, while digging her heels into his back, urging him to continue.

He tongued her again, this time swirling around,

laving until she pulled on his hair, a moan rising from her throat.

Ghost remembered how she had given herself to him so completely when they were younger, yelling out his name in the throes of their shared passion. He wanted to capture that same sense of abandon.

While his tongue took control of her nubbin, he thrust one of his fingers into her slick channel, reveling in how wet she already was, knowing it would ease him inside her soon. He added a second finger in with the first and stretched her, feeling her muscles contract, gripping his fingers.

Teasing and tasting, he licked, swirled and flicked that amazing bundle of nerves that made her crazy with desire.

And she responded by raising her hips, pumping them upward, pulling on his hair to keep him focused on her pleasure.

He didn't need the encouragement. Making her come apart was his goal. If he read her right, she was nearing her climax.

Charlie's body tensed, her heels dug into his back and she thrust her hips upward.

Ghost didn't relent, continuing his frenzied assault until he stormed past her resistance.

Charlie's fingers curled into his scalp and she cried out softly, "Ghost!" as she gave in with abandon, her body shaking with her release.

Ghost continued to stroke her with his fingers and tongue, slowing the movement as she relaxed and sank back to the mattress.

"Oh, my," she said, her head tossing from side to side. "I didn't know it could be even better than before."

Ghost chuckled and scooted her up farther on the

bed. He lay beside her, his hand cupping her sex, his shaft throbbing with his need. He wanted her to be sure.

She finally looked into his eyes, her own narrowing. "Why did you stop?"

"I want you to be sure."

"Sweet heaven. I've never been more sure." She dragged him over her, parted her legs and let him slide between them. "Please. Don't make me wait another minute."

Releasing a long breath, he eased up to her entrance, dipping in slowly. "Tell me to stop and I will."

"Don't you dare." She raised her legs, clamped them around his waist and dug her heels into his buttocks, urging him to take her. "I want you. All of you. Inside me. Now."

Unable to hold back another second, he drove into her, thrusting all the way until he was completely encased in her slick, tight wetness.

He bent to kiss her, taking her tongue with his as he moved out and back into her. Slowly at first, then faster and faster until he pumped in and out of her like a piston in an engine.

The faster he went, the harder he got, the tension building, pushing him to the edge. One. Last. Thrust. And he shot into the stratosphere, spiraling to the stars, his body exploding with electric shocks that spread through him from his shaft to the very tips of his fingers. He dropped down on her, still buried deep inside and held steady until his shaft stopped throbbing and he could breathe normally again.

At long last, he rolled to his side and pulled her with him, curling her up against his body.

Charlie laid her cheek against his chest and chuckled. "Your heart is racing."

"You do that to me."

She sighed and circled her fingers around his hard, brown nipple. "I'd say I could get used to this, but I can't."

"Can't, or won't?"

"Does it matter?" she whispered. "You're here today. But you'll be gone soon."

"What if I come back?"

"In another seven years?" She snorted and shook her head.

"How about in a couple of months?"

"Would it be fair to Lolly?"

He thought about it. "I want to know my daughter. I want to watch her grow."

"You can't do that if you aren't here."

He knew what she said was true. But lots of SEALs had families willing to be there when they got home.

"Charlie, I want you—"

She pressed a finger to his lips. "Shh. I just want to hold you for tonight. We don't have to talk. In fact, I'd rather not ruin what we shared with words we might regret."

Ghost clamped his teeth down on his tongue, wanting to say more, wanting to force her into some kind of commitment, but he didn't want her to kick him out of her bed. For that night, he would shut up and hold her. Tomorrow, they'd have to make time to talk. They had too much at stake to remain silent for long.

Chapter 8

Charlie lay in the warmth of Ghost's arms, listening to the beat of his heart. This was where she'd always wanted to be. She didn't want the night to end. For a long time, she lay awake, until her eyes closed and she drifted into sleep.

A sharp ringing sound jerked her out of a lovely dream, jarring her awake. She sat up, thinking it was the smoke alarm. When it stopped and then rang again, she realized it was the phone on the other side of the bed.

Ghost grabbed the phone from the cradle and handed it to her.

She took it, almost afraid to answer. "Hello," Charlie said, her voice hoarse with sleep.

"Ms. McClain, Hack here. You wanted me to call when we got a hit on the IP address."

Charlie sat up straighter, pushing the fog of sleep out of her head. "Whose is it?"

"We traced it back to a man who died several months ago, but I have one of our guys headed out to the physical address. Apparently it's local. I thought you'd want to know."

"I do. Is that all?"

"So far. I'm still tracking some of the people in that chat room. When I have more, I'll let you know."

"Thank you." She handed the phone to Ghost and he set it back on the charger.

"They're sending someone out to the physical address associated with the IP address," she said, draping her arm over her eyes.

Ghost rose up on his elbow and stared down at her. "Whose was it?"

She moved her arm and stared up into his eyes, her own narrowing. "That's the strange part. Hack said it was registered to a dead man."

"A what?" He brushed a strand of her hair from her face, tucking it behind her ear.

She leaned into his hand and kissed his palm. "Someone who'd died several months ago."

Ghost bent to kiss her forehead. "I would like to know if he died of natural causes, or if he was murdered." Then he kissed her nose.

Charlie closed her eyes, loving the feel of his lips on her skin, while blocking the thought of someone who might have been murdered for his connection to an IP address. She opened her eyes. "What time is it?"

Ghost leaned back to glance at the clock on the nightstand. "Nearly seven o'clock."

Her heart leaped. "Lolly will be up any minute." She shoved against his chest. "You have to get out of here."

"Why?"

"She's super curious and asks a lot of questions. Frankly, I'm not prepared to answer any about you."

"Like, 'Mommy, why are you in bed with Mr. Caspar? And why are you naked?'" He lowered the sheet and tweaked the tip of her nipple.

Her core responded with an answering ache. But she couldn't allow herself to go for round two with the chance of Lolly running in and jumping into the bed, like she did so often. As much as she would have liked to see his tweak and raise it to a much more satisfying conclusion, she didn't feel like facing a lot of questions from her daughter.

"Out." She rolled away and shot out of the bed.

Ghost got up and stretched, his body naked in the light peeking around the edges of the curtains. God, he was gorgeous.

A sound from the room down the hallway made her race to her closet, grab the first pair of jeans she could find and jam her legs into them. "For the love of Mike, cover yourself," she hissed. "Lolly's awake."

Ghost grabbed his boxers from the floor and slipped them up his thighs.

Charlie pulled a sweatshirt over her head and ran for the door. "I'll distract her while you find more clothes."

His laughter followed her out the door and down the hallway to Lolly's room.

Her chest swelled with an unbidden joy at the sound. The joy faded when she thought about the end of the week and his ultimate departure. She wasn't certain her heart could take the pain again. Refusing to think that far ahead, she entered Lolly's room and found her standing by the bed, pushing her bright auburn hair out of her face. "I'm hungry," she said.

"Let's get you dressed and then you can help me fix

breakfast." Charlie spun her daughter away from the door and walked her over to her dresser.

As Charlie helped Lolly choose an outfit, out of the corner of her eye, she saw Ghost pass by in the hallway, with a big grin and a little wave.

When Lolly was dressed in a hot pink shirt, jeans and her pink cowboy boots, she was hard to hold back.

Charlie stepped out of her way, hoping Ghost was completely dressed and presentable. Apparently he was, because she heard Lolly in the kitchen talking to him.

With a few minutes to herself, Charlie washed her face, brushed her hair and her teeth and dressed in something more attractive than jeans and a bulky sweatshirt. Feeling a little more put together in dark jeans, a white blouse and her cowboy boots, her curly hair secured behind her head in a barrette, she entered the kitchen to find Ghost and Lolly waiting for her, the stove cold, the kitchen table empty.

"We're going to have breakfast at the tavern," Lolly said, grinning.

"We are?" Charlie's gaze met Ghost's, her brows rising.

"We are. My treat," he said. "Shall we go?" He took Lolly's hand in his and cupped Charlie's elbow.

"Actually, it sounds good." She hadn't treated herself or Lolly to a breakfast out in a very long time. Eating at a fast-food restaurant in Bozeman on her way to drop Lolly at the daycare didn't count.

Ghost insisted on taking his truck, moving Lolly's booster seat into the back center seat of the crew cab. Lolly liked being high above the ground, claiming she could see everything.

Charlie climbed into the passenger seat and waited

for Ghost to slip into the driver's side and start the engine. "Anything else from Kevin?"

He shook his head. "No."

"We could stop by there on the way home, if you like."

With a nod, he reversed, turned around and headed down the road to the tavern.

Since it was early on a regular workday, the tavern parking lot was full, with vehicles lining the street, as well.

Charlie suspected they might not get a table as full as it was. But once inside, they waited for only ten minutes before they were seated in a booth near the door.

"Hi, Charlie." Lisa Lambert, a young, bleach-blonde waitress, set a cup in front of Ghost, one in front of Charlie and poured coffee into both. She winked at Lolly. "Juice or chocolate milk?" she asked.

Lolly rocked in her seat. "Chocolate milk!"

After Lisa left, Charlie tried to focus on the menu, when she'd rather stare at the man she'd made love to the night before. When the waitress returned with Lolly's chocolate milk, Charlie still didn't know what she wanted to eat.

"We don't see you in here for breakfast often, Charlie. Who's your fella?"

Charlie's face heated. "He's not—"

Ghost stuck out his hand and smiled at Lisa. "Jon Caspar. Nice to meet you." He leaned close to read her nametag. "Lisa, is it?"

She shook his hand, blushing. "That's right. You must be new in town. I know I'd remember you, if I'd seen you around."

"I'm not actually. But I'm so much older than you, you wouldn't remember me. I'm back in town for a visit." He reached across the table and laid his hand over Charlie's. "Charlie was good enough to put me up for the week."

"Are you thinking of moving back?" Lisa asked, taking a pad and pen out of her apron pocket.

Charlie's breath caught in her throat and she leaned forward, wanting to hear his answer, even though she knew he was putting on a show for Lisa.

He gave Lisa a friendly smile. "I don't know yet. It depends on the job."

"We're ready to order," Charlie interrupted.

"Oh, right." Lisa pressed her pen to the tablet. "What would you like?"

They placed their orders and Lisa left, her cheeks flushed with color from the smile Ghost gave her before she turned away.

Charlie wanted to smack the grin right off his face. She'd slept with him the night before. How could he flirt with the waitress in front of her?

"Nice one, that Lisa," he said, with a smile playing around his lips. "Why don't I know her?"

Charlie's lips thinned. "Because she was practically in diapers when you were in high school."

He cocked his brows. "Jealous?"

"Not in the least. She's barely out of high school. What use would you have with her? She's not much older than Lolly."

Lolly glanced up from her chocolate milk, her gaze curious.

Ghost's smile faded. "Okay, I'll behave myself, if you'll stop being so serious. Deal?" He held out his hand.

Charlie took his, knowing as soon as they touched, she'd feel that electric shock running through her body. And there it was, searing a path straight to her heart. "Deal."

* * *

Ghost didn't know why he'd flirted with the young waitress. He supposed he wanted to get a reaction out of Charlie when she was holding him at arm's length that morning.

He didn't let go of her hand immediately, staring across the table at her. "Just to set the record straight, you're the only woman who interests me."

"For now," Charlie added, trying to pull her hand from his.

He held tight, refusing to release her yet. "For always."

"Please." She finally freed her hand and placed it in her lap, out of his reach. "I find that hard to believe when you haven't been back for seven years."

She was right. He'd tried to forget her in those seven years, but he'd been unsuccessful. The intensity of his training and deployments had made the time seem to fly. But always in the back of his mind, she was what kept him sane and focused.

The tavern door opened behind Charlie.

Ghost glanced up, his gaze taking in the newcomers entering.

Charlie turned in her seat.

A man in a law enforcement uniform and a woman who appeared to be his wife stepped through the door. They waved at the man behind the counter and were shown to a seat at a table beside Charlie and Ghost's.

Charlie smiled at the man. "Good morning, Sheriff and Mrs. Scott."

The woman smiled. "Good morning, Charlie, Lolly. It's always a pleasure to see you two." She turned to include Ghost in her smile and greeting. "And you are?"

The sheriff nodded, his gaze narrowing on Ghost. "Aren't you Tom Caspar's son?"

Ghost nodded and reached across to shake the sheriff's hand. "Tom is my father."

"Used to be the foreman out at the Dry Gulch Ranch, wasn't he?" the sheriff asked.

"That was him," Ghost said.

"How's he doing down in Florida?"

Ghost grinned. "They love that they haven't had to shovel one scoop of snow since they moved."

The sheriff smiled, nodding. "That's good. Thinking about taking Fran down there for a vacation to see if it's something we'd like for our retirement."

"You should visit my folks," Ghost said. "I'm sure they'd love to see you."

"Might do that." The sheriff turned his attention to the menu.

Lisa returned with three plates of food, setting them in front of Charlie, Ghost and Lolly. "Enjoy," she said and walked away.

The door behind Charlie swung open again with a bang that shook the booth they were sitting in.

Ghost frowned, his gaze following the man who'd entered. He thought he recognized him. His father had met with him on more than one occasion to discuss trading bulls. He'd called him Vanders.

"Sheriff Scott, what are you going to do about the cattle thieves who stole my herd?" the man shouted.

Charlie spun in her seat. "LeRoy?"

He ignored her, his attention on the sheriff. LeRoy Vanders stomped toward the section where the sheriff and his wife sat. He planted his fist on the table and glared at the man.

"LeRoy, we've been over this. You signed on to

graze your herd on government property. You read the contract. So, they raised the rates. The contract you signed gives them the right. And it's still cheaper than leasing private property." Sheriff Scott tilted his chin up and narrowed his eyes. "Pay your fees and I'll bet they'll give back your herd."

"My family has been grazing our cattle on that land for over a century. As far as I'm concerned, the government stole that land and is extorting money from me." He pounded his fist on the table.

"What do you expect me to do, LeRoy? You have to take it up with the Bureau of Land Management."

"I expect you to arrest the rustlers who stole my cattle." LeRoy's voice rose. "I was due to take them to the sale. That's the money I use to feed my family and heat my house through the winter. How am I supposed to make do until spring without that money?"

"I can't help you. You have to pay your fees." The sheriff started to rise.

LeRoy pushed him back into his seat and pulled a gun from beneath his jacket.

Mrs. Scott screamed.

Charlie gasped and used her body to block any stray bullets from hitting Lolly.

LeRoy pointed the gun in the air. "I'm tired of being pushed around on my own land. I'm tired of the government taking what belongs to me. I'm tired of the law protecting the criminals and not me and my family."

Ghost eased out of his seat, keeping low, staying out of LeRoy's peripheral vision. He didn't want to startle the man into pulling the trigger. At the angle he was currently holding the gun, LeRoy would put a sizable hole in Ghost if he fired the weapon.

"LeRoy, put down the gun and discuss this like a reasonable man."

"I'll show you reasonable," LeRoy said. Before LeRoy could pull the trigger, Ghost grabbed the man's hand, jerked it into the air and yanked the gun from his grip. Then he twisted the rancher's arm up behind his back.

"Let go of me, damn you!" LeRoy shouted. "Mind your own business. This discussion is between me and the sheriff."

Ghost leaned close to LeRoy's ear. "This discussion stopped being just your business when you pulled the gun." Ghost nodded toward the sheriff. "You want to take him away, or should I?"

A young sheriff's deputy burst through the door. "Got a call from dispatch. Where's the perpetrator?"

The sheriff shook his head. "Over here, Matthews."

Matthews hurried to where Ghost held Mr. Vanders immobile. He snapped the cuffs on the man's wrists and led him toward the exit.

Vanders twisted out of Matthews's grip. "This isn't over by a long shot, Sheriff. I'm not the only one angry about what's going on. You just wait. This isn't the last you'll be hearing from us." He glared at Ghost and Charlie. "And we don't take kindly to interference."

Matthews hooked LeRoy's arm and dragged him out of the door.

Ghost waited until the man was out of the building before he relaxed.

Sheriff Scott held out his hand. "I'll take that. It's evidence."

Ghost gladly handed over the gun.

"Thank you for taking charge," the sheriff said. "I never would have thought Vanders would pull a gun on me. He used to be a reasonable man." He touched his hand to his wife's shoulder. "Are you okay?"

She nodded.

The sheriff sighed. "I'm thinking Florida is looking pretty good about now. How about you, dear?"

Fran pressed a hand to her chest, her face pale, her eyes worried. "People are getting crazy around here. I've never seen them so mad about so much."

A man rose from the table behind the sheriff and shook Sheriff Scott's hand. "You handled that well, Sheriff."

The sheriff frowned. "Should I know you?"

The man smiled. "Randall Gaither. I work with the Apex Pipeline Authority. It's good to see local law enforcement enforcing the laws."

The sheriff's brows twisted. "Just doing my job. Now, if you'll excuse me, I'd like to have breakfast with my wife."

The man nodded. "Of course. Of course." He resumed his seat at the table on the other side of the sheriff and lifted his coffee cup.

Ghost took his seat and stared down at his plate for a moment before he raised his chin and met Charlie's gaze.

Charlie stared at him across the table. "You're as cool as a cucumber." She lifted her glass and her hand shook so much orange juice spilled onto the table. "And I'm shaking like a leaf. You were amazing."

He shrugged. "I was hungry. I figured I wouldn't get to eat my eggs while they were hot, if someone didn't shut him up." He winked at Lolly. "How are your Belgian waffles?"

And just like that, they continued their breakfast as if a man hadn't just pulled a gun in a public place. The less he made of the incident, the better they all were. For Lolly's sake, he didn't let on that he'd been almost as shaken as Charlie. A man had entered the tavern with a gun. He could have started shooting and hurt Charlie or Lolly.

Ghost couldn't let that happen. Wouldn't let it. Hopefully, their problem was solved by the arrest of LeRoy Vanders. Maybe now, they could relax and enjoy the rest of the week.

He shook his head. Nothing ever was that easy. Hadn't Vanders said he wasn't the only one unhappy about the current state of government in Wyoming? If he was right, he might have been only the tip of the iceberg.

The week ahead didn't look like it was going to be a picnic.

Chapter 9

"Is today Mother's Day Out?" Lolly asked as they left the tavern.

Charlie had barely been able to choke down her food. After all of the excitement, the patrons of the tavern had either gotten up to leave or stayed to gossip about LeRoy's tirade and Ghost's handling of the situation.

Lisa had been all over Ghost. Forney, the tavern owner, had offered to give them their meal for free.

Ghost had insisted they could pay and did so. He didn't look comfortable with the notoriety. As soon as Lolly finished her meal, he hurried them out the door.

Charlie nodded. "As a matter of fact, today is Mother's Day Out. Would you like to go play at the center?"

"Yes, please. Can I go?" Lolly danced around Charlie, her eyes wide, her hands pressed together. "Please?"

Charlie glanced over her head at Ghost. "Think it would be okay?"

"Are they inside much of the day?"

"They have arts and crafts and play games in the center."

"It should be okay. We can give the teacher a heads-up to be watchful."

Charlie stared down at her daughter and sighed. The threats had been against her, not her daughter. With LeRoy detained, perhaps the problem had been solved. "Okay," she said to Lolly. "You can go for a couple of hours." It would give her time to meet with Kevin and his computer guy to see if they had anything more to tell them. She was anxious to hear what they found at the address Caveman was supposed to check out that morning.

"Do you remember where the community center is?"

Ghost nodded. "I think so."

"That's where they have the Mother's Day Out. Lolly goes three times a week to play with her friends during the summer." She started to help Lolly up into the truck, but Ghost nudged her aside.

He lifted Lolly, settled her into the booster seat and buckled the seat belt around her.

When he rounded the truck to hold the door for Charlie, he whispered in her ear. "Are you sure it's a good idea to leave her at the daycare?"

"The threats were against me," Charlie said. "Not Lolly. And she so looks forward to going. I hate to disappoint her." Though she'd had the same misgivings. "How about we let her stay long enough for us to do some digging here in town? We won't be far, if anything happens."

He nodded. "Okay." Ghost helped her up into the truck and climbed into the driver's seat.

The community center was on the edge of town, with a wide, open field used for baseball, soccer and football practice. The center was a converted US Army Armory. The inside was a gymnasium with basketball hoops on either end of the open room. Back when the US Army National Guard occupied the building, they had used the gym for formations on bad weather days and for hip-pocket training in buddy care and field stripping their weapons.

Now the gym was used by locals for the occasional game of basketball and for the Mother's Day Out program, offering the community children a place to play with others their age.

As they drove up to the center, Ghost commented, "Looks better than when I used to come here."

Charlie smiled. "We recently had a Fix It Day. Everyone turned out to paint and do much-needed roof repairs."

"What's with the signs?" He pointed to a grouping of signs outside the center, indicating other businesses besides the community center.

"The city overhauled the old armory offices. The mayor and the county treasurer occupy two of them and the others were rented out to a real estate agent and an insurance salesman. They have access to the outside without going through the gymnasium where the kids play."

Charlie remembered spending a lot of time in the community center as she was growing up. From the annual Halloween parties and Christmas craft shows, to the Fall Festival dances. The community center had been a hub of social gatherings in the Grizzly Pass area.

Ghost parked and helped Lolly out of her seat.

The little girl ran toward the entrance, her face alight with excitement. She had to wait for Charlie to enter the pass code to open the outer door. But once inside, she ran through the front lobby straight into the gym.

Ghost and Charlie followed at a more sedate pace.

Inside, a dozen children were playing four square on the wooden floor of the gymnasium, their shouts echoing off the walls.

Charlie found the woman who ran the Mother's Day Out, her friend from high school, Brenda Larson.

Brenda pushed a stray strand of hair out of her face and smiled as she weaved through a couple of smaller children to where Charlie and Ghost stood. "Charlie, I'm so glad Lolly was able to come today. Ashley and Chelsea missed her yesterday."

After hugging Charlie, Brenda stood back, her gaze raking over Ghost. She tipped her head, her eyes narrowing. "You look familiar…" Then her face lit. "Jon? Jon Caspar?" She flung her arms around him and hugged his as tightly as she'd hugged Charlie. "You look so much larger than life. You were all buff when you came through several years ago, but look at you." She stood back and ran her gaze over him again. "I barely recognized you. When did you get back in town?"

"Yesterday," he said. "It's good to see you, Brenda."

"What a wonderful surprise." She glanced from Charlie to Ghost and back. "Any special reason you're here?" She paused.

Heat rose up Charlie's neck into her cheeks. "No. Not really. He's here on leave."

Brenda's brows rose again. "Your parents moved south several years ago. I would think you would vacation in Florida with them."

Ghost shrugged. "I haven't been back here in a while. It's nice to be here and explore all of my old stomping grounds."

"I'm sure." Brenda's lips curled up on the corners. "Where are you staying?"

Charlie wasn't up for answering her friend's questions with Ghost standing beside her. "I'm only leaving Lolly for a couple of hours while I run some errands."

Brenda crossed her arms over her chest and nodded. "I see how it is. Ignore the questions and maybe she'll stop asking." She winked at Ghost. "Have it your way." She turned toward the kids. "We're making sock puppets today. I think Lolly will enjoy that. Don't forget we're going on a field trip tomorrow to the Yellowstone Nature Center. You won't want Lolly to miss that. We were able to get an educational grant from the state to fund the bus and the snacks for the trip. If you want to come and help supervise, I'd gladly take all the help I can get."

Charlie frowned. "I'd forgotten that was tomorrow. Lolly's been looking forward to the trip all summer."

"Have her here a few minutes early." Brenda touched her arm. "And don't worry if you can't come along. I know you work from home and it's hard to get away sometimes."

Charlie took Brenda's hand. "About Lolly. Could you keep an extra special close eye on her?"

Brenda glanced toward the happy child, bouncing a ball with three other little girls. "Is she not feeling well?"

Charlie explained the situation with the threats. "I don't know if she'll become a target because of my meddling."

"Wow." Brenda squeezed her hand. "I'm sorry to

hear this is happening to you. I'll be sure to keep her close. We don't plan on leaving the building until after lunch."

"I'll be sure to get her before then."

Brenda's lips twisted as she stared at the little girls. "She'll be disappointed that she won't get to go out on the play set with her pals." Charlie's friend turned back to the adults. "But I understand completely. I'd be leery, as well."

"Thank you, Brenda." Charlie touched her friend's arm.

"We should get together for a girl's night out in Bozeman sometime soon."

"I could use a break," Charlie agreed. "When this mess clears, you're on."

Brenda smiled. "You sure tall, dark and hunky won't mind?"

Charlie glanced up at Ghost. He wouldn't be around when that time came around.

"Whatever makes Charlie happy," Ghost said. His gaze met hers and held it for a long time.

A flash of hope filled Charlie's chest. If Ghost really believed that sentiment, he'd stay in Grizzly Pass with her and Lolly and give up his life with the Navy SEALs. But as much as he loved the path he'd chosen, the likelihood of him leaving it behind was slim to nada.

"Come on, we have some things to check on. And I really do have a job I need to work on. My boss is patient, but he likes it when I meet my project deadlines."

After one last glance in Lolly's direction, Charlie turned toward the door.

Ghost hooked her elbow and walked with her.

The familiarity of his grip on her arm gave her comfort at the same time as it fanned the smoldering embers burning inside. If they didn't have bigger problems to solve, she'd have him take her back to her house to make love to her until it was time to pick up Lolly.

And if wishes were horses…

He handed her up into his truck and closed the door. Then he rounded to the driver's side and climbed in behind the steering wheel. "Where to?"

The first word on the tip of her tongue was *Home*. But she tamped down the urge and answered, "Kevin's. I want to know what they've come up with."

Ghost drove back to the Blue Moose Tavern and parked in back of the building. Because it was broad daylight, he sent Charlie up first and followed, shortly after.

Garner answered on the first knock. "Come in. I'm glad you stopped by. And, by the way, thank you for disarming LeRoy before he shot through the ceiling and hit one of us or the computers."

Caveman rose from a chair beside Hack's and held out his hand.

Ghost shook it and nodded toward the computer screens. "Find anything at the physical address for the IP address?"

The D-Force man stretched and shook his head. "Nobody there, only a server and a satellite internet setup. What I gather from the neighbor a half a mile away is that Old Man Huddleston died in his sleep and no one found him until he'd stopped picking up his mail for two weeks."

Garner continued the story. "The mailman notified the sheriff who checked on him and found him in his lounge chair, dead. No one turned off the electricity or gas to the place and someone has been mailing in the payments with cashier's checks."

"The satellite internet is a hack job. Someone with a little know-how is tapped into several satellites. No subscription or paid service."

"Seems like a lot of trouble to keep a social media site up and running."

"And anonymous," Hack said.

"After the demonstration yesterday, I ran into Vanders's wife at the grocery store. She was stocking up on pantry staples, as if she was getting ready for a big snowstorm. I asked her if she'd seen the internet reports about the demonstration. She laughed and said she rarely looked at their computer and didn't know how to use it, anyway."

"That rules out Vanders's wife, but not Vanders himself as the one who'd been leaving threats with Charlie."

"You would think he would have singled me out more at the tavern, if he was angry with me," Charlie pointed out.

"We're still researching Don Sweeney. There's not much on him."

Caveman nodded. "He was the other name I came out of the demonstration with. He's younger and likes to hear himself get loud. He might be in his late twenties. I imagine he knows a little about the internet. Most kids under thirty have been exposed to computers and the internet. Hell, most of them can run circles around me."

Hack turned to face the others. "I found his name on a list of recent layoffs from the Apex Pipeline Authority. I traced him through state birth records. He's the son of a local cattle rancher, Raymond Sweeney, who fell on hard times and had to sell several hundred acres to pay for his wife's cancer treatments. Apparently Don wanted to work on the ranch but had to take a job with the pipeline as soon as he left high school. His mother died last year. Don was laid off this year when the oil prices plummeted."

Ghost narrowed his eyes. "Has he had any run-ins with the law?"

"He had a DUI when he was nineteen, right after his brother died in a farming accident," Hack said, "But other than that, nothing else showed up on his record."

"No tie-in between him and the server setup at the Huddleston place?" Charlie asked.

Caveman rubbed his fist into his opposite palm. "Want me to have a talk with the man?"

"Supposedly, he's up in Montana looking for work in Bozeman."

"Can you verify that?" Charlie asked.

"Already did. His credit card purchases are around the Bozeman area as late as this morning."

Charlie shook her head and drew in a deep breath. "I feel a need for more groceries."

"What?" Ghost shot a glance at her, wondering why the sudden urge to buy more food when she'd been to the store the day before.

A smile tilted Charlie's lips. "Mrs. Penders, one of the owners, is a notorious gossip. If anyone knows anything, she does."

"What are we waiting for?" Ghost turned toward the door.

"*I'm* going. Alone." She gave him a stern look. "She might clam up with both of us hitting her with questions."

Ghost frowned. "I don't like it when you're out by yourself."

"I've been managing on my own for years," she said.

Taking that punch to the gut, Ghost nodded. "Maybe so, but not with someone threatening your life."

"It's walking distance." She pressed her lips together for a moment before adding, "If you want to walk with me, you can." She held up her finger. "But you're *not* going in."

Caveman, Hack and Garner watched their interchange, their lips twisting.

Heat flooded Ghost's cheeks. He didn't like being told what to do. Still, Charlie didn't belong to him. He had no right to order her around. Even if he and Charlie were a thing, he wouldn't be able to control her. She had a mind of her own.

"She'll be okay," Garner reassured. "And you'll be right outside the store."

"Fine." He turned toward the door. "Let's go."

As they descended the stairs to the ground, Ghost worried. "I don't like leaving you unprotected."

"I'll be fine. I have my gun in my purse."

"You carry?"

"I have since before Lolly was born."

He stared at her. He'd taught her how to shoot a 9 millimeter pistol when he'd been back in town seven years ago. She'd been pretty good, even after only one lesson. "Do you practice?"

"Every chance I get. At the very least, I make it a point to go quarterly. I figure it's no use having a weapon if you don't know how to use it."

Ghost chuckled. "Okay. I feel a little better knowing you can defend yourself."

"And Lolly," she reminded him.

"And Lolly," he agreed. "But it doesn't hurt to have someone covering your six."

"Your six?"

"Navy speak for your six o'clock position," he said with a grin.

"Oh, you mean my back." She smiled. "I like it when you go all military on me. As long as you explain it to me. I don't know much about what you do."

His smile faded. "It's probably just as well. Most of it isn't pretty or something you write home about."

She touched his arm. "I hope someday you'll tell me about why you limp."

"That's easy." He shrugged. "Took shrapnel in my thigh."

She shivered. "You say that like it's no big deal."

"It happens in wartime situations."

"It must be hard to go into battle knowing you or some of your friends might not come out alive."

"Not as hard as thinking about the ones we leave behind. Most SEALs aren't worried about themselves."

"They're worried about their families," she said, finishing his thought. "Is that why you pushed me away when you were setting off for your first assignment as a SEAL?"

They walked along the sidewalk in front of the hardware store, their pace slowing as they neared Penders Grocery.

"I knew what I was getting into would be difficult. I couldn't ask you to wait for me. I'd already heard too many stories about SEALs' wives and girlfriends leaving them when they were on deployment. Some came back to an empty house. Others came back to find other men had taken up residence in their beds."

She stopped short, her hands going to her hips. "And you thought I would do that?"

"No. But other women cracked under the pressure of waiting, not knowing if their men were coming back alive or in a body bag."

"So you decided to spare me the pain?"

He nodded.

"Without giving me the choice." She stared at him a moment longer.

Ghost had left her, convinced he was doing the right thing by letting her live her life without the worry of losing him. Looking at the color in her cheeks, the anger blazing from her eyes, he decided he might have been wrong.

They'd arrived in front of the grocery store.

"Are you sure you don't want me to go in with you? I can keep my distance while you're talking to Mrs. Penders."

She dropped her hands from her hips, inhaled and exhaled before she responded. "I'm quite capable of taking care of myself, and making my own decisions. And have you ever considered that you might need someone back home to cover your six? To be there when you get back and to take care of you when you were wounded?"

He stiffened. "What if I'd lost my leg or an arm? Or hell—what if I came back a paraplegic?"

"You'd still be you where it counts." She touched his chest. "And Lolly would have had a father."

"Lolly has a father. And I want to be a part of her life."

Charlie nodded. "I was wrong to keep her from you, but now isn't the right time to break that to her. We have to figure out who the hell is stirring up trouble. When the dust settles, we'll figure out how to make sure you get to see her." She lifted her chin and stuck her hand out. "Deal?"

He took her hand in his and yanked hard enough to pull her off balance.

Charlie fell into his chest, her hand trapped between them.

"Deal." He pressed a kiss to her lips, taking her mouth with a searing-hot passion he hadn't felt since the last time they'd been together. Whatever happened with the stalker, Ghost refused to walk away from this woman ever again. It had taken him seven years to figure out what was wrong with him, why he felt like he was walking through life with a hole in his chest. He'd been missing a part of himself. The part that was Charlie.

He broke off the kiss, wanting to say so much to her, but the timing wasn't right. Somehow, it never felt right. "Go. Before I say to hell with it and take you back to your house and make crazy love to you."

She stared up at him, her tongue sweeping across her bottom lip. "And that's a bad idea?"

"When someone's after you and we don't know who it is?" He nodded. "Probably not a good idea. See if Mrs. Penders has anything to go on. Find out who has been having trouble besides Vanders."

She cupped his face with her palm. "After all of this, we need to talk."

"Damn right we do," he said. Then he turned her and gave her a gentle nudge toward the store entrance.

Chapter 10

"Charlie!" Mrs. Penders exclaimed.

Still reeling from Ghost's kiss, Charlie had barely entered the store when the older woman swept her into her arms and hugged her.

"I heard about what happened in the tavern with LeRoy." She stood back and stared at Charlie, running her gaze over her as if searching for injuries or blood. "You're not hurt, are you?"

"No, I'm fine. No bullets were fired. No blood was shed."

"I heard LeRoy went crazy with the sheriff and threatened to shoot him."

Charlie nodded, encouraging the woman to go on about the earlier tussle with the angry Mr. Vanders. "I can't get over how LeRoy behaved toward the sheriff."

"He's just the first rancher in the county to stand up to the law. The man has to be feeling pretty desperate. With his cattle confiscated, he has no way to support his family."

"He said there were others who felt the same. What did he mean by that?" Charlie asked. "Are there more people in the county struggling to make ends meet?"

"Oh, sweetie, there are so many."

"How could I not know this?"

"Most of them keep their troubles to themselves." Mrs. Penders leaned close. "But I hear things as they check out here at the grocery store."

Charlie almost felt guilty for prying into her neighbors' affairs. But it if helped to find Rebecca's attacker and her own stalker, then so be it. "What do you hear?"

"The Parkers are selling their prized, registered quarter horses to pay the mortgage on their place. Because of the increased fees per head of cattle, they aren't making enough off the sale of their steers to keep feeding all of their horses and pay the bills."

"Circle C quarter horses?" Charlie's stomach fell. "They've raised quarter horses for a century."

Mrs. Penders nodded. "I imagine Ryan's grandfather is turning over in his grave. And then there's Bryson Rausch."

"The richest man in the county? I remember his daughter driving a Cadillac convertible to high school. He's having trouble?"

Mrs. Penders nodded, glanced around at the store to make sure no one else was listening. "He bet on the wrong stock in the market and lost everything."

Mr. Rausch had always been very nice to Charlie when she'd run into him in town or at the county fair. Though she'd been envious of his daughter Sierra, she'd always liked Mr. and Mrs. Rausch and hated to know they were in financial trouble.

"Then there's Timothy Cramer," Mrs. Penders went on.

Charlie frowned. "Timothy?"

"Goes by Tim. You might have known his wife, Linnea."

"Oh, yes. Linnea." Her frown deepened. "Her second child died of SIDS not long ago."

Mrs. Penders nodded. "So tragic. It broke Linnea's heart and busted up their marriage."

"That's awful."

"Tim went on a drinking binge and disgraced himself with some floozy in Bozeman. Linnea tried to forgive him, but she couldn't. Not when he didn't even show up for the baby's funeral. She filed for divorce and took half of everything he owned. He's having to sell his grandmother's farm north of town because he can't afford to buy her out. And to add to his misery, he worked as an inspector for the pipeline and lost his job when he was caught falsifying reports.

"The Vanderses and the Parkers aren't the only ones hurting from the increase in range grazing fees. The Mathis family, the Herringtons, Saul Rutherford and the Greenways are all angry with the changes made by the Bureau of Land Management. They can't afford to pay the fees and they can't afford to lease private land. They'll end up selling their cattle at a loss and not having a way to support their families and pay their mortgages next year."

"I'm so sorry to hear that. It makes me sick to know so many are hurting."

"And some are more vocal than others. I wasn't surprised when I heard LeRoy was hauled off to jail. He was a powder keg set to go off. Thankfully someone stopped him from taking others down with him."

"Are there any others as angry and vocal as Mr. Vanders?" Charlie asked.

A customer walked into the store and waved at Mrs. Penders. She waved back and lowered her voice. "Oh, sure. Ernie Martin is angry because the government cut subsidies to his production of angora wool. He's been raising those goats for the past couple of years, making a killing and spending it as fast as he made it. But the money comes from the subsidies, not from the goats or the wool. Now that he's been cut off, he needs it more than ever to make payments on the second mortgage he took out to purchase all of those goats. Ernie's been madder than a hornet about losing the subsidies. He was forced to take a job with the pipeline company, but was laid off when the gas prices dropped. The poor man has had nothing but bad luck."

"Anyone else?" Charlie pushed, knowing she was running out of time with Mrs. Penders. As soon as her customer came to the counter, she'd be interrupted and remember she had a store to run and clean.

"Just about any of those folks who were tagged with bigger grazing right fees. None of them are happy. And they don't know where they'll get the money to pay the fees. Some of them have said they'll stand and defend their herds of cattle from being confiscated by the BLM. Some are willing to die." Mrs. Penders clucked her tongue. "I've never seen people so hot or determined."

"Mrs. Penders. Charlie, what are you ladies doing?" Linnea Cramer stepped up to the counter, carrying a quart of orange juice and carton of eggs. "You two look entirely too intense. What's going on?" Then her eyes widened. "Oh, wait. You have to be talking about the near-shooting at the tavern this morning. Is that it?"

Linnea leaned closer. "I heard that you were there when Vanders tried to shoot the sheriff. Someone said Jon Caspar was there and subdued the man. You weren't hurt, were you?"

Charlie smiled and shook her head. "I'm fine. I feel sorry for Mr. Vanders. He was not happy about his cattle being taken."

"We're all struggling a little from the economy tanking and the oil prices falling. People in this area don't have a lot of choices for jobs. That's why we lose so many young people to the bigger cities."

Mrs. Penders squeezed Charlie's hand. "I was so glad to see you come home to Grizzly Pass."

Charlie's eyes misted as she hugged the older woman. "Mrs. Penders, you're so sweet to say that." She moved away to allow Linnea to reach the counter with her purchases.

"I wish I could say I was happy to be in Grizzly Pass, but I'm not. As soon as my ex-husband sells his property, I'm free to go wherever I choose."

"And where will that be?" Mrs. Penders asked, adding Linnea's grocery items as they spoke.

"I think I'll move to Seattle. At least there I can go to the theater, visit a museum and see the ocean whenever I want."

"I thought you liked it here in Grizzly Pass," Mrs. Penders said.

Linnea's lips thinned. "I did. But things change." She shoved the items across the counter toward Mrs. Penders.

"Is this all?" the store owner asked.

"All I can afford for now," Linnea said.

Mrs. Penders placed the items into bags and counted out Linnea's change. "I hope things work out for you."

Charlie touched Linnea's arm. "I hope you find the happiness you're searching for."

"Me, too. And the same to you, Charlie. At least, in our daughters, we have someone to love, who loves us unconditionally. Count your blessings. I know I would." She gathered her bags and left the store in a hurry, her eyes suspiciously shiny.

"Poor woman. To lose her second baby and her husband all in less than six months. Thankfully, her first child keeps her grounded." Mrs. Penders transferred her gaze to Charlie. "Here I've been talking all this time. What did you come into the store to get?"

Charlie glanced at the clock on the wall. She'd been there the better part of half an hour. Already it was getting close to lunch and time to collect Lolly. She thought about everything happening in her community, the families falling apart, losing their homes and loved ones. All she wanted to do was gather hers closer. She couldn't wait until her parents were back from their river cruise in Europe. For now, she wanted to spend time with Lolly and Ghost. "I was wondering if you had something I could take out on a picnic. I'm feeling the need to spend time with my family."

Mrs. Penders smile spread across her face. "All of the gloom and doom talk getting to you? You're a smart woman to put your family first." She grabbed Charlie's hand and walked her to the bakery section of the store where she and her husband stocked the glass cases with fresh bread and pastries. "Let me make up some sandwiches and a tub of potato salad and baked beans for you to take with you."

While she waited, Charlie thought about all of the people she knew who had reason to be mad at the world, who might want to take it out on the government. Their list of suspects had grown from one or two to what felt like an entire town. Her heart ached for all of them. But it made it abundantly clear that she, as a mother, needed to focus on what was most important. Her family.

Ghost had found a bench in front of the hardware store and settled back to keep an eye on Penders Grocery. In the meantime, he watched as people passed in cars, trucks or on foot. Some stopped to say hello and renew acquaintances with Ghost, taking him for a short stroll down memory lane before they moved on to conduct their business or duck into the tavern for an early lunch.

He'd been there for five minutes when a man around his own age, stopped by and sat next to him. "Heard you were back in town." He held out his hand. "Tim Cramer. You might not remember me. I was a couple years ahead of you in school."

"I remember. You were our star quarterback. You helped the Grizzlies win state that year for the first time in nobody could remember how long."

Tim's lips turned upward on the corners. "That was a long time ago. Back when nothing could stop us." He stared out at Main Street. "What about you? What brings you back to this hellhole?"

"Felt like visiting the place I grew up," Ghost said.

Tim's lip lifted in a half smile bordering on a sneer. "Not someone in particular?"

Ghost shrugged. "Not really." Not at first, anyway. Now that he was there, he wanted to spend all of his time with Charlie and Lolly.

"Didn't you join the Navy?" Tim asked.

Ghost nodded.

Tim glanced his way. "What happened with that?"

"Injury sidelined me."

"Sorry to hear that." He leaned back again. "I hope you're not looking for a job. You'll have to get in line. Half the men in the county are unemployed or barely making it by."

"That's what I'm hearing," Ghost said. "They don't have to worry about me taking their jobs. I won't be here more than a week."

"Yeah, well, enjoy your vacation and tell Charlie hello. See ya around." Tim rose from the bench and walked away, his hands in his pockets.

Ghost remembered Tim as being a lot bigger. Or was it that Ghost had been a lot smaller, being three years behind him in high school? The man had been cordial and friendly, but something about him struck Ghost wrong. He tried to pinpoint it, but he couldn't. Soon Charlie emerged from the store with a sack full of food.

"What did you find out?" he asked.

"Let's go to Garner's loft before we talk." She crossed the street and stopped at Ghost's truck. He unlocked it and helped her load the bags into the back seat.

She led the way up the stairs to where they found Hack and Garner bent over a computer screen.

"Anything?" Charlie asked.

"We did some digging into LeRoy Vanders's family. Seems his sons have been in trouble with the law on more than one occasion. Some of their arrests include driving under the influence." Hack read through a report he had up on one of the monitors. "Both Vernon and Dalton have a couple of DUIs each. Vernon has been arrested on multiple occasions for hunting out of season and poaching on federal land. Dalton has been in several fistfights and has a restraining order against him. LeRoy's oldest son did some time in federal penitentiary, for shooting at a law enforcement officer."

Garner nodded toward Charlie. "What did you learn from Mrs. Penders?"

She listed a number of names and circumstances that made the men potential suspects. One jumped out at Ghost.

"Tim Cramer?"

Charlie nodded. "Divorce. He's losing his daughter and half of everything he owns, including the land and house his grandmother left him."

"I spoke with him while waiting for you to come out of the store."

Charlie's eyes narrowed. "What did he say?"

Ghost shrugged. "Nothing incriminating. He asked if I was looking for work and told me I'd have to get in line since half the men in the county were unemployed. He also told me to say hello to you." He captured Charlie's gaze. "I couldn't read anything into what he said."

"I ran into his ex-wife in the store. Was he watching for her to come out, do you think?"

"Was that the woman who came out before you did?"

"Yes."

"No, he was gone before she emerged."

"We'll look into his background and see if we can come up with anything." Garner half sat on the edge of a table, his leg dangling over. "I feel like we're searching for the needle in the haystack."

"I checked the Vanderses' utility bills," Hack said. "They have a phone line and internet. They are all on the same plan. They might be involved in whatever takeover they're planning, but we don't know if it's one of them, or all of them. And we don't know if they are computer savvy enough to tap into Charlie's webcam. That takes more sophistication and technical knowledge."

"Check Cramer, Rausch and Parker," Charlie said. "Any one of them would have to be computer savvy to do their business. Raising prized horses would require a website and email in these times. A man who makes and loses his wealth in the stock market is heavily involved with technology. And a man working for the pipeline as an inspector has to have the ability to communicate using modern technology."

"On it," Hack said.

"In the meantime, we're heading out to lunch," Charlie said.

Ghost shot a glance her way. "We are?"

She nodded. "After we pick up Lolly."

As they descended the stairs, he asked, "Where are we going for lunch?"

She responded, "Out."

Ghost wasn't sure he liked the vague answer, but he went with it. "Just promise me we're not going into the lion's den."

She shot a sideways glance at him. "Huh?"

"You know. We're not taking Lolly into a potentially dangerous location where crazy men wield guns."

Her lips twitched and a smile spread across her face.

Ghost swallowed hard on the constriction in his throat. This was the Charlie he remembered from seven years ago. Happy, carefree and in love with life.

"Uh, Ghost, we've already done that today. You remember. The tavern?"

He would have laughed at her teasing, but the thought of LeRoy Vanders shooting that gun inside the restaurant where Lolly and Charlie were close enough to be killed with a single bullet made his chest hurt. "Yeah."

She was right, but it wasn't funny.

Lolly was in the middle of playing hopscotch with her girlfriends when they arrived. She dragged her feet, her bottom lip sticking out just a little. "Can I stay longer?"

"No, sweetheart," Charlie said, taking her daughter's hand. "But I have a special surprise I think you'll like."

Lolly's face perked and she hopped up and down. "What is it?"

"My question, exactly," Ghost muttered.

"Now, it wouldn't be a surprise if I told you, would it?" Charlie winked at Lolly and lifted her chin when she glanced toward Ghost.

He liked this teasing, fun Charlie. She didn't seem as weighted by responsibility. She appeared to be making an effort to include them in the fun.

Ghost went along with her. "Come on, sugar bear." He swung Lolly up in his arms and carried her toward the truck. "The sooner we get going, the sooner we discover what this big surprise is."

Minutes later they were on the road heading toward Charlie's house.

As Ghost neared the turn, Charlie put her hand on his arm. "Keep going."

"Where to?" he asked.

"I think you'll know when you get there." She sat back in her seat. "Follow the highway heading south out of town."

He increased his speed as he left the town limits and hit the open road. Before long, his instincts knew where they were going without Charlie telling him. "We're going to the Dry Gulch Ranch, aren't we?"

She smiled.

His chest tightened, his mind filling with memories of growing up on the Dry Gulch Ranch. Five generations of Whitakers had owned the ranch. Ghost's father had worked for the fourth of the five. Ghost had grown up with Trace Whitaker, riding horses, swimming in the creek, hunting and fishing on the Dry Gulch. They'd been best friends even though his father had worked for Trace's father.

"Has Trace returned from his stint in the Army?" Ghost asked.

"Not yet. But the foreman is aware we're coming out and Trace left word with him that you're welcome to have run of the ranch anytime you're home on leave."

"I haven't been back since my parents moved away."

"It hasn't changed a whole lot. I came out once to help the foreman's wife set up her new computer."

Ghost focused his attention on maneuvering through the huge gate with the cattle guard over the road. Then he drank in the view leading up to the first place he'd ever called home. The winding drive through pastures with the mountains as a backdrop was forever seared into his memory.

He rolled down the window to smell the scent of the pinion pines as he neared the ranch housing compound. The drive wove through a stand of trees. At the last curve, the trees seemed to part and the big rock-and-cedar house with the wide porches and huge expanses of windows appeared.

To Ghost, it felt like coming home. He turned before he reached the house and drove around to the back where the foreman's quarters sat near the huge old barn.

Charlie had been right. Nothing much had changed, except one major item. His parents wouldn't be there to welcome him and he wasn't home. This was another foreman's lodgings now.

Still, the surprise was one he could enjoy anyway.

Jonesy, the wiry cowboy with salt-and-pepper hair who'd taken over from Ghost's father, met them in front of the barn with a friendly smile.

Charlie helped Lolly out of the truck while Ghost went to greet the older man.

"Jon Caspar, you're a sight for sore eyes." Jonesy had been one of the ranch hands Ghost's father had trained to take over his position as foreman. He'd been there as Ghost was growing up on the ranch.

Ghost engulfed the man in a hug. "How are you and Mrs. Jones?"

"The missus is doing fine. She would have been here, but she's in Bozeman picking up some ranch supplies and some fabric for her quilting bee or some such nonsense." He stepped back and looked at Ghost. "You look great. The Navy must be treating you right." His smile slipped. "Heard you were injured." He tilted his head from side to side, his gaze skimming over Ghost. "Nothing permanent, I hope."

Ghost laid a hand on his leg. "Took a bit of shrapnel to the thigh. I'll be okay." He didn't go into the detail of how long the doctors spent in the operating room removing all of the shards of metal and reattaching major veins. Or the physical therapy it took to get him back to where he was, standing on his own two feet, with only a limp.

He knew he still had a long way to go before they

would allow him to return to his unit. Hell, he still had to face the Medical Review Board. They might decide to medically retire him. He refused to think of that now. Not when the sun was shining and he could smell the hay in the barn and the earthy scent of horse manure.

"I saddled a couple of horses and a pony for your ride. I think you'll like the ones I picked." Jonesy's brows drew down. "I didn't think about it, but can you ride with your injury?"

Ghost wasn't sure. "I'll let you know after I've given it a try."

"I gave you a gentle gelding, and Charlie has one of our sweetest-tempered mares."

"What about me?" Lolly asked, her eyes wide, excited.

Jonesy bent to Lolly's level. "You get to ride Annabelle, a rescue pony Mr. Whitaker insisted on giving a home. She's just the right size for a little girl like you." He straightened and gave Charlie a direct look. "Annabelle is very well trained and will behave herself with the little one."

Charlie smiled. "I know you wouldn't give Lolly anything she couldn't handle. She's been taking riding lessons at the Red Wagon Stables on the other side of town, so she knows a little bit about sitting in the saddle and handling the reins."

"That's great. You can't start them too young. If you ever want to come ride, you can come out here. Mr. Whitaker would like knowing his horses are getting some exercise besides what me and the missus are giving them."

Charlie shifted the bag she carried into one arm and hugged the man with the other. "Thank you, Jonesy. It's good to see you. I don't get out here nearly enough."

She glanced down at what she was carrying. "I brought the food for a picnic. I don't suppose you have an old blanket and some saddlebags?"

"A picnic?" Lolly clapped her hands. "We're going on a picnic."

"When you called to tell me what you wanted to do, I got things ready for you. The saddlebags are on Jon's horse and the blanket is tied to the back of yours."

"Thank you." Charlie kissed the older man's cheek.

A moment later, Jonesy brought out the horses and the pony and tied them to a hitching post.

Ghost helped Charlie put the food in the saddlebags and then he stood at the ready while Lolly mounted the chocolate brown pony with the cream-colored mane and tail. Annabelle stood patiently while Lolly settled into the saddle.

Jonesy adjusted the stirrups to fit her legs and handed her the reins. "If you tap her gently with your heels, she'll walk. Pull back on the reins when you want her to stop."

"I learned this at my lesson," Lolly said. She tapped her heels and the pony moved forward.

Lolly's grin filled Ghost's heart with joy. He'd never thought about children of his own, but deep down, he'd wanted them, and he'd wanted his children to ride horses and have a love of the outdoors.

Ghost held the mare's head while Charlie mounted. Then he approached the gelding, praying he could hoist himself into the saddle. Thankfully, it was his right leg that had been damaged the most. He set his boot in the stirrup and swung his leg over. So far, so good. He had trouble setting his right foot in the stirrup, but eventually managed. "Where to?"

Charlie shook her head. "You know the ranch better than I do. Lead the way."

Jonesy opened the pasture gate for them and waited as Charlie and Lolly passed through. When Ghost rode abreast of him, he leaned toward him. "Take them to the pool in the creek where you and Trace used to swim. That's about the prettiest place on all of the ranch."

Ghost nodded. "You're right. I will."

Jonesy glanced up at the clear blue sky. "The weatherman calls for rain this afternoon."

"We'll be back before then," Ghost said.

"If you get caught up on the mountain—"

"I know of a place we can hole up until we can get down."

Jonesy smiled and nodded. "You should. You spent most of your youth in those hills." His smile faded. "Keep an eye out for bears. I've seen bear scat and claw marks on trees out that direction. They're around."

"Will do," Ghost promised.

Jonesy closed the gate behind them and headed back to the barn.

Ghost nudged the gelding into an easy trot to catch up with the others. When they came abreast, he was glad when the horse settled into a steady walk. The constant jolt of a trot was too hard on his recovering leg.

The three of them ambled across the pasture, their pace set by the pony.

Ghost pointed to wildflowers and trees, naming them for Lolly. She asked questions, curious about the birds and the ground squirrels they saw along the way. They spied antelope in the distance and admired a bald eagle flying overhead.

By the time they arrived at the creek pool it was well past lunchtime. As soon as they tied the horses to the bushes, they worked to spread the blanket over the grass and set out the food Mrs. Penders had prepared for their picnic.

Ghost ate in silence, enjoying the sounds of the birds and the rustle of leaves as a gentle breeze rippled through the branches. When they finished, they packed the leftover food in the saddlebag and set it aside.

Charlie stretched out on the blanket, her arms crossed behind her head, a smile lifting the corners of her lips.

Lolly played nearby, skipping stones in the pool.

Ghost leaned up on one elbow, his gaze on Charlie, Lolly in his peripheral vision. "I understand why my parents moved to Florida, but I can't help thinking that this is as close to heaven as you can get."

She closed her eyes, her smile widening. "I thought you might like to get away from town for a little while."

"What made you think of coming here?"

Her smile slipped as she looked up at him. "After listening to Mrs. Penders talking about all the troubles people were having, I needed a pick-me-up, and I figured you could use one, too. Life's too short to go around looking for what's wrong with it. If you just open your eyes, you can see the beauty all around you."

Ghost nodded, soaking in the beauty that was Charlie. "I agree."

"Seriously, look around us. Have you seen anything more beautiful?"

"Never."

She turned toward him. "You're not looking at the trees and the sky."

"No. I'm not." He touched her cheek with the back

of his knuckles. Her skin was as soft and smooth as it had been seven years ago. And her lips… He bent to taste them.

She didn't resist. Instead, she opened to him and met his tongue with her own in a long, languid caress that stirred his blood and made his heart beat faster.

Eventually, he lifted his head to stare down at her.

"Remember the last time we were here?" she asked, cupping his cheek with her palm.

He nodded. "We skinny-dipped in the pool."

She smiled. "Uh-huh. I think this is where Lolly was conceived."

He shook his head, his heart full to bursting. He glanced across at Lolly, the beautiful little girl with hair as fiery as her mother's.

A movement behind the child made Ghost refocus his attention on the dark brown woolly mass on the other side of the pool, rearing up on its hind legs.

Grizzly!

Chapter 11

Ghost lurched to his feet. "Lolly," he said, his voice low and urgent. "Lolly," he said a little louder.

She was bending over picking flowers.

Charlie rolled to her feet and stared in the direction Ghost was looking. Her gasp indicated she'd seen what he was looking at. She started forward, but Ghost put out a hand to stop her. "Get to the horses and be ready to mount with Lolly. I'm going to distract the bear while you two get away."

"You can't run on that leg. I should distract her while you and Lolly get away."

"Just do it," he said, his voice low, his tone unbending.

Charlie left the blanket and the saddlebag and eased toward the horses, quickly untying them from the bushes.

Lolly had yet to see the grizzly. She glanced up and

looked in Ghost's direction. "Aren't these pretty?" she called out.

Ghost froze, his gaze on the grizzly across the pool from Lolly. Then he saw movement in the brush behind the big bear. Two cubs emerged.

Holy hell. It was a mama grizzly and her two cubs. Lolly was in mortal danger.

"Lolly, look at me," Ghost said. He bent to gather the saddlebag and blanket. "Sweetheart, go to the horses." In a commanding tone, he said, "Now."

She frowned, looked down at the flowers and back up at him, "But—"

"Now," he repeated swinging wide, away from Lolly toward the narrower end of the pool. If the grizzly charged, it would be slowed by the deeper water. In which case, Lolly would have time to run to the horses. Hopefully, Charlie would get her in the saddle and the hell out of there before the grizzly cleared the pool.

If the bear was smart enough to go around to the shallow end, she'd focus her ire on Ghost and he'd use the saddlebag and the blanket as distractors to give himself time to get away.

That was the plan and the backup plan. It was up to the bear to make the first move.

Lolly frowned and started toward the horses.

The grizzly mama roared and ran into the water.

Lolly spun toward the sound, saw the grizzly and screamed.

"Run!" Ghost yelled.

"Run, Lolly!" Charlie said. She had the horses' reins in her hands. They'd spotted the grizzly and were dancing backward, pulling her away from Lolly.

The girl seemed to be frozen for a moment. Then

she dropped the flowers, turned and ran as fast as her little feet could carry her, straight for her mother.

The grizzly started into the water. When it got too deep, she changed direction toward the shallow, narrow end where Ghost was waiting. He waved the blanket, catching her attention.

The bear roared again and ran toward him.

Ghost took off, pain shooting through his bum leg. Too late, he remembered he wasn't as agile as he used to be. He sure as hell couldn't outrun a grizzly. His only hope was to fool her into attacking the blanket while he climbed a tree. He wasn't fool enough to believe she wouldn't climb up after him, so he'd have to make the blanket convincing enough to keep her occupied while he made good his escape.

The mama bear roared again and charged out of the deeper water toward him.

Ghost ran for the brush. As he passed a big bush, he lifted the blanket letting it catch the wind enough to spread it out, then he laid it down over a tall bush and ran behind it.

Moving from bush to bush, he ran as fast as he could, careful not to let the grizzly see him. When he reached a tree he thought he could climb, he popped his head above the bushes enough to locate the grizzly.

She was mad, slapping at the blanket and the bushes with her murderous claws. Once she'd ripped the blanket to shreds, she reared up on her hind legs again and gave another terrifying roar.

Ghost eased himself up into the tree, reaching only for the branches on the far side of the thick trunk. Several times he leaned around the side to spy the grizzly sniffing through the bushes, trying to find him.

He kept climbing, higher and higher. The narrower

the branches, the less likely the grizzly could reach him. Despite common misconception, he knew grizzlies could climb trees. It was harder for them than for the black bears, because of their giant claws, but they could climb. His best bet was not to draw attention to himself.

When he'd gone as high as he could, he stopped and remained absolutely still.

The bear kept coming, her nose to the ground, sniffing for him. When she reached the base of the big tree, she circled it several times, sniffing and looking up into the branches.

Ghost held his breath, praying she didn't see him and hoping Charlie and Lolly had gotten far enough away that the grizzly couldn't easily catch up to them.

Several minutes crept by. The bear reared on her back legs and hugged the base of the tree. For a heart-stopping moment, Ghost thought she would climb.

Then the sound of a cub calling out in the woods came to him and the grizzly at the same time.

For a moment, she continued to stare up into the branches of the tree. With one last roar, she dropped to all fours and hurried toward the sounds of her cubs.

Ghost watched her until he couldn't see her anymore. Then he gave it another two or three minutes before he eased his way down through the branches. As he got close to the ground, he paused, took a moment to scan the area. When he was absolutely positive the bear had gone, he slipped to the ground and crept through the woods, making his way toward the pool. The grizzly and her cubs had moved on.

Ghost walked back along the trail they had arrived on earlier, hoping to catch up to Charlie and Lolly. His leg ached and the clouds had settled in over the hills.

Soon fat drops splattered on the ground and in his face. Part of him hoped Charlie and Lolly had gone back to the barn. Another part hoped they were just ahead of him on the trail.

The drops turned to a deluge of cold rain soaking through his clothes, chilling him to the bone.

He was wiping his eyes for the tenth time when he glanced up to see dark masses blocking the trail ahead. For a moment his heart skipped several beats. His first thoughts were of the bear and her cubs. Then he could make out the shapes of two horses and a pony, a woman leading them and a little girl huddled close to her mother's legs.

Limping faster, Ghost hurried toward them. "Charlie! Lolly!"

They turned as one and ran toward him, flinging their arms around him.

"We were so scared," Lolly said, her words coming out on a sob.

"Are you all right?" Charlie asked, rain streaming down her face. She leaned back and studied him, her gaze going over him from head to foot.

"I'm fine. I don't think I've climbed a tree that fast since I was a kid." He grinned and lifted Lolly into his arms. "Come on, I know of a hunting cabin close by. We can take shelter until the storm passes."

He settled Lolly on the pony, helped Charlie into her saddle and pulled himself up onto his horse.

Within a few minutes, he'd found the cabin they'd used during the fall hunting season, years ago. The door opened easily and the inside was dry, even if it wasn't warm. Fortunately, someone had stacked dry cordwood next to the potbellied stove. Matches and tinder were right where they had always been. Soon

Ghost had a fire going and the interior of the cabin grew cozy warm.

The one-room structure had two twin beds, the thin mattresses folded over to keep the dust from settling on the surface.

Charlie stood at the window, staring out at the rain coming down. "It doesn't look like it will let up soon and it'll be getting dark soon."

Ghost removed his soaked shirt and hung it on a nail on the wall, close to the stove. "We might as well get comfortable. Looks like we'll be spending the night."

Lolly sat on one of the two chairs, her eyes wide. "Will the bear find us here?"

"No, sweetheart," Charlie reassured her.

"If she does, will she break down the door?" Lolly shivered.

"You'll be okay here in the cabin," Charlie said. "She only chased us because she was protecting her babies."

"I'm scared," Lolly whispered, a violent shiver shaking her body.

Charlie smoothed a hand over her daughter's damp head. "You know what I do when I'm scared?"

Lolly shook her head.

"I get busy." She drew Lolly to her feet. "Let's get these beds ready to sleep in."

Ghost pitched in to help them shake the dust from the mattresses. They found sleeping bags rolled up in an airtight plastic container in one of the corners. On one of the shelves they found cans of beans and corned beef and hash. Another shelf contained a pot and an old, manual can opener. Soon, they had dinner of beans and corned beef and hash.

Charlie stripped Lolly out of her damp clothing and

tucked her into a sleeping bag. She hung the items near the stove to dry.

With the warmth of the fire, a full belly and the people he loved surrounding him, Ghost couldn't think of a place he'd rather be.

Could he have a different life than that of a SEAL? Was he ready to leave it to the younger, more agile men coming out of BUD/S training?

He looked around at the small cabin, tucked away from the world and realized this was his world. These were the people he cared most about. He wasn't sure of what he'd do career-wise, but he would take into account the need to be with his daughter. If Charlie gave him a second chance, he'd spend the rest of his life making up to her for the past seven years.

Charlie arranged the sleeping bags over the thin mattresses and settled Lolly into one of the small beds.

Lolly reached out for her mother's hand. "Will you sleep with me?"

"You bet." Charlie had already decided the beds were too small for her to sleep with Ghost. With Lolly in the same room, she didn't think it right for her to be in bed with a man who was more or less a stranger to her daughter.

She lay down beside Lolly, pulled her close and sang the soft ballad she'd sung to her daughter since she was a tiny baby.

Ghost settled in the bed beside them and turned on his side, his gaze on her and his daughter.

Soon, Lolly's breathing grew deeper and her body went limp. With her hand tucked beneath her cheek, she slept.

Charlie stared past her to the man who'd risked his

life to save them from being mauled by a grizzly. With an injured leg, he'd run through the woods, providing a sufficient distraction for them to get away.

Her heart squeezed hard in her chest like it had when she'd ridden away with Lolly, not knowing if he would escape the bear. For all Charlie knew, Ghost might have been killed or wounded so badly, he could have been lying on the ground bleeding to death.

She and Lolly had ridden hard, putting half a mile distance between them and the pool where the grizzly had appeared.

About that time, the clouds lowered on them. It began to drizzle and Charlie couldn't go any farther without knowing. She'd turned back the way they'd come, determined to find Ghost. Lolly had been just as worried about him, insisting they go back.

The sky had opened up, dumping rain on them. They couldn't see ahead and the horses slipped on the trail. She'd gotten down from the saddle and set Lolly down beside her. If Ghost was to be found, she had to be close enough to the ground to see him.

When he'd emerged from the deluge, walking toward them, Charlie's heart had nearly exploded with the joy she'd felt.

She and Lolly had run to him, hugging him close. At that moment, Charlie knew she was still hopelessly and irreversibly in love with the man.

And she'd been terribly wrong to keep news of his daughter from him.

"I'm sorry," she whispered, capturing his gaze in the soft glow coming from the potbellied stove.

His brows dipped. "For what?"

She smoothed a hand over her daughter's drying hair. "For keeping Lolly from you."

"I didn't make it easy for you to come out and tell me," he said. "I'm sorry I was so selfish when I left, that I didn't consider what I was leaving behind."

"You were just starting your career. You didn't need to be saddled with the worry of a family."

"And you shouldn't have had to go it alone with a child to care for."

"We made mistakes," Charlie said.

"The question is, do we continue to make the same mistakes, or do we make things right?"

His words were softly spoken, but they were heavy, weighing on Charlie's mind. "You still have a career with the military. I can make sure you see Lolly on holidays."

"I want to be with her more than that."

Charlie's gut clenched and her breath caught in her throat. Was he going to sue for custody? God knew he had a right to.

"Being back…being with you…makes me want more." He swung his legs over the side of the little cot and winced. "Being a SEAL used to be everything to me. The training I went through made me want to prove something to my team and to myself. But after the first year or two, I realized there will always be another battle and another enemy to fight. I didn't think it would be right to bring someone else into my personal life, when my life wasn't guaranteed."

"Nobody's life is guaranteed," Charlie argued. "I could be hit by a bus tomorrow. Or worse, we could be targeted by homegrown terrorists. You can't live thinking about what *could* happen. You have to muddle through with what you know and what you have."

"I know that, but a SEAL's life expectancy is a hell

of a lot lower than most people's. It wouldn't be fair to subject a loved one to the constant worry."

Charlie stiffened, the heat of anger rising in her chest. "So you make that determination unilaterally? Have you ever thought it isn't fair to exclude a loved one from the decision?"

His lips twisted. "I thought it was the right decision."

"Well, you might be the only one who thought it. If you bothered to include all involved in the decision-making process, you might have come to an alternate conclusion."

Charlie flipped over onto her other side. Her eyes stung and she swallowed hard. She wouldn't cry another tear for Ghost. The man could be so thickheaded. The way he was thinking would doom them to the same mistake they'd made seven years ago. When would he ever learn?

With a child to care for and protect, she couldn't spend her days mooning over a man who couldn't commit.

"Charlie, I've never stopped loving you," he said.

"Yeah, yeah," she muttered, without turning over. "You have a funny way of showing it." The last of her words came out garbled as she choked back a sob.

"Please don't turn away from me," he said.

"I have a job, Lolly has plans for tomorrow and I need sleep. I have two lives to think of. Figure out your own life."

"But—"

"Please," she whispered. "Just leave me alone. I'm too tired to think or argue."

"We're not through with this conversation," he said, his tone firm.

She lay silent, tears slipping down her cheeks. She refused to sniffle. He couldn't know that he was breaking her heart all over again.

Charlie lay awake, pretending to be asleep long after Ghost settled back in his bed.

She hurt so much it was a physical pain she couldn't ignore. Before the sun rose, she was up, looking out the window at the gray light of predawn.

"How long have you been awake?" Ghost whispered.

"Not very." She didn't face him. She couldn't. Her heart weighed heavily in her chest and one little word from the man she loved and she might burst into tears.

"I'm hungry," Lolly said. She stretched in the bed and rubbed her knuckles against her eyelids. "Are we going home?"

"As soon as you get your clothes and boots on, we can start back," Charlie said.

Lolly rolled out of bed and dressed in her dry clothing and then pulled on her pink cowboy boots. "My boots are still wet."

"We'll get you into some dry clothes and shoes when we get back home."

"And breakfast?" Lolly asked.

"And breakfast." Charlie forced a smile to her lips and turned in Lolly's direction. "Ready?"

Ghost had his boots on and had tucked his shirt into his waistband. Without saying a word, he left the little cabin, gathered the horses and waited for Charlie and Lolly to mount before he swung up onto his horse.

They rode down the mountain as the sun edged over the horizon.

Charlie's gaze scanned the hillside and the brush for grizzlies, not wanting a repeat of their encounter from the day before. The ride remained blissfully uneventful.

Jonesy greeted them at the barn, leading a saddled horse, his brows furrowed. "I was just about to ride out to find you three."

"We had a grizzly sighting and got caught in the rain," Ghost informed the man.

Jonesy shook his head. "I'd noticed bear scat in that area, but I'd hoped you wouldn't run into one."

"It was a mama and her two cubs," Lolly said. "She didn't like it that we were around."

"Glad you got away without injury. Some aren't as fortunate." Jonesy grinned. "Did you stay in the hunting cabin?"

Ghost nodded. "I'll bring some canned goods and firewood to replenish what we used."

"No, don't do that. I was going to run some up this week anyway. Glad you found dry wood and something to eat."

"We are, too," Charlie said. "Otherwise it would have been a much more uncomfortable night." She slid out of her saddle and started to lead the horse into the barn.

"I'll take care of the horses. You three look like you could stand some breakfast. The missus has extra scrambled eggs if you're hungry."

"I'm hungry," Lolly exclaimed.

"Are you sure it's not a bother?" Charlie asked.

"She'd be happy to have someone to fuss over," Jonesy reassured her.

"We can't stay long," Charlie glanced down at Lolly. "Today is the day for the field trip to Yellowstone National Park. We have to be there early."

"I'll hurry," Lolly promised.

They made their way to the foreman's little cottage where Mrs. Jones had breakfast waiting on the table.

"How did you know we were coming?" Lolly asked.

Mrs. Jones blushed. "I was watching through the window."

"We don't want to burden you," Ghost said.

She waved her hands. "It was no trouble at all. We get so few visitors, it's a pleasure to cook for someone else."

Ghost, Charlie and Lolly took seats at the table and dug into the scrambled eggs and thick slices of ham Mrs. Jones served.

Charlie hadn't felt much like eating, but the ham and eggs hit the spot and helped lift her flagging spirits. By the time she left the Dry Gulch Ranch, she was resigned to whatever happened.

Lolly's chatter filled the silence on the drive home.

While Lolly took a quick shower, Charlie changed into dry clothes and shoes, washed her face and brushed her hair back into a ponytail. She'd considered wearing makeup, but decided it was too late to impress a man who wasn't going to stick around. Resigned to going without makeup, she ducked into her office and powered up her computer. Once the monitor flashed to life, she clicked on the URL of the Free America group and scrolled through the messages. She'd just about reached the bottom when Lolly called out.

"I'm ready." Her daughter entered her office wearing jeans and her community center T-shirt and sneakers.

"You were fast," Charlie remarked. She glanced at the computer one last time and frowned.

A message popped up on the group that caught her attention.

Let it begin with a meeting of the mines

A chill slithered down Charlie's spine as she turned toward Lolly. The message wasn't directed at her, this time. It was directed toward the Free America group. So much for assuming LeRoy Vanders was the leader. He was safely in jail with no access to the internet.

Though Charlie wasn't sure what the message meant, one thing was certain, something was about to start. What, she didn't know.

"Come on, Mommy. We're going to be late and miss the trip." Lolly spun on her heels and ran down the hallway.

Charlie rose and met Ghost by the front door where he held Lolly's hand.

What did it mean? Had they meant to spell mines or had it been a misspelling intended to be minds? The hills were dotted with abandoned mines from the gold rush era. "Ready?" Charlie asked, her mind on the message, her stomach churning.

"Yes!" Lolly jumped up and down. "We're going to Yellowstone today. We get to ride on a bus."

Her excitement brought a small smile to Charlie's lips. As she gathered her keys and purse from the hallway table, the phone next to them rang.

Charlie froze, almost afraid to answer. Would it be another harbinger of potential doom? She lifted the phone from the charger. "Hello."

"Charlie, Kevin here."

"Hey, Kevin," she said. "What's up?"

"We have some satellite images that might interest you and Ghost."

Her gaze met Ghost's and a tremor of awareness rippled through her. "We're on our way to town. I have to drop off my daughter at the community center, then we'll be there."

"See you in a few, then." Garner ended the call.

Ghost met her gaze with a question in his eyes.

"He has some satellite images he wants us to look at." She looped her purse over her shoulder and followed Ghost and Lolly outside.

"We can take my Jeep. I feel like driving." She might as well get used to being that single parent again. It wouldn't be long before Ghost left.

Ghost didn't argue, but moved the booster seat from his truck into the backseat of her Jeep and buckled Lolly in.

Once again, Lolly jabbered away. If the adults weren't responding, the little girl was too excited about riding in the bus to notice.

As they neared town, Charlie pulled up in front of the tavern first. "Why don't you get started reviewing the images? I'll be back in less than five minutes."

"I can wait," he said, not budging from the passenger seat.

"Please," she said, staring straight out the front window without looking into his eyes. "I need just a few minutes alone."

He hesitated.

In her peripheral vision she could see his jaw harden and his lips press into a thin line. Then he leaned into the backseat and chucked Lolly beneath her chin. "Have a great time at Yellowstone. Don't pet any bison while you're there."

"Don't be silly. Bison are wild animals," she said.

He climbed out of the Jeep and stood on the sidewalk watching as they drove away.

Charlie felt as if she was leaving him for good, knowing perfectly well she'd be back to study satellite images. But she couldn't help looking at him in the rearview mirror. He looked so sad, and that made her heart hurt even more.

What were they going to do? How could they fix a relationship that wasn't meant to be?

More immediately, she worried about the message. *Let it begin with a meeting of the mines.*

Chapter 12

Ghost wanted to kick himself. Hard. Last night he could have made things right with Charlie. He could have told her he loved her and wanted to be with her more than he wanted to breathe. Instead, he'd fumbled the pitch and struck out.

She'd dropped him off like she wanted nothing to do with him. If he didn't know better, he'd bet she didn't come back to view the images Garner's team had come up with.

And then there were the threats against Charlie that had him worried. She ran around town without him as if no one would attempt to harm her. And maybe no one would, but that didn't make Ghost any more confident. He had half a mind to jog down to the community center and make sure she was all right. It was only a few blocks. But wait. He wasn't quite up to jogging. Not without a whole lot of pain.

He didn't believe LeRoy Vanders was the one posting the threats. Frankly, the man didn't seem technologically advanced enough to track her back to her webcam. But if not Vanders, then who?

Yeah, he was being foolish. Instead of following her, he climbed the stairs to Garner's office and knocked.

Caveman opened the door. "Good, you're here. You'll want to see this." He stepped aside.

Garner, Caveman and Hawkeye stood at the large monitor mounted on the wall, staring at a satellite image.

Garner glanced over his shoulder. "Ghost, glad you made it. Where's Charlie?"

"She went on to the community center. She'll be here in five minutes."

"Do you want us to wait until she gets here to go over what we found?"

"No, she said to get started without her." Ghost stepped up beside Garner. "What's this a picture of?"

"The mountain between Grizzly Pass and the highway turnoff that leads to Yellowstone National Park. The image is from a week ago." Most of the mountain was dark and dense with lodgepole pine trees. Garner pointed to a place that appeared to be a gash in the landscape. "See this?"

"Looks like an old mining camp," Ghost noted.

"It is. We looked it up. It's the abandoned Lucky Lou's Gold Mine. It played out about forty years ago and has been closed since." Garner glanced back at Hack. "Show two nights ago."

Hack clicked his mouse and the screen in front of the others flickered. For a moment, it appeared unchanged. Until Ghost leaned closer and noticed a change in the mine area.

"Are those vehicles?"

Garner nodded. "We counted half a dozen. And if you look here at that bright dot, we think that's a camp-fire, and next to it are people. Show the infrared shot," he called out.

Hack clicked and another image appeared with green spots of color. Where the campfire had been was brighter, almost white.

Garner pointed to several smaller dots of green lined up from the back of one vehicle to the side of a hill. "Why would they be lined up at the back of one of the vehicles and all the way to the mine entrance?"

"Are they unloading something?" Ghost asked.

Garner nodded. "That's the only thing we could think of. Caveman, Hawkeye and I are headed out this morning to check on it."

"I want to go," Ghost said.

"Do you think Charlie will be okay without you to keep an eye on her?"

Ghost wrestled with his desire to go with her and his desire to find out what someone was storing in an old mine in the middle of the night. "I'd better stay."

The phone rang in Kevin's office.

Hack lifted it. "Yeah." A moment later, he held it up. "It's for you, Kevin."

The DHS team leader grabbed the phone. "Kevin, here." He listened for a moment and nodded. "Are you sure you'll be all right?" He paused. "Okay. I'll tell him." The man handed the phone back to Hack and turned to Ghost. "That was Charlie. The woman who was scheduled to go with the field trip got sick and couldn't make it. Charlie offered to go with them."

Ghost stiffened. "When are they leaving?"

Garner looked at him. "Now. Do you want to try to catch up to them?"

Ghost hesitated. He didn't have transportation to follow the bus and if he risked running to the community center, he might miss them. Apparently Charlie wanted a little more time to herself without him. "No."

"She should be all right. No one was expecting her to be on that field trip."

"I guess it will have to be all right."

"You could take my SUV if you want to follow and make sure they're safe," Garner offered.

"No." Ghost shook his head. Charlie hadn't wanted him along. "Let's go see what's in that mine."

Garner grabbed his keys. "We can go in my vehicle." He stopped at a large safe near the door and twisted the combination back and forth until it clicked and he opened it. Inside was an arsenal of weapons. He reached in and pulled out an AR-15 military-grade rifle and handed it to Ghost. "We don't know what we're in for at the mine. If they have stashed something illegal or deadly, they might have guards positioned there." He reached in again and handed Caveman another AR-15. To Hawkeye, he handed a specially equipped sniper rifle with a high-powered scope.

Then he moved to a footlocker beside the safe and unlocked the padlock with a key and threw it open. Inside were rifle magazines and boxes of ammunition.

"Most of the magazines are already loaded. Grab what you think you might need. You can load everything into these duffel bags. We don't want to alarm the natives as we carry them out to the SUV."

Ghost wasn't sure what they'd run into at the mine. Being armed to the teeth was better than being outgunned.

Once they had everything they could possibly need

for a prolonged standoff with a small army, they headed out the door and down the steps.

Caveman carried the duffel bag with the rifles, Ghost and Garner carried gym bags filled with ammo. Hawkeye carried the case with the sniper rifle. One by one, they loaded them into the back of Garner's SUV.

With the smell of weapons oil in his nostrils and the hard shell of armored plating strapped around his chest beneath his shirt, Ghost closed the hatch.

He'd started around the side of the SUV when an explosion rocked the street.

Ghost automatically dropped to the ground and rolled beneath the SUV. His pulse pounded and flashbacks threatened to overwhelm him with memories he preferred to forget.

For a moment, he was back in that Afghan village, being fired on by a Soviet-made rocket-propelled grenade launcher manned by a Taliban fighter positioned on top of one of the stick-and-mud buildings. He lay pressed to the ground, trying to breathe past the panic paralyzing his lungs.

Chapter 13

Charlie sat beside Brenda Larson in the front seat of the bus headed north toward Yellowstone National Park, wondering what Kevin had found that they'd needed to see. Though she knew Ghost had their best interests at heart, she would have liked to have been there to gauge for herself the importance of the new information.

They were ten miles out of town and the children had settled back in their seats when Brenda hit her with, "So what's up between you and Jon Caspar?"

"What do you mean?" Charlie stalled, not really wanting to talk about Ghost or what was or wasn't happening between them.

"He's back. You're in love." Brenda sat back, her brows raised, her gaze direct, unflinching. "When can we expect an announcement?"

"There won't be an announcement." Charlie stared

out the window, her chest tight, her eyes stinging. A tear slipped free and trailed down her cheek. Damn. And she'd promised herself she wouldn't cry that day. The field trip was all about the kids, not her pathetic excuse for a love life. She swiped at the tear and grit her teeth to keep others from falling, hoping Brenda wouldn't see them. Then she glanced at her reflection in the window and Brenda's beside it. Too late, Brenda could see everything in her reflection.

Her friend laid a hand on her arm. "What's wrong, Charlie?"

What was the use holding back now? And she really needed a shoulder to lean on. "He's going to leave again and I love him."

Brenda's face brightened. "Maybe he'll take you with him? Not that I want you to leave Grizzly Pass. Friends our age are hard to come by around here."

"He doesn't think his life is conducive to having a family." Charlie sniffed and wished her voice hadn't sounded so wobbly.

Brenda tilted her head to the side and touched her finger to her chin. "He might have a point. They move around a lot."

Charlie frowned. "You're not helping. Besides, I already knew that."

"He's a Navy SEAL. They are in a high-risk job. He might get killed on a deployment." Brenda smiled. "Perhaps he doesn't want you to be just another military widow."

"He won't give me that choice."

"Would you be okay with him staying in the military?"

"Of course."

"Would you move to be with him when he's not deployed?"

Charlie nodded.

Brenda raised her hands, palms up. "Then what's the problem?"

"He hasn't asked." Another tear slipped down her cheek.

"Have you given him a chance?" Brenda chuckled. "I've seen you when you get all stubborn and hard-headed. It's pretty intimidating."

Charlie thought about how she'd shut Ghost down the night before and how she hadn't encouraged a frank conversation since. "Maybe not."

"Then wipe your tears, have fun with the kids today and when you get home, hit him up with how you feel. If he feels the same, he'll ask you to go with him. If he doesn't, at least you will know and you can stop crying over him."

"You're right." Charlie wiped her tears and straightened, forcing a smile to her face.

She squeezed her friend's hand. "Thank you. I needed someone to talk to."

"Glad to help. Anytime."

The bus lurched, flinging her forward.

Kids screamed and the brakes smoked.

"What the—" Charlie glanced up in time to see a big, army-style dump truck straddling the highway in the middle of a curve.

The bus driver had jammed his foot on the brake and now stood on it in an attempt to stop the bus before it slammed into the truck.

"Hold on!" Charlie yelled and braced for impact.

Brakes smoked and the bus skidded across the pavement toward the truck. With a bluff on one side and a drop-off on the other, they didn't have a choice.

As if in slow motion, the bus went from fast to slow, the truck rising up before them, filling the windshield. Charlie braced herself, but couldn't close her eyes as the bus slowed, slowed, slowed but not fast enough for her. Just when she thought they would crash into the truck, the bus stopped, its front bumper scraping the side of the truck.

When the smoke from the brakes cleared, Charlie sat up and glanced back at the children, her gaze darting to the seat Lolly had occupied with Ashley Cramer and Chelsea Smith. At first she didn't see them. Then, one by one, their heads popped up over the top of the back of the seat in front of them and they looked around.

The rest of the children crawled up off the floor and into their seats, some crying, others looking frightened and disoriented.

Brenda stood and walked toward the back. "Hey, guys. Everyone okay?"

Most children nodded. One little boy shook his head, his nose bleeding, tears streaming down his cheeks.

"Come here, Elijah." Brenda gathered him up into her arms. "For now, stay in your seats until we figure out what's going on. Everything will be all right."

Charlie leaned over the back of the seat and touched the bus driver, Mr. Green's, shoulder. "Are you all right?"

He nodded. "Didn't see that coming." The old man wiped the sweat from his brow and peered through the windshield. "That could have been really bad."

Charlie looked to either side of the truck for a driver to find out why the truck was parked in the middle of a dangerous curve. Movement around the rear of the truck captured her attention and she watched as a man emerged, wearing camouflage pants, camouflage jacket and a black ski mask. He carried a military-grade rifle with a black grip and stock and he was headed straight for the door of the bus.

Charlie's heart fluttered and a cold chill shivered down her spine. "This doesn't look good. I think the truck is the least of our worries."

Another man dressed from head to toe in camouflage followed the first, also wearing a ski mask and carrying a rifle with a curved magazine loaded in it.

They stopped at the bus door.

"Open the door," the guy in front ordered.

The bus driver shook his head, shoved the shift in Reverse and pressed the accelerator.

"Go. Go. Go!" Charlie said.

He popped the clutch in his hurry and the bus engine stalled.

The men holding the rifles pointed them at the door and opened fire.

Charlie staggered backward, the seat hit her in the backs of her knees and she sat hard.

Mr. Green grunted and slumped forward over the steering wheel.

One of the men kicked what was left of the door open and entered the bus. "Stay down and don't move!" he yelled and waved his rifle at the occupants of the bus.

Charlie wanted to go to Mr. Green, but was afraid if she moved, the attackers would open fire in her direction and hit one of the children. So she stayed down, praying Lolly would remain seated.

The second man entered the bus, pulled the driver

out of his seat and dragged him to the side. Then he slipped into the driver's seat and started the engine.

The dump truck engine roared to life. The big vehicle turned away from them and lumbered north along the highway until they reached a dirt road on the left. The truck turned onto the road and disappeared between the trees.

Charlie held her breath, as the bus turned as well and followed the dirt road the truck had taken. She wanted to go to Lolly and hold her in her arms, but she didn't want to draw any attention to herself or the children.

The kids sat in silence or softly sobbing, holding on to the seatbacks in front of them as they bounced along the rutted road.

Where were they going? What was going to happen to the children?

Charlie wished Ghost was with them. He'd know what to do. With only two men wielding guns, surely he would have been able to subdue them before they shot Mr. Green. She glanced down at the old bus driver, her stomach knotting.

The man's face was even paler than before and his chest didn't appear to be moving. Dear God, he was dead.

Charlie closed her eyes briefly and prayed for a miracle. Then she opened them and focused on the road ahead. She had to keep her wits about her to ensure the safety of the children.

The bus slowed around a curve in the dirt road and came to an open clearing, facing a giant hill that had been carved away at the base. It appeared to be an old mine.

The hills and mountains of Wyoming were dotted with the remnants of old gold mines from the gold rush era of the 1860s. This was just one of many that had been abandoned when the gold played out.

The man driving the bus slowed, as he headed toward the entrance to the mine.

Charlie leaned forward, her heart leaping into her throat. "What are you doing?"

"Shut up!" the man wielding the rifle backhanded her, knocking her across the seat.

She picked herself up and watched in horror as he drove right up to the mine, parking the bus so that the door opened into the mine entrance.

The driver parked the bus and clicked on a flashlight.

"Everyone out!" he yelled. He grabbed Mr. Green and dragged him down the steps and into the mine.

Charlie pressed a hand to her bruised cheek. "What are you going to do with us?"

"You have two choices—shut up and get out, or die." He pointed his rifle at her chest.

She raised her hands. "I'm getting out." Charlie eased to the edge of her seat. The rifleman backed up, giving her enough room to pass.

For a moment, she thought of all the self-defense classes she'd taken. None of them had prepared her for the possibility of children being used as target practice or shields. Her instinct was to jam her elbow into the man's gut and shove the heel of her palm into his nose. But she couldn't. If he jerked his finger on the trigger, he could shoot a kid.

Charlie could never live with herself if her actions were the cause of one of these babies being killed. She glanced back at Lolly as she stepped down off the bus.

The man with the flashlight waved Charlie to the

side. "Do something stupid and one of these kids will get hurt."

She raised her hands. "Please don't hurt the children. Just tell me what you want me to do. I'll do it."

"Stand over there and keep quiet." He shone the flashlight toward a stack of crates.

Charlie followed the beam and stopped when the light swung back toward the bus.

Three children dropped down from the bus, huddling together, sniffling in the dark. The flashlight swung her way.

Charlie opened her arms and the kids ran into them.

She counted them as they emerged, one by one. When Lolly reached the ground, she looked for her mother.

Charlie nearly cried. Again the flashlight swung her way and Lolly ran to her. Charlie held her in her arms, smoothing her hand over her hair. "It's going to be all right," she whispered. "I promise." Somehow they'd get out of this in one piece. She refused to break her promise to her daughter.

Brenda brought up the rear with Lolly's friends Chelsea and Ashley.

Another man joined the two in camouflage. This one was dressed all in black with a matching black ski mask. He stood beside the other two as Brenda walked by with the two little girls.

He grabbed Ashley and swung her up into his arms. "I'll take this one."

Brenda leaped forward. "Don't you hurt her!"

The man with the flashlight swung it, clipping Brenda in the side of the head.

Brenda crumpled to the ground and lay still.

Chelsea dropped down beside her, crying hysterically.

"Take the brat before I hit her, too," Flashlight Guy shouted.

Charlie rushed forward and dragged Chelsea back to where the rest of the children huddled. She told them to stay where they were and then she eased forward to where Brenda lay with her face down, her eyes closed.

"Get back!" the man with the gun yelled.

Charlie inched back to stand with the cluster of kids and waited for the men to leave or at least back up enough to let her get to Brenda and the bus driver.

The bus moved away from the opening of the mine and a triangle of sunlight shone in.

Charlie studied everything around her, looking for an escape route, counting the number of men involved, evaluating her options and coming up with no plan that would save twenty children.

Yet another man wearing camouflage stepped into the cave entrance where the original captors stood. He was bigger than first two, and he carried a 9 millimeter pistol. "Where's Cramer?"

"Hell if I know. He drove the truck," Flashlight man said.

"He was here a minute ago," the rifleman said. "Took one of the kids and walked out."

The man muttered a curse. "Dalton, find him. Vern, help me move the plate in place."

"What about them?" Vern said.

"If one of them moves, we'll shoot them," the big man said.

Based on the names they were calling each other, Charlie knew who they were. The Vanders brothers. And it appeared Tim Cramer had come along for the ride in order to steal his daughter away. Charlie would bet Cramer had already escaped the compound with his girl. Dalton wouldn't find them.

For the next few minutes, the two men worked to move a huge metal plate into position over the entrance of the mine.

Charlie took the opportunity to study the boxes lining the walls. She reached into an open one. Inside were sticks of dynamite and dozens of empty cartridge boxes. She searched for a weapon among the boxes, only to find more empty boxes. Another crate contained empty cases of what appeared to have at one time contained new AR-15s. More than the number carried by the men holding them hostage. A lot more. In one crate alone, she counted over twenty empty AR-15 boxes. And there were a lot of crates lining the walls of the mine. What were they planning? A total takeover of the state?

Once the metal door was in place, most of the light was blocked. A little at the top and sides gave just enough for Charlie to make it over to Brenda and Mr. Green. She felt for a pulse on the bus driver. His skin was cold, he lay very still and no matter how long Charlie pressed her fingers to the base of his throat, she couldn't find a pulse. The man was dead.

Her heart hurt for his wife. They were a childless couple who loved each other and their menagerie of dogs.

Moving to Brenda she touched the caregiver's shoulder. "Brenda."

Brenda moaned.

"Sweetie, please. Wake up and tell me you're all right."

She moaned again and rolled onto her back. "Why is it so dark?" she croaked.

"We're in a mine."

"Oh, God." She tried to lift her head but dropped it back to the ground. "The kids?"

"All here and okay, except Ashley Cramer."

"Where's she?" She rolled to her side and tried to push to a sitting position. "Linnea will be frantic."

"I think Tim took her."

"That bastard." Brenda pressed her hand to her lips. "Sorry."

Charlie wanted to say a whole string of curses, but it wouldn't get them out of the mess they were in. "Tim was in on this."

"What is *this*, anyway?" Brenda asked, blinking her eyes before staring around at the walls of the mine.

"The Vanders brothers have taken us hostage. We're in some mine shaft."

"Those idiots?" She tried to get up, but couldn't quite make it on her own. "What do they hope to accomplish?"

"I don't know." Charlie helped Brenda to her feet and she staggered over to the children where she collapsed to a sitting position.

The children gathered around her, all wanting to be held and comforted, every one of them frightened out of their minds.

Charlie knelt beside Lolly. "Are you doing okay?"

She nodded. "Are those bad men going to let us out of this cave?"

"I don't know if they will, but someone will find us and let us out." She hoped it was true. As far as she knew, nobody would know where to look for them.

"Mr. Caspar will find us. He's a real hero."

Charlie hugged her close. "Yes, Lolly, he is." That's what he did. He fought for his country. For her and Lolly and everyone else. He was the real hero.

"Miss Brenda told me." Lolly snuggled against Charlie. "I'm cold."

Charlie rubbed her arms and pulled her closer.

"I hope my daddy comes soon."

Charlie swallowed the lump in her throat to say, "Your daddy?" Had she overheard them talking about her? Had she put the pieces together and guessed?

"Mr. Caspar. He's nice and he's a hero. I want him to be my daddy."

"Oh, baby." Charlie held her tight and fought the tears. She wanted Ghost to be Lolly's daddy, too. And Charlie wanted him to be her husband. If she had another chance, she'd get right to the point and ask him if he would marry them. If he said no, she'd figure out how to live without him. But on the slim chance he said yes, she'd be the happiest woman alive and follow him to the ends of the earth, if that's what it took.

"What the hell was that?" Caveman called out from behind a parked pickup.

The sound of the Delta Force soldier's voice penetrated the fog of memories and yanked Ghost back to the present and Grizzly Pass, Wyoming.

Caveman and Hawkeye had sought cover behind vehicles while Garner knelt near the corner of a brick building. Ghost waited a moment, trying to determine where the sound had come from. When no other explosions shook the ground, he rolled from beneath the SUV and stood.

"Sounded like it came from the south end of town," Garner said.

A siren wailed from the north, heading toward the tavern.

Ghost hurried toward the front of the building in time to see a sheriff's vehicle racing south along Main Street.

"Come on," Garner said. "Let's go check it out."

All four men climbed into the SUV and took off after the sheriff.

At the other end of town people were coming out of their homes and businesses, standing in clumps, talking to each other, holding their small children close. The sheriff's car was positioned at the end of Main Street, blocking traffic from entering or leaving town.

Garner parked a block away. The men piled out and hurried toward one of the abandoned buildings on the edge of town. The front wall had been blown out, the bricks scattered across the street.

Behind them, another siren sounded and the volunteer fire department engine truck rolled down the street, passing them to stop next to the sheriff's vehicle. Firefighters jumped to the ground and started unrolling a long hose.

The sheriff emerged from the building, covered in dust, shaking his head. "You won't need that. Looks like someone set off a stick of dynamite. No fire, no smoke, just a big mess."

Ghost inhaled and let out a long, slow breath and asked, "Why?" He turned to Garner and the others. "Why would someone want to blow up an old building in a little town?"

"Kids bored in the middle of summer?" Caveman offered.

No. Ghost wasn't buying it. Someone had deliberately set that dynamite to blow in that particular building at that particular time.

"It didn't do much damage." Hawkeye studied the scene. "It was an old building not worth anything. Whoever did it, did the town a favor, getting the demolition started."

"Why would they pick this building on the south end of town?" Ghost asked, his mind wrapping around the possibilities and coming up with one. "Unless they were creating a diversion to draw all of the attention away from something."

The radio clipped to Sheriff Scott's shoulder chirped with static. "Sheriff, we have a problem," came the tinny voice.

Sheriff Scott touched the mic. "Give it to me."

Ghost's attention zeroed in on that radio and what was being said, his gut clenching.

"Someone's demanding LeRoy Vanders's release."

"Demanding?" The sheriff snorted. "On what grounds?"

"They want to negotiate his release in exchange for a busload of our kids."

The words hit Ghost like a punch in the gut.

The sheriff's face paled and everyone standing in hearing range of the sheriff's radio froze.

"What is he asking for?" Sheriff Scott asked.

"He wants you to bring LeRoy Vanders to Lucky Lou's Gold Mine in one hour, in a helicopter. If you aren't there in exactly one hour, they will blow up the entrance to the old mine with dynamite. With the children inside."

Ghost grabbed Garner's arm. "That's my woman and my kid on that bus."

"We have to work with the sheriff to get those kids

to safety," Garner said. He stepped toward Sheriff Scott. "Sir."

"Don't bother me now. I have a crisis to avert." The sheriff hit his mic. "Who the hell can we call with a helicopter?"

Garner got in front of the sheriff. "I can get one in under an hour."

The sheriff looked at Garner and nodded. Then he keyed the mic. "Get Vanders ready. I'll let you know when the helicopter lands." He stared at Garner. "If you're wrong, you might cost us the lives of those kids."

"I can get one from Bozeman in thirty minutes." He gave the sheriff instructions on how to contact his resource at the Bozeman airport. A helicopter would be dispatched in less than ten minutes.

Ghost paced the pavement, desperate to do something. "We can't wait for them to make the trade. What if they decide to bury those kids in the mine anyway? They could have that whole place rigged with explosives."

"We'll make the exchange," the sheriff said. "We can't risk the lives of the children."

"Sheriff." Ghost planted himself in front of the sheriff. "You have four of the most highly skilled military men at your disposal. Let us get in there, recon the situation and report what we see."

"I don't know." The sheriff shook his head. "If they see you, they might detonate the explosives."

"We know how to get in without being seen. We can get a count on the number of combatants. You'd be better off knowing numbers in case they start shooting at the men delivering Vanders."

"He has a point," Garner added. "Let us be your eyes and ears while you're putting the exchange in place."

The sheriff stared at Garner. "How do I know you won't do something stupid?"

Ghost grabbed the man's arm. "The woman I love and my little girl were on that bus. I wouldn't do anything that would cause them harm. Please. Let us do this."

The sheriff stared into Ghost's face. "I've known you for a long time. I knew your father. He was proud that you made it through SEAL training. From what they say, only the best of the best can be a SEAL." He stared at the others. "I trust Jon Caspar. If he trusts you, I guess I have to, as well. Go."

Ghost turned to run.

The sheriff snagged his arm. "We have to bring those kids back alive. One of them is my grandson."

Ghost nodded and took off for the DHS agent's SUV. Hawkeye, Garner and Cavemen beat him to it, climbing in. Ghost settled in the seat and leaned forward, staring through the front windshield as they blew through town and north toward Lucky Lou's Gold Mine. He prayed they could get in without being seen and that none of the passengers on the bus had been hurt in the hostage takeover.

Chapter 14

Lolly fell asleep, leaning against Charlie.

Unable to sit still without coming up with a plan, she eased Lolly to the floor and stood, stretching the kinks out of her muscles. She wondered how long it had been since they'd been captured. Thirty minutes? An hour? More?

Some children were still sniffling, huddled up to Brenda, seeking comfort from each other.

Charlie crossed to the metal plate covering the opening of the mine and strained to hear what was happening outside.

"They'll be here on time if they want to see those kids again," a voice said.

Charlie recognized it as the man who'd been carrying the flashlight, Dalton Vanders.

"What if they bring in the feds?" The slower, deeper voice of Vernon Vanders said. "We aren't equipped for a standoff."

"We have the detonators." The third voice could only be the man in charge. The oldest of the Vanders brothers, GW. "The mine entrance is rigged to blow. If they don't give us what we want, we blow the entrance."

Charlie gasped. If they blew the entrance, everyone inside could be buried alive. Should, by some miracle, they live through the blast, they might suffocate before anyone could dig them out.

"They better hope they bring Dad in that helicopter," Dalton said.

"Ten minutes. If they don't show by then, we blow and go," GW said, his voice moving away from the mine entrance.

Ten minutes. Charlie looked around in the limited lighting. They had ten minutes to figure out how to get out of the mine.

Going deeper without lights was suicide. They could fall down open vertical shafts in the floor, or die due to poisonous gases. She went back to the boxes and searched for something, anything she could use to move the door enough they could slip out.

The only thing she could find was a broken slat from one of the crates. If she could use it as leverage, she might be able to move the heavy metal plate that had taken two men to slide in place.

Charlie jammed the slat into the sunlit gap at the base of the metal barrier. Holding on to the end, she leaned back as hard as she could, putting all of her weight into it. The plate budged, but only half an inch. She pulled the slat out and lay down on the floor.

She could see a little bit of daylight and movement. A couple of yards from the entrance, stood someone wearing camouflage pants and black work boots.

She didn't know where the others were, but she

couldn't wait for them to appear. She had to get a wide enough gap to slip the children out and away from the men before they got really stupid and detonated the charges that would seal twenty children and the adults in the mine.

Fitting the slat back in the gap, she pulled again, the gap widening until a four-inch opening stretched from the top to the bottom of the entrance.

On her third attempt, the slat cracked and broke. Charlie fell on her butt with a bone-jarring thud and groaned. The additional space she'd gained was less than another inch. Five inches wide might get a small child out, but not Brenda and Charlie. And the children would need to be guided into the nearby trees and underbrush to hide. Without the leverage of the slat, she'd have to work with her bare hands. As heavy as the metal plate was, she doubted she'd get far, but she had to try.

The sky darkened, as if clouds had blocked the sun.

Charlie crawled to the widened gap and peered out. She spotted all three Vanders brothers. They stood near the dump truck. Two of them held the AR-15s. The one she figured was GW had the 9 millimeter in a holster on his hip and his hand wrapped around a small gadget Charlie assumed was the detonator.

Her teeth ground together. Any man who could contemplate blowing up the entrance to a mine with children trapped inside was no man at all. He was an animal.

She looked to her right and her left. If she remembered correctly from their drive in, the mine entrance had several bushes growing next to it and a young tree sprouting near the base of the hill. If they could get the kids to the bushes they might make it to the forest before their escape was discovered. The men outside must have felt pretty confident in the ability of the rusty metal plate holding their hostages inside. Either that or they were too busy watching for whatever they'd demanded to arrive to keep a close eye on a bunch of kids and two women.

Charlie leaped to her feet. Time was running out. She had to get the children to safety before the crazy brothers sealed their fates inside a mine shaft tomb.

Brenda disentangled herself from the children and rose to assist. "Let me help," she said.

With her heart pumping adrenaline through her veins, Charlie grabbed the metal plate.

Brenda curled her fingers around the rusty steel.

Together they leaned back, straining to move the heavy sheet of metal. By God, they'd move that barrier if it was the last thing they did.

Charlie prayed it wasn't.

Armed with a headset radio and an AR-15 rifle, Ghost lived up to his nickname and eased up to the edge of the mine compound, clinging to the brush. "Three targets, two carrying rifles and one with the prize."

"I got one vehicle leaving by road." Caveman was working his way toward the mine by paralleling the road in and out. "Notifying 911. They have the state highway patrol on standby. They should pick him up on the highway."

"I'm in position in the bird's nest," Hawkeye said from his position on a ridge high above the mine clearing.

"Ready when you are," Garner added.

The big guy in the middle had his fist closed around

a small box of some sort. If it was a detonator, they'd have to get him to let go of it before they took out the other two men. It would do no good to kill any of them, if the guy holding the key to the show pressed that button.

He studied the layout. An older model dump truck was parked a couple of yards away from the mine entrance. One of the men stood near the rear of the truck, watching the road in. Another used the other end of the truck as cover, also monitoring the only road in.

The man with his hand on the detonator pulled what appeared to be a satellite phone off the web harness he wore and hit several buttons.

"Where's Vanders and our bird?" he demanded. "My thumb is a hair's breadth away from the ignition button." He listened for a moment. "I don't care if it takes time to get a helicopter here. Five minutes. That's all that's left between you and those kids. Five." He jabbed the phone, ending the call. "Get ready. Either they'll show up with him and the bird, or we set off some fireworks and get the hell out of here."

"I think I hear something coming," one of the men shouted.

"'Bout time," the guy at the other end of the truck said. "I need a beer."

The sound of rotor blades beating the air came over the top of the hill.

"Got my sights on the prize holder," Hawkeye reported.

"Do not engage," Garner reiterated the sheriff's instructions. He was positioned to the right of Ghost and twenty yards to his rear. He was to transfer data to the sheriff as the others took their positions.

"Holding steady," Hawkeye reassured.

Ghost scanned the area for other bad guys but was surprised there were only three. It didn't take an army to take a school bus full of children and unarmed adults. And with the lives of those children held in the balance, these men could demand the world and get it.

The helicopter crested the hill and hovered over the mine.

"What are they waiting for?" one of the men shouted.

"I don't know," the man holding the detonator yelled back over the roar of the helicopter.

"There's someone with a gun in there!" One of the men with a rifle pointed his weapon at the helicopter.

"Don't shoot!" detonator man yelled.

"They've got a gun!" He raised his weapon to his shoulder and fired.

Ghost shook his head. Just what they needed, a trigger-happy bad guy firing at the helicopter carrying their bargaining chip. "The situation has escalated, request permission to move in and take out the targets," Ghost said.

"Sheriff said do not engage," Garner reminded him.

"The sheriff didn't get the word to the bad guys. Things are about to get really bad." Ghost bunched his muscles, ready to charge into the gray.

"I've got the shooter in my sights," Hawkeye reminded them.

"I'm in position and have the other dude with the gun in mine," Caveman said.

Ghost couldn't wait for the men to freak out and blow up the mine entrance. "I'm going in for the man with the prize. Boss, either you're with me or you're not."

"I got your six, coming up on your left," Garner said. "Sheriff gave the go-ahead. They're lifting off."

As the helicopter climbed higher into the sky, the team moved in.

Hawkeye took out the man firing at the bird. Caveman fired at the other, nicked his leg and sent him to the ground. Unfortunately, he still had his gun in hand and was firing back in the direction of Caveman.

Ghost was almost across the open ground when the man with the detonator turned toward the mine entrance and raised his hand.

Making a flying tackle, Ghost hit the man in his midsection, sending him staggering backward. He stumbled and hit the ground flat on his back. The detonator flew from his grasp and skittered across the dry ground, landing in front of the man firing at Caveman.

He flung his rifle to the ground and low-crawled toward the detonator.

Ghost punched the man he'd tackled in the nose and scrambled to his feet, flinging himself at the man as he reached for the detonator.

Before he could get to him, the man's hand slammed down on the red button.

The world erupted behind Ghost, sending him flying forward and slamming him to the ground. He laid for a moment, stunned, his ears ringing. The man who'd hit the button lifted his head and stared at him, then reached for his rifle.

Ghost lurched to his feet and kicked the rifle out of the other man's grip.

A shot rang out behind him and the big guy he'd tackled stood facing him, his eyes wide, blood spreading across his camouflage shirt. He took one step and fell forward like a tree toppled by lumberjacks.

Garner lay on the ground nearby, his rifle up to his shoulder. "Told you I had your six."

Ghost scanned the area. Caveman came out of the woods, the helicopter dropped lower and landed on the other side of the dump truck and people rushed toward the mine entrance.

"Charlie. Lolly." Ghost's head still rang and his leg ached, but none of that mattered. The woman he loved and his only child were trapped behind the rocks and rubble blocking the entrance to the old mine.

He ran toward the jumble of boulders and rocks. Dust swirled in a cloud making it hard to see clearly. Or were those tears clouding his vision?

"Charlie! Lolly!" Oh, dear God, how was he going to get them out of there? He lifted a boulder and tossed it to the side. He lifted another and threw it to the side, too.

"Ghost!" Hawkeye said his name several times before he heard the sound through his headset.

"They're in there," Ghost said, his heart ripped to shreds, his mind numb. "They're in there, and I can't get to them."

"Ghost, listen to me," Hawkeye said. "I have them in my sights."

"What?" Ghost straightened from the pile of rocks. "How?"

"They're in the woods to the south of the mine. I count more than a dozen kids and two adults."

From desperation to hope, Ghost left the rocks and ran toward the south side of the mine. He crashed through brush, tripped over logs and fell several times before he spotted something pink through the dense foliage.

When he broke through the underbrush, he stumbled and fell to his knees in front of all the children and two women. "Charlie! Lolly!" He coughed, choking with the dust he'd inhaled and the emotion he couldn't hold back.

"Ghost?" Charlie ran forward and knelt beside him. "Is that you?" She rubbed her hands across his face, her fingers getting coated with a fine layer of dust. "Oh, thank God." She flung her arms around him and kissed him, dirt and all.

He held her close for a long time. His leg hurt like hell and his ears still rang, but Charlie, Lolly and the rest of the kids were okay.

"Mr. Caspar?" Lolly inched forward, her brows knit, her cheeks streaked with dried tears.

"Lolly, baby, come here." He held out an arm, making room for her in his embrace.

She ran to him and wrapped her arms around his neck. "I was so scared."

He laughed. "So was I." He kissed her cheek with a loud smack. "But we're okay now."

She leaned back and stared at his face. "You're dirty."

He laughed out loud, his heart filled with so much joy, he was afraid it might explode. "Yes, I am. And I'm so happy you and your mama are all right."

Her eyes filled with tears. "Mr. Green didn't come out with us."

Charlie smoothed a hand over her hair. "No, sweetie, he didn't. But the sheriff will make sure they get him out of there. You'll see."

Ghost's gaze connected with Charlie's.

"The bus driver," she whispered and shook her head, her eyes filling.

He nodded. With Charlie's help, Ghost lurched to his feet and straightened his leg, the pain shooting up into his hip. He ignored it, looking at the children huddled around another young woman. He shook his head, thankful they were all alive. "How did you get them out of the mine?"

Charlie held up her hands, stained with rust and marked with cuts and scrapes. "Brenda and I moved the metal plate they'd used to block the entrance. They thought it could keep a couple of women with a bunch of children contained." She snorted. "They didn't count on the adrenaline rush we'd get at the mention of blowing the entrance." Charlie lifted her chin and smiled at the other woman. "The important thing is, we got it open enough to get all of the children out while the Vanders brothers were shooting at the helicopter. It was close, but we were able to get all of the children out of the mine before the explosion."

Ghost shook his head, a grin spreading across his face. "You are amazing."

"And you should have seen Lolly, herding the kids into single file like the little soldier she is." Charlie smiled down at their daughter. "She's so much like you it hurts sometimes."

Lolly stared up at Ghost. "Mr. Caspar, will you be my daddy?"

Her words hit Ghost in the gut and he sucked in a breath before responding. "I don't know." He turned to Charlie. "What does your mother think about the idea?"

Charlie's eyes filled again, tears spilled over the edges and her bottom lip trembled. "I was going to wait until I was wearing a pretty dress and my hair was fixed." She stared down at her wrecked hands. "And after a manicure." She laughed, the sound coming out as more of a sob. "But I don't want to wait another minute to know." She dropped to one knee and took Ghost's hand.

"What are you doing?" he asked. He tried to lift her back to her feet, but she resisted.

"Jon Caspar, you big, sexy SEAL, with a heart as big as the Wyoming sky, will you make an honest woman of me and marry me?" She stared up at him, tears running down her dirty face, her hair a riot of uncontrollable curls, her clothes torn and smeared with rust. She was the most beautiful woman in the world.

Ghost's heart swelled in his chest to the point he thought it could no longer be contained.

Lolly clapped her hands together, her eyes alight with excitement. "Please say yes!"

Ghost laughed and drew Charlie up into his arms. "I would have liked a shower before I proposed to you. But since we're here, the sun is shining and I'm holding the most beautiful woman in the world, I can't think of a better answer than yes." He drew in a deep breath and bent to kiss the tip of her nose. "Yes, I'll marry you. Yes, I'd love to have Lolly as my very own daughter. And yes, we'll work things out, somehow, because that's what people do who love each other as much as we do. I love you, Charlie, from the tips of my toes to my very last breath."

"Jon, I've always loved you," Charlie said. "From our first date, I knew you were the one for me. I just had to wait until *you* knew I was the one for you."

He brushed a strand of her hair out of her face and tucked it behind her ear. "I've always loved you, but I didn't want to hurt you by dragging you through the life of a SEAL's wife."

Charlie laughed. "So you hurt me by leaving me behind?" She shook her head. "That's man thinking." She cupped his face and leaned up on her toes to kiss him. "I'd follow you to the ends of the earth, and I'd always be there for you when you came back from deployment."

"Me, too." Lolly hugged him around his knees. "I love you, too. I'm going to have a daddy of my own." She looked up at him with his blue eyes and her mother's red hair and grinned. "We're going to be a family."

"You bet, we are." Ghost lifted her up on his arm and wrapped the other around Charlie. Together, they led the others out of the woods and back to the clearing in front of the mine.

Charlie felt as if she'd gone from one movie set to the other and wondered if she had been dreaming through all that had happened. She had a hard time wrapping her mind around all of it from having the bus hijacked to being trapped in a mine, to the fairy-tale proposal in the woods and back to the cacophony of every kind of motor vehicle and dozens of uniformed personnel filling her vision.

A fire truck had arrived, along with rescue vehicles from across the county. Every sheriff's deputy on duty was there along with the Wyoming Highway Patrol. The sheriff was in the middle of all of it speaking with the DHS representative, Kevin Garner.

When Charlie emerged from the woods with Ghost, Brenda and all of the children, a round of applause erupted from the rescue personnel.

Paramedics rushed forward to check out the children, Brenda and Charlie.

She suffered through the delay of having her hands cleaned and bandaged, while Ghost carried Lolly over to where the sheriff directed the remaining efforts.

Charlie hurried over as soon as she could break away.

Tim Cramer was tucked into the backseat of one of the Wyoming Highway Patrol cars, his face angry, his hands cuffed behind him.

A deputy escorted a pale and shaky Linnea Cramer into the fray where she was reunited with her daughter, Ashley, in a tearful reunion.

"Thank God, they got Ashley back," Charlie said as she joined the group gathered around the sheriff.

"We had a roadblock set up on the highway headed toward Montana. We figured he'd make a run for Canada with the child," the sheriff said. "Wyoming Highway Patrol picked him up. If he thought he had problems before, he's in a heap more trouble now. Rebecca Florence came to this morning and said it was Tim Cramer who'd attacked her in the library. He'd worn the ski mask he was found with today, but she knew it was him when he told her it was her fault he was losing his wife."

Charlie frowned. "What do you mean it was her fault? I didn't think she and Linnea were even friends."

The sheriff's mouth twisted. "Apparently, Ms. Florence was in Bozeman for a library conference staying at the same hotel where Cramer was entertaining a young lady who wasn't his wife in a room on the same floor as Rebecca's."

"And she told Linnea." Charlie nodded. "So he beat her up for squealing on him."

The sheriff nodded.

"What about the Vanders brothers?" Charlie asked, looking around as paramedics loaded a sheet-draped body into the back of one of the waiting ambulances.

"Dalton is dead, Vernon and GW will live to face time in the state prison," the sheriff said.

Charlie couldn't feel sorry for any of them. How

long would it be before the children got over the terror they'd faced on the bus and in the dark mine? "I hope they get what they deserve."

Ghost slipped an arm around her.

She leaned into his strength, glad he was there.

"If not for Garner's team, it could have been a whole lot worse," Sheriff Scott said. "The chopper took hits from Dalton's gun. The pilot is being treated for a gunshot wound to his leg and Dalton shot his own father." The sheriff shook his head. "LeRoy Vanders took a bullet to the chest. They're working on him now and loading him into the helicopter his son tried to shoot down. I doubt he'll make it all the way to the hospital in Bozeman."

"What about Mr. Green?" Charlie asked. Her heart ached for the old man who'd done nothing to deserve being killed for driving a busload of kids. "He's still inside the mine." She shook her head. "He didn't make it. Vernon took him out on the bus."

The sheriff's lips thinned and released a long sigh. "His wife will be devastated." He pinched the bridge of his nose before continuing. "I ordered excavation equipment in case we had to dig you and the kids out. It's on its way. We'll get him out."

Charlie nodded.

Sheriff Scott shot a glance at the crumbled mine entrance. "What I don't understand is where they got all the explosives and detonators."

Ghost's jaw tightened. "From what I saw of the detonator, it was military grade. I knew the Vanderses had an arsenal of guns from all the hunting they do. But the explosives are an entirely different game."

Charlie touched the sheriff's arm. "I found at least a dozen wooden crates in the mine. They were filled with empty boxes from what appeared to be a large number of rifles, boxes of ammo and the curved magazines I've seen used with the semiautomatic weapons the military use. What would the Vanders brothers need with that many weapons?"

"Unless they aren't the only ones stockpiling weapons," Kevin Garner said. "We have infrared satellite photos of a group of people unloading items from a truck into the mine. It was from only a few days ago."

"Those crates were empty except for the boxes the weapons came in."

"Where did all of those guns and ammo go?" the sheriff asked. "And who shipped all of them? There has to be a paper or money trail."

Garner nodded. "I have my tech guy working on that. In the meantime, getting into that mine and going through those crates might help us trace the weapons back to the buyer."

The sheriff's face grew grim. "Sounds like someone is trying to build an army."

"Then we better find out who before they succeed," Garner said.

Charlie shivered in the warm country air. Her peaceful hometown of Grizzly Pass, Wyoming, had darker secrets than she'd ever expected. She began to wonder if bringing her daughter there to raise had been a good idea after all.

Ghost tightened his hold around her waist, reminding her that if she hadn't come back, she wouldn't have found Ghost again.

Everything happened for a reason. And she couldn't be happier that she now had her family back together. Whatever the future held, wherever they went, it would be as a family. Anything else, they could deal with, as long as they were together.

An hour later, Kevin Garner loaded his team of specialists into his SUV along with Charlie and Lolly and took them back to town.

He dropped Charlie, Lolly and Ghost at the community center where Charlie had left her Jeep.

Charlie handed over her keys. "If you don't mind, my hands are shaking too much to drive."

He took the keys in exchange for a kiss and helped her and Lolly into the vehicle.

Once they were all inside, he glanced over at Charlie and took her hand. "Just so you know, I plan on staying until the situation is resolved here in Grizzly Pass. After that, I hope you'll be patient and flexible with where we go next."

Charlie squeezed his fingers. "I'm one hundred percent okay with that plan. As long as you're here with us. I don't think we've found the people at the crux of what's been going on around here."

"Me either," he said. "But I know one thing."

"What's that?"

"I'm not leaving until we do. And when I do leave, you and Lolly are coming with me." He lifted her hand and pressed a kiss to the backs of her knuckles.

"Good," Charlie said. "Because I'm not letting go this time."

"How do you feel about being a Navy wife?"

"I couldn't be prouder, as long as my Navy husband is you."

"Good, because once we've completed this assignment, I want to rejoin my unit in Virginia."

"I've always wanted to go to Virginia," she said, a happy smile spreading across her face.

"And if the medical board invites me to leave the military?"

She turned her head toward him. "We could come back to Wyoming."

"I'm glad you feel that way. Being back reminded me how much I love this state. More than that, it reminded me of how much I love you."

* * * * *

It wasn't long before they were arriving at the ranch. He
grabbed her overnight bag, and they walked inside.

"We both need to get a few hours' sleep," he said. "I'll
take the couch and you can have the bed."

She walked toward the bedroom but turned at the
door. "Come with me. Just to sleep together like before."
Those big green eyes studied him as she reached her hand
out toward him.

There was nothing he wanted more than to curl up
with her in his bed. But with his anger and frustration so
close to the surface, he couldn't discount the fact that he
might wake up swinging. The thought of Bree being the
recipient of his night terrors made him break out into a
cold sweat.

"Never mind," she said quickly, misreading his hesitation,
hand falling back to her side. "You don't have to."

Damn it, he'd rather never sleep again than see that wounded look in her eyes from something he'd done.

He stepped toward her. "I want to. Trust me, there's nothing I want more. But…I just don't want to take a chance on waking you up if I get called back in to Risk Peak early." That was at least a partial truth.

The haunted look fell away from her eyes, and a shy smile broke on her face. "I don't mind. I'll take a shorter amount of sleep if it means I get to sleep next to you."

He would have given her anything in the world to keep that sweet smile on her face. He took her hand, and they walked into the bedroom together.

They took turns changing into sleep clothes in the bathroom, then got into the bed together. The act was so innocent and yet so intimate.

Tanner rolled over onto his side and pulled Bree's back against his front. He breathed in the sweet scent of her hair as her head rested in the crook of his elbow. His other arm wrapped loosely around her waist.

She was out within minutes, her smaller body relaxing against him, trusting him to shelter and protect her while she slept. Tanner wouldn't betray that trust, even if that meant protecting her against himself.

Besides, sleeping was overrated when he could be awake and feeling every curve that had been haunting his dreams for months pressed against him.

Definitely worth it.

Don't miss
Security Risk *by Janie Crouch,*
available August 2019 wherever
Harlequin® Intrigue books and ebooks are sold.

www.Harlequin.com

HIEXP0719

SPECIAL EXCERPT FROM

*In order to clean up his player reputation, rodeo champ
and cowboy Nico Laramie asks his best friend,
Eden Joslin, to pretend they're an exclusive couple.
But one kiss with the woman he's always kept at a
distance and Nico knows this fake relationship is about
to turn into something very real...*

Read on for a sneak peak at
Sweet Summer Sunset
part of the Coldwater Texas series from
USA TODAY *bestselling author Delores Fossen.*

"You've been avoiding me," Eden added, and she set the grocery bags on the small kitchen counter.

"I have," he admitted, and he wanted to wince. This was the problem with crossing a line with a friend. He wasn't used to putting on mouth filters when it came to Eden. "I wanted to give us both some time."

Her eyebrow came up, and she huffed before she mumbled some frustrated profanity under her breath.

"See?" he snapped, as if that proved all the arguments going on in his head. "We're uncomfortable with each other, and it's all because of the kiss that shouldn't have happened."

She stared at him a moment, caught on to a handful of his shirt and yanked him to her. She kissed him. Hard.

Nico felt his body jolt, an involuntary reaction that nearly made him dive in for more. After all, good kisses should be deep and involve some tongue. It was like stripping off a layer of clothes or going to the next level. But those were places that Nico stopped himself from going. Before their tongues could get involved, he stepped back from her, and she let go of him, her grip melting off his shirt.

He felt the loss right away when her mouth was no longer on his. The loss and the realization that Eden was a real, live, breathing woman. An attractive one with breasts, legs and everything.

Oh man.

He didn't want to realize that. He wanted his friend. And he wanted that friendship almost as much as he wanted to French-kiss her.

"Now we can also be uncomfortable because of that kiss I just gave you," she said, as if that proved whatever point she'd been trying to make. It proved nothing. Well, nothing that should be proved anyway.

Nico stared at her. "Eden, you're playing with a thousand gallons of fire," he warned her—after he'd caught his breath.

"I know, and I'm going to be honest about that. In fact, I'm going to insist we be honest with each other so that we don't ruin our friendship."

That was very confusing, and Nico wondered if this was some kind of trick. Except Eden wasn't a trick-playing kind of person. "What the heck do you mean by that?"

Her gaze stayed level with his. "It means if you want to kiss me, you should. If you don't want to kiss me again, then don't."

He was still confused. About what she was saying anyway. Nico was reasonably sure that the wanting-to-kiss-her part was highly charged right now.

"I just don't want you to avoid me because you're struggling with this possible curveball that's been tossed into our friendship," Eden went on. "That kiss makes us even," she added with a firm nod.

Don't miss
Sweet Summer Sunset by Delores Fossen,
available July 2019 wherever HQN books
and ebooks are sold.

www.Harlequin.com

PHDFEXP0719